A Bed
of Roses

Vicki,
I hope your
future is "A Bed of
Roses!"

Ann Marie Jameson

A Bed of Roses

A Novel

ANN MARIE JAMESON

Cover art: Kathryn Shoultz
Book layout: Pattie Steib

ISBN-10: 1535021616
ISBN-13: 978-1535021616

Printed in the United States of America

10 9 8 7 6 5 4 3 2 1

First Edition, September 2016

*In loving memory of my mother, who instilled in me
a love of reading and who always believed in me
and my talent as a writer. She encouraged me to follow
my dreams and to trust in God to get me there.*

ACKNOWLEDGEMENTS

Thank you to my sister whose idea it was for me to tell "our" story. She pleaded with me and pleaded with me until I could no longer say no. If it were not for her, "A Bed of Roses" would never have been written. She held up her end of the bargain by holding my hand all the way through the process. She critiqued each chapter as I went and gave me wonderful ideas along the way. She was my cheerleader and my confidant. She gave me so much moral support when I needed it the most.

Thank you to my brother who came up with so many of the humorous twists and turns in the story. Every time I got stumped on what to write next, he would come up with another one of his outlandish ideas! He also critiqued each chapter and gave me very helpful constructive criticism along the way. He advised me on business decisions and looked out for my best interests.

Thank you to all of my other sisters and brothers, my aunts, uncles and cousins and my friends who lent their personalities to me as inspiration for each of my characters. I hope you will all enjoy reading about your alter egos. Also, thanks to all of you who volunteered to read each chapter of my manuscript along the way and gave me your "unbiased" critique of it from a reader's prospective.

Thank you to my illustrator, Katie, my editors, Joan and Amy, my formatter, Pattie, and my legal advisor, Jim, for all your expertise and help in getting my novel to print. I could never have done it without you!

Thank you to all the wonderful business owners and people of Natchitoches who welcomed me with open arms into their lovely town and helped me with my research. Natchitoches is the perfect setting for "A Bed of Roses!"

Thank you to my husband for his patience, love and understanding while I obsessed for hours in a day at the computer typing away often until late at night and to my children and grandchildren for their unconditional love and moral support.

And most importantly, I thank God for all his blessings in my life, for surrounding me with angels in the form of family and friends and for giving me the gift of writing. I truly believe that He was standing over my shoulder guiding my hands as I typed every word of this story. He was my collaborator and my inspiration. Without Him I could never have written "A Bed of Roses."

LIST OF CHARACTERS

Jacques Pierre Bordelon, Sr. - Jack
Margaret Myrié Perot Bordelon - Maggie

Jack and Maggie's Children and Their Spouses:
Myrié - A veterinarian from West Palm Beach, FL
Mary LeBlanc - Owner of a B&B (A Bed of Roses) in Natchitoches
Todd LeBlanc - Mary's husband, a retired insurance claims adjuster
Martine Broussard - A nurse from Alexandria, LA
Dave Broussard - Martine's husband, a computer programmer
Jacques (JJ) Bordelon, Jr. - A Cajun chef from Philadelphia,
PA Veronica Bordelon - JJ's wife, an insurance executive
Joseph (Joe) Bordelon - A missionary priest from AZ
Madeline (Maddie)-An HGTV host from Charlotte, NC
Garrett - Maddie's husband, a real estate lawyer
Jacob (Jake) Bordelon - A Delta Airlines pilot from Atlanta, GA
Mallory - A high school principal from Arlington, TX
Troy - Mallory's husband, a high school football coach

Myrié's Adult Children and Their Spouses:
Sean - Air Force Veteran from Virginia.
Andrea - Sean's wife
Seth - Active Duty Air Force from Virginia
Celeste - Seth's wife
Samantha - Elementary teacher from California
Scott - Satellite technician, single from Colorado

Mary's Adult Children and Their Spouses:
Beau - Active Duty Marine stationed in Jacksonville, NC.
Eva - Beau's wife
Blake - Reserve Duty Army Soldier, private detective from Texas
Allison - Blake's wife
Brett - Marine Veteran, refinery supervisor from Morgan City, LA.
Danielle - Brett's wife

Martine's Adult Children:
Kathryn - College student
David - College student

Maggie's Siblings and Their Spouses:
Mary Theresa Savoie (Aunt Tess) - Maggie's twin sister
Isaac Savoie (Uncle Isaac) - Tess' husband
Thomas Perot (Uncle Tommy) - Maggie's brother, hay farmer
Doris Perot (Aunt Doris) - Tommy's wife
Robert Perot (Uncle Robby) - Maggie's brother, horse rancher
Pauline Perot (Aunt Pauline) - Robby's wife
LA Senator Theodore Perot (Uncle Teddy) - Maggie's brother
Joy Perot (Aunt Joy) - Teddy's wife
Adele Daigle (Aunt Adele) - Maggie's sister
George Daigle (Uncle George) - Adele's husband

Others Characters:
Lillian Mae Bordelon (Lilly) - Jack's second wife
Charlotte - Lilly's oldest daughter
Caroline - Lilly's second daughter
Roy Landry - Lilly's Lawyer
Henry Babin Sr. - Bordelon Family Lawyer
Henry Babin Jr. (HB) - Henry's son and Bordelon family lawyer
Douglas Lambert, Jr (Doug) - Funeral Home Director
Sara Morgan Gentry - Mary's best friend, owns a property
management company
Ellie Roberts - Mary and Todd's housekeeper
Lola Savoie - Tess' daughter-in-law, owns Lola's Sweet Creations
Bakery
Jason Savoie - Aunt Tess and Uncle Isaac's son and Lola's husband
Richard - Caretaker for Bordelon Property
Judge Laura Parker - Judge assigned Bordelon case
Sheriff Daryl Jackson - Sheriff of Natchitoches Parish, Lilly's
nephew
Dixie Owens - Bordelon tenant, an artist
Trevor Gardener - Dixie's fiancé, construction worker

A BED OF ROSES

Very Minor Characters:
Fr. John Martinez - Pastor at Immaculate Conception Church
Aunt Isabelle (Issy) - Jack's sister
Wayne Dugas - Lilly's boyfriend before she married Jack
Susan Dugas Lirette - Wayne's daughter
Douglas Lambert Sr. - Doug Lambert's father and Jack's friend
Jane - Henry Babin and HB Babin's secretary
Angela Lasyone - Friend of Mary, owner of Lasyone's Restaurant
Nancy Rutledge - Friend of Mary, owner of The Good House B&B
Payne Williams - Friend of Mary, owner of Samuel Guy House B&B
Kathy - Owner of Maglieaux's On the Cane Restaurant & Sweet Cane B&B
Lacey - Jason and Lola's daughter, Works in bakery with her mother
Amanda - Uncle Robby's daughter, Bordelon cousin
Juliet - Uncle Tommy's daughter, Bordelon cousin
William Taylor - Friend of Teddy Perot, Perot family lawyer
Bill and Joanne Morgan - Old friends of Jack and Maggie, Sara's parents
Jim and Donna Neville - Old friends of Jack and Maggie
Paige Neville St. Germaine-Childhood friend of Maddie, insurance agent
Paul and Amy Robichaux - Old friends of Jack and Maggie
Dr. Julian Goudeau - Jack's neurologist
Peter Lockhart - Friend of HB, lawyer from New Orleans
Logan and Karen Miles - Friends of Todd and Mary from New Orleans
Sylvia and Dean Hebert - Friend of Todd and Mary from New Orleans
Gail - Friend of Mary's from New Orleans
Claire - Friend of Mary's from New Orleans

PROLOGUE

The annoying beeping of the alarm clock woke Mary at six-thirty on the morning of March 10, 2015. She felt like she had barely fallen asleep just six hours before. As she got out of bed and staggered to the bathroom, the events of the last month passed through her head in a blur. It was hard to believe it had finally happened. Her invincible father had passed away two days ago, after fifteen long years of declining health following a massive stroke that had left him partially paralyzed. It had all culminated in the last month with a trip to the emergency room, followed by a stay in the intensive care unit then hospice. At least God had been merciful in only letting Jack linger four days in hospice care before he released him from his pain and called him to join his wife, Maggie. Now Mary, the second of Jacques (Jack) and Margaret (Maggie) Bordelon's eight children, was left with the dubious task of corralling her four sisters, Myrié, Martine, Madeline and Mallory, and three brothers, Jack Jr., Joseph and Jacob together so that they could plan the funeral.

After growing up, all seven of Mary's siblings had moved away from their home town of Natchitoches, Louisiana, and had scattered themselves from one end of the country to the other. Even Mary had moved away for a time, only moving back in 2005 to help with her parents' care. Now, coordinating arrangements to get everyone home in time for their father's funeral had been a logistical nightmare. Only two, Martine and Mallory, had managed to make it home in time to say their goodbyes to their father.

Martine, a nurse, was Jack and Maggie's third child. She had driven from her home in Alexandria, one hour away, to Natchitoches a week before when Mary had called to tell her things were not looking good for their father. She had stayed with Mary to help her take care of Jack all the way to the end, which had been a godsend. With her medical background, she had been able to explain to Mary and the rest of the family all the medical jargon that the doctors were using, and she was especially helpful with administering the morphine that Jack needed when he came home. She had left the night before to go home and take care of a few things and to be available to act as chauffeur to some of the siblings who were flying into Alexandria.

Mallory, a principal of a Catholic high school in Arlington, TX, was the baby of the family. She looked like a young version of Maggie. She had her mother's dark brown hair and eyes and her creamy olive skin that was the Perot family trademark. Mallory had flown in four days ago after Mary had called to tell her that their father had been placed in hospice care. By the time she arrived, Jack had already slipped into a semi-conscious state in the hospital bed set up in the living room of the family home.

Jack and Maggie had built the home on the fifteen acres of land that Maggie had inherited from her parents forty years ago. A few years later Jack and Maggie bought fifteen more acres from Maggie's brother, Teddy. The land was part of a one-hundred-fifty-acre farm belonging to Maggie's parents. It was originally part of the nine-hundred-acre Willow Rose Plantation that had belonged to Maggie's grandfather and had been in the Perot family for generations. When both of Maggie's parents died, the farm was divided into ten plots for their ten children. Some of the siblings moved away or were not interested in owning so much acreage, so they sold their shares, but always to a family member, as it was agreed by all the siblings that they would make every effort to keep the land in the family for as long as possible. However, that was now all in jeopardy.

CHAPTER ONE

MISS LILLY

Only six months after Maggie's death eight years ago, Jack had announced to his still-grieving children that he was marrying Lilly Mae Johnson. Miss Lilly and her husband, Sam, who had died five years before Maggie, had been friends with Jack and Maggie since before Mary was born. Jack and Lilly started seeing each other four months after Maggie's death. Within a couple of months, they came to the conclusion that, since they were both alone, it just made sense for them to get married so that they could take care of each other. They also reasoned that, since they weren't getting any younger, they needed to do it sooner than later.

Mary and her siblings were shocked at the news as they never dreamed their father would remarry. For that matter, they never dreamed he would outlive their mother. His health had been going downhill for years due to diabetes and other health issues. When he suffered his first stroke, Maggie was left with having to care for him despite the fact that she was just finishing up chemotherapy treatments for breast cancer. Five years later Maggie's breast cancer returned and she developed dementia, which made it impossible for her to care for Jack, although, that fact seemed to elude his understanding. To make matters even worse, Jack had another stroke in 2005. By that time something had to be done, so Mary moved back home and stepped in as her parents' main caregiver. Therefore, the idea of anyone wanting to marry a man in Jack's physical condition seemed implausible. What his children failed to take in to account was that Jack's financial assets made him a prime target for a woman looking for financial security or a quick payday.

Both Mary and her brother, Jack Jr. (JJ), a renowned Cajun chef living in Philadelphia, had tried to talk to their father about how this move would affect the family legally, as well as emotionally, but their father, who had been in deep mourning after Maggie's death, had suddenly become like a teenager in love and did not want to hear any dissenting voices.

Before Jack's children had time to adjust to the idea of their father's impending marriage, Jack, then seventy-five, and Lilly, seventy, married in a grand ceremony. Then Lilly took over their beloved mother's house and that was that. Needless to say, not only did the Bordelon siblings have some unsettling feelings about this sudden change of events, but so did their mother's five surviving siblings, three of which lived on the surrounding property. To put it mildly, there were more than a few ruffled feathers to go around.

A week before the marriage, in an effort to smooth over some of the dissent, Jack and Lilly loudly proclaimed that all the property and assets in the Bordelon family would remain in the Bordelon family. However, at the same time, Jack was quietly working behind his children's backs to have JJ replaced by Lilly as his executor with power of attorney. JJ learned of the changes just days before the wedding when he received a certified letter from their father's lawyer informing him that his services were no longer needed in his father's affairs. This did not go over well with JJ. It is safe to say that that letter capped off the already stormy relationship between Jack and his namesake.

Just months after Jack and Lilly's wedding, everyone's concerns became reality when Jack revealed that he was rewriting his will and that Lilly would be inheriting a portion of Belle Rose upon his death.

Most people assumed Maggie had named the family property Belle Rose after her family plantation, Willow Rose, but it was actually Jack who had named the property Belle Rose. Roses were Maggie's passion so she started planting rose bushes all around the house and property shortly after she and Jack built their family home there. One day Jack started complaining to his wife about all the thorny bushes she had planted to which she responded, "Roses are so beautiful, you can never have too many." After that Jack started teasing Maggie by referring to the house and property as Belle Rose, which means beautiful rose in French. The children picked up the name and they started using it as well. Before long everyone was referring to the property as Belle Rose.

Now, the Bordelon children had no say in the decision to hand over a piece of Belle Rose to Lilly, as Maggie had left all her worldly possessions to Jack in her will. At the time of their mother's death none of the children had any reason to contest the will, even though Maggie was clearly suffering from advanced stages of dementia, as they never dreamed such a thing would happen. By this time JJ and his brother, Jacob (Jake), the seventh of the eight Bordelon children, a confirmed bachelor and a pilot for Delta Airlines, had exhausted all means of reasoning with their father. However, Mary did not want to throw in the towel quite yet so she solicited the help of her brother Joseph (Joe), the fifth Bordelon child who was a missionary priest currently working on a Indian reservation in Arizona.

Joe always had a way with his father from the time he was little. Where Jack and JJ's relationship had always been rocky, Jack and Joe's had always been smooth. This was partly because Joe had the kind of personality that made everyone feel at ease. Plus, he always knew exactly what to say and he would say it in such a way that no one could dare take offense, not even Jack. Joe could usually get Jack to do just about anything, but he rarely played that card. No one in the family had been that surprised when Joe announced after his high school graduation that, instead of taking the baseball scholarship he had been offered to Northwestern University in Natchitoches, he would enter the seminary to become a priest. Maggie was over the moon with the news, but Jack was not as excited about it. That was one of the few times Joe had played his card and he won Jack over in no time.

This time, however, even Joe's efforts fell on deaf ears. As Jack had so eloquently put it, everything that he and Maggie had accumulated over the fifty years of their marriage now belonged to him and he could do whatever he damn well pleased with it! Besides, he said now that Lilly was his wife, it was his responsibility to provide for her in the event of his death.

Jack had preached to his children for as long as Mary could remember, the importance of keeping Belle Rose in the family. So much so that, when Mary and her oldest sister, Myrié, had divorced and were contemplating getting married again, he had strongly advised his daughters to take legal precautions to insure that whatever they inherited from the family did not get put into community property with their new husbands. He was adamant about making sure that his grandchildren's inheritance would not fall in the hands of their new husbands should either of his daughters die first. Yet, here he was, doing exactly what he had warned them against doing. It made utterly no sense to any of his children.

Jack's hasty marriage after Maggie's death and his subsequent behavior dealing with his children forever fractured the strong relationship he had had with his children and, while most of them continued to check up on him from time to time in phone calls to Mary, few called him directly or made the long trip home to visit him. At first Jack took the withdrawal of the children from his life as a personal affront to him and to Lilly, blaming them for not being able to accept his new wife who was in his eyes an "angel" sent to him by God. As Lilly became his full-time caregiver, she also became his lifeline. Subsequently, she controlled his world. Whatever Lilly wanted she got. Whatever she told him, he believed without question. Jack, who had once been an astute and shrewd businessman, husband and father, had a definite blind spot in all matters related to Lilly and the blind spot extended to her daughters, Charlotte and Caroline; and all three used this to their full advantage. Charlotte and Caroline even convinced Jack to allow each of them to build a cottage on the family property. This, of course, only upset his children more and widened the divide between them and their father. It also enraged the aunts and uncles on Maggie's side of the family.

Maggie's brother, Tommy, had bought up most of the land from his siblings over the years and even some from a few of his

Perot cousins. Altogether, he had one-hundred-fifty acres on which he grew hay and raised cattle. All three of the Bordelon boys had worked summers baling hay for their uncle when they were in high school. Maggie's youngest brother, Robby, had thirty acres on which he bred and trained horses. Myrié and Mary loved going to their uncle's ranch when they were young to ride horses with their cousin, Amanda. Uncle Robby had even given them a palomino horse named Silver when they were teenagers. The remaining fifteen acres were owned by Maggie's twin sister, Mary Theresa, or Aunt Tess as everyone called her, and her husband, Isaac. Their land held the original house built by Maggie's parents in 1918 and the Perot family cemetery.

As kind and loving as Jack was to Lilly and her daughters, he was just the opposite to his own children. Jack constantly lashed out at his ungrateful children for their seeming abandonment of him in his old age. Whenever any of them did visit him, he would angrily complain about his other children being so unreasonable, never accepting any of the blame for the situation himself. Even Mary and Martine visited less and less, as they dreaded the inevitable conversations with their father. However, Mary never quite gave up, and finally, with her constant nudging along with a lot of praying, Jack, just a year or so before he died, became more open to seeing how his behavior had played a role in the demise of his relationship with his children. He even expressed to Mary some amount of remorse but he still could not fully grasp the magnitude of what he had done to deserve his children's rejection.

Mary took this as a good faith effort on his part and used it to convince most of her siblings to give their father another chance. Because of this, most of them were at least speaking to their father, even if it was mostly by phone, in the final year before his death. Two of Mary's sisters had even made the long trip home to visit Jack in that last year. Myrié, a veterinarian, had come all the way from West Palm Beach, Florida, and Madeline (Maddie), a rising star on HGTV and the sixth of the eight children, had come all the way from Charlotte, North Carolina.

After hospice stepped in and Jack was moved from the hospital to the family home, Lilly turned over the majority of his care to his children. She said it was so that they would have an opportunity to spend as much time with their father as possible before he passed away. She also decided that they should handle all of the funeral arrangements as she was just "too overwhelmed in her grief" to do so herself. Mary and her siblings were thankful to have the authority to do so, though it all seemed a little too convenient considering their past experiences with Lilly.

As Jack slowly slipped away, family and friends came to pay their last respects. Jack's only living sibling, his eighty-seven year old sister, Isabelle, or Aunt Issy as her nieces and nephews called her, made the two hour trip from Cottonport so that she could see her baby brother one last time. It was heartbreaking to see her sitting next to Jack's bed, holding his hand and talking to him as if they were both children again.

People paraded in and out of the house expressing their condolences to Lilly, Mary, Martine and Mallory with puffy eyes and tear stained cheeks. Most told stories of their fond memories of Jack and the important role he had played in their lives. Just hours before his death, Fr. John Martinez came to administer the Last Rites.

When the final moments came, Mary and Martine had just stepped out of the room and Lilly and Mallory were the ones by Jack's side. As soon as it happened, Mallory ran to get Mary and Martine. All three rushed back into the room where their father's now lifeless body lay. As they hugged and consoled each other, all the hurt feelings they had experienced at the hands of their father temporarily drained away.

CHAPTER TWO

THE HOMECOMING

Mary and her husband, Todd, ran a Bed and Breakfast out of their circa 1890, Acadian style home. The house had five guest bedrooms and there was a cottage in the back with three additional bedrooms which meant that they would be able to accommodate most of the family members who would be coming in for Jack's funeral. Mary only had a couple of reservations coming up in the next few days so she had called one of her B&B friends, Payne Williams, who owns the Samuel Guy House Bed and Breakfast, and made arrangements with him to have her guests stay at his B&B. She also called Nancy Rutledge, another of her B&B friends, who owned The Good House Bed and Breakfast, and made arrangements with her to accommodate Martine and Myrié's children.

Around nine o'clock on the morning of March 10, Mary and Mallory were busy preparing the bedrooms for the arrival of the rest of the Bordelon family when the phone rang. Mary answered it and a lady on the other end of the line introduced herself as attorney Roy Landry's secretary. She said that Mr. Landry was representing Lillian Bordelon in the matter of her husband's will. She went on to say that Mr. Landry would like to know if Mary and the other Bordelon children would like to meet with him on Thursday morning to look over their father's Last Will and Testament. She said that Lillian had informed Mr. Landry that most of Jacques' children lived out of the area and would only be in town for a short time so he wanted to accommodate them as much as possible.

Mr. Landry was not the lawyer that Jack and Maggie had used for years before Maggie's death. He was Lilly's lawyer and she had convinced Jack to switch to him after their marriage. This too had been a not so subtle sign to the Bordelon children that Lilly had had an agenda from the start. When Mary first found out that Jack had switched lawyers, she had called her parents' long-time family lawyer, Henry Babin, to see what she could find out. When his secretary, Jane, forwarded her call to Mr. Babin, Mary was surprised to hear not Henry Babin's voice on the other end of the line, but his son, Henry Jr.'s voice instead.

Henry Jr., or HB as he was called, and Mary had gone to school together. She heard that he had moved to New Orleans to work for a large law firm there after graduating from Loyola Law School. HB told Mary that his father had a car accident about a month ago and was still home recuperating. He said that the accident had been a wakeup call for his parents and him and that he had decided to move back home to be closer to them and to work in his father's practice. He added that his father would be semi-retiring at the end of the year and would just work a few cases from his home office. HB asked Mary if she wanted his father's home phone number. She was reluctant at first to take it for fear of intruding on his father's recovery but HB assured her it would be fine if she called him.

Mary was relieved when Henry Babin answered the phone and sounded genuinely happy to hear from her. After some small talk, Mary asked him the question she was calling about. Mr. Babin told her that he wasn't at liberty to discuss with her the specifics of her father's legal business with him due to confidentiality laws. However, because of his love and admiration for Maggie, he went out on a limb to tell her, in a roundabout way, that he suspected the reason her father had switched lawyers was due to the fact that, when Jack and Lilly had come to see him about switching Jack's power of attorney and executor designate, he had advised Jack against doing so. He said this seemed to upset Lilly and that writing the letter to JJ informing him of the change was the last legal work he had done for Jack.

Mary asked Mr. Landry's secretary to hold on for a minute while she briefly explained to Mallory what was going on. They both agreed it would be a good idea to schedule the appointment, so Mary told the secretary that she and her siblings would be available to meet with Mr. Landry at ten o'clock Thursday morning. After she hung up the phone, Mary and Mallory discussed what they thought would be in the will. Their father had made it pretty clear that he was leaving Lilly a sizable amount of his estate but no one really knew how much.

After arguing with Jack to no avail, the Bordelon children had all pretty much washed their hands of the estate. They all had successful careers and they all, with the exception of Mary and Martine, lived far away from the family homestead. So none of them were that interested in taking over Belle Rose, however, they would like to see it stay in the family. Mary's three boys had all been very close to their grandfather and had shown some interest in the land, especially her oldest son, Beau, who was planning on retiring from the military in a couple of years. A few years before, Beau had told his grandfather that, after he retired, he would like to come home and build a house on the family property. Jack had told Beau he thought that was a wonderful idea but now that seemed highly unlikely.

Mary and Mallory decided second-guessing was not going to do them any good and that they had more pressing things to do. They still had to finish getting the bedrooms ready for the family and they had to write their father's obituary. They decided that Mary would continue working on the bedrooms while Mallory continued working on the obituary. By noon Mary had finished up the rooms and was making a light lunch of tuna sandwiches when Mallory walked into the kitchen and said, "What's that I smell cooking? It smells delicious!"

Mary replied, "It's chicken and sausage gumbo, but you can't have any of it right now."

"Why not?"

"Because Todd is making it for supper tonight." He just went to take a shower so I am supposed to be keeping an eye on it for him."

Mallory went over to stir the gumbo.

She mumbled, "Man, there is enough gumbo here to feed an army! I don't know why I can't have one small bowl of it."

"Because for starters it isn't done yet and, secondly, by six o'clock tonight we will have an army here, that is, if no one's flight gets held up."

Mary explained that JJ and Veronica were supposed to be landing in Alexandria at four o'clock and Myrié's flight would be arriving at four-fifteen. Martine and Dave were supposed to pick them up at the airport. Maddie and Garrett said they would be arriving between five and six o'clock depending on their work schedule.

"At least they will be driving in in their company motor home," Mary said. "That is one less bedroom we will need. Jake picked up Joe in Tucson this morning in his personal plane and they are supposed to be landing at the airport here between three and four o'clock. That makes ten of us for supper tonight so here, eat your tuna sandwich and pretend it is a catfish po'boy."

Mary handed Mallory a plate with a sandwich and chips on it and a glass of iced raspberry tea. She got her own plate and glass of tea, then they both sat down to eat. When they finished, Mallory took out her laptop and showed Mary the text for the obituary she had been working on. Mary said it looked good to her and they crossed it off their "To Do List". Mallory said she would forward it to the funeral home for their approval. Next on the list was getting all the pictures together for the video and picking out the music. After discussing several songs, they decided on, "I Did it My Way," by Frank Sinatra. It seemed to fit their father more than any other song they could think of.

Mary left Mallory to work on the video while she made some phone calls. First she called Immaculate Conception Church and made an appointment for Joe to meet with Fr. John the next morning at nine o'clock to go over the funeral Mass arrangements. Next, she called the church choir director to make an appointment for Myrié to meet with her at the same time to go over the music. Just as she hung up the phone, Todd came into the kitchen to resume his job of cooking gumbo.

Todd and Mary had been married for twenty years. It was a second marriage for both of them and it had not always been smooth, but they had weathered the storms along the way and had come out of them stronger than ever. Mary's first marriage had been a disaster, but her three sons had come from it so she wouldn't do it differently even if she could. Todd had one son from his first marriage, but he and Mary did not have any children together. Todd was twelve years older than Mary, but Mary had always felt closer to his age than her own as she always felt like she was an "old soul" in a younger body.

Todd was a "Cajun" in the truest sense of the word. Mary had met him when she was living in New Orleans and they had connected almost immediately. At the time, Mary was going through a divorce from her first husband and was not looking to jump into a new relationship. However, two years later they couldn't imagine their lives without each other, so they decided to get married. A few years later Mary's father had his first stroke and Mary started thinking about moving back home to help her parents. When Mary first brought up the idea to Todd, he was very much against it so Mary would make the trip home as often as she could, all the while continuing to work on getting Todd to change his mind. It was an uphill battle for a while as Todd just couldn't see himself living anywhere else but New Orleans. However, he finally gave in when Hurricane Katrina hit the city and everything was destroyed for miles and miles around. At that point Todd couldn't bear to see his beloved city in ruins so he gave in and they packed up what was left of their belongings and moved to Natchitoches.

Mary had always wanted to open a B&B and Natchitoches was a B&B haven, so she convinced Todd to let her take the insurance money they had collected on their house in New Orleans and invest it in a large run down historical home near the center of town and they began the ominous and painstaking job of renovating it. Maggie loved helping Mary with the project and it gave her something to focus on during that last year when she was dealing with the devastating effects of cancer. Mary and Todd opened the doors to "A Bed of Roses" just a month after Maggie's death in 2007.   Mary had named the B&B in honor of Maggie and her love for roses. However, she had gotten the actual name from a saying her mom used to recite to her children when they were young. She would say "Life isn't always going to be a bed of roses. It's going to be up to you to make the best of whatever life throws at you."

Mary had so much wanted to share the special day with her mom, but she could feel her mom's spirit looking over her shoulder when she cut the ceremonial ribbon for her new business.

When they opened the B&B, Mary retired from teaching to run it full time while Todd continued working as an insurance claims adjuster. His work required some traveling, but whenever he was home, he helped Mary in the B&B, mostly with the cooking and the lawn care. He just recently retired, and now days he spends much of his time playing pool on his regulation, nine foot pool table, hanging out at the local pool hall and watching pool tournaments and sports on television.

As Todd continued working on his gumbo, Mary filled him in on what the plans were for the evening. As they were talking, the phone rang and Mary looked at the caller ID. It was her sister, Madeline.

"Hello, Maddie. Where are you and Garrett now?

Maddie replied, "We're in Jackson, Mississippi."

"Do you think y'all will make it here in time for supper? Todd is making a big pot of gumbo."

"Oh, Mary, I wish I could say yes but we have hit a snag. Our producer wanted us to stop off in Jackson to meet a real estate agent here so he could show us a piece of property he has listed that might be a good project for our show next season. Well, you know how these things go. One thing led to another and it ended up taking longer than Garrett and I anticipated. I hope Garrett can get this wrapped up soon so we can get back on the road."

Mary quickly reassured her sister, "Don't worry Maddie. I understand and I am sure all the others will too. Just drive carefully and get here when you can. You know where to park the RV so if you come in in the middle of the night just pull in and we will see you in the morning."

"Ok, thanks, sis! We will be there soon! I promise! Tell Todd he had better save me some of that gumbo or else!"

Mary laughed as she responded back, "Don't worry. There is plenty, but I'll make sure he saves you some."

Maddie said, "Love, you!" and Mary replied back, "Love you too, a bushel and a peck!"

Maddie smiled to herself as she completed the old fashioned phrase, "And a hug around the neck!"

Mary and her sisters had picked up the family saying from their grandmother years ago. There were numerous pecan trees around the Perot property. When Mary was young, her grandmother, her mother, her aunts and all the little kids would collect pecans in the fall by the bushel and the older kids would take them to the Farmer's Market in town to sell on Saturday mornings. As they picked up the pecans her grandmother would say to the little ones, "I love you a bushel and a peck and a hug around the neck." They all got such a kick out of it. Later, their mother carried on the tradition by saying the phrase to her children and grandchildren, and her daughters did the same.

When Mary looked back at Todd, he was rolling his eyes at her.

Mary's smile turned into a frown as she retorted, "I know, I know. You don't have to say it. If Maddie ever makes it here when she says she will it will be a miracle. I guess that is what we have to put up with having a celebrity in our family."

With that they both smiled just as Mallory walked into the room. She looked at both of them and asked suspiciously,

"What are you two smiling about?"

Mary responded, "Nothing, we were just discussing Maddie. She called a few minutes ago."

Mallory shot back, "Oh, wait. Don't tell me. I bet she and Garrett had to stop off somewhere and they are going to be late."

Mary and Todd cracked up laughing and Mallory joined in. They were still laughing when the phone rang again. Mary picked it up. This time it was Joe. She answered the phone still laughing.

"Joe said, "Hey, Mary. What's all the commotion about?"

"Oh, nothing. Are you and Jake already here?"

"Yep, we just got here. Who's coming to get us?"

Mary thought for a minute and then said, "I'll send Todd. He's just finishing up with his gumbo. He should be there in about twenty minutes."

"OK, sounds great! See you soon."

As Mary hung up the phone, Todd turned the fire down under the gumbo and told Mary to keep an eye on it. He went over to the key rack by the door, picked up his truck keys and grabbed his Saints ball cap from the coat rack.

As he walked out the door Mary yelled after him, "No stopping off at The Dry Bean, Todd! You had better bring my brothers straight back here!" Mallory looked at Mary and said, "He sure left in a hurry! Do you think he heard you?"

"Oh, he heard me alright. The question is, will he do what I told him. If I know Todd and our brothers we'll be lucky if they get back in time for supper. Oh, well, it's my own fault. I should have known better than to send him to pick those two up."

With that Mary and Mallory walked out of the kitchen and went to Mary's office to finish working on the video. They were still working on it when they heard Martine and Dave's SUV pull up in the gravel driveway. They immediately got up and ran back into the kitchen.

JJ came barreling through the door first yelling, "Anybody home?"

Myrié was next with, "Where's my drink?"

Veronica, Martine and Dave brought up the rear. Everyone quickly started hugging each other and laughing out loud in traditionally, boisterous Bordelon fashion.

JJ was dressed in his signature jeans and cowboy boots and Veronica looked as neat and fashionable as always in her designer pantsuit and heels. She and JJ were such a contrasting couple, he with his southern Cajun drawl and country boy appearance and she with her upscale, northern, executive flair. Myrié was dressed in a colorful attire that only she could pull off and make it look chic. She was the flamboyant one in the family and had been ever since Mary could remember. Martine and Dave were both in their dressed down jeans and LSU T-shirts as usual. Martine was the quietest of all the brothers and sisters and often got lost in the shuffle with all her more outspoken siblings. She was the tallest of the sisters which wasn't saying much as the rest of them were barely five feet. They were all so different, but Mary loved them all dearly and was so happy to see them!

Mary thought, "Now if only Todd would hurry up and get here with my two baby brothers,..." and as if on cue, he and her other two brothers barged into the room, clearly showing signs that they had, indeed, stopped off at The Dry Bean. At least they had brought refreshments with them and again hugs were shared around the room as Todd took bottles of wine and beer out of paper bags and set them on the kitchen counter.

JJ went over to the gumbo pot and picked up the lid. He yelled across the room, "Hey, brother-in-law, are you attempting to make gumbo?"

Todd replied, "Why, you need my recipe? I bet that one you've been using in that fancy restaurant you run up north isn't passing for Cajun cookin' even with that funny name you slapped on it."

Everyone laughed as they started picking sides in the never-ending duel of the two Cajun chefs in the family. Drinks were poured all around and everyone started talking at once, which was another common occurrence whenever the Bordelon children got together. Myrié asked when Maddie and Garrett would be arriving, and Mary told her about her phone conversation with Maddie. No one was any more surprised at the news than Todd or Mallory had been earlier. The sisters all chipped in to help Mary get the rest of the food ready as the guys brought in all the luggage and stacked it in the hallway. They all sat down at the big farmhouse-style kitchen table and the conversation dropped slightly in tempo as everyone started eating the delicious soup with slices of hot, toasted French bread.

In between bites, Mary filled everyone in on the call she had received from Mr. Landry's secretary. This brought to the forefront the topic of their father's will, a topic that most of them had long ago decided to put in their rear-view mirror, but now that their father had died, it was staring them all in the face.

Their father's will was a sore subject for a multitude of reasons but the main one was that he had used his will as a tool to manipulate all of them, and even on some occasions, to turn them against each other. When he wanted something from one of them, he would make grand promises of what he would be leaving them in his will, and when they did not do as he wished, he would threaten to take them out of it or to leave their share to one of the other siblings. When he really wanted to threaten them, he would say that he had decided to leave all his estate to the Catholic Church. When they were all young adults, these tactics had some influence on them, but as they got older, they began to see through his games. They started comparing notes with each other and realized what he was doing. They tried to make him understand that he didn't need to buy their love or loyalty and that threatening them was counterproductive, but their father never seemed to get the message.

After he married Lilly and started making statements about rewriting his will, most of the siblings tried to reason with him. They didn't complain about the money, but they tried to get him to understand the importance of keeping the land in the family. Contrary to what their father believed, they did not want the land for its monetary value, but because of what it represented. They wanted to protect their mother's family legacy, a legacy that he had strongly supported as well as encouraged up until his marriage to Lilly. However, after they realized he wasn't budging, they all stopped showing any interest in the land, as they realized, as long as he thought they wanted it, he would continue to use it to manipulate them. When he realized that none of his wayward children were going to play his games anymore, he recorded himself lecturing them about how disappointed he was in them and mailed copies of the CD recording to each of his children. Since neither their father nor

Lilly knew anything about recent electronic technology, the siblings strongly suspected that Lilly's daughters had a big part in this endeavor. However, they never confronted their father, Lilly or her daughters, choosing silence as their only response. When his children refused to even acknowledge receipt of the CD's Jack became even more enraged. However, after a period of time he finally gave up and realized he could no longer control his children. Now they were all going to find out just how far he had gone to make his point and to have the last word on the matter.

Of course the Bordelon children knew that Lilly was far from blameless in the whole will scenario. Mary had learned through a cousin that Lilly had dated a man named Wayne Dupree shortly after her husband, Sam, had died. He, like her father, had recently become a widower and was in poor health. When Mary found out about Wayne and Lilly, she tracked down Wayne's daughter, Susan. Mary had been in Girl Scouts with Susan when she was young, and she remembered Susan's father, then a firefighter, coming to one of their meetings and giving the young scouts a lesson on fire safety. She got in touch with Susan on Facebook and invited her to lunch.

Over the course of the meal, Susan poured her heart out to Mary as soon as Mary told her about her father and Lilly. Susan told Mary that she and her brother hated Lilly and her two daughters for what they had done to their family. She went on to tell Mary the entire story. Susan said shortly after her father began dating Lilly, Lilly convinced him to move out of his house and to move in with her so that she could take care of him. After he did, she took over his checkbook and began paying all of her expenses out of his account. Then Lilly convinced him to buy a large storage building and put it on her property behind her house so that he could store some of his things in it. Eventually, Lilly convinced him to empty out his house and move all of his belongings to the storage building so that he could sell the house. Luckily, Susan's mother did not leave a will so Wayne had to have his children's consent to sell the family home since they now owned half of it. When Wayne went to his children to get their consent, they immediately suspected Lilly was behind it all and that she wanted their father to sell the house so that she could get her hands on the money from the sale. Susan and her brother refused to give their consent which upset Lilly but she couldn't do anything about it. Lilly tried to get Wayne to marry her, but when he told his children about the idea, they got very upset so he put her off.

Shortly afterwards, Wayne became seriously ill and had to be hospitalized. At that point, Susan, who still had power of attorney, stepped in and demanded Lilly turn over her father's checkbook. When Wayne died a couple of weeks later while still in the hospital, Susan and her brother went to Lilly's house to get their father's suit so he could be buried in it. When they arrived at the house, they were met outside by Charlotte and Caroline. The sisters handed Susan and her brother two boxes containing some of their father's clothing and a few of his personal belongings and told them in no uncertain terms that they were not welcome on the property. When they asked about getting the rest of their father's belongings they were told by the sisters that they would not be getting anything else. Before Susan and her brother could take legal action to obtain any of their father's things, Lilly and her daughters held a garage sale without their knowledge and sold all of their father's things, including most of their family antiques. By the time Susan finished her story, she was in tears and Mary was, too.

After Mary spoke to Susan, she called all of her siblings and relayed to them the information she had just learned. They all concluded that Lilly must have decided she would not make the same mistake with Jack as she had with Wayne. They strongly suspected that she planned from the start to convince their father to marry her as soon as possible so that she would have full control of his finances with no pesky interference from his children. Furthermore, they highly suspected that she had planned from the start to eventually get their father to change his will to make her his sole beneficiary and they suspected her daughters were in on the plot.

As the siblings sat around the table discussing the ins and outs of the situation, they all expressed more concern for their aunts and uncles than themselves. They all prayed that somehow their father had come to his senses before he had died and only gave Lilly usufruct of the land in his will. They knew how much it was going to hurt their mother's family, especially their Aunt Tess, if Lilly inherited the land that had been in the Perot family for generations. Aunt Tess hated Lilly living on the property in Maggie's house from the start, and she was adamant that she did not want to see Lilly inherit even a small part of it. She thought it was a slap in the face to her beloved twin sister's memory, and she had told Jack as much on more than one occasion but he had refused to listen to her concerns just as much as he had his own children's.

The Bordelon family finally decided to drop the subject as discussing it was not getting them anywhere. They all agreed that they would have to deal with their father's will soon enough when they met with Mr. Landry on Thursday, but until then, they would not let the subject of their father's will ruin the little time that they had together this week. They had not all been together in one place since their mother's funeral eight years ago and that had truly been a sad time for all of them.

As everyone started getting up from the table the usual complaints started about how miserable they all were from having eaten too much. Everyone, including JJ, complimented Todd on how good the gumbo was. While Myrié, Martine and Veronica went upstairs to unpack Mary and Mallory cleaned the kitchen. After depositing the suitcases upstairs the guys came back down and headed to the game room. On the way they started making bets as to which one was going to come the closest to beating Todd in a game of nine ball. Todd was already there chalking up his pool stick as he prepared for the slaughter.

He said in his thickly-accented, Cajun drawl, "Well, boys, which one of yous am I a gonna have to make cry first?"

Maggie's Coffee Cake

Batter Ingredients
2 cups self-rising flour
½ cup sugar
¼ cup butter
2 eggs
1 cup milk
1 tsp. vanilla

Topping Ingredients
1 tbsp. cinnamon
½ cup all-purpose flour
1 cup sugar
¼ cup softened butter
¼ cup chopped pecans

Pre-heat oven to 350 degrees. Mix batter ingredients together and pour into square 9x9 pan. Mix topping ingredients together and sprinkle on top of batter. Cook for 30 to 45 minutes until golden brown.

Note from Myrié: This is a Bordelon family favorite whether it is for breakfast or as a go-to dessert when we need something not too sweet and in a hurry!

CHAPTER THREE

THE CONFRONTATION

Wednesday morning Mary's alarm clock went off again at six thirty, but she didn't get up for a while. She rolled over and hit the snooze button as she slowly began to focus in on why her head was pounding. The events of last night started appearing in slow-motion in her foggy brain. She remembered everyone coming in last night. She remembered them all sitting around the kitchen table. She gradually started remembering a few other things like staying up until after midnight reminiscing with her sisters and Veronica as they drank glasses of wine. They all retold story after story of things that had happened in their childhood, alternating between tears and laughter as each one brought up a memory of their past. They especially enjoyed enlightening Veronica on some of the more sordid details of JJ's teenage years. Veronica thought that she had already heard most of the juicy stories there were of JJ's youthful escapades, but JJ's sisters told her a few new ones.

Mary finally got up and headed to the bathroom. Thankfully, she had bought pastries from Lola's Sweet Creations Bakery the day before because she was not up to cooking breakfast for everyone this morning. They were going to be lucky to get a homemade cup of coffee.

By the time Mary made it to the kitchen it was seven forty-five and Todd, Myrié, Martine, Dave and her three brothers were already there. This didn't surprise Mary as they had all been early risers since Mary could remember, unlike herself. Todd had already made coffee so Mary poured herself a cup, added some cream and sugar and set down at the kitchen table next to Todd. As she leaned over to kiss her husband good morning, she noticed a half-eaten cake sitting in the center of the table. She immediately surmised that either Myrié or JJ had gotten up especially early to make their mother's famous coffee cake.

As Mary cut herself a slice, she sarcastically commented, "Glad to see y'all haven't forgotten how to make yourselves at home."

JJ shot back, "Well, if we want anything to eat around here we better know how to fix it ourselves because we would starve waiting on Sleeping Beauty to fix anything for us before lunch time."

Jake chimed in, "Yeah, I thought this was a Bed and Breakfast," putting added emphasis on the word, breakfast.

Mary replied, "This Sleeping Beauty only gets up early to fix breakfast for her paying guests," putting added emphasis on the word, paying.

Myrié spoke up, "Well, I just thought since we are not paying guest we should at least chip in and help out as much as possible."

Mary replied, "Thanks Myrié. I should have known it was you and not JJ who made the coffee cake. I really do appreciate it. You know how much I love Mom's coffee cake and you know how to make it better than any of us."

JJ quickly jumped in, "Hey, I can make Mom's coffee cake just as good as Myrié can, maybe even better."

Just as Joe started to add his two cents to the conversation, the siblings' bantering was interrupted by Maddie who walked into the kitchen slamming the back door behind her.

Maddie was a whirlwind in a tiny body. She was the shortest of the sisters at only four foot, ten inches, but what she lacked in stature, she made up for in personality. Mary jumped up and ran over to give her sister a big hug.

Then she turned back to the table and yelled, "Why didn't any of you tell me Maddie was here?"

Jake responded, "Well, you didn't give us a chance. Besides, you just came downstairs a few minutes ago. If you hadn't slept all morning, you would have known they pulled in about an hour ago."

Mary ignored Jake's comments as she sat Maddie down at the table and went over to pour her a cup of coffee. As she handed the cup to Maddie she said, "You must be exhausted! Did you and Garrett drive all night to get here? Where is Garrett?"

Maddie replied, "Yes, we drove most of the night, but Garrett did most of the driving, so he's sleeping right now. I slept some last night because I knew I was going to want to hit the floor running this morning. I know you, Marty and Mallory have been doing so much, especially you, Mary, and I feel terrible for not being able to make it in sooner to help."

Mary gave Maddie a motherly look as she said, "Oh, Maddie, do not worry one bit about that! I am just so glad to have all of you home."

Just then Mallory and Veronica came down the stairs and into the kitchen. They took turns hugging Maddie, then pouring themselves cups of coffee. Everyone sat around the table eating coffee cake as Mary started dishing out the assignments for the day. She told Joe about the ten o'clock appointment he had with Fr. John and Myrié about the ten o'clock appointment she had with the choir director. Veronica offered to help Mallory finish the video work and put it on a CD to take to the funeral home. Mary asked Marty to call the funeral home to confirm the appointment with Doug Lambert, the funeral director, for two o'clock this afternoon. The meeting was for the family to go over the final arrangements for the wake service which was already scheduled for Thursday night and the funeral which was already scheduled for Friday morning. Mary asked Myrié and Maddie if they would like to accompany Martine, Mallory and herself to the funeral home. She warned them that Lilly and her daughters would also be at the meeting. Myrié said she wouldn't miss it for the world and Maddie seconded her response. Next, Mary assigned Maddie to call the president of the Ladies Altar Society at the church, to go over the arrangements for the reception following the funeral. The ladies club was in charge of organizing all the donated food for funeral receptions, and the potluck meal was usually held in the church activity center.

JJ and Todd volunteered to plan all the family meals. Mary told them not to worry about Thursday night as she had already reserved a private dining room at The Landing Restaurant on Front Street for the family after the wake. Todd and JJ said they would also make out a grocery list and go shopping for whatever they needed that Mary did not already have on hand. Mary thanked them wholeheartedly as they were going to have a lot of mouths to feed over the next four days. Mary's three boys, Beau, Blake and Brett and their wives, Eva, Allison and Danielle, were all driving in today, and Myrié's four children, Sean, Seth, Samantha, and Scott, and two of their spouses were expected in on Thursday as were Marty and Dave's two children, Kathryn and David. Mallory's husband Troy also would be driving in on Thursday but would be leaving their two young children with his sister. JJ and Veronica's three children and Maddie and Garrett's two children would not be coming. So, by Thursday evening, there would be a total of twenty-five family members present. Since all the bedrooms in the main house were now occupied, Mary planned to put her kids in the cottage out back and send Myrié and Martine's kids to The Good House B&B.

After making sure their services were not immediately needed, Jake and Dave said they were going to take a ride out to Perot Country to visit the aunts and uncles. Maddie and Martine asked the guys to wait for them to finish their phone calls so that they could go with them. Everyone scattered to take care of their assignments while Mary picked up the dishes from the table and started cleaning the kitchen. At nine thirty Joe and Myrié left to go to the church and Jake, Dave, Marty and Maddie left to go visit the aunts and uncles. JJ and Todd were still in the kitchen arguing over the menus. They must have finally come to an agreement because Mary heard Todd's truck pull out of the driveway around ten thirty and she assumed they were headed to the grocery store. Mary used the next couple of hours to straighten up the house and make sure everything was in order in the cottage for her boys and her daughters-in-law. By twelve thirty Garrett had joined the family and everyone was back at the house eating a chicken casserole someone had dropped off for lunch. Joe gave a rundown of all the arrangements that he had made with Fr. John, and Myrié informed everyone what songs she and the choir director had picked out. Afterwards, the sisters all piled in the B&B SUV and left for their meeting at the funeral home.

When the sisters arrived at Lambert Funeral Home, they were immediately greeted by Doug Lambert. Doug's father and Jack were close friends and his family's funeral home had handled the funeral arrangements for most members of the Perot and Bordelon families including Maggie's funeral. Doug's father would have personally handled Jack's funeral if it were not that he had retired from the family business a couple of years earlier and was now suffering from the onset of dementia.

After expressing his heartfelt condolences, Doug escorted the sisters into a conference room. Lilly was already seated at the long mahogany table, and Charlotte and Caroline sat a few feet away in side chairs. The sisters all greeted Lilly and her daughters with courteous pleasantries and stiff hugs. Then they each took a seat at the table. Mallory handed Doug the CD copy of the video she, Mary and Veronica had put together. He thanked her and said that he was sure it would be perfect. He also thanked her for forwarding him Jack's obituary and said he had made copies of it for everyone to review. As he was speaking he passed the copies out to everyone sitting at the table. They all looked down at their copy and proceeded to skim over the contents of the article. Lilly was the first one to comment.

"I think there must be a mistake here. Under the list of Jack's children's names there is no mention of either of my daughters' names."

Mallory immediately responded, "That's because they are not Jack's children."

"Well they are my daughters, and I was Jack's wife so that makes them his step-children, and therefore, they should be listed in the obituary along with his other children."

Myrié turned to Lilly and said, "Lilly, your daughters were adults in their fifties when you married our father. Do you really believe it's necessary to put them in our father's obituary as his step-children?"

Lilly began to sob as she replied, "Yes, I most certainly do! They were very close to Jack and they did a lot for him. He loved them as his own and I know that, if he could be here, he would tell you so himself!"

Mary turned to Charlotte and Caroline and said, "Since we are talking about Charlotte and Caroline, let's ask them how they feel about it, but first, I want them to think about something before they answer. If your mother had died before our father, would you want to list all eight of us in your mother's obituary?"

Charlotte and Caroline looked at each other, then at their mother. They were obviously uncomfortable.

Charlotte spoke first. "This is all news to us. We had no idea that our mother expected us to be in the obituary. We never even thought about it one way or the other. As far as what we would do if the tables were turned, I do not think we would put all of you in our mother's obituary. That being said, I understand how our mother feels, and I do not want to see her so upset."

Caroline interrupted her sister. "It doesn't matter to me if we are in the obituary. She turned to Lilly and said, "Mom, it's OK. It isn't a big deal. Just let it go."

But Lilly wasn't ready to let it go. She turned to Mallory and snapped, "This is your doing isn't it? You're the one who wrote the obituary and you intentionally left my daughters out of it! You are just trying to get back at me for marrying your father! I bet your brothers, JJ and Jake, are behind it, too."

Mallory was so hurt and angry over Lilly's accusations but she did not want to say something she would regret later, so instead, she got up and walked out of the room. Out of concern for her sister, Martine quickly got up and followed her out the door.

Maddie, trying to ease the tension in the room, diplomatically said. "Lilly, we are not trying to get back at you. I admit some of us have stronger feelings on the subject than others but Mallory is in no way trying to get back at you for anything and neither are any of the rest of us."

She turned to Doug and asked, "Is there any precedent for such a situation?"

Doug slowly replied, "Not really. I have seen it done both ways. It is really up to the individual family or families."

Mary cut in, "You know, it really is all up to Lilly." With that, she looked straight at Lilly and without blinking an eye she said in a slow, matter-of-fact tone, "You are the wife, so you have all the authority here, just as you have had for the last seven years. Whatever you want, that is what it is going to be, so it is really all up to you." Every time Mary used the word "you" she put a little more emphasis on it. By the time she finished speaking, all eyes in the room were directed at Lilly.

For a few moments no one spoke. Then suddenly Lilly wailed, "Well, this is just great! I lose, no matter what I do. If I say I insist on having my daughters put in the obituary, then I look like the horrible stepmother, but if I give in, then I don't get what I want. She wiped the tears from her eyes with a tissue, then noisily blew her nose as everyone waited to see what she would do next. Finally, she blurted out, "Just forget it! Do whatever you want!"

Myrié and Maddie looked at each other in disbelief. Mary had just played Lilly and came out on top.   Doug, trying to salvage the difficult situation, quickly said, "Well, I guess that settles it. The obituary is accepted as written. Let's move on to what kind of casket you would like. We have several to choose from."

Myrié, Mary and Maddie, in an effort to soothe things over, agreed with the casket Lilly picked out. They did the same with the flowers she wanted and the other decisions that needed to be made. They even agreed to have Lilly be the one presented with the flag that was going to be draped over their father's casket because he was a veteran of the Korean War.

Last, Doug asked which one of the Bordelon children would like to deliver the eulogy for their father at the wake service. This caught the remaining sisters off guard as they had not even thought about doing such a thing. Doug recommended JJ do it since he was Jack's oldest son. The sisters looked at one another and read each other's thoughts. They all three knew that would be a bad idea so Maddie quickly offered, "Myrié will do it. She's the oldest in the family so it should be her."

Myrié shot Maddie a look that could kill but she knew that it really was her responsibility, so she reluctantly agreed. By the time the meeting was over, Lilly had calmed down and everyone was cordial in saying their goodbyes.

Myrié, Mary and Maddie rushed out of the room to look for Mallory and Martine. They did not see either sister in the waiting area so they went outside. There they spotted them standing in the parking lot next to Mary's SUV. As soon as they saw them, they went over to Mallory and all three gave her a bear hug at once.

They all cried in unison, "Are you alright?"

Mallory responded, "Yes, I'm fine. I shouldn't have let her get to me like that."

Marty asked, "What happened after we left?"

Maddie replied, "You missed it. Mary talked Lilly down and won!"

Mallory said, "You mean Lilly backed down?"

Myrié responded, "Yep."

Mallory hugged Mary as she said, "I don't know what you said to get her to back down, but whatever it was, I love you for it!

Myrié cut in, "Well, I think we need to go out and celebrate the victory!"

Mary replied, "Myrié, it is only three thirty in the afternoon and I have to get back to the house so I will be there when my kids start coming in."

Myrié and Maddie both shot back, "It's five o'clock somewhere!"

All of them laughed but Mary stuck to her guns. "Come on. Y'all get in. We still have wine at the house if you want to celebrate and, if you're nice to me, I might make you some peach daiquiris."

At that, they all piled in the SUV and headed back to the house as they talked and laughed and teased Mary about her wonderful performance. Mary humbly insisted that they were making too much of her part in the fiasco. She told them that getting Lilly to back down had been a joint effort. To take some of the spot light off of her, she told Martine and Mallory about

Myrié agreeing to deliver the eulogy for their father at the wake. With that they all started teasing Myrié about what she was going to say. Myrié had no earthly idea what that was going to be.

When they arrived back at the house it was four o'clock and JJ and Todd were in the kitchen cooking shrimp étouffée. For once they seemed to be getting along without arguing over who knew more than the other about how to cook anything and everything. JJ was at the stove stirring the creamy concoction while Todd was washing dishes. They were trading "Thibodaux and Boudreaux" jokes and laughing so hard they could barely get out the punch lines. Veronica and Dave were sitting at the table watching them and laughing at them more than at their jokes.

They looked up at the sisters as they came through the door and Veronica asked, "Well, how did it go?"

JJ and Todd stopped trading jokes long enough to turn their attention to the sisters to see what they had to say.

Myrié said, "It was a cage fight but we outnumbered them."

Mary replied, "I don't know if I would go that far."

Just then Jake and Joe entered the room. Jake said, "Did I hear something about a cage fight?"

Maddie proceeded to tell the story, embellishing it ever so slightly and ending it with praises to Mary, once again, for her performance. Mary took a bow and everyone clapped for her.

Todd yelled, "That's my girl!"

Mary blushed and tried to change the subject by asking if any of her children had called while she was gone. Veronica answered that Eva had called to say she and Beau should be here about five o'clock.

Mary replied, "That means they should be getting here soon! What about the others?"

"Several other people called but not any of your other children. Mostly it was friends calling to express their condolences and asking if there was anything they could do. A few said they wanted to come by and drop off food, but I told them to call the church and make arrangements to drop it off there on Friday. Between what JJ and Todd are cooking up and all the casserole dishes people have already dropped off and the two cakes Aunt Doris and Aunt Pauline sent, I didn't think you would want more dishes to clutter up your refrigerator. I hope that was OK."

Mary answered, "That's great! You did exactly what I would have done. Thanks for playing secretary for me while we were gone."

"No problem. It gave me something to do to feel useful. I wrote down all the names of everyone who called and put the list on your desk."

Mary thanked the ever efficient Veronica again as she looked at her cell phone. It had just beeped indicating she had a text message. She silently read the message and then told everyone that it was from Allison and that she and Blake should be arriving about six o'clock. Just as she put the phone down it beeped again. This time it was Brett. It said that he had to work late so they would not be coming in until tomorrow. They planned to get an early start and hoped to get in by noon. Mary again relayed the message to the others as she went over to the cabinet to pull out her blender. She said over her shoulder, "I guess I better make those daiquiris I promised Myrié and Maddie."

Jake said, "Now that sounds like a good idea to me!"

As Mary was passing out the frozen drinks, she heard a car pull up in the driveway. She immediately stopped what she was doing and ran to the door. Beau and Eva got out each side of the car and Mary rushed over to hug them both. The last time she had seen them and their kids was last summer when she and Todd had driven the twenty hour, two-day trip to Jacksonville, NC, where Beau was stationed. She was disappointed they did not bring her grandchildren with them so that she could see them, too, but she understood why they hadn't. Luckily, Eva was able to make arrangements on short notice with a close friend to watch the children so that she and Beau could make the trip themselves.

Mary said, "I am so glad you made it!"

Beau replied, "There is no way we were not going to come."

Mary understood exactly what he meant as she knew how much he loved his grandfather. As Jack and Maggie's first grandchild, Beau had shared a special relationship with the both of them, but especially with his grandfather. Even though Beau shared his own father's name, he looked more like his grandfather than any of Jack's own sons did. This fact even more endeared Beau to his grandfather. The two were both a short five foot seven inches tall with broad shoulders, a long torso, short legs and a round face. If one were to compare pictures of them at the same ages it would be difficult to tell them apart if it were not for Beau's lighter hair color. And, to top it off, Beau was born on his grandfather's birthday.

Mary escorted Beau and Eva into the house, and everyone took turns hugging them. Beau and Eva both complained about how long the drive was but they said it was worth every mile to be back home and to get some Cajun cooking.

As Beau shook Todd's hand, he said, "Mom told me you made a big pot of gumbo yesterday. You better have a bowl left over with my name on it."

Eva quickly added, "And one with my name, too."

Todd replied, "Sorry. Your greedy aunts and uncles ate the whole pot last night."

Mary quickly corrected Todd's statement saying, "You know that's not true, Todd. I made sure to save enough for all three of my boys and their wives and Maddie, that is unless someone got into it while I was gone."

JJ turned to Beau and Eva and said, "The reason there is plenty left over is because it wasn't very good. If I were you, I wouldn't eat any of it. Maybe you should wait until I make a pot, then you would be sure to get a good batch."

Mary said, "Oh no! Here we go again!"

Todd retorted back, "Funny, that's not what you said last night when you were wolfing down your second big bowl of it."

Everyone laughed and cut up as Mary resumed making daiquiris for everyone. The noise level in the room was so loud no one heard a car pull up in the driveway. They all turned their heads as Blake and Allison walked into the kitchen. As soon as they saw them, the previous scene was repeated, but when Blake made his way over to his Mom he picked her up, wrapped his arms around her and swung her around.

Blake was the tallest of Mary's children as he got his height as well as his looks from his father's side of the family. His six foot two frame towered over Mary's short four foot eleven inch one. She had been looking up to him since he was barely twelve years old. When Blake finally let his mother go, he walked over to Beau and they shared an extra-long hug as the two brothers had not seen each other in over two years.

After everyone finished with their greetings, Mary put out dishes and everyone helped themselves to the piping hot étouffée still sitting on the stove. They all crowded around the kitchen table and the snack bar to eat their meal and share conversation with their loved ones.

After everyone finished eating, Mary's sisters handled clean up duty while she took her kids to the cottage to get them settled. Afterwards, they all gathered in the pool room for a competitive couples' tournament of eight ball. Jake partnered with Mallory, and Joe partnered with Myrié. All the other teams were husband and wife. Everyone was grateful that Mary was Todd's partner as she was about as bad a pool player as Todd was a good one, which gave the rest of them a fighting chance. Sure enough, in the last game for the championship of all championships, Mary scratched on the eight ball and lost the game to Maddie and Garrett. There was whooping and hollering and high fives as everyone celebrated Todd and Mary's loss. Maddie and Garrett relished in their victory and graciously vowed to give Todd and Mary a rematch any time.

CHAPTER FOUR

THE READING OF THE WILL

Thursday morning breakfast was light with just coffee and the pastries Mary had picked up a couple of days before. Everyone ate in shifts as they got dressed for the day. All the Bordelon siblings had to be at Mr. Landry's office for ten o'clock. Mary assigned the rest of the family various duties around the house before she and her siblings loaded up in two vehicles and headed out. The sisters rode together in Martine's SUV and the brothers rode together in Mary's car with Joe at the wheel.

When they arrived at the law office, they were greeted by Mr. Landry's secretary. She said that Mr. Landry would be with them in a few minutes as she escorted them to a conference room. She asked if anyone wanted something to drink and they all replied no. JJ asked the secretary if she knew whether or not Lilly would be attending the meeting and she replied that she would not be. Everyone took a seat around the table and talked quietly until Mr. Landry entered the room a few minutes later. He introduced himself and the brothers stood up to shake his hand as they introduced themselves. Then, Mr. Landry walked over to each one of the sisters and lightly shook her hand as she introduced herself.

With the formalities out of the way, Mr. Landry got straight to business. He said that he knew their schedule must be tight with all the funeral arrangements, so he did not want to waste too much of their time. He stated that he had made copies of the will for each of them and, if there were no objections, he would pass the copies out and let everyone read the will to themselves. Then, if anyone had any questions, he would be glad to answer them. Everyone agreed, so Mr. Landry began passing out the copies, and as each one got their copy, they began to read silently.

After about five minutes time Mr. Landry said, "As you all can see, your father left all of his assets to his wife, Lillian Mae Bordelon."

No one spoke for several seconds.

Finally, JJ broke the silence. He addressed Mr. Landry with a question. "In your experience as a lawyer do you find it unusual for a man to leave his entire estate to a second wife and to completely leave out his children by his first wife of fifty years?"

Mr. Landry stuttered slightly as he answered JJ's question. "Umm, well, I, umm, really can't say. Each case is different."

Martine was the next one to speak up. She asked, "If we were to be inclined to contest this will based on the mental state of our father, what would we need to do?"

Mr. Landry replied. "I assure you Jack was perfectly sane and in full control of his mental faculties when he had this will drawn up, and if you were to make such a claim, I would testify in court that I am one hundred percent sure of that."

Most of Jack's children suspected that their father was likely not completely sane at the time he had signed this will, and probably had not been for sometime, but they had never challenged their father or Lilly in court regarding the matter and did not want to now. To the average person, Jack had seemed to be perfectly sane, but Mary and most of her sisters had long suspected that the four strokes he had suffered over the years damaged his processing skills and were the cause of his apparent inability to accept reasoning that he would have easily seen prior to the strokes. In their eyes this fact affected his mental competency. However, JJ and Jake had felt that it was just their father being the usual stubborn, dominating and arrogant person he had always been. Either way, though, they were all in agreement that before their father married Lilly, he would have never let Belle Rose go to anyone who was not a descendant of the Perot family.

Mary was the next one to speak up. "Mr. Landry, do you not find it odd that our father specifically stated in this will that, should he and Lilly die together or should Lilly die before him, that her daughters would inherit a portion of the land, **and** in so doing, he listed each of her daughters by their full names. Yet, in the part where it states who would be getting the remainder of his estate in such circumstances, it only states that it would go to his **"descendants"**? In other words, why would our father list his wife's daughters by their full names and not so much as list any of his own children or grandchildren by their full names but only mention them collectively as his descendants?"

Mr. Landry replied to Mary's question in a defensive tone. "I can't tell you why he did so, but it really is not relevant since he preceded his wife, Lillian, and therefore, she inherits everything."

"Mary replied, "Well, I'll tell you what it suggests to me. It suggests that the will was arranged by Lillian, and our father just signed it without having any input into its contents."

Mr. Landry fired back, "I beg your pardon! I can assure you that was not the case!"

Myrié asked, "How do we know that this is, in fact, our father's Last Will and Testament? It is dated September 15, 2010. Who's to say that he did not write another will after this one?"

Mr. Landry's responded to Myrié's question in an even more defensive tone. "Myrié, if your father had another will, I would have known about it as I was his lawyer, so he would have come to me if he wanted to update his will."

Myrié challenged Mr. Landry's statement, "No, you see, that is the problem here. You were not our father's lawyer. Henry Babin was. You were Lilly's lawyer, and she brought our father to you after she married him."

Mr. Landry was getting flustered by this point. He felt like he was being interrogated. He thought about Myrié's statement for a few seconds before replying back, "Well, technically, that is somewhat true. I did represent Lillian before she married

Jacques, but I did become Jacques' lawyer shortly after his marriage to Lillian, and besides, Henry Babin died about a year ago so he could not have represented your father at the time of his death."

Mary knew this to be true because she had read about Mr. Babin's death in the newspaper. His obituary had said he died of a massive heart attack. Mary had immediately called HB to offer her condolences and had sent flowers to the funeral home in the name of the Bordelon family. Afterwards, she had called her father to inform him of Mr. Babin's death. Jack had seemed genuinely saddened to hear the news about his old friend. She had asked him if he wanted to attend the funeral with her, but he declined as he was recuperating from the flu at the time. Despite all of this, Mary thought of something else that possibly could have happened. She asked, "Who is to say that sometime after September 15, 2010, but before Mr. Babin's death in 2014, that our father did not go back to see Mr. Babin and did not, at that time, have another will drawn up?"

Mary knew this was highly unlikely, but she was beyond frustrated about the whole situation and was just trying to wrap her head around the idea that their father could have done such a horrible thing as disowning his entire family. She could half way understand his anger towards some of his own children, but how could he have done such a thing to his own grandchildren who had never done anything but worship him?

When Mary's son, Beau was stationed in Louisiana for a three year stint as a Marine recruiter, he had gone through all kind of hoops to get assigned to a recruiting office in the Natchitoches area. He finally succeeded and was assigned to an office in Alexandria. Beau knew his grandfather's health was not good and that he may not have many more opportunities to be with him, so he wanted to do whatever he could to have quality time with him. He convinced his wife, Eva, to agree to live in Natchitoches. Then he somehow convinced her to agree to move, with their three young children, into a small two-bedroom cottage on his grandfather's property just so that Beau could be close to his grandfather and be available to help Lilly take care of him. However, between the time Beau spent in commuting every day to and from work and the long hours he was required to work as a recruiter, he was not home nearly as much as he had hoped to be. Fortunately for Lilly, Eva had stepped up in his place and helped with a lot of Jack's personal care.

Beau and Eva's children also adored their great-grandfather and spent a lot of time reading to him and entertaining him. So much so that Mary sometimes felt a little jealous of all the time Beau, Eva and her grandkids spent with her father, but she never complained because she knew how much it meant to her father and to them. They had all cried miserably when Beau completed his time as a recruiter and was reassigned back to the base in Jacksonville, North Carolina. Once in Jacksonville, Beau did not have any opportunities to come home again to visit as it was a long trip back to Natchitoches and he had since had to go on two deployments.

Since Mary's other two children, Blake and Brett, lived a little closer to Natchitoches, they had both come to visit as much as possible. Brett and Danielle had even dropped everything and took off a week of work so that they could come home and help Lilly care for Jack when he was hospitalized and Mary was out of town. Mary had frantically called them and told them that Jack was in the hospital in intensive care and was not doing well. She said that she was in Las Vegas with Todd at a pool tournament and could not get home right away to see about him. Without thinking twice, Brett and Danielle volunteered to go fill in for Mary and ended up staying even after she made it home. Mary told them they didn't need to stay, but they wanted to make sure their grandfather was out of the woods before leaving him.

Myrié's children also came to visit their grandfather on a few occasions. Just last Thanksgiving, Sean and Seth had driven more than twenty hours with their wives and young children to Natchitoches to spend the holiday with their grandfather. Myrié would have loved for them to come to Florida to see her instead, but she too had not complained when her children had told her they were going to see their grandfather for Thanksgiving. Her children had chosen to go to Louisiana, instead of sunny Florida, during Thanksgiving just to see their grandfather.

Mr. Landry replied to Mary's question in exasperation, "Well, I guess that is possible, but don't you think he would have told Lillian about it if he did? Besides, Henry Babin's son took over his father's office so he would have informed you if his father had a will for Jacques in his files. Plus, Mr. Babin would have more than likely filed a copy of the will at the court house and there is no such will on file."

Mary thought about all the points Mr. Landry was raising and quickly came to the conclusion that if Lilly knew about a new will, she certainly would not want to inform Mary and her siblings about it, especially, if it was not in her best interest. As far as Mr. Babin having filed it in the court house, her father may have explicitly instructed him not to file the will so that there would be no way that Lilly or her daughters could possibly find out about it. Mary decided to drop this line of questioning for now, but she made a mental note to herself to call HB as soon as possible to see if he knew if her father had visited his father prior to Mr. Babin's death.

Mary's thoughts were interrupted by a question from Jake.

"Mr. Landry, do you know about any life insurance policies our father may have had? Our father was an insurance salesman and he had a three hundred thousand dollar life insurance policy for several years, but he recently told us he had cashed it in a couple of years before our mother died."

Mr. Landry replied, "Life insurance is not included in a will so I do not know the answer to that question. You would have to ask Lillian or his insurance agent, but the information is confidential so the agent would not be able to tell you anything unless you were a beneficiary."

In hearing this, Mary knew asking Lilly for such information would be out of the question, but she made another mental note to call her insurance agent as soon as possible to see what she could find out. She and her father had the same insurance agent, and it was a long-time family friend. At least that is, if Lilly had not convinced him to switch agents like she had lawyers.

Maddie asked, "What about our mother's personal belongings and family furnishings that are in the house? Do we have any right to those?"

Mr. Landry responded, "Legally, no. They all became Lillian's property when your father died, but I will ask her about them and see what she wants to do. If she says you can come get them, I will have my secretary call you to set up the arrangements."

Joe had been silent through the entire meeting, but he finally spoke up and asked a very important question. "What about our mother's ashes that are entombed in a bench on the property by the meditation pond?"

Mr. Landry replied, "What about them?"

Joe responded, "Does Lilly now have ownership of our mother's ashes or can we have them removed from the property?"

Mr. Landry looked perplexed over the question. He said, "Well, as long as the ashes are on the property she has the rights to them but I will speak to her about that too and get back to you."

Joe said, "Please ask her if we can have the bench with both of our parents ashes moved to the family cemetery located on our Aunt Tess' property."

Again, Mr. Landry said that he would ask Lilly and get back to the siblings. After that, no one spoke up to ask any other questions.

Mr. Landry, looking clearly relieved to have the session over with, said, "Well, I hope I have answered all of your questions satisfactorily. If there is anything else I can do for you, please, let me know. Your father was a wonderful man, and I am very sorry for your loss."

None of the Bordelon siblings believed that this man ever knew the real Jacques Bordelon. He certainly did not know the side of him that they all did, and as far as their loss, it is doubtful that he meant it in the way that they were experiencing it at that moment. However, the siblings held their tongues and begrudgingly thanked him for his time as they got up and walked out of the room, through the office lobby and out into the parking lot. All eight of them were emotionally spent and practically speechless.

JJ was the first to regain his composure. He said, "As far as I am concerned it is done. I never wanted anything from him and I could care less about anything he owned. As far as our mom's ashes, I would like to see them moved but I could care less about his."

His siblings understood his feelings on the subject but they were too emotionally raw to respond. They all got back in the vehicles they had come in and rode home in silence, or at least the sisters did. As for the brothers, no telling what choice words were being spoken concerning their father and Lilly.

CHAPTER FIVE

THE WAKE

When Mary and her siblings returned home around noontime, Mary was excited to see that Brett and Danielle had just arrived. They were still exchanging hugs and greetings with the others at the house when Mary and her siblings walked into the kitchen. Brett walked over to his mother and picked her up in a huge bear hug. Next he exchanged hugs with his aunts and uncles and Danielle followed suit behind him. None of the siblings were up to sharing what had just happened at the lawyer's office with the rest of the family. They had a wake to go to in a few hours and they were going to need all the composure they could muster to act civilly in front of their, supposedly, bereaved stepmother and her family.

Mary asked Todd what was on the menu for lunch. He told her they were having meat pies as her friend, Angela, had come by earlier with a whole box full of the pies from her family restaurant, Lasyone's. Everyone cheered at that and all their attention went towards getting ready to eat. As they ate, the conversation was light and mostly centered around Mary's children. The aunts and uncles asked them numerous questions about how their lives were going and how their children were doing. All the boys and their wives were more than happy to swap stories of the trials and tribulations of young parenthood and the married aunts and uncles all laughed and laughed with the added relief of having escaped that period of their lives mostly unscathed. That is, except for Mallory, who was still in that period herself.

By the time they were finished with their meal, Myrié and Martine's children had drifted in. First Sean and Seth and their wives, Andrea and Celeste, arrived. They had made the long drive in together as they lived close by each other on the east coast. Next Samantha, Scott, Kathryn and David came in. Samantha had flown in from California and Scott had flown in from Colorado. They had rendezvoused at the airport in Alexandria, and Kathryn and David had picked them up. Then they had all ridden together to Natchitoches. Hugs were shared all around again, and the aunts and uncles repeated their questions to the newest bunch of nieces and nephews, laughing once again at the married couples humorous stories of parenthood. Sean and Andrea had two children, Seth and Celeste had four children and Samantha had two children. Scott and David were still eligible bachelors and Kathryn was also single. For these three, the aunts and uncles offered words of advice, some good and some not so much. All was received graciously, though, and the now overly crowded kitchen became extremely noisy with everyone trying to talk at once.

Finally, around two thirty, Mallory's husband, Troy, arrived. She was so happy to see him as she had started to get nervous thinking he might not make it in time for the wake. After everyone welcomed the last member of the family to arrive, Mary reminded them that they all needed to be dressed and ready to go to the funeral home by four thirty. That left a little less than two hours for everyone to get dressed. Mary told Myrié and Martine's kids that she had reserved rooms for them at The Good House. They thanked her and Todd volunteered to take them over to the B&B and help them get checked in. They told him it really wasn't necessary, but he insisted, so they all left the house and the rest of the family headed to their prospective bedrooms to get ready, with the exception of Myrié who stayed to help Mary pick up in the kitchen.

At four thirty everyone reassembled in the kitchen to decide who was riding with whom. Fifteen minutes later they all piled in their assigned vehicles and drove the short distance to the funeral home. When they arrived they were once again greeted by Doug Lambert. Most everyone knew Doug but Mary introduced him to the members of the family who didn't. After the formalities Doug ushered them into a side room of the funeral home so that he could go over some minor details and last minute instructions regarding the wake service and the funeral the next morning. He asked Mary if the pallbearers still planned to do the military salute at the church following the funeral. Mary said yes and each of the pallbearers stepped up to identify themselves. They were Beau, Blake, Brett, Sean, Seth and David. All of them but David would be wearing their official military dress uniforms for the ceremony as Beau was an active duty Marine, Blake was a reservist in the Army, Seth was an active duty Airman, Sean was an Air Force veteran and Brett was a Marine veteran. Doug took them aside to go over some specific instructions regarding their duties as pallbearers. Afterwards, he escorted all the family into the chapel where the wake would be taking place.

As soon as they walked into the room, they could hear Frank Sinatra singing, "I Did it My Way." In the front of the room was a large flat screen TV and playing on it was the slide show video that Mallory had given Doug the day before. As the song played in the background, pictures flashed across the screen of Jack; first of him as a young boy, then as a young man, then pictures of he and Maggie together as young adults and on their wedding day, then pictures of he and Maggie and their children, and then the grandchildren and great-grandchildren. Last, there were pictures of Lilly and Jack together.

Lilly and her family were already in the chapel seated on the left side so the Bordelon family sat in the pews on the right side of the room. After a few minutes, Doug came over and told them that this would be a good time for them to view the body before the wake actually started. He said that Lilly and her family had already done so and that now it was their turn. The family members formed a line and walked one at a time over to the casket to take one last look at their father and grandfather. It was difficult for all of them to look at the now lifeless body of the once strong and dominating figure that had been the patriarch of the family for so long.

All of Jack's grandchildren and their spouses, unaware of what had transpired earlier in the day at the lawyer's office, walked over to Lilly and warmly greeted her and her family. However, all of Jack's children kept their distance, not trusting themselves to be able to maintain the necessary level of decorum required in such a setting.

After a few minutes, friends and family started drifting in to pay their respects and the Bordelon family members spread out to greet them. It wasn't long before the room was overflowing with people and nearly everyone the family spoke to expressed fond memories of Jack and commented on how beautiful the video was.

All of Maggie's surviving siblings and spouses were there. Even Maggie's eighty-four year old brother, retired Louisiana Senator Theodore Perot, or "Uncle Teddy" as everyone called him, and his wife, Joy, had come in from Baton Rouge, and Maggie's sister and her husband, Adele and George Daigle, had come in from Lake Charles to pay their respects. The Bordelon children were so happy to see all of their dear aunts and uncles even if it was on such a sober occasion. Dozens of the Perot cousins were also in attendance and the Bordelon children were happy to see all of them as well.

There were so many longtime family friends that came to pay their respects that it would be impossible to list them all. There were several members of the Morgan family there. They and the Bordelon family went back at least three generations. Bill Morgan's first job as a teenager was as a delivery boy for Jack's father who was a butcher. Bill and his wife, Joanne, were about ten years older than Jack and Maggie and had been mentors to them as young parents. Bill Morgan's daughter, Sara Morgan Gentry, was ten years older than Myrié. Myrié and Mary had babysat Sara and her husband, Terry's children when they were teenagers. Later, Sara and Mary had become best friends with Sara serving as her mentor when she became a young mother. They had remained best friends to this day. When Mary saw Sara, the two friends embraced without speaking for they knew each other so well that words were not necessary. Mary knew she could count on Sara to be there for her when all of her family had to go back home.

There were also several members of the Neville family there. Jim and Donna Neville had been Jack and Maggie's best friends. Jim had been tragically killed in a car accident leaving behind a pregnant wife and five children. When the accident happened, Jack had taken all of Jim's children under his wing and served as their substitute father for years. Donna would be the first one to say she could never have made it without Jack and Maggie's help. Two of the Neville children, unlike Jack's own children, had followed his footsteps and became insurance agents for the same company he had worked for. Paige Neville was Maddie's best friend from kindergarten all the way through high school. Now she was Mary's insurance agent and, as far as she knew, Jack and Lilly's too.

Paul and Amy Robichaux were there. They had been friends of Jack and Maggie for at least forty years. Their son, Mike, had been Joe's friend in high school. Amy was a psychologist and had counseled Mary when she was going through her divorce. She and Paul had come out to visit Jack and Lilly on several occasions after their marriage and they were present at the Bordelon home when Jack passed away.

Logan and Karen Miles had driven in from New Orleans to pay their respects. They were longtime friends of Todd and Mary and they, along with several other friends from New Orleans, had evacuated from Hurricane Katrina and followed Todd and Mary to Natchitoches where they all stayed for weeks at Belle Rose until they could return to their homes in New Orleans. Jack and Maggie had welcomed them all as they went about setting up a makeshift hurricane shelter at Belle Rose. Everyone quickly signed up for various duties such as cooking, laundry and garbage detail. Belle Rose became like a little village unto itself, and by the time everyone had to leave, they all had become so attached to Jack and Maggie, and Jack and Maggie had become attached to all of them as well. All of the close knit group had come up for Maggie's funeral and would have definitely come up for Jack's funeral too had it not been that another member of their group lost her mother the same week. So, they all stayed in

New Orleans to attend that funeral while Logan and Karen volunteered to make the trip to Natchitoches and represent everyone else in the group at Jack's funeral.

At six o'clock, Doug requested that both Lilly's family and the Bordelon family take their seats so that they could begin the vigil service. When the families were all seated, everyone else followed suit and Donna Neville came up to the podium to lead the families and friends in the reciting of the Rosary. Afterwards, she said a few words about her dear friend, Jack Bordelon, and how much he had done for her and her children after her husband's tragic death. Then Doug motioned to Myrié to come forward. She nervously walked up to the podium and looked around at all the faces staring back at her. She said a quick silent prayer that she could pull this off and then began her speech, referring to her notes as she went.

"My siblings and I would like to thank all of you for coming here this evening to help us honor our father, Jacques Bordelon. As we went around the room a little while ago, talking to all of you, many reminded us of the wonderful man our father was. You all had such fond memories of how he had touched your lives in so many ways, but especially, in his acts of generosity, both with his money and with his time. You see, our father didn't just take care of his own children but he took care of a community. He truly embraced the saying in the bible, "You are your brother's keeper." When someone he knew wanted to send their child to a Catholic school but couldn't afford it, he paid their child's tuition. When someone he knew fell on hard times and needed money to pay their rent and feed their family, he gave them a personal loan. When someone he knew wanted to start a business on the Cane River but didn't have the money to buy the land, he gave them a lot he owned himself on the River. When someone he knew had a sick child and needed a way to transport that child to a hospital out of town, he showed up at their door in his motor home and chauffeured the whole family to the hospital miles away. Once he befriended a homeless man and took him home with him. He gave him clothes out of his closet and got him a job working at a local restaurant. Then he let him stay with us until he got his first pay-check. He drove the school bus when the Catholic school we attended couldn't afford a bus driver. When my best friend, Janice, lost her father, he took her and her brother under his wing. Then, as Donna Neville just told you, when his best friend died a couple years later, he took on the added responsibility of being a father figure to six more children."

"I could go on and on with these stories but you all get the main idea. Our father was a bigger than life person in this community. Everyone knew him, loved him, trusted him and respected him. He was asked on several occasions to run for mayor, and if he had, I am sure he would have won by a landslide but he said politics was not his thing. Politics may not have been for him, but he served on numerous boards and committees usually as president of them."

Myrié paused for a second to catch her breath, then she continued.

"However, there were times that we, as his real children, did not see him for days at a time because he was out doing what he loved best, helping others. We all worked odd jobs from the time we were old enough to babysit or mow lawns or wait tables so that we could save up money for a special outfit or to go to a movie because we all knew better than to ask our father for money for frivolous things. Helping the downtrodden was a more fitting use of his money. When we grew up, married and had kids of our own, he stuck to that same philosophy. If we needed money for something, it was always in the form of a loan to be paid back in full and on time, and if on some occasions it wasn't, he took issue with us. I am not going to lie. There were times I, and my siblings, resented our father for some of these things, but now, looking back on it, I would have to say that we all benefited greatly for the lessons our father taught us. We learned to be self-reliant. We learned to be hardworking and responsible. Most importantly, though, we learned to be grateful for everything we had in life for we were taught that life owed us nothing, and because of that, we are all truly grateful that we were raised by two wonderful people in a strong Christian environment. We are grateful that we never had to worry about having a roof over our heads or food to eat. We are eternally grateful that we had and still have an amazing extended family and a tight-knit circle of sisters and brothers. For all this we are very thankful to our father, Jacques Bordelon, as well as to our mother, Margaret Bordelon."

Suddenly Myrié's speech was over. She had gotten through it and had honored her father in the best way that she could. Some of the people listening may have found what she said to be disingenuous at best but she spoke from the heart and she had spoken the truth and that is all that anyone should expect of her. When she got back to her pew and sat down next to Maddie, her sister squeezed her hand and leaned over to whisper in her ear, "I knew you could do it! Great job! None of us could have said it any better!"

As Myrié turned to look at her other siblings they were all giving her the thumbs up. It made her feel so good to have their approval and she was relieved that she had been able to represent them all without falling flat on her face. If anyone felt her speech was disrespectful to her father, then so be it.

Next Fr. John addressed the family and friends. After Myrié's speech, what he had to say rang a little hollow. He spoke about all the wonderful deeds Jack had done for the church and praised him for being a good and faithful soldier in God's army. Last, he read a couple of Bible scriptures and gave a short homily. Afterwards, the extended family members and friends slowly filed out of the chapel and Doug approached the children to ask if they wanted to take one last opportunity to view the body. All of them declined the offer so he went over to Lilly and her family and asked them the same question. As the Bordelon family made their way out of the chapel they could hear Lilly crying as she stood by their father's casket with both of her daughters at her side.

Out in the parking lot Mary and Todd gave directions to The Landing. When they arrived at the restaurant they were directed to the private dining room Mary had reserved. After everyone ordered, JJ, now the new patriarch of the Bordelon family, and Mary stood up to address their family. Mary spoke first. "There will never be a good time to tell you all this news, but it is something that has to be done. As you may already know, we had a meeting with Lilly's lawyer today to read your grandfather's will and what we found out was quite disappointing. We all knew going into the meeting that it probably was not going to be good news, but it was the worst case scenario. According to the will presented to us, our father saw fit to leave his entire estate to Lilly."

All of Jack's grandchildren in the room looked from one to the other in total shock and dismay. It broke Mary's heart to see the look of betrayal on their faces.

Beau spoke up first. "How could he do that? The land has been in the Perot family for generations. Paw Paw preached to us the significance of the land staying in the family for as long as I can remember. He was so happy when I told him that Eva and I wanted to come home after I retire and build a house on it."

The other grandchildren echoed what Beau had just said.

Sean spoke up next. "What about all of Maw Maw's brothers and sisters? How are they going to deal with the situation?"

Mary replied, "Probably not very well, but we haven't had a chance to tell them yet and we probably will not have a chance until after the funeral. I know that they all suspect it as Aunt Tess has asked me several times over the last seven years since our father married Lilly what I thought was going to happen when he died. As you all know, your grandfather was very stubborn about this subject, and any effort we made to address it over the years fell on deaf ears."

The next one to speak up was Blake. "Is there anything y'all can do about it, legally?"

JJ replied, "We are going to look into a few things but it is hard to say right now. We just got the news ourselves today. Personally, I think the witch put him up to it."

Veronica touched JJ's arm to get his attention and said in a soft but stern voice, "Not now, JJ."

JJ looked at Veronica, gave her a little smirk of a smile and then turned back to address his family again. "OK, umm, where was I? Oh, yeah, we are not going to let this define us as a family. Despite what happened with our father after our mother's death, our parents raised us to appreciate family and that is the true legacy that they both left us with. It is the same legacy that your parents have instilled in all of you. Whatever financial or material things your grandparents accumulated in their lifetime, it is not nearly as important as the family they left behind. We will all deal with this as a family and we will go on as a family no matter what happens with the land or the estate."

Mary added, "We are all going to get through the funeral tomorrow and we will do it with grace and integrity. We will treat Lilly and her family as politely as possible and we will hold our heads up high. If you do not have it in your heart right now to do it for our father and your grandfather, then do it for our mother and your grandmother. She was the most gracious and loving person we will ever know in our lifetime, and we are her children and grandchildren, so we will act like it.

Everyone in the room clapped as Mary and JJ sat down. A few minutes later the waitresses started bringing the food into the room. Everyone started eating and talking among themselves, but the conversation was not nearly as boisterous as it usually was when they were all together as it had taken on a much more somber tone.

CHAPTER SIX

THE FUNERAL

There it was again, that awful alarm clock! Mary rolled over and turned it off as she sat up in bed. No time to hit the snooze button this morning. The funeral wasn't until ten thirty, but the boys had to be at the church for nine o'clock and the rest of the family had to be there for ten o'clock. Mary had a lot to do before then, starting with serving breakfast to twenty-five hungry people. At least she had prepared three Stuffed French Toast casseroles last night and put them in the refrigerator so all she had to do was pop them in the oven. She didn't hear the shower running so she hoped that meant Todd was already downstairs and had made coffee. She slowly got up, made her way to the bathroom and turned on the shower.

Mary could smell the bacon and the coffee before she even got to the kitchen. Todd was standing at the stove and he looked up at her as she walked into the room. He already had her three casseroles sitting on the counter waiting to go in the oven and the coffee pot was full. "God bless you!" she said as she went over and kissed her husband on the cheek on her way to the coffee pot. After she fixed her coffee she turned on the oven and set the temperature at three hundred fifty degrees. She turned to Todd and asked, "Where is everyone? It's already seven o'clock." Mary knew all her siblings except Mallory were early risers.

Todd replied, "Some already came down and got coffee. That's actually the second pot I've made this morning. I think they are just getting dressed for church before they come down for breakfast. I told them you were cooking your signature

French Toast Casserole so you know they will all be down in a little while."

Mary, absentmindedly looked out the kitchen window and commented, "I think it is supposed to be a sunshiny day today. At least that is a blessing." Then she turned back to Todd and asked, "Have you seen any of the kids yet this morning?"

Todd answered, "Nope," as he took crisp strips of bacon out of the pan and put them on a plate sitting next to the stove. Just then Jake walked into the kitchen and snatched a piece off the plate. Before Todd could say "Be careful, it's hot." Jake had put it in his mouth. He immediately made a face. Todd said, "Serves you right!" A second later, the back door opened and all three of Mary's boys walked in. They each walked over to their mom and took turns kissing her on her cheek as they made their way over to the coffee pot.

Mary popped all three casseroles in the large, over-sized oven as she asked her sons, "Are the girls up yet?"

Brett responded, "Yes Ma'am. They should be in in just a few minutes."

Beau asked, "When's breakfast going to be ready? We have to hurry up and eat so we can go get dressed in our uniforms."

Mary replied, "I am putting the casseroles in the oven now. They should be ready in thirty minutes. Will that give you enough time?"

Beau answered, "That should work but that means we need to eat first before the rest of the gang gets here."

Blake and Brett added, "Yeah, that's right!"

By the time the French toast was ready everyone had assembled once again in the kitchen. Mary started serving generous slices of French toast dripping in praline sauce to each of her guests. As she handed each one their plate, they looked for the nearest available chair or stool and sat down to eat.

By eight forty-five the boys were pulling out of the driveway headed to the church and the rest of the group had gone to their rooms to finish getting ready. By nine thirty everyone was again assembled downstairs and getting their car assignments. By nine forty-five, the caravan of cars pulled out of the B&B parking lot headed to the church.

When Mary got out of the car the first thing she noticed was her boys and her nephews standing outside looking so sharp in their military uniforms. The sight of them made her feel so proud! She went over and gave all of them a quick hug before she entered the church. She and the rest of her family met Doug inside and he instructed them to wait at the back of the church so that they could greet extended family members and friends as they came in. Lilly and her daughters were also standing in the back and they greeted their family members and friends as they came in the church as well. Finally, it was almost ten thirty and Doug told both Lilly's family and the Bordelon family that it was time for them to take their seats at the front of the church. The Bordelon family let Lilly's family go first, then they filed in behind them. They took their seat in the second from the front, right side pew behind Lilly and her family as the soloist in the choir began singing "Amazing Grace." When she finished the boys marched in carrying their grandfather's casket in full military style. It was an impressive sight to say the least! After the casket was secured in the front of the church and the pallbearers took their seats in the front left side pew, Fr. John began the mass. It was a traditional funeral Mass with Bible readings and music centered around the afterlife. In the homily, Fr. John talked about what a wonderful husband, father and friend Jack had been and how loved he was by all.

At the end of the funeral Mass, the pallbearers went back to the casket, lifted it up and carried it down the aisle and out of the church. Fr. John and the altar boys, then the two families, and then the mourners followed behind. When everyone had exited the church, two of the uniformed pallbearers ceremoniously removed the flag from the casket and folded it according to the official military flag code. Then Beau formally presented the folded flag to Lilly. Afterwards, he walked back to the casket and took his place at the side of it. Then the pallbearers lifted the casket and carried it one last time to the waiting hearse. The final act the uniformed pallbearers did for their grandfather was the military salute. They formed a drill line with Blake in the command position. They performed a drill arrangement, and then the salute. As they held their salute position the hearse drove away with their grandfather's body. The whole salute ceremony was magnificent to watch! Jack's departure from his time on Earth had been in as grand a style as he had lived his life on Earth. It was the most moving part of the entire funeral.

Since Jack had requested to be cremated, there was no graveside ceremony. His body was taken back to the funeral home where he would be privately cremated. In a few days Doug would bring the ashes to Lilly and he would assist her in putting them in the urn inside the left side pedestal of the marble bench sitting in front of the meditation pond on the Bordelon property now owned by Lilly. The right side pedestal of the bench housed Maggie's ashes which were now also owned by Lilly.

After the funeral, everyone made their way next door to the church activity center. The slide show video that was played at the wake was again being played on a flat screen TV mounted in a corner of the activity center's main room where the potluck meal was being served by the Altar Society ladies. Mary's friends Nancy and Angela, both members of the Altar Society, were helping out with the serving. There were two long tables covered with all kinds of food dishes. There were foil pans filled with jambalaya, dirty rice, red beans and rice and fried chicken. There were baskets of rolls, cornbread muffins and sliced French bread. There was a side table with two five gallon containers, one labeled sweet tea and one labeled un-sweet tea. There was another side table covered with desserts, including banana pudding, peach cobbler and several different kinds of cakes, cookies and pies.

Everyone went through the line, got a plate of food and a glass of tea, then made their way over to one of the many tables lined up around the room. The Bordelon siblings did not all sit together as they attempted to spread themselves out among their extended family members and friends. JJ and Veronica sat at the table with the uncles and aunts. Martine and Dave sat at the table with some of the cousins. Myrié sat at a table with her friend Janice and some other high school friends. Jake sat at the table with an old high school football buddy and his wife. Maddie and Garrett sat at the table with her high school friend, Paige, and the rest of the Neville family. Todd and Mary sat at the table with

Logan and Karen Miles and the Morgan family. Joe sat at the table with the Robichaux family. All the grandkids sat together.

Finally, around one o'clock, most of the people had finished eating, said their goodbyes and cleared out of the activity center and both Lilly's family and the Bordelon family were free to go. They all sincerely thanked the Altar Society Ladies as they filed out of the building. Before leaving they went back to the church to get the many plants and flower arrangements that friends and family members had sent. They loaded them in the back of Mary and Martine's SUVs and, then headed back to the B&B.

By one thirty, the Bordelon family was back at the B&B and most went straight to their rooms to change out of their dress clothes and into something comfortable. Myrié and Martine's children went to The Good House B&B to change but they were back in less than thirty minutes. Everyone assembled in the kitchen and Todd set out bottles of beer, wine and soda on the island counter top while Mary got out wine glasses that had once belonged to her mother.

After everyone had gotten their drink of choice Myrié proposed the first toast. "To us, for holding our heads up high and holding our tongues in front of Lilly and her family." Everyone raised their glass high, tapped them to each other's glasses and took a sip of their drink.

JJ was the next to make a toast. "May the witch get what's coming to her and I'm not talking about our father's money or land!"

This time Veronica refrained from correcting him and everyone laughed as they again raised their glasses, tapped and sipped. However, Joe must have felt a little guilty because his toast was slightly more appropriate. He piously said, "May God put upon Lilly and her daughters' hearts the desire to do what is right by the Perot and Bordelon families." Everyone gave him a sideways glance but no one made any comment. They just again raised their glasses, tapped and sipped.

Mary made the final toast to her father. "To Jacques Pierre Bordelon. May he rest in peace and may God have mercy on his soul and allow him to enter heaven's gate so that he can join our beloved mother, Margaret Myrié Bordelon, in eternal life."

Everyone performed the toasting ritual one last time. Then they all started talking at once in their signature Bordelon communication style.

Eventually, the conversation got around to what they should do now. Mary said the first thing that needed to be done was to speak to HB Babin. She wanted to rule out any chances of a second will. She said that she had spoken to HB earlier at the reception following the funeral but she didn't mention anything about the will at the time because she didn't want to bring it up until she could speak to him privately. It was getting close to five o'clock on a Friday afternoon so she volunteered to go to her office and make a quick phone call to see if she could reach him before he left his office. After she found out what he had to say they could decide the next step. Everyone agreed that she should make the call so she headed to her office while the others stayed in the kitchen and continued with their socializing.

The phone rang once and was immediately answered by HB's secretary. As soon as Mary told Jane who she was, Jane told her how sorry she was for her loss. She said Jack had always been so nice to her and that every Christmas Maggie had brought a large tin of delicious homemade cookies and pecan pralines to the office for her and Henry. Mary thanked her for her kind words and asked her if she could speak to HB.

Jane said, "You most certainly can, sweetie. He was on another phone call a few minutes ago but I think he is off now. Can you just hold on a minute while I check?"

Mary replied, "Certainly," then she heard Louis Armstrong's voice singing in her ear as Jane put her on hold. In just a few seconds the music stopped and she heard HB's voice at the other end of the line.

"Hello, Mary. This is a surprise. I just saw you a couple of hours ago."

Mary responded, "I know, but I really couldn't talk to you about legal matters at the time, so I waited until I came home and you had had time to get back to your office. I thought then we could speak more privately."

HB asked, "So this is a business call I take it?"

Mary answered, "Yes."

HB replied, "OK. I am guessing this has something to do with your father's death."

Mary answered again, "Yes."

HB said, "Ok, shoot."

Mary quickly filled HB in on what had transpired at Mr. Landry's office the day before. She concluded with, "So, my question to you is do you think it is possible that my dad could have gone to see your father before his death and had him draw up another will? Then, he had your father keep it secret even from you to make sure Lilly, nor any of us, knew about it?"

HB thought about it for a minute, then, responded, "Mary I would like to tell you yes, as I hate that your father did what he did to you and to your sisters and brothers, but I really don't think that he did because, when I took over my father's law practice, I went through all of his old files with Jane and the only will I found in your father's file was an old one that left all of his personal assets to your mother. It had not been updated after your mother's death so I asked my father about it and he said that Jack had gotten a new lawyer after he married Lilly and that he thought he had probably updated his will with him. I wanted to be sure so I checked at the court house and there was a new will on file for your father. I forgot the exact date of the will but I think it was in 2010 and it was filed by Roy Landry."

Mary sighed but continued to push the issue. "I understand what you are saying but my dad could have contacted your father at home after 2010, but before your father's death and had him draw up the will in secret and then asked your father not to tell anyone, including you, about it for fear of Lilly or us finding out about it."

HB felt so sorry for Mary. He could hear the desperation in her voice. He gently responded back, "Mary, that is possible I guess, but if he had, don't you think your father would have contacted me after my father passed away to make sure I was aware of the will in case of his death?"

Mary saw HB's point but she pressed on anyway. "Maybe he didn't think about it or didn't trust letting anyone else know about it. Did your father have any files at his house when he died?"

HB replied, "Yes, he had a small file cabinet with a few files but I retrieved those files shortly after his death."

Mary knew she sounded delusional but she couldn't help herself. "Do you think he could have had some other files that he kept somewhere else in his office or in another room in the house?"

HB responded, "I don't think so, Mary, but I will ask my mom. I will let you know if I find out anything from her that might be helpful."

Mary thanked HB for his time and patience. He told her not to think twice about it. He apologized for not being able to help her more and told her to call him anytime if there was anything else he could do for her. Mary thanked him again and told him to give his mother her regards.

When Mary returned to the kitchen, everyone was laughing and having a good time. She hated to interrupt the happy moment but she needed to relay the information she had obtained to the others so she yelled over the noise to make her entrance known. When she finally got everyone's attention, she told them what HB had told her, ending with the part about him volunteering to talk to his mother and get back to her as soon as possible.

Jake turned to Garrett, the only lawyer in the family, and asked, "So what would you suggest we do now?"

Garrett looked a little surprised that Jake was speaking to him as everyone turned their attention towards him to see what he was going to say. Garrett replied, "Well, first of all I am a real estate lawyer so I don't do much work in the area of will litigation unless we are buying a piece of property that is part of a succession, but even then, the studio has lawyers who deal with that kind of thing on retainer and they handle most of the legal work. Also, there is the issue of differences in laws from state to state. Laws concerning will litigation and successions are different from state to state and I know nothing about Louisiana law. My advice to you would be that you should wait at least until you hear back from this HB guy to see what his mother might know before you make any decisions or plans. Then, if you need further legal advice, I would hire him to represent you."

Everyone realized that what Garrett was saying made sense but they all planned to go home in the morning and, then they would all be scattered from one end of the country to the other again. Of course they could communicate via phone and email but it would be a little more difficult for them to pursue a unified line of defense regarding the will situation after they were back home. They hated that much of the follow-up would fall on Mary's shoulders once again. Also, they would still need to figure out what action to take after Mr. Landry notified them of what Lilly's answers were to the questions they had asked at the meeting. He said that he would call Mary's house to give them the answers as soon as Lilly responded to their requests concerning their mother's personal belongings, their family furnishings and their parents' ashes. Since it was the weekend, that likely would not happen until sometime next week. Then, there was the issue of what to tell the aunts and uncles. JJ said they were all asking him questions at the reception when he sat with them to eat. He said it took every ounce of self-discipline he could muster to not let on about the meeting they had with Roy Landry the day before.

After discussing all of these angles in the puzzle, it was decided that JJ, Myrié, Martine and Mary would meet with the aunts and uncles tomorrow morning to explain what was going on, as JJ, Veronica and Myrié's flights did not leave until tomorrow afternoon at four o'clock. Jake had to fly out first thing in the morning as he was scheduled to fly a Delta red-eye flight to London tomorrow night. Since Joe was catching a ride with him he would be leaving in the morning also. Maddie and Garrett had to be back in Charlotte the next day for a meeting with their producer, so Garrett planned to get up and start driving around five o'clock in the morning before the rest of the family was even up. Everyone else needed to be on the road by nine o'clock so that they could get back home to their respective jobs and children.

As soon as Mary told her sibling that she got the information back from Mr. Landry regarding Lilly's answers to their questions and from HB regarding the possibility of another will at his parents' house, she would hold a conference call so that they could discuss their options and decide what to do from there. With this much settled, they decided to resume their socializing and try to make the most of the little time they had left together. Maddie asked Mary and Todd if they were up to a pool game rematch and the trash talk started.

Mary, with the help of her daughters-in-law, put together a couple of snack food trays while Todd and her boys got more bottles of beer, wine and soda out of the storage room refrigerator and carried them to the game room. JJ made a quick phone call to Aunt Tess to invite her and the rest of the aunts and uncles over for breakfast around nine o'clock in the morning. Aunt Tess said she and Isaac would love to come and that she would relay the information to the others. She said that Adele and George were spending the night at her house and Teddy and Joy were spending the night at Robby's house so they would be able to come too. JJ said that would be great. Right before they hung up, Aunt Tess told JJ to let Mary know she would be bringing a pan of homemade biscuits to breakfast so not to cook any. JJ said he would be more than happy to relay that message. When JJ got off the phone, he gave Mary the message about the biscuits, then, everyone headed to the game room and the pool tournament was on.

This time Mary and Todd were victorious but they had some stiff competition from Joe and Myrié. Everyone teased Joe about how he came to be so good at shooting pool in his line of work. Around eleven o'clock Garrett said he needed to get to bed if he was going to be getting up at five o'clock to drive back to NC. He went around the room hugging everyone and saying his goodbyes. Maddie told him she would be coming to bed soon after. Myrié and Martine's kids were the next to make the rounds saying they needed to head back to The Good House so they could get a decent night's sleep. They would all be leaving out bright and early, too, so they did not plan on coming back to Mary's before they left town. Around eleven thirty, Maddie said her final goodbyes to her siblings and her nieces and nephews. All the sisters cried as they hugged her before allowing her to leave. By midnight the rest of the family headed off to their bedrooms hugging each other along the way.

CHAPTER SEVEN

THE AUNTS AND UNCLES

This time when Mary's alarm clock went off, she was already awake. She had awakened around five o'clock to the sound of Maddie and Garrett's RV pulling out of the driveway and could not get back to sleep. All she could do was toss and turn while so many thoughts about the last few days ran through her head like a late night movie with her family as the actors. She could hear the shower running so she decided to go to the kitchen and get a cup of coffee while she waited for Todd to finish up in the bathroom. When she got there, she saw Myrié standing in front of the island cracking eggs into a big mixing bowl. JJ was standing in front of the refrigerator holding the door open and looking inside for something.

Mary said, "Myrié, you didn't have to start breakfast for me. I told you last night that I was going to throw together a couple of sausage and egg casseroles this morning."

Myrié looked up from what she was doing and said, "I know, but I couldn't sleep so I got up. Then I figured, since I was up, I might as well get breakfast started for you."

Mary went over and gave Myrié a squeeze and said, "Thanks, I really appreciate it!" Then she turned to JJ, who was still standing in the door of the refrigerator, and asked, "What are you looking for?"

JJ replied, "The andouille sausage."

Mary said, "It's in the bottom drawer." as she walked over to the coffee pot, poured herself a cup, added cream and sugar and sat down at the table.

As Mary sat sipping her coffee, she rationalized, "Well if you two are going to take over making breakfast I am just going to sit back and watch."

JJ gave Mary a sideways look as he responded, "I'm sure we can find something for you to do."

"Mary replied, "How about I supervise?" Just then Todd walked into the kitchen. When Mary saw him she sarcastically continued, "Oh, sorry, I have to go take my shower now. I am sure Todd can help with whatever you need," to which JJ complained, "That sounds like a cop out to me."

Todd added, "I'm used to it," as he poured himself a cup of coffee. Mary commented, "Life is tough around here."

Myrié looked up from scrambling the eggs long enough to say, "By the time you finish showering and getting dressed, I should have the casseroles put together and one in the oven cooking. Then I am going to run upstairs to shower and get dressed myself."

Mary said, "Sounds good. I shouldn't be long." as she walked out of the kitchen, coffee cup in hand.

By the time Mary returned an hour later, Jake, Joe, Mallory, Troy, her three boys and her three daughters-in-law were all sitting at the table eating breakfast. What was left of one of the egg and sausage casseroles sat in the middle of the table, along with a basket of store bought biscuits. The other casserole was sitting on the stove waiting to be cooked. Todd, JJ and Veronica were sitting at the snack bar drinking coffee. Mary went over to the coffee pot and poured herself another cup, then went to sit at the table next to Blake. She lamented, "I really hate to see y'all leave so soon. It seems like you just got here. I wish we could have spent more time together."

Blake responded, 'I know, but we all have to get back home to see about the kids and our jobs. I promise we will try our best to come back with the kids to see you in the summer when they are out of school."

Beau added, "Mom, Eva and I will see what we can do, too. Hopefully, I will not have to deploy again for a while."

Brett echoed his brothers' promises and even Mallory, jumped in saying, "Yeah, 'Mom,' me, too."

Everyone laughed at Mallory's referral to Mary as "Mom" but the comment was fitting as, of all the sisters, Mary was the most like their mom. Since Maggie passed away, she had been the glue that had kept the family together and they all loved her for it. When Mallory called Mary "Mom" it warmed Mary's heart and she said with tears in her eyes, "I don't want any of y'all to feel, now that our parents are both gone and Lilly is in our family home, that you no longer have a place to come home to. You will always have a home here with Todd and me."

Jake said, "Well, if you and Todd are now our 'surrogate parents,' does that mean you are taking us all to Disney World?"

Todd replied, "Don't push your luck or you're going to be disowned again."

Everyone started laughing as Myrié, walked in the kitchen and said, "What's so funny?"

JJ replied, "Todd and Mary just adopted all seven of us."

Myrié said, "Well that's nice to know. When are we going to Disney World?"

This time the laughter was so loud it filled the entire room. It was finally interrupted by Mallory when she said, "I hate to be the party pooper, but Troy and I need to get on the road. The others at the table quickly repeated her assessment and everyone started getting up from the table. They each carried their dishes to the sink and started saying their good-byes.

Troy went upstairs to get his and Mallory's luggage while the boys went to the cottage to do the same. When Mallory came to hug Mary, she broke down in tears. It suddenly hit her that she really was parent-less and she whispered in Mary's ear, "I am too young not to have parents anymore!"

Mary whispered back as she hugged her baby sister tighter, "You aren't parent-less remember? Todd and I just adopted you."

They both laughed through their tears as Mary whispered, "I will always be here for you and don't you ever forget that!"

Mallory squeezed her sister back and they both reluctantly let go of each other, but not before Mary added, "I love you a bushel and peck!" and Mallory responded back, "And a hug around the neck!" They both wiped away their tears as they turned to hug other family members. Mary cried even more when she hugged her own children goodbye.

By eight thirty everyone had left except for the ones who were staying for the meeting with the aunts and uncles. Myrié had put the second casserole in the oven and they were all sitting around the table waiting for their guests to arrive. As they waited, they discussed the best way to break the news to their mother's siblings. They all agreed that JJ should be the one to do it, but Veronica warned him to keep it clean. He begrudgingly promised her and his siblings that he would.

At exactly nine o'clock they heard the vehicles pull up in the driveway. By the time all of the aunts and uncles had gotten out of their cars and trucks and made it to the back door, Mary was standing in the doorway welcoming them. Aunt Tess, true to her word, was carrying a big pan of homemade biscuits. JJ quickly jumped up to take the pan from her. As he did he said, "Man, these sure smell good!" Then he leaned over and gave his favorite aunt a kiss on the cheek.

Aunt Tess responded, "Well, I hope they are. I am getting so old I can't remember how to cook like I used to."

JJ replied, "Now Aunt Tess, you know you are not a day older than sixty."

Aunt Tess laughed as she answered back, "JJ, you know that's not true, but I'll take it anyway."

JJ put the pan of biscuits down on the island counter as all the others in the room exchanged hugs and handshakes. Todd motioned for the elder family members to sit at the table while the younger ones sat around the snack bar. Myrié and Veronica were in the kitchen getting everything ready. After everyone was served, had eaten until they couldn't hold another bite and had praised all the cooks for the wonderful breakfast, the light conversation grew more serious.

No one was surprised when Uncle Teddy, a retired lawyer as well as a politician, spoke first. "Alright, kiddos, out with it. We know why y'all invited us over here, so stop pussy-footing around and get on with it."

Aunt Tess continued, "Yes, we need to know what we are up against."

Knowing he couldn't put it off any longer, JJ stood up and began, "Well, we want all of you to know right up front that we all tried our best to talk sense into our stubborn father from the time he told us about Lilly..."

Aunt Adele interrupted, "We know all that. God knows how hard you all tried and so did we, but right now, we just need you to give it to us straight. The suspense is killing us!"

JJ took a deep breathe then preceded to tell his dear aunts and uncles the devastating news that he knew would break all of their hearts.

Uncle Tommy was the first to respond. He turned to his older brother, Teddy and asked, "So where does this leave us? Legally I mean."

Teddy gloomily answered, "Not in a very good place, that's for sure. We don't even have a leg to stand on here. It all falls on Maggie and Jack's children as his supposed heirs, but honestly, they don't have much of a leg to stand on either. Our sister, Maggie, God rest her soul, left everything to Jack, and now our scoundrel of a brother-in-law has seen fit to leave everything that she and he owned and worked hard for their entire lives to his no good, gold digging wife."

No one spoke for a few seconds as they let what Teddy said sink in, then Adele asked, "What about the legal settlement from our brother, Louis?"

Louis had been the oldest of the Perot children, and he had never married nor had any children. At least none that anyone knew of. He was an investment tycoon and had accumulated quite a portfolio in his lifetime. He had passed away just a few months before Maggie and had left a will leaving all of his assets to his siblings or their legal heirs. However, his estate was very complicated and had taken years of legal litigating. The lawyer who was handling everything had told Louis' siblings about six months ago that the settlement was almost completed and that they should be receiving a check for their individual inheritances soon. He was surprised when Teddy, a friend of his for years, had come to see him and had asked him if there was any way he could drag his feet with getting the settlement awarded. Teddy explained to him that the family wanted to keep Jack from getting Maggie's share of the inheritance due him as her sole heir for as long as possible. They knew if that happened, Lilly would assuredly get her hands on it, and they were just as sure that Louis and Maggie would be turning over in their graves if that happened. Teddy and his siblings knew Jack's health was not good so they had selfishly prayed that they could out last him and that the money would somehow find its way to Maggie's children, her rightful heirs, instead of to Jack and his greedy new wife. Now all their procrastinating had been for nothing. It looked like, not only was Lilly going to get all of Jack and Maggie's hard-earned money and the family land, but she would be getting their brother, Louis' money too.

Teddy silently kicked himself for having sold his fifteen acres to Jack and Mary over thirty years ago. At the time Jack had assured him that the land would stay in the family and Teddy had no reason to doubt him as Jack had always been a firm believer in the land remaining in the Perot family. Once, after Teddy learned of Jack's engagement to Lilly, he had questioned Jack again about the issue and Jack had assured him that he would honor the promise he had made to Teddy years before. When Tess had called Teddy and told him Jack was making threats to his kids about leaving a portion of his estate to Lilly, Teddy had called Jack up right away and asked the question one more time, to which Jack had, once again, reassured him that he would never leave the land to anyone outside the family. So, while all Teddy's siblings had come to him complaining over the last seven years that this day could come, he had not worried about it. He thought he could trust Jacques Bordelon to be a man of his word, but now he realized his siblings' fears were not in vain.

Everyone was staring at Teddy as he had not answered Adele's question. He shook off his personal thoughts and finally responded, "I am afraid that if Jack's will said he left everything to Lilly, then that means everything, including our brother's settlement." One could actually hear the heaviness in everyone's hearts as the magnitude of what Jack had done to the family sunk in. Even though the Bordelon children knew about the settlement, none of them had thought about it until now. The blows from their father's will just kept coming.

Last, JJ reluctantly added salt to his aunts' and uncles' already festering wounds when he told them about their sister's ashes. God knows he didn't want to do it as he was afraid they could not bear one more ounce of bad news. Just as he feared, as soon as he told them Aunt Tess and Aunt Adele started crying.

Aunt Tess said in between her sobbing, "How can this happen? How can someone "own" another person's ashes?"

Uncle Isaac put his arms around Aunt Tess in an effort to calm her, but she just kept sobbing uncontrollably. Uncle George did the same to Aunt Adele and got the same results.

Finally, Uncle Robby, the baby of the Perot family who had not said anything so far, spoke up. "Well, the hell with waiting on Lilly to give us our sister's ashes back! Tommy and I will just go over there ourselves and get them! I dare that Black Widow to stop us!"

Tommy quickly responded, "Sounds like a good plan to me. I'm in."

To which Aunt Doris, immediately replied, "You certainly are not! You are not going to do any such thing!" Aunt Pauline echoed the same remarks to her husband.

All hell was starting to break loose among Maggie's siblings. In an effort to calm everyone down, Mary stood up and said, "Why don't we just wait and see what Mr. Landry says about Lillie's answer to our questions concerning the ashes and our Mom's personal..."

But before she could finish her statement, Aunt Tess interrupted, "You mean you all have to ask that woman for your own mother's personal effects, too!"

Aunt Adele shouted, "So help me God!" as she made the sign of the cross.

Everyone was finally silenced by JJ's booming voice. "Ok, ok, everyone. Calm down. We understand how you all feel about this and we are doing what we can to deal with it accordingly. We are looking into the possibility that our father may have come to his senses before he died and wrote another will with his old lawyer, Henry Babin, after he wrote the will that Lilly's lawyer presented to us. When we get an answer to that question and the answers to the other questions, we will decide where to go from there."

Uncle Robby remarked, "I thought Henry Babin retired years ago, and besides, I think I read in the paper that he passed away last year."

Mary said, "He did, but his son took over his practice and he is looking into the matter for us. There isn't any other will on file at the court house but we have reason to believe that Dad may have been hiding the new will from Lilly, so he may not have had Mr. Babin file it."

Uncle Teddy said. "Well, his son should have a copy of it in his file at the office."

Mary patiently replied, "We asked him that and he said there isn't one, but he is checking with his mother to see if possibly the will would be among some of his father's personal papers at home."

Aunt Tess asked, "Didn't he and his mother go through his father's personal papers after he died?"

Mary had been trying to sound optimistic about the chances of a second will but she knew it wasn't working. She addressed her upset aunts and uncles once again. "Yes, they did, but it will not hurt to have them take a second look. When they looked through Mr. Babin's personal papers after he died, they were not specifically looking for our father's will. Besides, if Dad was paranoid enough not to let Mr. Babin file the new will at the court house, he could have been paranoid enough to have him hide it somewhere where even his son or wife would not readily come across it."

Uncle Tommy said. "Don't you find all this line of thinking a little far-fetched?"

Feeling sorry for Mary, Myrié jumped in to defend her. "We all know that it is far-fetched, but we also know how shrewd our father was. It is not that far-fetched to think that he could have just have easily tried to get one over on Lilly as he had us. Uncle Teddy, you said yourself that Dad promised you he would not do what it seems he did. Dad breaking promises to us is not uncommon, but it is harder to believe he would break a promise to you."

Teddy thought about what Myrié was saying for a brief moment before responding, "I hope you're right, Honey, 'cause if you aren't, we Perots got a war on our hands." Teddy's siblings seconded his remarks as the Bordelon siblings tried, once again, to calm them all down. Finally they were able to get the heated discussion shelved until they could get some answers to their questions. Mary promised to let them know the minute she heard anything. A little while later all the aunts and uncles said their goodbyes as they hugged all their nieces and nephews and made JJ, Veronica and Myrié promise that they would come back home soon.

After closing the door behind them, JJ said, "Boy, that was painful!"

Everyone agreed wholeheartedly.

Mary quietly said, "I sure hope we get the answer we want from HB because, if not, I am going to have to be the one to break it to them and it isn't going to be pretty."

Martine, who had been silent most of the morning, patted Mary on the back and said, "If the answer isn't what we hope for, don't tell them anything until I can drive over to help you break the news to them."

Mary thanked her for her offer and JJ and Myrié apologized for not being able to be there too. Mary said that she understood and that she knew they would be with her and Martine in spirit if not in person.

Dave looked at his watch, then leaned over and said to his wife, "I hate to interrupt your family meeting, but if I am going to get JJ, Veronica and Myrié to the airport in time, we need to leave in a few minutes." Martine turned to say something to the others but they were already up and headed to the stairs.

JJ said as he walked away, "Don't worry brother-in-law. It won't take us long. We are already packed." True to JJ's word, they were back downstairs, suitcases in hand in less than five minutes. Again there were more goodbyes and hugs as the family members all bid farewell to their host and hostess for the last four days. They thanked Todd and Mary profusely for their wonderful southern hospitality and hugged them one last time right before they drove off.

As Todd and Mary stood in the driveway waving goodbye, Todd wrapped his arms around his wife and held her for a few seconds longer than usual until he could feel the tension in her body start to drain. Mary wiped away the tears, kissed her husband on the cheek and they both walked, hand in hand, back inside their now empty house.

CHAPTER EIGHT

GETTING ANSWERS

It was Wednesday morning and Mary's alarm clock went off at its usual time. Mary jumped up and hit the floor running as she had several things she needed to get done. She had been so busy in the last three days since her family had left just getting her house back in order and ready for her weekend guests. Yesterday Sara had called and insisted Mary take a break from her household duties so they could go to lunch together. The two friends had met at their favorite restaurant, Maglieaux's On the Cane on Front Street. They sat on the outdoor patio overlooking the Cane River, eating their shrimp salads and drinking glasses of wine, while Mary told Sara all about the will situation. Sara's response was classic "Big Sister Syndrome". She was appalled that Mary's father would have done such a thing and she had a few colorful words to describe Lilly. Mary told Sara about her family's hopes of a second will and Sara said that she would be praying they found one. The friends ended up spending most of the day together which is one of the reasons why Mary had so much to do today. For starters she had a million thank you notes to write for the flowers people had sent to her father's funeral, donations they had made in his name to Immaculate Conception School and for Masses they had said at Immaculate Conception Church. She also had to go into town to do her grocery shopping, and to pick up a birthday cake at Lola's Sweet Creations Bakery. She had ordered the cake for her housekeeper, Ellie.

Ellie had been Mary's parents' housekeeper for years. She started working for them when Maggie was pregnant with

Mallory and was having difficulty. The doctor had ordered Maggie to bed for the last two months of her pregnancy. So, with seven children already in the household and the youngest one only two years old, Jack decided he needed to get some help fast. He hired Ellie who was, at the time, the part-time housekeeper at the church rectory, to help out in the Bordelon household. Ellie had worked for Jack and Maggie ever since and she practically raised Jake and Mallory. When Maggie died, Ellie stayed on to take care of the house and of Jack, that is until he married Lilly. Once Lilly moved in, everything changed. Ellie was used to doing things the way Maggie liked them being done, but Lilly wanted things done her way. Ellie tried to please her, but no matter what she did, she could never make Lilly happy. Once, after a particularly bad day, Ellie came to visit Mary. Ellie was in tears as she told Mary she didn't know if she could take one more day working for Jack's new wife. She told Mary that Lilly talked down to her like she was the "hired help". Of course, Ellie knew that she was, indeed, the "hired help" but Maggie had never treated her that way. Maggie had always made her feel like she was family.

It was just a coincidence that Ellie had picked that day to come talk to Mary. Mary had just told Todd that very morning that their B&B business was starting to really pick up and she thought it might be a good idea to hire some part-time help. She offered Ellie the job right on the spot and Ellie gladly accepted her offer. Ellie called Lilly while still sitting at Mary's kitchen table and told her she would not be working for her anymore. She told Lilly she had been offered another job but she did not say with who. When Jack found out that Ellie was working for his daughter, he had a fit! Mary didn't visit him again for over a month while she waited for him to cool down. When she finally did go to see him, he started ranting and raving, but Mary stood her ground, and in the end, he dropped the topic altogether. They never spoke about Ellie again.

Hiring Ellie had been one of the best decisions Mary had made for her B&B business. All the guests loved her and she was so much help to Mary. She came on Mondays, Wednesdays and Fridays to help Mary with the general housework, but she did so much more for Mary than just housework. Whatever Mary needed her to do, Ellie did and she never once complained. And best of all she was a fantastic cook! Even better than Todd, but Mary would never tell him that.

Ellie had been out of town when Jack passed away. She had gone to Atlanta with her daughter to see her granddaughter's new baby. When Mary called to tell her the news, Ellie offered to fly home immediately, but Mary had insisted she stay. Ellie had felt so bad that she had not been there for Mary and her siblings. When she returned on Monday, she apologized over and over to Mary. She felt even worse though for not having had the opportunity to see all the Bordelon children while they were in town. When Mary told Ellie about her father's will, she was beside herself with anger towards Jack and Lilly.

Ellie said, "Mary, I had a terrible feeling about that woman the minute she walked into your dear mother's house! I didn't trust those daughters of hers either. They're all like a bunch of snakes in the grass! And to think Mr. Jack would do such a thing to his own children! It just ain't right, Mary, it just ain't right!" Mary did her best to calm Ellie down, but in the end she just let her be. She figured Ellie needed time to process what had happened just like the rest of them.

As soon as Mary showered and dressed, she went to the kitchen, grabbed a cup of coffee and a pecan muffin and went to her office to write the thank you notes. Right at nine o'clock she heard Ellie come in the back door. Mary yelled out, "I'm in the office."

Ellie came in and said, "Good morning, Sugar. How are you doing?"

Ellie always called Mary and her sisters "Sugar". That is, except for Mallory. She had a special name for her that she had called her since Mallory was born. She called her "Mon, Cheri" which was Cajun French for "My Darling."

Mary told Ellie she was fine but busy. Ellie asked her what she could do to help. Mary said she could start upstairs with putting the freshly laundered sheets back on the beds. Without another word, Ellie rushed out of the room and up the stairs to do as Mary had asked and Mary went back to writing her thank you notes.

Finally, around noon, Mary put stamps on the last of the notes and put them in a small shopping bag so she could take them to the post office. She went in the kitchen and found Ellie making chicken salad. Mary loved Ellie's chicken salad and she knew that was exactly why Ellie was making it. She was trying to mother Mary any way she could and Mary loved her for it. Mary poured them a glass of iced tea while Ellie made chicken salad sandwiches for the two of them and the two women sat at the kitchen table eating and talking about what the schedule was for the weekend. Their meal was briefly interrupted by a phone call by someone wanting to make a reservation.

As soon as Mary heard the phone ring, she jumped. She had been doing that for the last three days thinking it might be Mr. Landry or HB, but it never was. Mary took down the information from the young lady on the other end of the line and told her she would be looking forward to their arrival next month. When she hung up the phone she made a mental note to stop by HB's office while she was in town. She couldn't take the suspense any longer. She would also stop by Paige Neville's office to see what she could find out about her father's life insurance policy. She was undecided if she would stop by Mr. Landry's office to see if he had spoken to Lilly yet. She would decide that later. After they finished eating, Ellie helped Mary with her grocery list. By one thirty Mary was headed out the door to run her errands.

Since the suspense was getting the best of her, Mary decided to make HB's office her first stop. When she walked into the office, HB was standing in the lobby shaking hands with an older, distinguishing looking gentleman. Mary assumed he was another client of HB's. As the two men turned to look at her, HB said, "Hello, Mary, I didn't know you were coming by today."

Mary replied, "Oh, I'm so sorry. I didn't call to make an appointment. I can come back another time if you are busy."

Mary silently kicked herself for not thinking of calling ahead but HB quickly reassured her that it was quite all right.

He said, "No problem, Mary. Mr. Taylor was just leaving."

Mr. Taylor turned towards Mary and addressed her in a pleasant voice. "Are you Mary LeBlanc, Jack and Maggie Bordelon's daughter?"

Mary responded, "Yes, I am but I'm sorry. You have me at a disadvantage. I'm afraid I don't recognize you. Have we met before?"

Mr. Taylor said, "Yes, but I am not surprised you don't remember. I was an old friend of your Uncle Louis, and as far as I know, I am still an old friend of your Uncle Teddy. I met you years ago at your mother's funeral. Teddy introduced us. I knew both of your parents but not well. Teddy told me your father passed away last week. I am so sorry for your loss."

Mary apologized again to the charming gentlemen for not recognizing him. He just laughed softly and said, "It is completely understandable, my dear. You were going through a lot that day. Let me introduce myself to you again. My name is William Taylor. I actually live in Baton Rouge but I come to Natchitoches from time to time to do business."

Mary asked, "Oh, what kind of business are you in Mr. Taylor?

He replied, "I'm a lawyer like HB but, please, don't hold that against me."

It was Mary's turn to laugh this time. She assured him that she wouldn't, and with that, he said his goodbyes and left the office. HB turned to Mary and escorted her into his inner office."

Mary took a seat in the over-sized, leather armchair in front of HB's desk while he walked around to the other side and sat down. As he did he asked Mary how she and her siblings were doing and she said they were fine. Mary didn't want to be rude, but she wanted to get right to the reason she had come in the first place, so she abruptly asked, "Did you have a chance to speak to your mother yet about what we discussed on the phone a few days ago?"

HB responded, "As matter a fact, I did. I am sorry I didn't call you back sooner but I was hoping I might have better news if I waited."

"What do you mean?"

"Well, I talked to my Mom and she said that she remembers Jack calling the house a few weeks before my dad had his heart attack. She said my dad took the call in his home office and that he was on the phone for quite some time. When he came out of the office he told her that he was going to drive out to see Jack the next day. She said the next day, when he came back from his visit with Jack, he seemed a little preoccupied but when she asked him what was wrong, he said, "Nothing." She asked him how his visit with Jack had gone and he said "fine", but when she tried to get more out of him, he didn't seem to want to talk much about it."

Mary started getting her hopes up. She said, "That all sounds pretty suspicious. It means my Dad very well might have spoken to your father about his will, and maybe, even had him write another one up like we all hoped was the case. By any chance did your mom say whether or not you father mentioned if Lilly was home when he went to see my dad?"

HB replied, "I know what you're thinking and I thought the same thing, so I asked her that, and she said that he did make a comment about Lilly not being there. Mom said she remembered it because Dad said he was relieved when he got there that Lilly wasn't home. She said Jack told my dad that Lilly had gone to Alexandria to do some shopping with her daughters. She said Dad was glad he did not have to see her because he knew Lilly did not like him ever since Jack had brought her to his office and he had advised Jack against changing his will."

Mary was beside herself now with excitement over what HB had told her so far, but her excitement was short lived, as the next thing he told her was that he and his mother had looked all over his dad's office and had not found any copies of any wills, let alone one for Jack. He said that was why he had put off calling her with the, supposedly, good news of their fathers' impromptu visit. He said he was hoping that he or his mom would eventually find a will for her father among his father's old papers and things but that they had run out of places to look.

Mary was so disappointed. Everything HB had told her sounded so good, up until the last part. She thanked him for all of his and his mother's efforts, though, and HB apologized to her for not being able to do more. He promised her that he and his mom were not giving up looking for the will and that if they came across anything he would let her know right away. He went on to say that his mom was just as eager to find a new will for Jack as anyone. He said that, from the little bits she knew of Lilly, she did not like her and that his mom couldn't understand how any woman could do to anyone what Lilly had done, let alone to a family as nice as the Bordelon family. He said that his mom had called it down right disgraceful!

As disappointed as Mary was, she couldn't help feeling a little better, after HB told her what his mother had said about Lilly. It made her feel like her family wasn't in this alone and that other people understood what they were going through, too.

HB said that if there really was another will, he wished his dad had shared it with him and that he couldn't understand why Jack would not have called him about it when he had heard his father had passed away. Mary said that they may never know the answers to those two questions, but knowing how secretive her father was about certain things, she wouldn't be surprised. It would be such a tragedy, though, if her father had written a new will but it never got found and Lilly got everything anyway. Mary didn't want to think about that. She chose instead to think positively, at least for now. She thanked HB again and left his office taking with her a little ray of hope that, just maybe, her father didn't disinherit his family after all.

When she left HB's she headed straight to Paige Neville's insurance office. Paige's last name was actually St. Germaine now, as she was married to Jessie St. Germaine, a very good electrician who Mary had hired to do all the electrical work when she was renovating her house. As soon as Mary walked into Paige's office, she came over and gave Mary a big hug and asked, "How are you doing, Mary?" Mary was getting tired of everyone asking her that question, but she knew that they all meant well, so she responded with her usual answer, "I'm doing fine. I hope I am not catching you at a bad time."

Paige replied, "Oh, of course not! Come in and have a seat." Paige motioned Mary inside her office and she took a seat across from Paige's desk just as she had done in HB's office. Paige sat behind her desk and said, "Now, what brings you here today? Do you need to change something on one of your policies?"

Mary replied, "No. I am actually here to talk to you about my dad." Paige didn't say anything so Mary continued, "My dad had a three hundred thousand dollar life insurance policy but he told us he had cashed it in a few years ago to do some renovations on his property. However, my brothers and sisters and I think he may have just told us that. You know how our dad could be about certain..."

Paige interrupted Mary and said, "Mary, I am so sorry, but all I can tell you is that your dad did have a life insurance policy with me at the time of his death, but I am not able to disclose the amount of the policy or the beneficiary other than to say that it isn't any of his children or grandchildren."

Paige looked so sad to have to be the bearer of bad news that Mary almost felt sorry for her. It didn't take a rocket scientist to figure out who the beneficiary was if it wasn't any of the children or grandchildren. She thanked Paige for her time and left her office as quickly as she could. She didn't want to think about the life insurance money for now. There were more important things for her to be concerned about like their family land, their parents' ashes and their mother's personal things. Mary decided she needed to go see Mr. Landry. She rationalized that his office was just around the corner on Church Street so why not stop in while she was close by.

When Mary got to Mr. Landry's office, his secretary informed her that he was not in and that she did not expect him to come in the rest of the day as he was in court. Mary asked her if she would let Mr. Landry know that she had been by and to please call her at his earliest convenience. The secretary said that she would give him the message when he checked in with her. Mary left the lawyer's office and headed to the post office. Once she dropped off her thank you notes, she headed to the grocery store. She hated grocery shopping. She just hoped the store would not be too crowded when she got there. Luckily, it wasn't bad and she was able to get in and out quickly. She had one last stop to make and that was to pick up the birthday cake for Ellie.

Mary loved coming to Lola's Sweet Creations Bakery. It always smelled like fresh baked cookies and homemade pies and Lola made the best cakes in town. Lola was married to Mary's cousin, Jason, who was Aunt Tess and Uncle Isaac's son. Jason and Lola were like two peas in a pod and they were the nicest country folks you could ever meet.

After Lola and Mary exchanged hellos, Lola went to the back of the shop to get the cake Mary had ordered. When she returned with it, Mary couldn't believe how pretty it was. Lola always out did herself with her creations and this time was no exception. Mary thanked Lola and told her how beautiful the cake looked. Lola smiled broadly as she rang up Mary's purchase. Mary paid for the cake, then told Lola she needed to run as she had groceries in the car.

Mary was so glad Ellie was nowhere in sight when she got to the house. She quickly brought in all the groceries and the cake. She put the groceries away and sat the round cake decorated with yellow roses on the island counter top. She had gotten a pineapple cake because she knew it was Ellie's favorite and she had told Lola to put yellow roses on it because they were her mother's favorite and she knew Ellie would understand the sentiment of the roses the minute she saw them. She put seven candles on the cake, one for every ten years. It was hard to believe Ellie was going to be seventy years old tomorrow! She didn't look a day over sixty and she could run circles around Mary.

Todd walked in the house and came over to the island where Mary was standing to give her a kiss. As he did he noticed the cake sitting in the center of the island. He asked Mary who it was for and she reminded him about Ellie's birthday. Just then they heard Ellie coming in the back door. She must have been cleaning the cottage.

Mary, hurriedly, lit the candles as Todd distracted Ellie by saying, "So Ellie, I hear you have a birthday tomorrow. Mary said you are going to be forty-nine years old."

Ellie smiled at Todd's remark, then, her face lit up as she noticed the cake. She exclaimed, "Mary, you shouldn't have but I am so glad you did! I bet that is one of Lola's cakes isn't it?"

Mary replied, "Of course! Do I ever buy a cake anywhere else? And it's a pineapple cake, your favorite!"

Ellie took one look at the yellow roses and then looked back at Mary. She said with tears in her eyes, "Your mom's favorite!"

The two women hugged each other as they smiled ear to ear. Then, Todd and Mary sang Happy Birthday to Ellie as she blew out her candles. Mary got a knife out and cut three generous slices of the cake. They sat at the snack bar eating the delicious confection while Mary filled them both in on all that she had found out. By the time they were finished eating and Mary was finished talking, it was nearly four o'clock. Ellie normally worked until five but Mary told her to go home early. Ellie started to argue with her but Todd stepped in, and between the two of them, they convinced her to go home to her husband, Arthur. Mary put the cake back in its bakery box and gave it to Ellie to take home with her.

As Mary picked up the dishes, the phone rang and she absently picked it up without looking at the caller ID. She said, "A Bed of Roses. How can I help you?"

The other voice on the end of the line said, "Um, this is Roy Landry. May I please speak to Mary LeBlanc?"

Mary was surprised to hear Mr. Landry's voice. She had not expected him to call her until the next day as his secretary had said he would be in court the rest of the day. She quickly replied, "This is Mary LeBlanc."

Mr. Landry said, "My secretary told me you came by and that you wanted me to call you."

Mary responded, "Yes, I did. I was wondering if you have spoken to Lilly yet concerning our Mother's things and our parents' ashes."

Mr. Landry replied, "I spoke to her this morning and she said that you and your siblings could come by on Saturday to get what is left of your mother's personal effects and some family furnishings, but she said the bench with your parents' ashes will be staying by the pond. According to her, that is where your parents wanted them to be kept and she wants to honor their wishes."

Mary was only half satisfied with Mr. Landry's answers to their inquiries but she thanked him for getting back to her and she asked him to please let Lilly know that she would come by Saturday at eleven o'clock to get their mother's things and the furnishings.

When Mary hung up the phone, she started thinking about how she was going to break the news about her mother's ashes to her aunts and uncles. She quickly decided to take Martine up on her offer to come with her so that they could do it together. Mary called Martine and told her everything that she had found out. Martine agreed to meet Mary at her house for ten thirty Saturday morning. They decided they would wait until after they got their mother's things out of the house before they went to talk to Aunt Tess and Uncle Isaac. They figured it would be easier if they just sat down with the two of them instead of the whole gang. After they talked to Aunt Tess and Uncle Isaac they would let Aunt Tess break the news to the others. Martine volunteered to call Aunt Tess to let her know they would be coming by some time Saturday afternoon. Mary gladly accepted her offer as it was one less thing on her plate to take care of. Mary waited until after supper to make a conference call to all of her siblings.

Since Mary ran a business out of her home she had set up a system on her phone where she could handle conference calls. All she had to do was inform the necessary parties as to when to call in and give them her code. At the designated time she would place the call and the others would call in using the code. The system had come in handy many times over the last few years when she needed to communicate with all of her siblings to let them know about things involving their father. Now she sent a text out to all her brothers and sisters to call in at seven o'clock. When everyone was on the line, Mary filled them in on what she had found out and what hers and Martine's plan was for Saturday. Everyone thanked her and Martine for taking care of getting their mother's things and wished them luck with dealing with Lilly and their aunts and uncles.

Mary's Stuffed French Toast with Praline Sauce

Ingredients:
¼ lb. (half stick) of butter
1 cup brown sugar
2 tbsp. light corn syrup
⅓ cup chopped pecans
1 loaf French or Italian bread

6 eggs
1 cup milk
1 tsp. vanilla
ground cinnamon

Filling (Optional)
2 ounces softened cream cheese
1 banana mashed
¼ cup pineapple or strawberry preserves

¼ cup chopped pecans

In saucepan bring butter, corn syrup and brown sugar to a boil. Continue boiling for one minute, stirring constantly. Remove from heat and add pecans. Pour mixture into 9x13 baking pan sprayed with PAM. While cooling, cut bread into one inch slices. If you want to add filling, mix all filling ingredients in small bowl, then put a slit in top of each bread slice and spoon in filling. Nestle slices into syrup mixture. Combine, eggs, milk and vanilla in a blender and whip for 15 seconds. Pour over bread slices. Sprinkle with cinnamon. Let sit for at least ten minutes so bread can absorb the egg mixture. Bake at 350 degrees for 35-40 minutes or until light brown on top. (Can be refrigerated overnight, then baked in the morning for convenience.) When serving, turn upside down so that syrup is on top. You can sprinkle with powdered sugar right before serving if you want to make an even bigger impression! (Serves about 8 people)

Note from Mary: My family likes a lot of praline sauce so I increase or double sauce ingredients. Hope your family loves this breakfast treat as much as mine does!

CHAPTER NINE

THE FEUD BETWEEN
THE UNCLES AND MISS LILLY

Thankfully for Mary, the next couple of days went by so fast she hardly had time to worry about her aunts and uncles or Lilly. A young couple from Texas had shown up Thursday afternoon as a walk-in. They only needed a room for one night as they were just passing through on their way to New Orleans, but before they left, they reserved the same room for the following Monday night when they would be back in town on their way home. Her reservation for a business man who was coming to town for a medical conference showed up right after Mary had finished checking in the young couple. His secretary had made the reservation for him for Thursday and Friday night. On Friday a party of six women from Shreveport checked in. They had reserved the cottage for a girls' weekend getaway. They were all so excited just to be away from their husbands and children for a couple of days.

Mary had asked Ellie to come in on Saturday instead of Friday so that she could help with breakfast Saturday morning. Mary was glad she had done so because now Ellie would be at the house to look after the guests while she went with Martine to get their mother's things and to talk to Aunt Tess and Uncle Isaac. She was going to need Todd to go with them so he could bring the truck to put the furniture in that Lilly would, hopefully, see fit to let them have.

Maggie had given Mary some family heirlooms and antique pieces of furniture for her Bed and Breakfast before she died. She had also given her a set of china and a set of sterling silverware along with her silver tea set and some other silver serving pieces. At the time Mary had felt bad about taking the expensive items from her mom before her death but Maggie had insisted that she wanted Mary to have them. She had told Mary it was her way of leaving a piece of herself with Mary so that she could be with her daughter, if only in a small way, as she entered the exciting life of owning and running a B&B. Mary, graciously, took the items from her mom and she cherished them more than anything else she had bought for her B&B. After her father announced he was marrying Lilly, Mary was so glad she had listened to her mother. Otherwise, Lilly would now be in possession of those things too.

Maggie had left special instructions for her other daughters to get some of her things, after her death. Myrié had gotten her wedding china and her sewing machine, Martine had gotten her Christmas china. Mallory had gotten her wedding ring. Maddie was supposed to get her diamond cross necklace, but when they looked in Maggie's jewelry box, they couldn't find it. Maggie had also left instructions for JJ to get her "mother's ring" so that he could pass it on to his daughter, Valerie. Since Jake and Joe were not married, nor had any children, their mother had not left special instructions for anything to be given to them.

Right before Lilly moved in to their mom's house, Jack had invited his children over to get some of Maggie's dishes and small personal items so there was not a lot they wanted except for an antique secretary desk that had once belonged to Maggie's mother and their mom's dining room table and hutch. Jack had promised Maddie the desk when they could not find Maggie's cross necklace. It was the only thing Maddie had really wanted besides her mom's cross. She said that she remembered seeing her mom sitting at it writing out various things like her grocery list and letters to loved ones ever since she was a little girl. The dining room set was important to all of them because they had eaten all their holiday dinners over the years sitting at the dining room table. If Mary could get the dining room set, she wanted to save it for Myrié so that she could put their mother's china back in the hutch where it belonged. She was also hoping Lilly would give her their father's shot gun that he had promised JJ and his two hand guns he had promised to Jake and Joe. None of the guns were worth much, but it was the sentiment of having them that was important to Mary. She wanted her brothers to have something of their father's. She knew that they might not want them right now but she hoped that one day, when the sting of what he had done faded, they might decide they wanted them after all.

Martine and Dave arrived at Mary's house Saturday morning at ten thirty. Mary and Ellie were just finishing up serving their guests breakfast. As soon as Ellie saw Martine, she ran over and gave her a hug. Just then Todd walked into the kitchen and greeted Marty and Dave as well. Mary gave a few last-minute instructions to Ellie before leaving. Then, she and Todd got into his truck while Martine and Dave got into their SUV and they headed for Belle Rose for the first time since Jack's death nearly two weeks ago.

In less than ten minutes, they were driving down the Perot property's private main road and into the long driveway of what was now Lilly's property. For Mary and Martine it was such an eerie feeling to know that Belle Rose no longer belonged to their family, or at least not for now. They were doing their best not to give up hope that another will would turn up soon.

Mary tentatively knocked on the familiar door with the stained glass window that one of her cousins had made especially for Maggie. The glass had a white dove perched on an olive branch etched in it. Todd, Martine and Dave stood close behind her. Charlotte opened the door and motioned for them to come inside. Lilly was sitting at the table and Caroline was standing next to her. Mary said hello to the three women and thanked them for allowing her and Martine to come get some of their parents' things. It was not easy for her to stand in her family home and have to ask Lilly for her own parents' things but she swallowed her pride and did so as politely as she could. She told Lilly what furnishings they would like to have and the guns they wanted. At first Lilly didn't say anything. She just sat there as if she didn't really want to give them what they had asked for but she didn't know exactly how to tell them no. Mary and Martine held their breath as they waited for her response. Finally she agreed to let them have everything Mary had requested. While

Mary and Martine helped Todd and Dave move the furniture, Charlotte and Caroline went with Lilly to retrieve the guns. When they returned, Charlotte and Caroline were each carrying a box and Lilly was carrying the shot gun. The box Caroline was carrying was filled with some personal things that belonged to Maggie and Jack and some family photo albums. The box Charlotte was carrying contained the two hand gun cases.

After everything they had come for was loaded in the truck and SUV and they were getting ready to leave, Lilly brought up the situation with the ashes.

She said, "Roy told me you requested the marble bench with your parents' ashes in it be moved to your family cemetery. I really wish that I could accommodate you, but that is not what your parents wanted. Your father left me explicit instructions to put his ashes in the bench with your mother's and he wanted the bench to stay right where he had put it when your mother died. He built that pond just for that reason."

Mary responded, "Lilly, you must realize how difficult it will be for us or our aunts and uncles to come visit our parents' grave site if the ashes remain on this property."

"No, I don't understand why that would be a problem. I have no intention of keeping you off the property. You are welcome to come visit your parents any time."

As soon as Lilly said this, Charlotte added. "Of course you would need to call our mom or one of us first before coming on the property." That was exactly what the Bordelon children were trying to avoid. They did not think it was right for them to have to ask permission every time they wanted to come on the property to visit their parents and they knew their mother's siblings didn't either.

Mary tried another tactic. "Lilly, what's going to happen to the bench if you decide to sell the property or if, God forbid, something happens to you?"

Lilly replied, "Well, if that happens Charlotte or Caroline will get in touch with Tess or one of you and make the arrangements to have the bench moved to your family cemetery."

Mary decided to let it go for now as Lilly had been more than cooperative so far with allowing them to get their mother's things and she did not want to push her luck. Plus, she didn't feel she was going to change Lilly's mind and she was in a hurry to get out of the house. She and the others told the three women goodbye and made a hasty retreat. Now came the even harder part.

When they pulled up to the big white farm house with green trim they saw Aunt Tess and Uncle Isaac sitting on the front porch swing. Mary had always loved the house. She had so many fond memories of being here with all of her family members. They would gather here for holidays and family occasions. They always had a big family reunion on the property every Fourth of July.

Aunt Tess and Uncle Isaac got up to greet Mary and the others as they walked up the steps to the porch. Hugs were shared and Aunt Tess invited them inside. Before they reached the kitchen, they could smell the wonderful aroma of fresh-baked rolls. Aunt Tess had told Martine she would be making lunch for them when Martine had called to tell her they would be dropping by Saturday around noon, but as usual, Aunt Tess had outdone herself. There were several homemade dishes laid out on the kitchen counter including fresh vegetables from her garden. She told them to make themselves at home while she poured everyone glasses of iced tea. After fixing their plates, they all sat around the kitchen table eating the delicious meal and making small talk for a few minutes before Mary got up enough courage to address the subject she had been dreading.

Mary finally told her aunt and uncle everything she had learned on Wednesday. She also told them about their visit with Lilly before coming to their house. She saved the part about the ashes until last, knowing that it would be the hardest part for Aunt Tess to accept. After listening intently to everything Mary said, Aunt Tess remarked that she was glad Lilly had done the right thing in giving them the items they had requested out of their parents' home but she was adamant that leaving her sister's ashes with Lilly was not going to fly with her or her other siblings. As for the possibility of another will looking a little more likely than before, she and Uncle Isaac still expressed skepticism. They said they couldn't wait around on HB or his mother to locate a will that may or may not even exist while that "Black Widow" as they had all begun to refer to Lilly, took over their family land.

Aunt Tess also had some news of her own to share with Mary and the others. She told them that their family lawyer, Mr. Taylor, had come by to see her Wednesday concerning Louis' estate settlement. Immediately, Mary recognized Mr. Taylor's name from her visit with HB. She thought to herself, "So, the business he was in town for was her family business." She wondered why he or HB didn't tell her that. Mary's thoughts were interrupted by what Aunt Tess was saying, "Mr. Taylor also paid a visit to Lilly. He said that, despite his best efforts to convince her otherwise, Lilly had not agreed to allow Maggie's share of the settlement to go to Maggie's children instead of to herself."

Aunt Tess went on to say that the settlement was going to come to around forty thousand for each of Louis' siblings. Aunt Tess speculated that the reason Lilly had been so cooperative with giving Mary and Marty their parents' things today was because she had had a momentary feeling of generosity knowing that she was going to be coming into even more Bordelon money courtesy of the Perot family settlement in a couple of weeks. She said that Mr. Taylor had exhausted all means of postponing the paperwork any longer and the checks would be coming out by the first of the month. It wasn't about the amount of money that upset Aunt Tess and her siblings. It was the point of where the money came from and where it was going that angered Maggie's siblings. As Aunt Tess spoke you could see the tears welling up in her eyes. She was so beside herself in frustration over the whole ordeal that Mary was starting to worry about her and the strain she was under. She knew that Aunt Tess had a weak heart, and she knew none of this was helping. Mary tried to calm her down by saying that there was still a chance that their father had left another will and that it would be found soon. Martine spoke up and said that maybe they should be the ones to tell the rest of the aunts and uncles the news instead of letting Aunt Tess tell them, but Aunt Tess assured them that it would be better coming from her, so Mary and Martine reluctantly agreed to let her do it as planned. After a few more minutes of discussion, Mary and the others thanked Aunt Tess again for the wonderful lunch and kissed her and Uncle Isaac goodbye.

On the ride back to the house, Mary took out her frustration with her father on Todd. Todd, understanding what his wife was going through, wisely, kept quiet. When they got back to the house, Todd and Dave unloaded the furniture in the garage and Mary and Martine took the two boxes and the shot gun inside. After Mary put the guns in Todd's gun cabinet for safe keeping, she and Martine went through the photo albums separating the pictures into stacks for each of the siblings and put them in individual manila envelopes to be mailed out. Then, they sifted through the other items and decided what to do with each one. Last, they placed a conference call to their siblings to relay all the events of the day.

By the time they were finished, it was after six o'clock. Todd and Dave had already come in over an hour earlier and had gone straight to the game room. Ellie had left after filling Mary in on the events of the afternoon at the B&B. Mary got up and warmed up the shrimp pasta and squash patties Ellie had made for them. After eating, Martine and Dave thanked Mary for the supper and Mary and Todd thanked them for making the trip over to help with the day's events.

After Martine and Dave left, Mary cleaned up the kitchen and prepared a breakfast casserole for her guests so all she would have to do is pop it in the oven in the morning. It had been a long day and she was exhausted, mentally as well as physically. She checked her email for reservations, then went to her bedroom and got ready for bed. As her head hit the pillow she could hear the rain drops hitting the tin roof.

In the morning Mary rushed around getting breakfast served to all of her guests, cleaning up afterwards, then checking everyone out. All of the ladies who had stayed in the cottage raved about the wonderful time they had and promised they would be back again next year. By noon everyone was gone and she decided to leave the room cleaning until in the morning when Ellie would be there to help her. She had just sat down on the couch to watch a movie with Todd when the phone rang. She looked at the caller ID and saw that it was Lilly. She couldn't imagine why Lilly was calling her, unless, maybe, she had second thoughts about giving them their parents' things yesterday. She picked up the phone and, tentatively said, "Hello".

Lilly's voice came shrieking over the line. "Mary, you need to come over here right now!"

Mary responded, "What for?"

Lilly wailed, "Because there is a tractor in the middle of the main road blocking my driveway and I know it must belong to your Uncle Tommy! When I came home from church, there it was, just as pretty as you please, right in front of my driveway! I had to drive around it so that I could get to the house! My car almost got stuck in the wet grass! You know how soft the ground gets here when we have a heavy rain like we had last..."

Mary interrupted, "Lilly, this is all very interesting but why are you calling me about it?"

"Because you need to come over here right now and have him move it! Better yet, just call him and tell him it needs to be moved right away!"

"Why didn't you call him yourself instead of calling me? I am sure he must have a reasonable explanation as to why he left the tractor in the middle of the road. Maybe it broke down and he couldn't get it started again."

"I can't call him! You know none of Maggie's family likes me. I bet they all cooked up the idea of putting that tractor in the middle of the road just to aggravate me. I don't know if they told you about the visit I got from their lawyer, Mr. Taylor, last week but I am sure that this tractor business has something to do with it!"

Mary assured Lilly she had no idea what she was talking about even though she did. Lilly was not any more happy with Mary than she was with Tommy by the time she hung up and it had taken all of Mary's control not to laugh out loud at her as she said goodbye. As soon as she got off the phone, Todd asked her what it was all about. After she relayed Lilly's story to him, he laughing said, "I have to hand it to your Uncle Tommy, that's a good one!"

Mary replied, "Let's give him the benefit of the doubt before we jump to any conclusions."

Todd laughed again as he responded, "Yeah, right, Mary, you do that." With that he turned back to watching the movie and Mary got up and went into the kitchen to call Aunt Tess to see if she could find out what was going on.

Mary suspected Lilly and Todd were right about Uncle Tommy's motives but she wanted to be sure. As soon as she explained her phone call with Lilly to Aunt Tess, her aunt denied knowing anything about the tractor situation, but Mary could tell by the tone of her voice that she was lying. Aunt Tess is as honest as the day is long and not practiced in the art of lying. Besides, Mary knew Aunt Tess went to church every Sunday morning so she would have had to pass by the same spot in the road Lilly had to get to her own driveway, so something was definitely up.

After Mary hung up with Aunt Tess, she called Uncle Tommy. He said that his tractor had, indeed, broken down and, since it was a Sunday, he couldn't get anyone to come out and look at it until the next day. Despite what Mary had said to Todd she suspected this was a lie as she knew her Uncle Tommy could fix just about anything that could go wrong on his tractor except for a broken part, of course. While it was possible a part had broken, for it to have happened right in front of Lilly's driveway, was a major coincidence, especially just one day after her conversation with Aunt Tess. Nevertheless, Mary asked Uncle Tommy to please get the tractor moved as soon as possible and he promised her that he would.

Next, Mary placed yet another conference call to her siblings. All but Joe called in as he was probably tied up with church business on a Sunday. By the time she finished telling them about all three of her last phone conversations, they were all laughing hysterically. JJ said that it sounded like there was a feud brewing and his money was on his uncles and aunts. They all agreed and told Mary to be sure to keep them posted. They wanted to know every last detail.

By now Mary had lost all interest in the movie she was supposed to be watching with Todd so she decided to go for a walk. When she returned, it was almost four o'clock. She went to take a shower and get dressed for evening mass. When she returned home, Todd told her Lilly had called back. He said that she was upset because Tommy was not answering her calls. He guessed that Lilly would be calling back any minute because he had told her Mary was at church and should be home around seven o'clock. No sooner had he finished speaking than the phone rang. As soon as Mary could get a word in in between Lilly's ranting, she told Lilly that she had spoken to Uncle Tommy and she gave Lilly the explanation he had given her. Lilly was not happy with it, but at this point, Mary really didn't care.

The tractor standoff lasted three days before Uncle Tommy finally moved the farm equipment. Mary thought that would be the end of it but it turned out to only be the beginning. On Friday afternoon, just two days later, Lilly called her again even more hysterical than on Sunday. This time she claimed Uncle Robby had come down the road with a large load of hay in the back of his truck and several bales had fallen off right in front of her driveway blocking it once again. She said when she tried calling him to ask him to come back and clean up the mess, Aunt Pauline had answered the phone and had apologized to her for the accident with the hay but she said Robby couldn't come over right now to clean it up. She told Lilly that unfortunately Robby had just gotten thrown by one of his horses while he was trying to break it and hurt his back. She said he couldn't get out of bed right now but that he had told her to tell Lilly he would try to get someone out to clean up the mess as soon as he could. Before hanging up the phone, Lilly threatened, "You tell your uncles that if this doesn't stop I will take legal action!"

Lilly hung up the phone without even allowing Mary to say goodbye.

Mary couldn't believe what her uncles were up to. She knew how good of a horseman her Uncle Robby was and she knew there was no way he would risk getting on a horse that might throw him before he had done the proper amount of ground work with it. She was afraid things were going to get ugly if her uncles didn't stop their shenanigans.

Mary called her Uncle Robby's house and Aunt Pauline answered the phone just as she had with Lilly. When Mary asked her what had happened, she repeated the story she had given Lilly. Mary knew the story was a bunch of bull but she didn't know how to accuse her aunt of lying so she feigned concern for her poor, hurt Uncle Robby and asked if she should come over right away to check on him. Aunt Pauline quickly reassured her that was not necessary. She said she had everything under control and that Dr. Holmes had already come to check Robby and the horse out. She said the vet had told them that the horse was fine and that Robby should be back on his feet in a few days. Mary sarcastically thought, "Well, who am I to question the advice of Dr. Holmes concerning Uncle Robby's medical condition? After all he is a veterinarian!"

As soon as Mary hung up with Aunt Pauline she called her cousin, Jason, and asked him to go over and clean up the hay. However, as soon as she explained the situation to him, he started laughing and told her he didn't think he should get in the middle of it. He said that his mom and dad were probably in on the whole thing and they would not appreciate him screwing up their plan. Mary figured he was right about that so she let him off the hook.

When Ellie came downstairs, Mary told her what the latest development was with the now heated feud between Lilly and her mother's siblings. As soon as she did, Ellie said, "Well, aren't your uncles the sly ones! I am happy that evil woman is getting what's coming to her! She deserves whatever they dish out and more!"

Thankfully, the weekend went by without any more calls from Lilly. Mary took care of her guests and went to church on Sunday evening as usual. On Monday morning she put a call in to HB's office just to let him know what was going on with Lilly and her aunts and uncles. Lilly had threatened to take legal action in their last phone conversation if the pranks didn't stop. Mary didn't think there was anything Lilly could really do, legally, to her aunts and uncles but she thought it might be a good idea to make sure. She knew that when her parents built the house they had a predial servitude or right of passage agreement drawn up and her Uncle Tommy had signed it to grant them unencumbered access to their driveway from the private main road that was actually on Uncle Tommy's property, but she didn't know if the agreement was transferable to new property owners should her parents no longer be the owners. Since the property was supposed to stay in the family, she never gave it much thought. It was likely that the agreement had been drawn up by HB's father since he had been her parents' lawyer for as long as Mary could remember.

When HB answered the phone, Mary told him about the situation. Of course, he found it amusing, but after a few teasing comments, he took Mary's concerns seriously and said that he would go to the court house and see if the document Mary was referring to was on file. He told her that filing such documents at the court house isn't required, but it was probable that, if his father had handled the contract, he had done so. He warned her that usually such agreements are transferable, but he would check just to be sure.

Around four o'clock the same day, HB called her back. He said he had found the document she had told him about at the court house and that he was relieved to finally be able to give her some good news for a change. He said that Uncle Tommy did not grant transferable rights to a new owner in the agreement with her parents, so he could do whatever he wanted on his property as long as he didn't go on Lilly's property. He said that Lilly would need to get Tommy to sign another right of passage agreement for her to have unencumbered access to her driveway.

Mary, silently, said to herself, "Thank you, Jesus!" Finally something had gone her family's way in all of this mess with Lilly. She knew Uncle Tommy was as likely to sign a new right of passage agreement with Lilly as hell was to freeze over. She thanked HB again for his help and told him to be sure to send her a bill for his legal services.

He said, "Don't worry. I will!"

After hanging up with HB, Mary wondered if Uncle Tommy remembered signing the agreement with her parents so long ago, and if he did remember, did he also remember not making the agreement transferable. She also wondered why he decided all those year ago not to make the agreement transferable. She decided to call Uncle Tommy and ask him about it. When she placed the call her Aunt Doris answered the phone. After a few minutes of small talk with her aunt she asked to speak to her uncle. Aunt Doris told her he was still out in the field but she would have him call her as soon as he came in. Mary thanked her and hung up the phone just as Ellie came in the back door.

Ellie said, "Well, Sugar, the cottage is all cleaned and ready for guests. Do you want me to fix you and Todd something for supper before I leave?"

Mary replied, "Oh, no, I can do that, but sit down a minute so I can tell you what I just found out."

As soon as Mary filled Ellie in on what she had learned from HB, Ellie slapped her knee in excitement. "Finally, that woman is gonna get some of what's comin' to her! I bet those uncles of yours have a few more tricks up their sleeves. Miss Lilly should have known better than to mess with the Perot family!"

Mary had to laugh at Ellie's excitement, but she hoped she was wrong about the part where her uncles had more tricks up their sleeve. A little while later Ellie left and Todd came in. Mary repeated what she had learned from HB and Todd had much the same reaction as Ellie but his remarks were a little more colorful. While they were talking, the phone rang. When Mary looked at the Caller ID and saw that it was Lilly she said, "Here we go again!" as she picked up the phone and sweetly said, "A Bed of Roses. How can I help you?"

Lilly replied, "Mary, it's me, Lilly."

"Oh, I'm sorry Lilly, I didn't take time to look at the caller ID. To what do I owe the pleasure of your phone call?"

"I warned you to tell your uncles to stop all their nonsense or I was going to seek legal action!"

"What's the matter Lilly? Did Uncle Robby not send someone to clean up the hay in the road?"

"No, that isn't it. Someone came and cleaned up the mess yesterday."

"Then what's the problem now?"

"Now there's horse manure all over the road in front of my driveway!"

Mary had to put her hand over her mouth to keep from laughing out loud. She could just picture Lilly driving up to her driveway and finding horse manure everywhere. However, after listening to Lilly rant a little while longer, she found out it was even worse than she had pictured. Lilly said she had come home after dark so she had not seen the manure in the road. She said that she drove right through it and when she pulled up into her garage and stepped out of her car, the manure was all over her tires and her garage smelled horrible!

Mary was speechless.

Lilly asked, "Mary, are you there? Are you listening to me?"

Finally, Mary composed herself. "Yes, Lilly, I heard every word you said and I can only imagine how upsetting that must have been for you. I hope you were able to get everything cleaned up."

"Of course I didn't clean it up! I got Richard to do it for me, and I can tell you he wasn't anymore amused by it than I was!"

Richard was the caretaker that took care of the Bordelon property. He had worked for Mary's parents for several years before Maggie died and had continued working for Jack after that. He had moved into the two bedroom cottage on the property after Beau and Eva moved out of it so he could be more readily available to help Jack out. Ellie had told Mary once that Richard didn't like Lilly and he had talked about quitting but he felt guilty leaving Jack without any help.

Mary could hear Lilly rambling on the other end of the line. She was saying something about not being able to get the smell out of the garage. Mary finally interrupted her. "Lilly, you keep threatening to take legal action. Why don't you call Mr. Landry and see what he can do?"

Mary suggested this because, thanks to HB, she knew what Mr. Landry was going to tell her. Mary's statement caught Lilly off guard.

She hesitated a few moments and then replied, "That is exactly what I am going to do and you can tell your awful uncles I said so!" With that, Lilly slammed the phone down in Mary's ear.

As Mary hung up the phone she said out loud to no one but herself, "Well, you just go right ahead. We'll see where that gets you."

Todd immediately asked, "What now?" When Mary told him he replied, "Poor Miss Lilly. Bless her ever loving heart." They both started laughing and didn't stop until they heard the phone ring again. This time it was Uncle Tommy. When Mary answered it she was still laughing.

Her uncle said, "What's so funny?"

Mary answered, "I don't know. Why don't you tell me?"

Uncle Tommy impatiently replied, "Mary, I don't have time for your foolishness. I just came in from working all day out in the field. When I came in, Doris said you called lookin' for me, so you tell me what's going on."

Mary sobered up enough to say, "So, it is me that is being foolish now is it? I suppose you don't know anything about the hay that got dumped in the middle of the road in front of Lilly's driveway Friday or the horse manure that was put there last night?"

Uncle Tommy did not answer Mary right away and she thought she could hear the slightest sound of a snicker on the other end of the phone before her uncle cleared his throat and said in a serious tone, "Umm, Robby told me about the hay incident. That could have happened to anyone. Besides, he sent one of his guys over there yesterday to clean it up. As for the horse manure, I guess one of Robby's guys must have taken a ride around the property. You know a horse goes where a horse goes, Mary. You can't control that."

Mary said, "Right, Uncle Tommy. I am sure both incidences were purely coincidental just like your tractor breaking down in front of Lilly's driveway."

"That's it, Mary, purely coincidental. Besides, I don't know if you realize it or not, but Perot Road is a privately owned road and it runs on the edge of my property line so if Miss Lilly has anything more to say to you about it just tell her to come talk to me. I am sure she and I can come to some agreement."

"Right, Uncle Tommy. I'll do just that. Thanks for clearing all this mess up for me."

"No problem, Mary. Anytime you or your brothers or sisters need anything, you know I am here for y'all. After all, what are families for if not to help each other out?"

With that Uncle Tommy said goodbye and hung up leaving Mary speechless once again. A few seconds after she hung up with her uncle, the phone rang yet again. This time it was her friend, Sara. She was just calling to check on Mary and to see how she was doing. When Mary told her about the things that had been happening to Lilly and her suspicions of her uncles being behind it all, Sara replied, "It sounds to me like your uncles and Lilly have a feud going on."

Mary said, "That's what I'm afraid of. I have tried to put a stop to it, but my uncles keep side stepping me. "

"Why are you giving your dear uncles such a hard time? Lilly deserves everything they can dish out and then some. You should be rewarding them for their ingenuity."

"With friends like you, who needs enemies?"

"What are friends for if not to set you straight when you are clearly in a state of confusion?"

Mary had to laugh at her friend's logic, but she decided she would change the subject, so she asked Sara if she had started shopping for her vacation to Europe yet. The two women started talking about shopping and completely forgot about Lilly and her crazy uncles.

CHAPTER TEN

RECOVERING THE ASHES

On Tuesday Mary decided to pay a visit to her Aunt Tess. She knew that if Uncle Tommy and Uncle Robby were up to anything else, Aunt Tess would know about it, and she also knew Aunt Tess would have an even harder time lying to her face than she had over the phone. Mary didn't call her aunt before going over because she wanted to catch her off guard before she could think up a story to tell Mary. When Mary drove up to Aunt Tess' house, she didn't see her aunt's car anywhere in sight so she guessed she probably wasn't home, but she got out of the car and went to knock on the door anyway. She figured maybe Uncle Isaac had taken the car in to town even though he usually took his truck. After a few seconds, Aunt Tess came to the door and opened it. She smiled a little nervously at Mary, but she said that she was glad to see her as she invited her in.

Aunt Tess said, "Mary, I wish you had called to let me know you were coming. I would have baked a pecan pie. I know that is your favorite."

Mary replied, "I know you would have and I didn't want you to go to the trouble, so, that is why I didn't." Mary half-guiltily thought, "Now who's doing the lying?" but her thought was interrupted by Uncle Isaac who walked into the room and said, "Hi, Mary. What brings you out this way other than to see two old people?"

Mary replied, "Hi, yourself. I didn't think you were home. I didn't see Aunt Tess' car in the driveway so I figured you had taken it in to town."

As soon as Mary finished her statement, she saw the uncomfortable look on her Aunt Tess' face and then the hesitant look that passed between her aunt and uncle. Mary knew she had already caught them in something and she wasn't going to give up until she got to the bottom of it. She put her hands on her hips and looked them both straight in the eyes. After a few seconds Aunt Tess slowly spoke up. "Well, Mary, you see I have been having some trouble with the car not starting so I drove it over to Twin Tire first thing this morning and Isaac followed me there so that I could leave the car for them to check out."

By the time Aunt Tess finished her explanation, she seemed a little more confident as she must have thought she had successfully convinced Mary that she was not hiding anything, but Mary was far from convinced. She asked, "What are the two of you up to? I already know Uncle Tommy and Uncle Robby have been pulling some pranks on Lilly and I came over here to see if the two of you have been in on it. I can tell by the looks on your faces that you must be involved in it somehow but I am not sure how it involves your car."

Uncle Isaac quickly replied, "Don't include me in that, Mary. I didn't have anything to do with it."

Aunt Tess tried to shush her husband, but it was too late. By the time Mary was finished with them she had what she thought was the full story. It seems that Uncle Tommy had made a new dirt road with his bush hog through the back end of their property and they had been using it to go back and forth to town so that they wouldn't have to go in front of Belle Rose where all the shenanigans were going on. Aunt Tess had parked her car behind the house since that is where the road was. Mary also found out that Richard had been in on everything from the start. He had come to see Tommy about a job after Jack died because he didn't want to work for Lilly. Tommy, seeing a good opportunity to have eyes and ears on Lilly and her daughters, told Richard he would pay him to keep working for Lilly and to report back to him whenever Lilly or her daughters did anything unusual. Richard had been more than happy to do as Tommy had asked and had provided a wealth of information. For starters, he had found out that Lilly did not get the three hundred thousand dollar life insurance policy that she had thought she was going to get. The policy she got was only for fifty thousand dollars, and some of that went towards paying for the funeral. Richard had overheard Lilly talking to her daughters about it and he said that they were not happy about it. He also told Robby that Lilly was now dating her lawyer, Roy Landry.

Mary was surprised to hear the news about Lilly and Roy Landry. She was not surprised that Lilly already had set her sights on someone new, but she had not expected it would be Roy Landry. He had to be at least ten years younger than Lilly. Plus, Mary didn't know his marital status, but he appeared to be in good health which didn't fit Lilly's MO. She usually set her sights on older sick widowers.

When Mary left her aunt and uncle's house, her head was swimming. She didn't know what to think about all of what she had learned. She tried to find out from Aunt Tess if her uncles had any other pranks planned for Lilly, but Aunt Tess swore she didn't know. She did say that Teddy had driven over from Baton Rouge a couple of days ago and that he had stayed the night with Uncle Robby. She said she was pretty sure he was in on things too. Mary asked her aunt if Aunt Adele knew what was going on and she said she had called her and told her about it, but she assured Mary that Adele had no other involvement.

Mary had not placed a conference call to her siblings lately. She had only emailed them. After her visit with Aunt Tess, she figured one was in order. Boy, were they going to be surprised to hear what their crazy aunts and uncles were up to! She was sure the horse manure story was going to get the biggest laugh.

When Mary got home, it was two o'clock and Todd was at the stove browning a pot roast for supper. She was glad he was taking care of dinner as she had other things on her mind. While Todd worked at making a roux for his gravy, Mary filled him in on the latest developments with the Perot brothers. No sooner than she had finished telling him everything that Aunt Tess had told her the phone rang. She looked at the caller ID and saw that it was Lilly again. She quickly told Todd to answer it and tell her she wasn't home. He argued with her for a few seconds, but finally did as Mary asked when she volunteered to stir the roux for him. When Todd picked up the phone, all Mary could hear was his side of the conversation. "Hello.... Oh, hi Charlotte. I thought you were Lilly.... No, she's not home right now. Do you want me to give her a message?... Did you say snakes?... Oh, I am sorry to hear that. Is Lilly OK?... I will certainly give Mary the message as soon as she gets home.... Bye."

As soon as Todd hung up the phone, Mary said, "What was the part about snakes?" Todd replied, "It seems Lilly was riding around the property today on the golf cart and she came across a family of grass snakes. She yelled at Richard and he came and killed them all but she was very shaken up by it. Charlotte seems to think your uncles are behind it and she said if they didn't stop harassing her mother, they were going to take legal action."

Mary thought about it for a minute and then concluded Richard must have put the snakes where Lilly would find them. She didn't think her uncles would have risked going on the property themselves but she would bet her bottom dollar they had put Richard up to it. They probably didn't tell Aunt Tess about it because they knew how much she hated snakes. If they had told her, she would have definitely put her foot down and insisted they scrap their plan. Mary had to put a stop to all of this before someone really did get hurt. She had no intention of calling Charlotte back so she spent the next few hours doing chores around the house to keep herself busy and her mind off the worsening situation until she could call her siblings.

Finally, at six o'clock sharp, she made the call. This time Maddie wasn't available. She was in the middle of a project and the production crew was filming her, so her assistant said she would have Maddie call her as soon as she could. It took Mary a while to relay everything that had gone on in the past few days. As she expected, they could not believe how creative their uncles had gotten and they were even more surprised to hear about Richard's involvement in everything. JJ and Jake said they might come down so that they could help the uncles out. They said they wanted to get in on all the fun. Mary and her sisters quickly advised against that idea. They were all glad to hear Lilly had not gotten the three hundred thousand dollar life insurance money that she had been expecting and the gossip about Lilly and Roy Landry really peaked their interests. After Mary promised her siblings she would keep them posted, she ended the call. However, JJ and Jake continued their conversation on a private call and, against their sisters' advice, they plotted on how they could get in on the action. They decided JJ would place a call to Uncle Tommy and report back to Jake.

When JJ placed the call, Aunt Doris answered the phone. She said how happy she was to hear from him. JJ didn't want to be rude so he talked to his aunt for a little while until he ran out of things to say, then he asked her if Uncle Tommy was home. She said he was and in a few seconds JJ heard his uncle's gruff voice on the other end of the line.

"Hey, there, nephew. To what do we owe this rare phone call?"

JJ replied, "I just spoke to Mary and it seems there is a lot going on in Perot Country these days."

"Well, I'm not sure what that sister of yours has been telling y'all, but it's just business as usual here. You know baling hay and feeding cows."

"Ah, come on Uncle Tommy this is me, JJ, you're talking to, not sweet little Mary. Jake and I think what you and Uncle Robby have been up to is ingenious and we want to get in on the action."

"Well, son, if you boys want to come down for a visit, why didn't you just say so? We'd love to have you anytime. Robby and I, we got a huntin' trip of sorts planned that you and Jake might want to go on. Robby and I can fill you in when you get here. About how soon you think that will be? You know, times a wastin' when it comes to huntin'."

JJ couldn't imagine what kind of hunting trip his uncles were planning but if it had to do with Lilly, he was all in and he knew Jake would be too as soon as he told him about it. He quickly told his uncle, "We can come just about any time. Jake flies into Philly on a regular basis. In fact, I think he is due in tomorrow around noon. I can catch a ride with him back to Atlanta, then we can take his plane from there and land at the airport right there in Natchitoches."

Uncle Tommy replied, "Sounds good. See you boys tomorrow night."

But before he could hang up JJ asked, "Uh, Uncle Tommy, do you think you could pick us up at the airport? I don't want to bother Mary right now. You know she is kind of stressed out already over all that's been going on."

Uncle Tommy laughed as he said, "Got your drift, JJ. Mum's the word. Just call me when y'all land and Robby or I will come get ya. Y'all can spend the night here, too. I'm sure Doris won't mind a bit."

"Thanks, Uncle Tommy! Oh, I almost forgot. Do we need to bring any of our hunting gear?"

"Nah, son, that won't be necessary. Robby and I got everything covered."

As soon as JJ hung up the phone with his uncle, he called Jake and told him all about the plan. The brothers couldn't imagine what their uncles had in store for them, but they couldn't wait to get there to find out.

When JJ and Jake landed in Natchitoches, JJ called his Uncle Tommy. His uncle said he and Robby would be at the airport to pick them up in about twenty minutes. Thirty minutes later they were loaded up in the back seat of their Uncle Robby's four door GMC pick-up truck and headed back to Perot Country. As they rode, Uncle Tommy filled them in on what exactly the hunting trip was all about. When he finished, JJ and Jake couldn't believe these two old men had orchestrated such a plot. Actually, it was three old men because Uncle Teddy was in on it, too.

Uncle Teddy had gone a couple of weeks ago to Lambert Funeral Home and ordered a memorial bench just like the one Jack had ordered from them when Maggie had died. It had just come in yesterday and Uncle Robby had picked it up and brought it to his house. There he had filled the urns inside each pedestal with ashes from his fire pit back behind the barn that he used to burn trash in. Their plan was to sneak on to the Bordelon property after Lilly had gone to sleep. Richard would be waiting for them by the meditation pond. There they would swap out the two benches, taking the one with Maggie and Jack's ashes and leaving behind the one with the ashes from the fire pit. They figured if everything went as planned, neither Lilly nor her daughters would ever have any idea the benches had been switched. Once they had secured the bench with the real ashes they planned to put it at the family cemetery on Tess and Isaac's property. The aunts and uncles hadn't agreed yet on whether or not they wanted to keep Jack's ashes. They said they were going to hold off on making a decision on that for a while to see how things played out, but they were thinking about maybe taking his ashes out to Cane River in Tommy's fishing boat and dumping them in the river.

JJ and Jake were dumbfounded. In all the speculating they had done on the flight over as to what their uncles had up their sleeves, they had never dreamed they were going to be "hunting" their own parents ashes! However, they wouldn't have given up this opportunity for all the crawfish in Louisiana.

When they got back to Uncle Robby's house, they went inside and greeted Aunt Pauline and Aunt Doris. The two aunts had fixed some boudin and a bowl of potato salad. Everyone sat down to eat, and as they did, Uncle Tommy went over the plan one last time to make sure everyone knew what to do. Aunt Pauline and Aunt Doris seemed a little nervous about the whole thing and they warned their husbands and nephews to be careful. As far as anyone knew, Lilly didn't have any guns in the house as she had given Mary and Martine all three of Jack's guns a few days ago. So, even if she woke up, heard something and came outside, they shouldn't be in any immediate danger. Their plan was that, if that were to happen, Richard would high tail it up to the house to ward her off before she could see anything going on at the pond.

After they finished eating, Uncle Robby took them into the den and had them change into some of his camouflage hunting clothes. He also gave them each a black knit cap to wear and some gloves. They really did look like they were going on just another ordinary hunting trip. By now it was ten o'clock, but they wanted to be sure Lilly was asleep, so they hung out at the house for another couple of hours. While they were sitting around talking, JJ started asking his uncles questions about the incidents that had been happening at Belle Rose lately. Hearing their uncles telling the stories was so amusing, even though he and Jake had heard them all from Mary already. That is until they got to the story about the snakes. It seems there was one minor detail Charlotte had left out when she called and spoke to Todd about the incident. According to Uncle Tommy, who got his information from Richard, Lilly had been so frightened by the snakes that she wet her pants right there on the golf cart. He said that she had run into the house yelling, "Damn, those Perot boys!" When Uncle Tommy told them that part of the story, they burst into laughter. After JJ finally gained some control he said, "Poor Lilly, Bless her little heart." They all burst out laughing again and didn't stop for a full minute or more.

Around midnight Richard called to say all the lights in the house had been turned off at ten thirty and had not come back on since, so they decided it was time to put their plan into action. They all got back in the truck and Uncle Robby drove it around to the barn where the new bench was. They loaded it into the back of the truck with the help of a dolly and a make-shift ramp. Afterwards, Uncle Robby threw the dolly and the ramp into the back of the truck with the bench. Then, they started down a narrow, dark, dirt road behind Uncle Robby's house. JJ and Jake had never been on the road before. They asked Uncle Robby about it and he told them Tommy had made the dirt road with his bush hog and that it led from his property to the back end of Belle Rose. Uncle Tommy said he had also made dirt roads from each of their properties to the main road so that they no longer had to pass by Belle Rose to go into town. JJ and Jake stared at one another and just shook their heads.

The road was so dark that, even though Uncle Robby had his bright lights on the entire time, they had to go really slow. When they finally got to the back of the Bordelon property, they had to get out and unload the bench on to the dolly. They couldn't drive the truck on to the property because of all the pecan trees lining the back of the property. Thankfully, the meditation pond wasn't that far from where they had to park. Uncle Tommy had brought flash lights so they could see as they pushed the dolly forward past the pecan trees and towards the pond. Soon they could see Richard up ahead holding a bright lantern. By the time they got to the pond they were all out of breath from pushing the heavy marble bench in the grass. JJ and Jake wondered how these two old men had planned to do this without their help. There is no way they could have done it without getting some back up.

As quickly and as quietly as they could, they unloaded the new bench and swapped it out for the old one. Just as they were loading the old one on to the dolly, Richard saw a light come on in the house and he alerted the others. They quickly turned their flash lights off, which meant the only light they had was Richard's lantern, but Richard took off towards the house to make sure Lilly didn't come outside and notice anything going on. Then they were left in total darkness. They clumsily finished loading the bench on to the dolly, and slowly moved towards the back of the property. When they got to the cover of the pecan trees, they turned their flashlights back on. They hoped and prayed Lilly didn't come outside, and if she did, Richard was able to make up some story to explain what he was doing out so late. By the time they got back to the truck they were again out of breath and drenched in sweat. They loaded the bench into the back of the truck and jumped into the cab.

As they rode back down the dirt road towards Robby's house, they were giving each other high fives and laughing at how they had pulled off the heist of a lifetime. They wondered what the rest of the family was going to think about what they had done. When they got back to the house, the women were inside waiting anxiously. They rushed to the door as they pulled up and asked them how it went. Jake replied, "When the Perot and Bordelon boys go huntin' do they ever come back empty handed?" All the others laughed and slapped each other on the back.

Uncle Tommy turned to JJ and Jake and said, "Good work boys. We couldn't have pulled it off without y'all."

Uncle Robby seconded his brother's statement, "Yeah, when Tommy told me JJ had called and wanted to come help out I couldn't believe my ears. That's when we knew we could put our plan in to action."

JJ said, "Hell, we wouldn't have missed this for the world! Right, Jake?"

Jake responded, "Hell, no!"

Just, then, Tommy's cell phone beeped and he checked to see who was texting him this late at night. It was Richard and the text message read, "The Black Widow is in her nest and all is quiet on the home front." Tommy read the message out loud, then, they all high-fived each other again.

The next morning Uncle Tommy drove JJ and Jake to the airport and the brothers left Natchitoches without anyone else knowing they had even been in town.

CHAPTER ELEVEN

THE WITNESS

Thursday morning Mary woke up with a start. It was ten minutes after six so her alarm had not gone off yet. Todd was out of bed and she could hear the shower running. She couldn't figure out what had awakened her, but she had a strange feeling. She thought maybe it had something to do with what she had been dreaming, but she couldn't put the dream all together in her head. It had something to do with Belle Rose and she could remember seeing her mom smiling down at her. She thought there was a birthday party going on, but she wasn't sure who it was for. All her brothers and sisters were sitting around a picnic table out by the pecan trees, and her mom was lighting the birthday candles on the cake.

Whenever Mary had a dream that her mom was in, she tried to hold on to it, so she could be with her, but the vision had slipped away as fast as it had come. She tried to go back to sleep so she could, hopefully, pick up the dream where she had left off, but she didn't have any luck, so she decided to get up.

Just then, Todd came out of the bathroom fully dressed and clean shaven. He said, "You're up early. I didn't even hear your alarm go off."

Mary replied, "It didn't.

Mary went into the bathroom and Todd headed to the kitchen to start the coffee just as Mary's alarm started buzzing. After breakfast, Todd left the house to run some errands. Mary decided she would bake some banana nut bread for her weekend guests. While the bread was baking, she went in her office to check her email for reservation requests and to catch up on some paperwork. Around nine thirty the phone rang. She looked at the Caller ID and it said "Lambert Funeral Home." She picked it up, assuming they were calling about something to do with her father's funeral. When she said, "Hello," Doug Lambert responded, "Hello, Mary, this is Doug Lambert."

Mary replied "How are you, Doug?"

Doug responded, "Fine," then he went on to say, "Mary, I am calling you to tell you about something that happened yesterday that I thought might interest you."

Mary said, "Oh, what's that?"

"Well, I was talking to my dad. I don't know if you know but he has dementia."

"Yes, I had heard that. I am so sorry. I know how difficult that can be on a family. We went through it with our mother."

"Yes, I had heard that too. I don't know if it was this way with your mother, but with my dad, he has good days and bad days. On the good days he is able to recall most things but on the bad days not so much."

Mary wasn't sure what this had to do with her but she felt sorry for Doug and his family. She knew much too well the toll a parent suffering with dementia took on a family. She said that she understood and confirmed that they had gone through similar days with her mother.

Then she waited silently while he continued with his story.

"Well, yesterday he was having a good day and he was talking about the good old days with all his old friends. He started talking about your father and Henry Babin, and in the conversation, he mentioned that the last time he saw Henry was at Jack's house. He said that while he was there, Henry had asked him to sign a form. He said he thought it was Jack's will." Mary almost fell out of her chair, but she didn't say anything as Doug kept talking. "I had heard that Lilly inherited everything from your father, but my dad seems to remember Jack saying something about him having a surprise up his sleeve for Lilly. Now I know my dad's memory isn't very reliable, but I thought maybe you should know."

Finally, Mary regained her voice and said, "Doug, thanks so much for calling and letting me know this. I have been working with HB Babin because my family has reason to believe that our dad had his father write up another will for him, but we haven't found a copy of it anywhere. I think your father may have really been at my dad's house and he may have served as the witness to my dad's official last will."

Doug replied, "I'm sorry I can't be of any more help to you in the matter. I wish my dad's memory was more reliable."

Mary quickly reassured him that he had been a big help and to please give his father her regards. She hung up and immediately called HB. When HB answered the phone, Mary couldn't get her words out fast enough. After she told him what she had just learned from Doug Lambert, HB replied, "Well, that is some story! I can't believe I didn't think of it before. Of course Dad would have needed witnesses to sign the will. In fact there had to be two, so if Doug Lambert was one of them, then who was the second one? It would really help if we knew who that was, but we still wouldn't be able to do anything until we found a copy of the actual will. When we find it, we will know who the other witness is."

Mary sighed, "Yeah, that's the kicker. We have to keep looking. I wonder if my dad hid a copy anywhere. He couldn't drive anymore and he hardly left the house so he couldn't have taken it anywhere, but I don't think he would've risked hiding it in the house since Lilly could have found it there. Where else would he have hid it and who else would he have had at the house that would have been available to sign it?" Mary thought, it couldn't be Richard because, if he had known about the will, he would have told them right away. As she thought about both questions, it occurred to her that just maybe her dad had hid the will in the garage. He liked to go out in the garage and piddle around. She even remembered a couple of months before he died, he and Richard had spent a whole week out in the garage cleaning and organizing it. She would have to ask Uncle Tommy to ask Richard to look for it there.

Mary hung up the phone with HB and started to dial Uncle Tommy's number, but she stopped when it occurred to her that he would be in the field this time of day. She decided to take a ride out to Aunt Tess' to give her the good news about what Doug

Lambert had told her. She grabbed her purse and ran out the door. She couldn't wait to let her aunt know that her father might not have disowned his family after all and that, just maybe, they would get Belle Rose back before it was too late.

When Mary arrived at Aunt Tess' house, she noticed Uncle Robby's truck in the distance by the family cemetery. She could see Uncle Robby and Uncle Tommy with a couple of other guys in cowboy hats standing in the cemetery leaning over something. She also saw Aunt Doris, Aunt Pauline, Aunt Tess and Uncle Isaac standing in the cemetery next to each other and Uncle Isaac had his arm around Aunt Tess. Mary wondered what was going on. She got out of her car and started walking towards the cemetery. As she got closer, she could have sworn the something the guys were leaning over looked very similar to the bench her father had bought that now had her parents' ashes in it. By the time she got within a few feet of the cemetery, everyone finally heard her approaching and they all turned around to look at her. It was, then, that she realized the something definitely was her parents' bench. Everyone just stared at her for a few seconds saying nothing. Mary demanded someone tell her what in the Sam Hill was going on! Uncle Tommy and Uncle Robby looked at Aunt Tess and she looked back at them.

Finally, Uncle Tommy got up enough nerve to speak up. "Well, Honey, you see it's like this. Um, you might better sit down."

Uncle Robby led his niece over to another bench on the side of the cemetery and Mary sat down. By the time Uncle Tommy finished telling her what they had done, she didn't know if she should yell at them or kiss them. She knew she wanted to clobber her two brothers for not telling her they were coming into town and for being a part of the plan without even letting her know what was going on. When she spoke up, her voice was shaky. Her Aunt Tess came over and sat down next to her and put her arms around her shoulders. With tears in her eyes all Mary could say was, "Thank you! I love all of you so much!"

With that, the men finished putting the bench in place next to their sister, Nina's, grave, and they all stood around it with their heads bowed while Aunt Tess lead them in a prayer.

Afterwards, they all went back to the house and had a cup of coffee and a slice of Aunt Tess' homemade pineapple upside down cake. While they ate, Mary told her aunts and uncles the news that she had gotten from Doug a couple of hours earlier. They all praised God for having made Jacques Bordelon come to his senses before his death and prayed that the new will would be found before the succession was completed. Mary told them about her idea of her father hiding the will in the garage and Uncle Tommy said he would have Richard start looking for it right away. Mary got up and went around the table hugging each of her aunts and uncles as she told them goodbye.

When Mary arrived back home, Todd was still gone. She figured he had stopped off at the pool hall in town and probably would not be home until time for supper. She called his cell phone, but he didn't answer. She left him a voice message to pick up something for supper on his way home because she was too wired to even think about cooking anything. She called Sara and as soon as she answered, Mary poured out the story of her parents' ashes and everything else that had happened over the last few days. Sara could hardly believe all that Mary was telling her. The two women talked for a while until Sara got another call from one of her tenants and had to hang up.

Mary couldn't wait until six o'clock to do a conference call with her siblings so she started a group text. Before she could finish the second text, her phone was ringing. It was Maddie. She wanted to know all the details so Mary filled her in on the latest news. Maddie was just as excited as Mary had been about what Doug had told her and she was blown away by what her two brothers and her uncles had done. Maddie said she was trying to make arrangements to get back to Natchitoches sometime in the next couple of weeks to get the secretariat desk. They talked a few more minutes, then, Maddie said she had to run, as she was in the middle of laying tile for a kitchen back-splash.

No sooner than Mary had hung up the phone with Maddie, JJ called. He said he knew she was mad at him and Jake so he was calling to man up and apologize. After giving him a hard time for a few minutes, she begrudgingly forgave him. They discussed the situation of the will for a while, then, JJ said he had to run but he said for her not to worry about calling Jake or Joe. He said he would make the calls for her. He said it was the least he could do to get back in her good graces. She thanked him as she figured she would be explaining everything at least three more times by the time the rest of her sisters called. Mary hung up the phone and waited to see who would call next.

About a half hour later, Martine called and Mary went through everything for the third time. Martine was as shocked as Maddie had been. Mallory called next and Mary repeated everything for the fourth time getting the same reaction as before. By five o'clock, Myrié called and Mary repeated herself one more time. She silently told herself she would wait to make the conference call next time so she would not have to repeat herself so many times. Myrié was so excited that she said she was going to figure out a way to get back to Natchitoches as soon as she could. She needed to come get the dining room set anyway and she wanted to personally thank her aunts and uncle for all that they had done to defend the Bordelon family.

Just as Mary hung up the phone with Myrié, Todd walked in carrying a to-go bag from Lasyone's. Mary knew without asking that he had gotten her a shrimp po'boy. He walked over and sat the food down on the kitchen island.

As he leaned over and kissed Mary on the cheek, he nonchalantly asked, "So, how was your day?"

Mary rolled her eyes and then began telling the story all over again. When she was finished, Todd said, "This gets juicer by the day! I can't wait to see what your aunts and uncles do next!"

Mary replied, "Let's hope they cool their jets for now. The most important thing we need to happen is for someone to find that will!"

Todd responded, "Well at least you and your brothers and sisters can rest easier knowing that your father didn't hang his own kids out to dry."

Mary agreed that was nice to know. Even if they never found the other will, at least they wouldn't go the rest of their lives feeling like their own father had disowned them.

Mary turned her attention to the to-go bag as Todd started taking out the contents. She was delighted to see that not only had he bought her a shrimp po'boy, but he had also brought her a slice of Angela's sinfully delicious pecan pie! It wasn't quite as good as Aunt Tess' but it was pretty darn close!

JJ's Dirty Rice

Ingredients:

2 to 3 cups uncooked rice

¼ to ½ pound of chicken livers

1 to 1½ pounds ground beef

1 to 1½ pounds ground pork

½ cup chopped green onions

1 clove fresh garlic

2 medium onions

1 medium bell pepper

2 stalks celery

salt & pepper to taste

Put rice on to boil. Grind raw chicken livers in a food processor or blender. Brown livers, beef and pork together in larger pot. Chop up garlic, onions, bell pepper and celery. Add to meat mixture. Add salt and pepper. Cook until vegetables are tender. Add cooked rice and mix well.

Note from JJ: We Cajuns like our dirty rice spicy so I usually add a little cayenne pepper or red pepper flakes to spice it up a little or a lot depending on who I am cooking for. However, if you decide to try these seasonings for yourself, be careful how much you add, especially if you are not used to eating spicy food! Also, sometimes I substitute gizzards for chicken livers.

CHAPTER TWELVE

THERE'S SOMETHING FISHY GOING ON

A whole week went by without any fireworks. Lilly and her daughters left town on Friday to go on their annual spring break trip to Corpus Christi, Texas, so Richard had free reign to search the garage all week, but he had come up empty-handed. However, things started heating up the following Thursday night, literally as well as figuratively. That night a sudden change in weather caused an oxygen problem in the pond. Richard had not looked at the weather report and had not thought to turn on the aerator in the pond. Friday morning, when he walked outside, he thought he smelled something slightly "fishy" in the air. When he got near the meditation pond he was shocked to see that nearly all of Lilly's gold fish and other expensive tropical fish were floating belly up all over the top of the pond. By the time Lilly and her daughters pulled up in the driveway Friday afternoon you could smell the dead fish all the way to the house even though the pond was a good sixty to eighty yards away. Of course Mary wasn't there, but she heard all about it from Aunt Tess.

Aunt Tess called Mary Saturday morning. She said Richard had called Uncle Tommy's house to let him know what had happened and Aunt Doris had called to tell her. Aunt Tess said that, according to Richard, Lilly and her daughters were fit to be tied. They said they just knew Tommy and Robby were behind it all. They were sure that the brothers had poisoned the fish so they called the Wild Life and Fishery office and they sent someone out to test the water. When the guy told them it was the oxygen level in the pond that did the fish in instead of poison, they didn't believe him. They had questioned Richard at length about whether or not anyone had come on the property while they were gone. Richard said no one that he knew of but he told them that he had left the house unattended for a couple of hours Thursday to go pick up some grass fertilizer at the Kaffie Frederick's General Store. They decided that must have been when the brothers had come on the property and poisoned the fish. Richard said a little while later he saw Roy Landry pull up and go inside the house.

Mary didn't know what to think about this newest twist in the ongoing saga with Lilly. If the water tests did not show any signs of poison but it did show a low level of oxygen coupled with the high temperatures last night there shouldn't be any way that Lilly and her daughters could come after her uncles. Mary hoped that Mr. Landry had told the three women just that and advising them not to go around accusing her uncles of anything that they could not prove. Thankfully, by Sunday, Richard said everything was back to normal at Belle Rose except that he had to spend all day Saturday cleaning out the pond. He didn't complain too much, though, since he felt a little guilty for all those poor fish that had died all because he had failed to check the weather report and turn on the aerator.

As for Mary's uncles, they thought it was great news and they celebrated the occurrence by throwing a big fish fry Sunday afternoon. That Sunday just so happened to be Easter Sunday, so, the uncles held the celebration at Aunt Tess' house and invited all the Perot relatives that lived in the area. Todd and Mary, along with many of her cousins and their children, were there. Lola made a beautiful cake covered with a bed of dyed green coconut grass and decorated with a chocolate Easter bunny and a basket of multicolored Easter eggs. The aunts cooked up several side dishes, and everyone ate until they couldn't eat another bite. After the festivities, Mary went with her cousin, Amanda, back to her dad's house and they went trail riding. Mary got to ride her favorite horse, Sunny. He was a fifteen-year old palomino gelding that was a descendant of her first horse, Silver. It was a wonderful day and a nice break for Mary from the stressful last few months.

Just two days later, on the following Tuesday afternoon, Aunt Tess paid Mary a surprise visit. Over a cup of coffee, Aunt Tess told Mary that she had gotten a call from Uncle Teddy who told her that he had gotten a call from his friend, William Taylor. It seems Roy Landry called Mr. Taylor on Monday to inform him that Lilly had had a change of heart and was, now, inclined to go along with Mr. Taylor's suggestion of releasing the money from Louis Perot's estate settlement to the Bordelon children. Mr. Taylor said that Lilly's lawyer had called him in the nick of time because the checks were scheduled to go out the next day. In fact, they would have gone out sooner but they were a few days late issuing them due to the Easter holiday. He also said that Mr. Landry had made a weird statement about Lilly hoping that this would put an end to all the nonsense that had been happening to her lately.

Mary could hardly believe what Aunt Tess had said. Despite everything her uncles had done to Lilly, the thing that changed her mind, in the end, was something they had nothing to do with!

After Aunt Tess left, Mary decided to call Sara and let her in on the latest news. Of course Sara was all ears, and after Mary finished telling her about the fish incident and Lilly's change of heart concerning the money from her Uncle Louis' estate settlement, Sara was thrilled. She congratulated Mary for winning a battle with Lilly even if it wasn't the whole war.

Mary asked Sara if she and Terry were getting excited about their upcoming trip. Sara said that they were but that she hated leaving Mary with all the drama going on in her life. However, when she asked Mary if she wanted her to postpone her trip, Mary exclaimed, "No, I definitely do not want you to do any such thing! Celebrating your fiftieth wedding anniversary only happens once in a lifetime and taking a trip to Europe has been your dream for years."

When Mary hung up the phone with Sara, she texted her siblings to let them know she would be holding a conference call at six o'clock. Then she anxiously waited until time to make the call. This time everyone called in. When she finished telling them the latest news, everyone began talking at once. As soon as they all calmed down, Maddie said that she had looked at her schedule and she thought she and Garrett could come home on April 11 to get the secretariat desk. Mary was surprised Maddie was coming so soon.

She asked, "You mean this Saturday in just four days?"

Maddie replied, "Yes, is that a problem?"

"No. I was just making sure I understood you right."

Then Myrié said, "I think I might come then too, so I can get the dining room furniture."

Maddie and Myrié decided they would both fly in to Alexandria Saturday morning from their prospective cities on a one way ticket. Then, each of them would rent a small U-Haul truck to carry their furniture back home. Martine volunteered to pick them up at the airport if they would coordinate their flights to land in Alexandria around the same time Saturday morning. They both readily agreed. If all went according to plan, they should be at Mary's house around noon Saturday.

CHAPTER THIRTEEN

THE MISSING INSURANCE MONEY

Mary had an older couple from France staying in one of her upstairs guest rooms and a young couple from Tennessee staying in another one. The couple from France were on a vacation traveling through Louisiana and planned to stay at A Bed of Roses for three nights. The young couple was visiting friends in town and they planned to stay two nights. Thursday morning Mary cooked breakfast for the two couples and cleaned the kitchen afterwards. She was planning on going to the grocery store to get some things for the weekend. While she was making out her grocery list, the phone rang. She looked at the Caller ID and saw that it was her son, Beau. Beau didn't call that often. He usually left "keeping in touch duties" to Eva, but, he especially didn't call during a week day as he was always at work. Mary's motherly instincts instantly kicked in as she picked up the phone and said, "Hello."

Beau responded, "Hey, Mom. What up?"

Mary replied, "You wouldn't believe it if I told you, but you first. Why are you calling me in the middle of the day on a Thursday?"

Mary had spoken to Beau, Eva and the kids Sunday for Easter and she had filled her son in on everything that had been going on then but she hadn't had a chance to tell him about her Uncle Louis' settlement yet. However, she wanted to know what was going on with him first.

Beau answered Mary's question with a question of his own. "Well, I'm calling to see if you know a guy by the name of Randy Tucker. He is an agent with Edward Jones Financial."

Mary replied, "No, I don't think so. Should I?"

"I'm not sure. The reason I am asking is because I got a call from him yesterday. He said that Paw Paw had been a client of his and that Paw Paw had a life insurance policy with Hartford Life that he serviced. He said it was a three hundred and twenty thousand dollar policy. He apologized for not getting in touch with me sooner, but he said he had just recently taken over Paw Paw's accounts from a retiring agent and that when Lilly had called him to notify him of Paw Paw's death, she had not mentioned the life insurance policy as she was unaware of it. Paw Paw had put the policy in my name. I guess because I am the oldest of the grandchildren and he had set up the monthly statements for the policy to go to a different address than Paw Paw's IRA accounts so there had been a mix-up there."

Mary thought, "The surprises just keep coming!"

Beau continued, "The beneficiaries of the policy are Paw Paw's sixteen grandchildren. Each one of us is supposed to get twenty thousand dollars."

Mary said out loud, "Thank you, Jesus!"

Mary's father's image was being redeemed in her eyes with every passing day. She told her son, Beau, how happy she was for him.

He replied, "Mom, you know it isn't about the money."

Mary understood exactly what he meant. She softly replied, "I know Beau."

He continued, "What it means to me is that Paw Paw didn't disown me or any of his other grandkids like we had all thought." Mary knew how important that was to him and it was just as important to her.

Mary told Beau about her uncle's estate settlement and he replied, "That's great news, Mom! I don't guess you found the other will yet, though, have you?"

"No, not yet, but we are still looking. We are not going to give up until we do."

"Well, I sure hope it turns up. Eva and I really want to build a house at Belle Rose when I retire if at all possible." Mary wanted that for her son, too, as it would mean that there would be Perot descendants living on the land once again.

Mary replied, "I know what you mean, Beau, and I will let you know right away if we find it." Beau said he had to go because he had to get back to work. He told his mom he loved her and said goodbye.

Mary wondered if Mr. Tucker had called her other two sons or any of her nieces and nephews about their inheritance yet. However, she decided she wouldn't call anybody right away to find out. Instead, she waited to see who would call her first. Sure enough, a few minutes later, her phone rang and it didn't stop ringing all day as both of her other sons called and all of her siblings called to say they had heard from their children or from Mr. Tucker themselves.

When Mary spoke to her siblings, they also told her they had received a five thousand dollar certified cashier's check the day before from Mr. Taylor for their share of their Uncle Louis' estate settlement. Mary had received her check yesterday as well. They all agreed that it would be a good idea if they put the money towards paying HB for any legal work that was needed to prove the authenticity of the new will, if and when it was found, and any other expenses that might come up.

When Mary went to bed Thursday night she said an extra prayer of thanksgiving that God had seen fit to change Jacques Bordelon's heart in the last year of his life. She thought she had seen glimpses of change in her father during that last year and God knew how hard she had prayed for it, but when they had been presented with the will in Mr. Landry's office, it looked like her prayers had not been answered. Mary had always believed in miracles and she felt like she was living out one now. She didn't want to seem greedy, but she asked God for just one more miracle and, if possible, to let it come soon.

Mary had no idea what was in the new will, but it had to be better than the one Mr. Landry had. However, with Mr. Babin being dead and Mr. Lambert having dementia, it was going to be an uphill battle to prove the new will was written when her father was completely competent. One thing she had on her side was that Lilly had made the statement numerous times to anyone who would listen that her husband was as competent as the day was long. In fact, she had said it the day her father passed away in front of several people including Aunt Issy and Paul and Amy Robicheaux. Mary had suspected at the time that Lilly was doing it because she knew all about the will that she had Jack sign leaving her everything and she thought the Bordelon children might question it. So she wanted to make sure everyone knew that her husband was completely sane and knew exactly what he was doing when he signed it. It had irritated Mary, Mallory and Martine when Lilly said it, but none of them had spoken up to dispute it at the time. Now, Mary was glad that they hadn't.

CHAPTER FOURTEEN

MYRIÉ AND MADDIE'S RETURN VISIT

Saturday morning Mary jumped out of bed as soon as her alarm went off. She was excited that three of her sisters were coming to see her even if it was for a short visit. The sisters didn't get an opportunity to be together very often so this was a special treat for Mary. She just wished Mallory was going to be coming, too. Then they could have a mini sister reunion! The Bordelon sisters started having reunions after their mother passed away, but they only had them every two years. The last one they had was the year before and they had gone to Myrtle Beach, South Carolina. They had a great time just sitting by the beach, drinking margaritas and talking about life. Of course, they had all been together last month but that didn't count since it was for their father's funeral. While they were together this weekend, maybe they would start planning where they wanted to go next year for their reunion.

Mary's thoughts were interrupted by Todd who came in the bedroom to ask her if she needed any help with breakfast. She said that would be nice and asked him to start frying the bacon. She told him she would be in the kitchen in just a few minutes. Luckily, she had opted to take her shower last night since she knew this morning was going to be hectic.

The young couple had checked out yesterday but the older couple from France was still here and she needed to fix breakfast for them. They would be checking out by noon today and her sisters should be coming in around the same time.

When Mary entered the kitchen, Todd was already frying the bacon and she could smell the biscuits cooking in the oven. She quickly put together two fruit parfaits in crystal glasses, added a whipped cream and yogurt topping and placed a strawberry on top. Last, she sprinkled the parfait with chopped pecans. She carried the parfaits into the dining room and set them on the table beside each place setting. Then she went back to the kitchen where Todd was sautéing onions, tomatoes and crawfish in butter for omelets. She lightly scrambled some eggs and handed them to him. Todd put the crawfish mixture into a bowl and poured half of the scrambled eggs in the skillet. After the eggs had cooked for just a couple of minutes, he added some of the crawfish mixture. Just before turning the omelet over, he added grated cheese. When the omelet was done, he repeated the steps to make the second one. Meanwhile, Mary took the biscuits out of the oven and put some of her homemade strawberry fig preserves into a small glass bowl. The older couple came downstairs just as Todd put the omelets on the plates Mary had set by the stove. When they took their seats at the table, Mary brought the bowl of preserves into the dining room, set it on the table and asked her guests if they would like a cup of coffee. They said they did so Mary turned over each of the cups by their place setting and poured coffee into them as she interacted pleasantly with the guests for a few minutes before returning to the kitchen. She returned with the plates of crawfish omelets, bacon and biscuits. She sat the plates down in front of her guests and asked them if there was anything else she could get them. They said no thank you, so she went back to the kitchen while her guests ate their breakfast but she checked on them a few more times during the meal. She refilled their coffee cups and thanked them when they complimented her and Todd on how wonderful the breakfast was. They also told Mary how much they had enjoyed their stay at A Bed of Roses and that they were sad to be leaving. They both said if they ever came back to Natchitoches, they would certainly be staying at A Bed of Roses again.

After the meal, the couple went upstairs to finish packing while Mary cleaned up the kitchen. Around ten o'clock the guests came back down and Mary checked them out. She hugged them goodbye as she did most all of her guests when they left. Even though her guests usually came as strangers, they all somehow seemed to leave as friends.

About an hour after Mary's guests left the phone rang and it was Martine. She said she just wanted to let Mary know she had picked up Maddie, Garrett and Myrié at the airport and that they were on their way to her house. Mary told her to be careful driving and not to stop for lunch because Todd was frying catfish.

When the four of them arrived, Mary met them at the back door with a hug. They laughed and talked a mile a minute until Todd interrupted them to say that the fried fish was going to get cold if they didn't sit down and eat. They all took his advice and fixed their plates while Mary took out the French bread from the oven. Garrett, Maddie and Myrié said they were famished as they had been up most of the night and hadn't eaten in hours. Throughout the meal the sisters and two brothers-in-law talked about all the crazy happenings that had been going on in Perot Country. After everyone had eaten, Todd went with Garrett to help him get the suitcases out of the car. There weren't that many since Marty was only staying one night and Garrett, Maddie and Myrié were only staying two. While Mary's sisters and Garrett went upstairs to freshen up, she and Todd quickly cleaned the kitchen. When everyone returned downstairs, they all piled in the B&B SUV and headed to Aunt Tess' house. On the way, they stopped in town at the U-Haul station so that Garrett and Myrié could make the arrangements to rent two small U-Haul trucks. After making sure the station was open on a Sunday and that they had the trucks available, they told the attendant that they would be back Sunday afternoon to pick both of them up.

When they arrived at Aunt Tess', she and Uncle Isaac were sitting on the porch waiting for them. They both got up to greet their visitors and Aunt Tess hugged them all. After a few minutes visiting, they all walked over to the cemetery to pay their respects to Maggie and Jack and to all the other Perot family members who were buried in the cemetery. This time Mary led them all in prayer thanking God for allowing their parents' ashes to come to rest in this sacred place.

Shortly after they walked back to the house, Uncle Tommy, Aunt Doris, Uncle Robby and Aunt Pauline came over. Mary had called them before leaving her house to let them know she and the others would be at Aunt Tess' in a little while and had asked them to meet them there. All the sisters and brothers-in-law teased the uncles about the shenanigans they had been up to over the last few weeks but, in the end, they made it clear how much they appreciated their efforts. They asked them if they should be expecting any new activities but the uncles said they were pleading the fifth. Uncle Tommy said the next thing on the agenda was finding that will and they all readily agreed. Around five o'clock Jason and Lola stopped by to visit with their cousins. An hour later Aunt Tess took a chicken casserole out of the oven and a green salad out of the refrigerator. They all sat around the table and enjoyed eating the meal together.

By the time Mary and the others returned to the B&B everyone was exhausted, especially, Myrié, Maddie and Garrett. As much as the sisters were tempted to stay up late drinking wine and talking until all hours of the night like they usually did when they were all together, they decided they needed to call it a night. By eleven o'clock, the only sound in the big house was the ticking of the grandfather clock in the front foyer.

Fortunately, Sunday morning Mary didn't have any paying guests to cook breakfast for, so she and Todd and her visiting family members ate a light breakfast, then dressed and headed to Immaculate Conception Church for ten o'clock Mass. There they saw some of their aunts and uncles, several of their cousins and a few old friends. After Mass they all stood in front of the church mingling for about ten minutes. When they returned home, everyone changed clothes and ate lunch. Ellie came by to visit with Myrié, Maddie and Garrett for a little while. Myrié and Maddie were as happy to see her as she was them but she couldn't stay long because she had to go to a birthday party for one of her grandchildren. Ellie fussed at them for not coming home more often and they promised her they would try to do better in the future. Before she left she gave all three of them a motherly hug and told them to be careful driving home. As soon as she was gone, Todd drove Garrett and Myrié to go pick up the U-Haul trucks. When they returned, they drove the trucks around back to the garage where the furniture was stored.

Todd and Garrett loaded the dining room furniture into Myrié's truck first. Next, they started to load the desk into the truck Garrett had rented. While they were putting the piece of furniture on the dolly the drawer of the desk fell out. When Maddie reached down to pick it up, she noticed something long and yellow taped to the bottom of it. She flipped the drawer over and saw that it was a manila envelope. She opened the envelope and found some legal papers inside along with a smaller white envelope. She realized right away that it was their father's Last Will and Testament! She quickly looked for the date on the document and saw that it was April 1, 2014, April Fool's Day. What a coincidence! She wondered if their father had done it on that date on purpose as an added "gotcha" gesture. By the time she saw the date Myrié, Martine and Mary had come over to see what was in the envelope, too.

They all screamed at once, "You found it!"

Myrié, excitedly, asked, "What does it say?" Maddie handed it to Garrett to read since he was the lawyer in the family. Garrett took a few minutes silently skimming the document while the others all looked on in eager anticipation.

Finally he looked up and said, "Well, basically it says that Lilly gets two hundred fifty two thousand dollars, which he states is thirty six thousand dollars for each year that they were married and that she took care of him. It says that the money will be awarded her through the beneficiary clause in his IRA account and that the rest of his IRA account will go to Immaculate Conception Church. He mentions the life insurance policy that he left for the grandkids and the fifty thousand dollar life insurance policy he left Lilly which he states is to go towards paying for his funeral expenses and the removal costs for Charlotte and Caroline's two cottages located on his property. All of his remaining assets and all of his property holdings including his five rental properties are to go to his eight children equally and it names Mary as his executor."

After Garrett finished telling them about what was in the new will, Myrié was the first one to speak up. She said, "Well, personally, I think he was a little too generous to Lilly but I can live with it. It's much better than the other will and at least Belle

Rose will be back in the Bordelon family. That's the most important thing. I guess he felt like he owed Lilly for taking care of him for seven years."

All of them agreed, then, Martine asked, "Who are the witnesses?" Garrett looked back down at the will, then said, "There is a Douglas Lambert, Sr. and a Nicole Renee Banks."

Mary commented, "We all know who Douglas Lambert, Sr. is but I don't have a clue who Nicole Renee Banks is."

Just then Maddie realized she was still holding the white envelope in her hand. She opened it and pulled out what looked to be a letter. It was dated June 10, 2014 and it was addressed to her. She read it out loud,

> Dear Maddie,
>
> If you are reading this letter that means I have probably died and you have found my Last Will and Testament. If Lilly is reading this, then all bets are off. Well, I am praying it is you.
>
> I assume you know by now that Lilly and her lawyer, Roy Landry, coerced me into signing a will leaving everything to her. I think they may be having a "fling" but I'm not sure. Speaking of flings, I know this is going to come as a shock to you and your siblings, but Lilly and I had a short affair years ago when your mother was pregnant with you. I broke it off shortly after you were born because I didn't want to hurt your mother and I realized I had really messed up. Lilly and I went on with our separate lives and we never spoke about it again, but when Maggie died, Lilly started coming over and taking care of me. I was

in such a state of depression without Maggie and having Lilly there lifted my spirits. We quickly rekindled our feelings for one another, or so I thought. I know all of you tried to warn me what was really happening, but I didn't want to see it. Lilly insisted we get married right away so that she could look after me and I was all for the idea as I knew how much I needed help. When you and your sisters and brothers didn't support my decision, I admit, I was bitter. I didn't think y'all understood what I was dealing with living alone and having to take care of myself in my condition. I was afraid y'all might eventually try to put me in a nursing home and I definitely did not want that!

I know I said and did some things I shouldn't have, but I can't go back and change that now. Mary helped me see that I was wrong, but by then I was in too deep. You see, when I was in my state of anger, Lilly took advantage of it and had Roy draw up a new will giving everything to her. Since I completely trusted her at the time, I didn't even read the will completely. I just signed it. I thought it said that she would get all my assets and usufruct of the property. Later, when I took the time to read it, I realized what I had done and I asked Lilly to have Roy come back over so I could amend the will, but she refused. She said that if I amended it, she would tell all of you about the affair and she would leave me. I was afraid of what you and the others and Maggie's family would think of me if they knew about the affair, but even more than that, I was afraid of what I would do if Lilly left me. You see, I need her to take care of me. I know if she leaves me I will have to go to a nursing home and I can't do that. So I'm doing the only thing I know to do at this time. I am letting Lilly think that I am not changing the will but I called Henry Babin and had him draw up a new will. I warned him not to show it to anyone and to keep it under lock and key. Poor Henry passed away recently and I am not sure if he shared the copy with his son who took over his practice so I am leaving you this copy as my back-up plan. I promised your mother's siblings I would not let the Perot land fall into anyone's hands but a Perot descendant, and I am trying to honor that promise. Now it is up to you and your siblings to keep my word.

Please tell all my children and grandchildren how much I loved them and how sorry I am that I hurt them.

Love, Dad

When Maddie finished reading the letter, everyone was stunned! JJ and Jake had once said they suspected their dad and Lilly had a past fling but none of the others believed it. Now that they knew it was true, they were angry that their father had left

Lilly anything, much less two hundred fifty two thousand dollars! By God! She had even tried to blackmail him and force him to disown his entire family! It wasn't about the money. It was the principle of it. Yes, she had taken care of him for seven years, but she had access to all of his money while they were married to do with whatever she wanted and she had spent most of it already on herself, her daughters and her grandchildren. The sisters decided they needed to make a conference call to talk to their other siblings about what they had just discovered. They left Garrett and Todd to finishing loading the furniture and went back into the house.

When all eight of the siblings were connected on the call, Maddie explained what she had found taped to the desk drawer. All four of them were super thrilled about the will and were as stunned about what was in the letter as the others had been. JJ and Jake were especially angry that their father had decided to leave Lilly a sizable amount of money after she had blackmailed him and they rubbed it in to the others that they had told them so concerning their father and Lilly's affair.

They all agreed that they needed to hire HB right away to represent them. Mary said she would call HB and set up a meeting with him first thing Monday morning. They all agreed to send her a thousand dollars each to put in a special account for legal fees and anything else she might need to do for the family.

After they hung up the phone, Martine said she needed to get on the road as she wanted to get home before dark. She hugged her sisters and told them goodbye, then left, leaving her sisters to deal with calling the aunts and uncles. Mary, Myrié and Maddie contemplated whether or not to tell their aunts and uncles about the letter, but, in the end, they decided they needed to tell them everything, for better or worse. However, they decided they would, again, just tell Aunt Tess and, then, have her tell the others, but they couldn't do it over the phone. This kind of news needed to be delivered in person. Todd and Garrett, who had already come back inside, asked if they wanted them to come along for moral support but the sisters said they needed to go alone.

By the time they got to Aunt Tess' house, it was dark. Mary knocked on the door and, after a few seconds, Uncle Isaac opened it. He looked surprised to see them but welcomed them inside. As soon as Aunt Tess walked into the room she knew something was up by the looks on her nieces' faces. She looked from one to the other and then said, "Whatever it is, just tell me."

Mary replied, "Maybe you should sit down first."

Aunt Tess sat down on the couch and Uncle Isaac set down next to her. Aunt Tess said impatiently, "OK, I'm sitting. Now tell me what's going on."

Maddie began, "We found the other will."

Aunt Tess' face lit up as she said, "Well, that's great news!" Then she looked at her nieces' faces and realized something wasn't right with the picture. None of them looked happy. She cautiously said, "This is good news, isn't it?"

Myrié replied, "Yes it is."

Aunt Tess asked, "Where did you find it?"

Maddie answered, "We found it taped under a drawer in Maw Maw's desk that she gave Mom. Dad had promised it to me and Lilly gave it to Mary and Martine when they went to the house to get some of our parents' things a few weeks ago."

Aunt Tess said, "OK, but what's the bad news? The new will can't be any worse than the last one."

Maddie responded, "Dad left two hundred, fifty-two thousand dollars to Lilly in his IRA account and the remainder of the funds in the account go to Immaculate Conception Church but everything else, including the family land, goes to the eight of us equally and it names Mary as the executor."

Aunt Tess thought about this for a few minutes. The sisters could tell by the look on her face that she was wrestling with her feelings and trying to decide how she would respond. Finally she said, "Well, it's better than the other will. At least the land and Maggie's house is protected. That's the main thing. How soon can you evict her?"

Mary answered, "I'm going to call HB Babin first thing tomorrow morning to see what we need to do."

Aunt Tess said, "OK, so is that it? Y'all still look like you swallowed a canary?"

Maddie said, "Well, you see, there's one more thing. Dad included a letter with the will explaining what happened. Maybe you should read it yourself instead of me trying to explain it to you."

Maddie handed her aunt the letter and she began reading it silently. By the time she finished, her face had turned red and tears were forming in her eyes. She looked up at the girls and said, "I didn't tell any of you before, but your mom confided in me years ago that she thought Jack had cheated on her, but she didn't know who the other woman was. Since she didn't have any solid proof she never asked him about it and we never spoke of it again. When your dad married Lilly I had my suspicions, but I didn't want to say anything since I wasn't sure."

The sisters were upset to learn that their mother had known about their father's indiscretion. They could only imagine what she had gone through with five children and another one on the way. How hurt she must had been! Back then, times were different. People didn't get divorced as much as they did these days, not to mention that Maggie was Catholic, and therefore, didn't believe in divorce.

Aunt Tess said how sorry she was that they and the rest of their siblings were having to deal with such unsettling news about their father. They were not surprised their aunt was so concerned about their family but they knew she was hurting, too. Mary quickly went over to her aunt and sat on the other side of her. She put her hand on Aunt Tess' knee and spoke softly to her.

"Aunt Tess, We are all big girls and boys now and we are going to deal with this the best way we can. We are going to hire a lawyer and take it from there."

Aunt Tess looked up at her nieces and said, "You know the Perot family will stand behind y'all one hundred percent."

Myrié replied, "We know that Aunt Tess and we love all of you so much for it."

Mary said, "Aunt Tess, are you up to breaking this news to the others or should we do it?"

Aunt Tess assured them that it would be better coming from her. She asked Uncle Isaac to go make a copy of the letter for her to keep. After he did, he returned the original to Maddie and the sisters left the house feeling drained and worn out from the emotional stress of the day.

When the sisters got back to Mary's house, they opened a bottle of wine and played a game of who could come up with the worst things they could do to Lilly without getting caught. Myrié won the game with the brilliant idea of sending Lilly a certified letter telling her she had won a Caribbean Cruise for two and all she needed to do was mail a check for five hundred dollars to the specified address to pay the port fees and taxes. They actually thought about carrying the idea out, but after joking around about it, they reluctantly decided they should keep their focus on getting Belle Rose back.

CHAPTER FIFTEEN

THERE'S A SKUNK IN THE HOUSE

Garrett, Maddie and Myrié left Mary's house bright and early Monday morning. Afterwards, Mary anxiously waited until she thought HB would be in his office before calling to give him the big news. By eight thirty she couldn't wait any longer. Jane answered her call on the first ring. Mary exchanged greetings with her, then asked if HB was in yet. Jane said that he was and asked Mary to hold on while she transferred the call. Mary waited a few seconds, then she heard HB's voice asking, "Mary, what can I do for you today?"

Mary jubilantly replied, "We found the will!"

HB responded, "That's great news Mary! Where was it?"

Mary told HB where they had found the will and she added the part about the letter, but she didn't tell him the contents of the two documents. She said that she would rather bring them to him so that he could examine them for himself. She told HB her family wanted to hire him to represent them in contesting the original will. HB said he would be honored to and asked her how soon she could bring him the documents to review. She said she could be at his office in fifteen minutes.

As soon as Mary hung up the phone, she grabbed the manila envelope and her purse off the snack bar and headed out the door. In her haste she practically ran over Ellie who was just coming up the steps. Mary halfheartedly apologized to Ellie then told her she was in a hurry and she would explain everything when she returned. Ellie gave Mary a bewildered look as she jumped in her car and sped out of the driveway.

When Mary walked into the law office she was greeted by Jane who said, "Mary, HB told me the wonderful news. I can't believe you found the will! I am so happy for your family!" Mary thanked the sweet woman as she led Mary into HB's office then she left the room, closing the door behind her. Mary immediately handed HB the envelope. He opened it up, took out the documents and began reading. She sat down in the chair across from his desk and waited anxiously for him to finish. When he finally looked up at her, he said, "Well, we definitely have a case. The will is in legal format. Everything is according to the requirements of an official Louisiana will. It has been notarized, with two witnesses and it is dated after the will Lilly has so it should be accepted by the courts as the rightful will on its face. Plus, the letter is hand written by your father so that, in itself, makes it legitimate and it backs up the legitimacy of the new will which is good because obviously my father can't testify and Mr. Lambert will not be a good witness if he were to have to testify considering his mental state."

The next thing HB said came as a surprise to Mary as she had never thought about it. He commented, "This letter could actually be a problem for Roy Landry as it states that he allowed your father to sign the will without disclosing to him the complete contents of it and it insinuates that he could have been having an affair with his client's wife."

Mary said, "Oh, my gosh! I never thought about that!"

HB replied, "Well, we will just keep that under our hats for now and only use the letter if we need it."

Mary agreed, not wanting to make this any uglier than necessary.

HB changed the subject and asked Mary, "Do you have any idea who this Nicole Banks person is?"

Mary replied, "I have no idea and neither do any of my siblings."

"Well I will see if I can locate her. Also, I need to find out where Roy Landry is in the process of completing the succession. I don't think he has gotten a judgment yet because I have been on the lookout for it and I haven't seen it filed at the court house. It usually takes a while because you have to wait for the death certificate to be issued and some other things. I am going to file an immediate petition to the court to contest the current will on file. That will allow us to address the court before a judgment can be rendered. I will get back to you as soon as I have anything to report."

Mary thanked HB for all his help and he smiling replied, "Mary, I am going to enjoy helping your family put Miss Lilly in her place!"

When Mary walked out of HB's office, she was on cloud nine. However, when she returned home, her mood was interrupted by Ellie who was waiting for her. Ellie asked, "What was so darn important that you drove out of here like a bat out of hell?"

Mary apologized once again to Ellie, but this time she did it a little more sincerely. Then she told Ellie about finding the will and the letter that was with it. Ellie suddenly forgot all about being upset with Mary and started jumping up and down in excitement, that is until Mary disclosed the part about Lilly getting the two hundred fifty-two thousand dollars.

Then Ellie stopped jumping and angrily replied, "That woman doesn't deserve one lousy cent of your family's money!" When Mary told her the part about the affair and the blackmail, Ellie went from angry to furious! She said what Lilly had done was shameful and that she was going to rot in hell for it! She even said Mary's father might have already suffered a similar fate for cheating on his wonderful wife, Maggie. It took Mary a while to calm the poor women down. Mary was happy when the doorbell rang and it was a couple looking for a room. The arrival of the unexpected guests forced Ellie to pull herself together. Mary asked Ellie to escort the couple upstairs and show them the available guest rooms. By the time the check-in process was completed and the guests had left to do some sightseeing, it was lunch time and Mary warmed up some leftover dirty rice for Ellie and herself.

Around three o'clock, HB called to tell Mary he had checked the probate court schedule and found out the Bordelon case had been assigned to Judge Laura Parker but the judge had not rendered a judgment on it yet.

Mary said, "Well that's good news."

HB remarked, "Yes it is, and we are lucky we got Judge Parker. She is a good judge for our case. You must have an angel looking over your shoulder."

Mary smiled as she replied, "I think I do and her name is Maggie Bordelon."

HB said, "You're probably right about that. I filed the petition this afternoon to contest the will on the grounds that it is not Jacques Bordelon's Last Will and Testament. Then I filed the new will. Lilly's lawyer will probably get the notice tomorrow. Once he tells Lilly about it you may get a phone call from her. If you do, don't discuss the contents of the will and, definitely, do not mention the letter. We aren't going to use it unless we absolutely need it."

"Got it. If she calls I just won't answer it."

"Good idea. Now, her lawyer will probably request that you come in for a deposition. He will probably want to depose the witnesses, too."

Mary interrupted, "How are they going to do that? Mr. Lambert has dementia and we don't know who Nicole Banks is, that is, unless you found her."

HB replied, "No, but I haven't had much time to look yet. I'll let you know as soon as I have anything else to tell you."

When Mary hung up the phone, she picked it right back up to call Aunt Tess. When Aunt Tess answered, the first thing Mary asked her was if she had told the others about the new will and the letter yet. Aunt Tess said that she had called them all last night and that they were all thrilled about the will but they were pretty upset about what Jack had said in the letter. She went on to say that she was afraid her brothers were going to do something else to Lilly to get back at her. Mary was afraid of that, too. She just prayed that, whatever they did, they didn't get caught and no one got hurt. Next, Mary told Aunt Tess about what HB had found out. Aunt Tess said she would inform the others and to, please, let her know as soon as she heard anything else from HB. Mary assured her she would.

When Ellie walked in the kitchen, she could see Mary was worried about something. She asked her what was wrong. Mary told her what Aunt Tess had said about her uncles wanting to get back at Lilly for what her father had revealed in the letter.

Ellie responded, "Well, of course they do, Sugar. It's only natural for brothers to want to defend their sister's honor. I don't blame them one bit."

Mary replied, "But what if they get caught or someone gets hurt?"

Ellie responded, "Don't worry about that. Mr. Tommy and Mr. Robby are pretty smart cowboys and they know what they are doing."

Mary said, "I hope you're right Ellie."

Ellie hugged Mary and said, "Ain't I always right, Sugar? Now why don't you and me whip up a batch of pecan pralines for our guests?"

Mary replied, "That sounds like a good idea to me!"

By the time the women finished making the pralines and had cleaned up the kitchen, it was almost five o'clock. Mary put a few of the pralines in a small container for Ellie to take home with her for Arthur. After Ellie left, Mary texted her siblings to let them know she would be holding a conference call at six thirty, then she threw together a chef salad for supper. When Todd came home, Mary told him the good news. Then, they took their salads into the den and ate on TV trays while they watched the evening news.

At six twenty-five, Mary went to her office to make the conference call to her siblings. This time Jake didn't call in. JJ said he thought he was on a flight to London and that he would try to reach him later. Mary thanked him, then, proceeded to tell everyone else the latest news. They were all very relieved to hear they had found the will in time. Mary reassured them once again that she would keep them all informed of any more news that came up.

After Mary wrapped up her call to her siblings, she called each of her children and delivered the news to them. She had not had a chance to talk to any of them since she and her sisters had found the new will so she had a lot to tell them. All three were delighted to hear the news.

The next three days went by as slow as molasses for Mary, that is until Friday morning. Lilly had tried calling Mary three times and Charlotte had tried twice. However, Mary didn't answer any of their calls just as she had promised HB. Which is why she did not find out until Aunt Tess called her Friday morning that her uncles had pulled yet another stunt on Lilly. This time they had caught a skunk in the woods and had given it to Richard to let loose in Lilly's garage. According to Aunt Tess who got her information from Aunt Doris, who got it from Uncle Tommy, who got it straight from Richard, Lilly had gone out to the garage to get in her car when she spotted the skunk. She screamed which startled the skunk and that's when he did what skunks do. The garage door was closed so the smell was pretty potent in the confined area. Lilly ran back into the house to try to escape the smell, but since the garage is attached to the house, and she forgot to close the door behind her in her haste to get away from the smell, it quickly spread into the house.

Richard said they opened the garage door and all the windows in the house but the smell had already gotten into the curtains, the carpet, the walls, and all the furniture upholstery. It had also gotten into the car upholstery. Richard had to drive the car to the detail shop in town to have the upholstery professionally cleaned. Then, with the help of Charlotte and Caroline, Lilly had to take down all the curtains and soak them in vinegar before washing them. They also wiped down all the walls and hard surfaces with a vinegar solution and steam cleaned all the upholstered furniture and carpet. The three women worked for two days trying to deodorize the house, and the entire time they were cursing the Perot family. Aunt Tess said that Charlotte had called Uncle Tommy and threatened to send her cousin, Sheriff Jackson, out to arrest him and Uncle Robby. This upset Mary. She didn't know what she would do if the sheriff arrested her uncles. She asked Aunt Tess if the sheriff had come out to get Uncle Tommy and Uncle Robby. Aunt Tess said he came out but there wasn't much he could do because he didn't have any proof Tommy or Robby were involved, but he warned them that if anything else happened to his Aunt Lilly that he would be back and, proof or no proof, he would haul them both off to jail.

As soon as Mary finished her phone conversation with Aunt Tess, she called Uncle Tommy to try to talk some sense into him. However, she wasn't surprised when Aunt Doris answered the phone and said that Tommy had gone to the feed store with Robby and probably wouldn't be back for a while. She asked Aunt Doris to have Uncle Tommy call her when he returned home. Aunt Doris said she would give him the message, but Mary figured her uncle wouldn't call back.

Mary went into the game room and told Todd what Aunt Tess had just told her. Todd couldn't stop laughing. Mary said, "It's not funny, Todd. What if they get arrested?"

Todd replied, "They aren't going to get arrested, Mary and, even if they did, the sheriff can't hold them without some kind of proof. What did you expect when they found out your father had cheated on their sister with Lilly? Did you think they would stand by and let that go without defending their sister's honor, not to mention that Lilly blackmailed your father and tried to swindle their sister's children out of their inheritance including the Perot family land?"

Mary sheepishly answered, "Well, I understand what you are saying but I just don't want anyone to get hurt."

"Don't worry. Your uncles haven't hurt anyone yet and they are big boys. They can take care of themselves."

"I know, I know. Ellie says the same thing. I just hope you are both right."

Mary went back into the kitchen and waited for Ellie to arrive so she could tell her what her uncles had done this time. She didn't have to wait long before Ellie walked in smiling and cheerful as ever. When Mary told her the story, she laughed so hard she had to run to the bathroom to keep from peeing in her pants.

Ellie's Southern Pralines

Ingredients
1½ cup sugar
¾ cup light brown sugar (packed)
½ cup milk or evaporated milk

6 tbsp. butter
1½ cups pecan halves
1 tsp. vanilla

Combine all ingredients under medium heat stirring constantly until you get to a "softball stage" (238-240 degrees). Remove from heat and stir until mixture thickens. (Mixture will become creamy and cloudy and pecans will be able to stay suspended in it.) Quickly spoon out on buttered wax paper, aluminum foil or parchment paper. (When using wax paper, be sure to buffer with newspaper underneath, as hot wax will transfer to whatever is beneath.) Makes anywhere from 20 to 50 pralines depending on how big you make them!

Note from Ellie: I learned to make pralines like this when I was just a little girl kneeling on a stool next to my mama. She wouldn't let me get too close to the stove but when she took the hot mixture from the stove I got to help stir it until it got to just the right consistency. That is the secret to a good praline. If you stir it too much it will get too hard and the mixture will be ruined. If you do not stir it long enough your pralines will be runny and never harden properly. However, if you stir it just long enough to be at the right consistency, you will have very creamy pralines!

Note from Mary: I thought I would share a little advice with those of you who might be novices at making pralines. Never get started making them if you think you might get interrupted. If you have to stop to answer a phone call or greet someone at the door you will end up with a ruined batch of pralines. Making pralines requires your undivided attention!

CHAPTER SIXTEEN

THE DEPOSITION

Friday afternoon Mary got a call from HB. He said that Roy Landry had made a formal request for Mary to appear in his office with her lawyer on Monday morning at ten thirty for a deposition. HB asked her to come to his office at nine thirty so that he could go over a few things with her before the deposition. Mary said that she would be there, and then she asked HB if he had had any luck finding Nicole Banks. HB said that he had hired an investigator to look for her and the investigator traced her to a home health company in town where she briefly worked as a nurse's aide. According to their records, Ms. Banks had gone to the Bordelon home on April 1, 2014 to perform the weekly home check on Jack Bordelon. Shortly after that, she had quit her job with the company and moved to Texas with her boyfriend who had been offered an oil field job there. The company had no forwarding address or phone number to reach her. The number she was using at the time of her employment was no longer working, and the address she had on file was an apartment. HB said that his investigator called the apartment complex and spoke to the manager there, but she said Ms. Banks did not leave a forwarding address with them either. HB said the investigator had even checked Facebook and Twitter but Ms. Banks did not have an account on either.

Mary said, "Well that makes sense that it was a nurse's aide that Dad got to sign the will. I don't know why I didn't think of that before. Dad had nurses and nurse's aides coming to the house regularly to check his blood pressure, sugar levels and other vital signs and to assist him with his personal hygiene care. What if we can't find her?"

HB replied, "Well, let's hope we will not need her to testify. We have the home health company's records saying that she was employed with them and that she went to the Bordelon home on the day that the will was signed, so that should back up the fact that she was present and that she did, in fact, witness Jack signing his will."

Mary responded, "Ok, that sounds good to me. I guess I will see you Monday morning."

When Mary hung up the phone with HB she called Aunt Tess and told her about the deposition and the information they had found out concerning Nicole Banks. Aunt Tess asked Mary if Lilly would be at the deposition. Mary replied that she didn't know. She had not thought to ask HB that question. She had mixed feelings about whether or not she hoped she would be. On one hand, she had no desire to be in the same room with Lilly, but on the other hand she would like to see her face when she started realizing she might not walk away with what she had so ruthlessly connived to get.

Aunt Tess said that if Lilly was going to be there, she would love to be there herself to witness it. Mary understood how her aunt felt. Her mother and Aunt Tess had been extremely close, and she took what Lilly did to her twin sister as a personal affront. Mary promised her aunt she would call her the minute she got out of the deposition and relay every detail to her.

At six o'clock Mary held a conference call with her siblings and all seven called in. Mary told them about the skunk incident first, but before she could even finish telling the story, they were all laughing so hard that it took her a while to get them calmed down enough so that she could finish it.

JJ said, "Well, I know one thing, I sure don't ever want to get on any of our uncles' bad sides!

They all wholeheartedly agreed with him on that and Myrié added, "It sure feels good, though, to know they have our backs!"

Again, everyone agreed. Mary told her siblings about her phone call with HB, and after a few more minutes of spirited conversation, they ended the call.

On Saturday and Sunday morning, Mary prepared breakfast for her guests, and on Sunday evening, she went to church. She had a hard time sleeping Sunday night as she was anxious about the deposition she had to give in the morning. Even though she tossed and turned half the night, she jumped out of bed as soon as her alarm went off. Fortunately, all of her guests had checked out the day before so she did not have to prepare breakfast for anyone. She showered and dressed, then went to the kitchen and poured herself a cup of coffee.

Todd was sitting in the den watching the news and drinking what was probably his second cup of coffee. He had cooked a breakfast of eggs, sausage and toast for her and left it sitting on a plate on top of the stove. She knew that it was his way of showing her he understood it was going to be a difficult day for her and he wanted to do something to help her get through it.

When Mary arrived at HB's office, Jane greeted her and explained that HB was on the phone with another client. Mary waited in the lobby for what seemed like a half hour but, in reality, it was only ten minutes. As soon as HB saw her he apologized for keeping her waiting. They got down to business right away with HB telling her what kinds of questions she should expect Roy Landry to ask and how she should answer them. He told her that her answers should always be short and to the point, only providing the specific information she was asked and no more. He said that, whenever possible, he would provide the information himself so that she did not have to speak any more than necessary. Last, he reminded her not to mention the letter unless she was asked a specific question about it. She asked HB if he thought Lilly would be at the deposition. He said she wouldn't be. Mary guiltily felt a little disappointed.

They left HB's office at ten fifteen and drove the five minute drive to Roy Landry's office in separate cars. Mr. Landry's secretary greeted them, then escorted them to the same room that Mary and her siblings had sat in when they had come to review their father's other will over a month ago. Mary noticed this time there was a video camera set up in the corner of the room and she wondered if the deposition would be recorded.

Mr. Landry entered the room followed by a women who he introduced as Cindy Palmer, a court reporter. Mr. Landry turned to Ms. Palmer and asked her to swear in the witness. After that was done, Mr. Landry informed Mary and HB that the deposition would be recorded, then began by stating, "I have here a copy of the will for Jacques Pierre Bordelon Sr. that was filed last week by Mr. Babin. Everything seems to be in order. It is dated April 1, 2014, which is after the date of the will that I had on file for Mr. Bordelon. It was properly prepared and notarized by Henry Babin Sr. who we all know is now deceased. It has two witnesses, which is the required amount by law, Mr. Douglas Lambert, Sr. and Ms. Nicole Renee Banks. I would have deposed Mr. Lambert but it is my understanding that he is now suffering from dementia. As for Ms. Banks, my office is still trying to locate her. It seems she has moved out of the state and did not leave a forwarding address."

HB interrupted Roy Landry, "Everything you have stated is correct. My office has not been able to locate Ms. Banks either but that shouldn't be an issue as you just pointed out yourself that the will in question was properly prepared and, therefore, should be accepted by the court on its own merit as a legitimate Last Will and Testament for Mr. Jacques Pierre Bordelon, Sr."

Mr. Landry somewhat testily replied, "Yes, I understand but I do have a few questions for Mrs. LeBlanc." He turned back to Mary and asked, "Mary, can you tell me how you came to be in possession of the will, dated April 1, 2014?

Mary answered, "On, Saturday, March 14th, my sister, Martine, and I, along with our husbands, went to our parents' previous residence to get some of their furnishings and other personal items from our father's widow, Lillian Bordelon. One of the pieces of furniture that we got was a desk. We took all the furniture and other things Lillian gave us back to my house and we stored the furniture pieces in my garage until my sisters, Myrié and Madeline, could come get them. Madeline and Myrié flew in on Saturday, April 11. On Sunday, while we were in the process of loading the desk into the truck Madeline had rented, the top drawer fell out. When Madeline, picked up the drawer she noticed a manila envelope taped to the bottom of it. When she removed the envelope and opened it, she found the will inside."

Mary didn't mention anything about the white envelope with the letter also being inside the manila envelope as HB had advised her not to. She held her breath to see if Mr. Landry was going to ask her if there was anything else inside the envelope but he didn't.

Mr. Landry replied, "Then what did you do?"

Mary breathed a sigh of relief as she continued, "Well, Madeline handed the will to her husband Garrett, who is a lawyer, and he read it, then, he told us, basically, what it said. After that we took the will into my house where I kept it until the next morning when I brought it to my lawyer's office and asked him to file it at the court house."

Mr. Landry continued, "OK. Now, Mary, were you or any of your siblings, to your knowledge, aware before you found this will, that your father had written it?

"No, I was not, but we all thought it was possible that he had written another will after the one that you presented to us."

"And why did you think that might be the case?"

"Because the will you presented stated that our father left everything to his wife, Lillian, and had left nothing to his children or grandchildren. I and my siblings thought it was odd that our father would do such a thing and we told you that at the time you presented it to us." Mr. Landry didn't comment so Mary continued, "We had our differences with our father over the last few years but he was very close to his grandchildren and we did not think he would have left them out of his will completely. Plus, the thirty acres of land where his residence is located is land that has been in our mother's family for generations, and he had made a promise to our mother and to her siblings that he would never allow it to go into the hands of anyone who was not a descendant of the Perot family. In fact, he had reminded all us on several occasions that, should he die, we were to also honor that promise."

Mr. Landry rubbed his forehead and then asked, "Didn't your father tell you at one point that he planned to leave his wife Lillian, the land?"

Mary replied, "No, he did not."

Mr. Landry looked surprised at Mary's answer. He raised an eyebrow as he asked, "Are you sure about that?" He looked straight at Mary as he said, "Remember Mary, you are under oath."

Mary quickly fired back, "What my father told me as well as his other children was that he planned to leave Lillian a **portion** of the land. He never said he was going to leave her all of it and, besides, we didn't know if we should take him seriously because he said a lot of things when he was trying to get a desired reaction out of us. We thought he might be bluffing and we hoped he would come to his senses and realize the implications of such a decision. We asked our father to consider only giving Lillian usufruct of the house instead of actual ownership of any of the property."

Mr. Landry interrupted, "And did your father agree to this?

"Well, he never verbally agreed to it, but we still hoped he would reconsider and honor the promise he had made to our mother and her family."

Mr. Landry, wrote down some notes then continued with another line of questioning, "Mary, did you think that your father was in his full mental capacity when he, supposedly, wrote the will dated April 1, 2014?"

Mary replied yes, but she knew this was somewhat of a lie because she suspected that her father had not been quite the same since his first stroke in October of 1999. However, she knew that Mr. Landry had told her and her siblings at the time he presented the other will that he was sure their father had been mentally competent at the time it was written, which was in 2010. Since they had not pursued a competency hearing at the time, she figured it was prudent to just continue with the assumption that her father was, in fact, sane all the way until his death as Lilly had very vocally professed. Just as she and her siblings had thought it would be an uphill battle to prove their father's mental competency a month ago, Mary felt it would be just as hard for Lilly to prove he was competent in September of 2010 but not in April of 2014. To Mary's knowledge, her father had not had any strokes between 2010 and 2014 so, whatever damage he may or may not have had due to his strokes, occurred either before Sept, 2010 or after April, 2014. Mary also knew that to the average person her father had appeared to be completely in control of his mental faculties all the way until his death. It was only the family that recognized the small differences in his personality and mental state. What his neurologist would testify to, she wasn't sure, but whatever it was, she felt it couldn't hurt their case because, in order to do so, he would have to state that the damage occurred after September of 2010 but before April of 2014 which Mary was pretty confident would not happen. So, she took the risk of stating yes under oath to Mr. Landry's question, even though she thought it was a lie but only a little white lie she rationalized.

Mary's thoughts were interrupted by Mr. Landry who was asking her another question. "Mary, didn't one of your siblings, umm I think it was Martine, ask me at the time you and your siblings were in my office reviewing the will originally on file, that you might consider contesting the will due to your father's mental competency?"

Mary replied, "I think what Martine said was that, "If we wanted to contest it, what would we need to do?" And I recall at the time that you, Mr. Landry, stated emphatically that you were positive our father was in full control of his mental capacity at the time he signed the will that you prepared for him and that you would testify in court to that if need be." Mary somewhat indignantly ended her answer with a question, "So, you tell me, Mr. Landry, which is it?"

Mary's question seemed to rattle Mr. Landry and he busied himself with looking at his notes for a few seconds. Then he changed direction and asked, "Mary, would you say that Lillian was a good wife to your father?"

Mary replied, "Well, that depends on how you define a good wife."

Mr. Landry's frustration with Mary seemed to grow as he sought to clarify his question to her. "Would you say that Lillian took good care of your father considering his limited physical condition and his medical needs?"

Mary answered, "To my knowledge she did an OK job."

"Do you think it would be fair to say that your father felt he owed a great deal to his wife, Lillian, for caring for him during the seven years they were married?"

"Yes, and that is why you see that he stated in the April 1, 2014 will that he designated her as the beneficiary of his IRA account in the sum of two hundred fifty-two thousand dollars which is thirty six thousand dollars a year for seven years."

Mr. Landry once again paused and looked through his notes before continuing his questioning. "I just have one last question, Mary. Did your brothers, Jacques Bordelon, Jr and Jacob Bordelon, refuse to speak to your father following his marriage to Lillian despite his requesting them to on numerous occasions?"

Mary replied, "Yes, that is correct but they did speak to him by phone on at least a couple of occasions before April 1, 2014 and after that time. In fact they both spoke to him by phone a few days before his death."

Up until now HB had not interrupted Roy Landry's questioning of his client despite the fact that Mary had been answering his questions with far more information than he had advised her to give. Frankly, he was enjoying the show as he thought that Mary was getting the better of Roy Landry. However, he decided it was time for him to speak up. "Well if that is all you have to ask my client..."

Mr. Landry interrupted, "Oh, just one more thing. I almost forgot. Mary do you know anything about some of the strange things that have been going on at Lillian Bordelon's residence in the last few weeks since your father's death?"

Mary didn't know how to answer that question. HB quickly interceded for her saying, "Roy, that question is irrelevant to the question of the validity of the will and you know it. I am instructing my client not to answer it and I think that we are done here." With that, HB got up and gestured to Mary to do the same.

Mr. Landry responded, "OK, HB, I guess that will be all for now. If I need anything else I will let you know."

HB replied, "You know where to find me."

HB and Mary abruptly left the conference room and walked silently out of the office. When they were outside Mary turned to HB and asked, "How did I do?"

HB answered, "You did great! You elaborated a little more on some of the questions than what I expected you to but it was all good."

Mary apologetically responded, "I know. I kind of got carried away but I didn't know what to say when he asked me that last question. You saved me on that one!"

HB replied, "Roy was just fishing when he asked you that. He should have known I wasn't going to allow it."

Mary said, "Well, thanks just the same. I guess I need to call Todd. It is almost noon and I told him I would call him so we could meet at The Landing for lunch. Would you like to join us?"

HB thanked Mary for the invitation but declined saying that he needed to get back to the office. He told her he would call her as soon as he knew anything else.

While eating a wonderful lunch of crab cakes and fried green tomatoes topped with crab meat and hollandaise sauce, Mary told Todd all about the deposition. Afterwards, they both returned home where Mary was bombarded by questions from Ellie. When she had answered every question to Ellie's satisfaction, she went into her office and emailed her siblings and her children, then called her Aunt Tess. Thankfully, her aunt did not have any reports of foul play going on in Perot Country.

Aunt Tess' Pecan Pie & Heavenly Pie Crust

Ingredients

2 large eggs

¾ cup sugar

1½ tbsp. all-purpose flour

1 cup Karo syrup
(½ light, ½ dark)

1 tsp. vinegar

1 tbsp. melted butter

1 tsp. vanilla

¾ to 1 cup broken pecans

Preheat oven to 375 degrees. Beat eggs. Mix the sugar and flour together, add to eggs and beat again. Add vinegar, butter, vanilla and Karo syrup and beat well. Pour into unbaked pie shell and drop pecans on top of pie. Bake for 40 minutes or until done.

Note from Aunt Tess: There are two secrets to making a great pecan pie. One is using vinegar and the other is using fresh pecans instead of store bought ones. When I make my pecan pies, I always use fresh pecans from my own pecan orchard and my trees put out some of the best pecans in the south!

Pie Crust (This recipe makes 5 pie crusts)

4 cups all-purpose flour

1 tbsp. sugar

2 tsp. salt

1¾ cup Crisco shortening

1 tbsp. vinegar

1 egg

½ cup water

Combine flour, sugar and salt in bowl. Cut in 1¾ cup shortening. In separate bowl, beat together vinegar, egg and water. Combine both mixtures and blend well. Form into large ball. Chill for 15 minutes in the refrigerator. Divide large ball into 5 smaller balls. Roll out each ball and put in a pie dish. You can freeze the balls you do not need for later use.

Note from Aunt Tess: Another secret to making a great pecan pie is using a great pie crust and most great pie crusts are made from scratch, but these days hardly anyone takes the time to make a pie crust from scratch. After all, why go to all the trouble when you can buy a store bought pie crust that will taste ALMOST as good? However, I promise you, if you use this recipe, the rave reviews you will get from your family and friends will make the time you put into it well worth it!

CHAPTER SEVENTEEN

THE CONTEST

Wednesday afternoon, Mary went into town to do some shopping. She stopped at Lola's Sweet Creations Bakery to pick up some danishes for her guests in the cottage. When Mary walked into the bakery, Lola turned to her daughter, Lacey, and instructed her to handle the front counter. Then she walked over to Mary and offered her a strawberry cupcake with dark chocolate icing. Mary gladly accepted the offer as Lola steered her to a table in the corner of the shop and the two women sat down to visit.

As Mary nibbled on the cupcake Lola chatted away. She said that Jason had been keeping her up to date on all the interesting things that had been going on over at Perot Country. She couldn't believe all the stunts the uncles had been pulling on Lilly! She said the news had spread to all the cousins and they all wanted to get in on the action. She informed Mary that Juliet, Uncle Tommy's daughter, and Amanda, Uncle Robby's daughter, had started a hot line for cousins to call in with suggestions that they could pass on to their dads for future prank ideas and they were even giving out rewards for the best ideas.

Mary couldn't believe this was the first she was hearing of her cousins' crazy contest and she asked Lola why she hadn't called her to let her know what was going on sooner. Lola said that she didn't want to bother Mary because she knew she had a lot on her plate. Mary asked if Juliet and Amanda were paying the reward money out of their own pocket or was someone funding the contest.

Lola meekly replied, "Well, actually, Lola's Sweet Creations Bakery is sponsoring the contest."

Mary looked at Lola in astonishment. "And whose idea was all of this?"

Lola replied, "I don't think I should say anything more on the grounds that I may incriminate myself or my husband."

Mary didn't know what to say. She would not have come up with anything like this in a million years! She asked Lola if Aunt Tess knew what they were up to. Lola quickly replied that as far as she knew her mother-in-law didn't know anything about it and she asked Mary not to tell her. About that time, the bakery started getting busier so Lola excused herself and went to assist Lacey.

When Mary returned home, Todd and Ellie were in the kitchen. Todd was cooking up a crawfish stew and Ellie was assisting. Mary told them what she had just learned at the bakery and Todd immediately asked if he could enter the contest. Mary gave her husband a sideways look and he went back to stirring his stew. Ellie said that she thought it was a brilliant idea. Mary gave her the same look she gave Todd, but it didn't faze Ellie. As Ellie washed dishes, she started speculating out loud what would be a good prank to pull on Lilly. Soon, Todd was joining her in the speculating. Mary gave up and went to her office to check her emails.

Mary's email reading was interrupted around four o'clock by the ringing of the phone. Mary looked at the caller ID and saw that it was HB. When she answered it, HB told her that the judge had set the hearing for next Monday afternoon at ten o'clock. Mary asked him what she should expect to happen. He said that he and Roy Landry would present their evidence and call any witnesses they had. Then the judge would take some time to review the evidence, hopefully no more than a couple of days, then render a judgment. He also told her that he had set up a deposition for Friday morning with the supervisor of the home health care center where Nicole Banks had worked and had subpoenaed their employee log for April 1, 2014. He said that he knew Mr. Landry had set up a deposition with Jack's neurologist, Dr. Goudeau, and subpoenaed all of Jack's medical records. He also said that he had added Paul Robichaux's name to the witness list after Mary had told him about Lilly making the comment concerning Jack's mental competence on the day he had died.

After hanging up the phone with HB, Mary called Aunt Tess to let her know about the hearing date. Aunt Tess said that she would tell all her siblings and that she was sure they would all want to be there to support Mary. Mary greatly appreciated her aunts and uncles' support but she suspected they would also be coming because they were just as interested in seeing justice served as she was, if not more so. Mary thanked her aunt for her offer of support and told her she would see her Monday at ten o'clock.

Next Mary texted her siblings and let them know she would be holding a conference call at six thirty. Everyone called in on time and Mary preceded to tell them about the contest going on among the cousins.

Myrié was the first one to respond. "Do we have a crazy family or what?

Jake said, "They're crazy as a fox!"

Maddie suddenly exclaimed, "I just got an idea! I am going to pitch Natchitoches to my producers as the perfect town for our small town segment next season! With all the Cajun country flair Natchitoches has to offer plus all our crazy cousins, uncles and aunts it is sure to be a hit! We just need to find the right property for it! Mary you need to start looking for me!"

Everyone jumped in at once with their opinion of Maddie's idea.

JJ said, "I don't think our uncles and aunts will want to have anything to do with it but you might get some of the cousins to participate. It would need to be a house that has a connection to one of them to make the idea work."

Jake added, "You know our cousin, Mark, is a contractor. He might be able to work on the project with you, Maddie."

Mary interrupted, "Now wait a minute, guys. We need to get all this mess settled with Lilly before we even think of such a project. Maddie, promise me you won't mention anything about your idea to your show's producers until we have our family home back and Lilly is long gone."

Maddie replied, "OK, OK, I promise. But I am not going to give up on the idea. I think it could really be a good project for my show, and it would be free advertising for Natchitoches and even your B&B, Mary."

Mary, thought about Maddie's idea for about two seconds before putting it in the back of her mind. She decided a change of subject was in order, so she told everyone about the hearing scheduled for Monday. Her siblings all took the bait and immediately dropped the subject of the show. They started asking Mary questions about the hearing and expressing regret that they couldn't all come in to witness it themselves. Mary told them that all of the aunts and uncles would probably be there and she said she wouldn't be surprised if some of the cousins showed up, too. She promised them she would text them as soon as it was over if there was anything Earth-shattering to tell them. Otherwise, she told them to plan on a conference call at six o'clock Monday evening so that she could give them a play by play of what went on in the hearing.

CHAPTER EIGHTEEN

THE HEARING

Mary had four of her guest rooms in the house and the cottage booked for Friday and Saturday night. They were all guests for a wedding at Immaculate Conception Church on Saturday evening. She had Ellie come in on Saturday and Sunday to help her with the extra cleaning and cooking. With all the guests to attend to, she hardly had time to worry about the hearing.

Monday morning she and Todd walked into the court room at nine forty. HB was already there and so were all their uncles and aunts. Within minutes several cousins arrived. Paul and Amy Robichaux and Jack's neurologist, Dr. Goudeau, were also in attendance. Mr. Landry, Lilly, Charlotte, Caroline and some of Lilly's other family members were sitting on the other side of the courtroom. Mary and Todd went over and spoke briefly to the Robichauxs and then went over to the aunts and uncles to speak to them. Todd shook hands with all the uncles and Mary hugged her aunts as they both thanked all of them for coming. Todd sat down by Uncle Tommy and Mary excused herself to go over to talk to HB. She took the seat next to HB just before the bailiff called the court to order.

Judge Parker briefly addressed the courtroom, explained what the procedures were and informed the lawyers that she had reviewed each will that the two parties had submitted. She said that both wills were properly written and acceptable to the court but, based on the dates of the two, it appeared that the will presented by Mr. Babin in the name of his client, Mary Frances Bordelon, was the legitimate Last Will and Testament of the deceased party, Jacques Pierre Bordelon, Sr. Therefore, it would be up to Mr. Landry as the legal counsel for Lillian Mae Bordelon to prove to the court why the will, dated Sept 15, 2010, should be accepted over the other will, dated April 1, 2014. Judge Parker asked Mr. Landry to present his case.

Mr. Landry entered into evidence the written transcript of the deposition he had taken of Mary and called her as his first witness. After Mary was sworn in, Mr. Landry asked her some of the same questions he did in the deposition. Mary gave much the same answers but this time she tried to shorten them as much as possible. Last, he focused on the question concerning whether or not Mary thought her father was mentally competent at the time he had written the second will. Mary answered yes as she had at the time of the deposition.

Mr. Landry pressed the issue saying, "Isn't it true, Mrs. LeBlanc, that your father had four strokes over the period of fifteen years and that those strokes could have impaired his judgment?"

HB immediately stood up and said, "Objection, Your Honor. My client is not a doctor, therefore, she has no medical expertise to be able to attest to the neurological effects of the strokes her father had on his mental capacity."

Judge Parker responded, "Sustained."

Mr. Landry quickly rephrased his question. "Mrs. LeBlanc, in observing your father on a regular basis over the last fifteen years or so, did he appear to you to be any different after he sustained his strokes than he was before he had had his strokes?"

Mary tried to answer the question as honestly as she could without giving Mr. Landry the answer he was looking for. She slowly tried to phrase her words in just the right way. "My father had four strokes, a major one in September of 1999, a smaller one sometime in 2005, another one in October of 2007 and the last one in August of 2014 following his open heart surgery. So I am not sure what time frame you are referring to. Could you be more specific?"

Mr. Landry didn't say anything for several seconds. He walked back to his notes and studied them for a few more seconds. Mary assumed he was starting to see the point she was trying to make. She thought he should have already realized Jack had not had any strokes in between the time he signed the first will on September 15, 2010 and the time he signed the second will on April 1, 2014. He should have known that if he had deposed Dr. Goudeau and subpoenaed all of her father's medical records as HB had told her he had. She couldn't figure out why he had not seen this coming. Finally, Judge Parker asked Mr. Landry if he had any more questions for Mrs. LeBlanc.

He reluctantly replied, "No, Your Honor."

Judge Parker turned to HB and asked him if he wanted to cross-examine the witness.

HB replied, "Yes, Your Honor." Then he stepped forward and asked Mary, "Mrs. LeBlanc, did your father's wife, Lillian Bordelon, ever make any statements in your presence concerning your father's mental health?"

Mary replied, "Yes, she said on many occasions that my father was as sharp as a tack and completely competent. She even said it on the day he died in front of several witnesses."

Mr. Landry stood up and shouted, "Objection, Your Honor. My client Lillian Bordelon is not a doctor, therefore, she cannot attest to the mental competency of her husband."

Judge Parker replied, "I will allow the question. Mr. Babin did not ask if Lillian Bordelon could ascertain the level of her husband's mental competency. He only asked the witness if she had heard Lillian Bordelon make any statements concerning the state of her husband's mental competence. You may continue, Mr. Babin."

HB smiled at the judge and said, "Thank you, Your Honor." Then, he turned back to Mary and asked, "Mrs. LeBlanc, on March 12, 2015, did you and you siblings go to Mr. Landry's office to review your father, Jacques Bordelon's will dated September 15, 2010?"

Mary answered, "Yes, we did."

HB continued, "And during that time did your sister, Martine Broussard, ask Mr. Landry that, if your family wanted to question your father's mental competence, what you should do?"

Mary replied, "Yes, she did."

HB, then, asked, "And what did Mr. Landry tell her?"

"He said that he was one hundred percent positive that our father was completely competent at the time he signed the will on September 15, 2010 and that if we were to contest that he was prepared to testify in court to that effect."

HB turned to Mr. Landry and smiled. Then he turned to the judge and said, "I have no more questions for Mrs. LeBlanc, Your Honor."

Judge Parker told Mary she could step down. Then she asked Mr. Landry if he had any other witnesses. Mr. Landry said he did and he called Dr. Julian Goudeau to the stand. The doctor took the stand and was sworn in by the bailiff. Before Mr. Landry started questioning Dr. Goudeau, he put in to evidence the written transcript of Dr. Goudeau's deposition and Jacques Bordelon's medical files. Then he began asking the doctor all kinds of questions pertaining to Jack's medical condition, especially those related to his strokes. In summary, Mr. Landry asked him if Jacques Bordelon's strokes could have affected his mental capacity. Dr. Goudeau said that it was possible and that many stroke victims experience some mental deterioration, especially in their ability to reason, but that each case is different. Mr. Landry asked if the types of strokes Jacques Bordelon had experienced had made it more likely that his mental capacity could have been impaired due to the strokes. Dr. Goudeau answered yes. Mr. Landry said, "I have no more questions for this witness, Your Honor."

Judge Parker asked HB if he would like to cross examine the witness. HB said that he would and he walked over to the stand.

HB asked, "Dr. Goudeau, did Jacques Bordelon have any strokes to your knowledge between September 15, 2010 and April 1, 2014?"

Dr. Goudeau replied, "No he did not."

HB continued, "Dr. Goudeau, did you have an opportunity to see Jacques Bordelon on or around April 1, 2014?"

"Yes, I saw Mr. Bordelon on March 26, 2014 for his bi-annual checkup visit."

"And during that appointment did Mr. Bordelon appear to be in control of his mental facilities?"

"Yes, he was as lively as ever. He commented on how my nurses seemed to get prettier with each visit and told me a joke about a priest, a rabbi and a minister going in a bar. He, also, talked some about politics. He seemed to be very informed. He answered all my questions concerning his health without hesitation."

HB asked one last question. "Dr. Goudeau, in your expert opinion, did your patient, Mr. Bordelon, appear to you to be suffering from any loss in his mental abilities at the time of his office visit on March 26, 2014?"

Dr. Goudeau replied, "No, he did not."

HB said, "Thank you Dr. Goudeau. Then he turned toward the judge and said, "I have no further questions for this witness, Your Honor."

Judge Parker turned to Dr. Goudeau and told him he could step down. She asked Mr. Landry if he had any more witnesses.

Mr. Landry said, "Yes, Your Honor. I would like to call Lillian Mae Bordelon to the stand."

Lilly slowly got up and walked across the room. She was dressed in a much more conservative attire than usual, giving herself the appearance of being older than she was. She also walked as if she was feeble and short winded. Mary knew it was all an act to try to gain the judge's sympathy.

After the bailiff swore Lilly in, Mr. Landry walked up to the witness stand and asked, "Mrs. Bordelon, did your husband, Jacques Bordelon Sr., appear to you to be mentally competent at the time he signed the will on September 15, 2010?"

Lilly replied, "Yes, Jack was most certainly mentally competent at the time he signed that will!"

"And on and around the time of April 1, 2014, do you recall what mental state your husband appeared to you to be in to the best of your knowledge?"

"Well, he had started to decline somewhat at the beginning of 2014. I think it had to do with some of the pain medicine the doctors had him on."

"Do you recall what pain medication the doctor had prescribed for Jacques and what the dosage was?

"Yes, it was Gabapentin, 600 mg, twice a day."

"And do you recall if Jacques took his medication on the morning of April 1, 2014?"

"Yes, I know he did because I gave it to him just like I did every morning."

Mr. Landry turned to Judge Parker and said as he handed her a piece of paper, "I would like to enter into evidence this list of side effects for the medication, Gabapentin. The information was obtained from the Physicians Medical Journal published in 2014." The judge looked over the list then accepted it into evidence. Mr. Landry turned back to Lilly and asked, "Now Mrs. Bordelon, when the pharmacist filled your husband's prescription of Gabapentin for you, did it come with a list of side effects that could be caused by the drug?"

Lilly responded, "Yes, it did."

"And do you recall if a state of confusion was one of those side effects listed?"

"Why, yes, it was!"

Mr. Landry turned to Judge Parker and said, "I have no further questions of this witness, Your Honor.

The judge turned to HB and asked if he had any questions to ask Mrs. Bordelon.

HB answered, "Yes, Your Honor." then he asked Lilly if she had said on more than one occasion, that her husband, Jacques Pierre Bordelon, Sr., was "as sharp as a tack "or "as mentally competent as the day is long."

Lilly stuttered and then responded shakily, "I don't recall making such statements."

HB turned to the judge and said, "I have no further question of this witness at this time, Your Honor."

Judge Parker turned to Lilly and told her she could step down, then she turned to Mr. Landry and asked if he had any more witnesses.

Mr. Landry replied, "No, Your Honor. We rest our case."

Judge Parker looked down at her watch then addressed the court room, "Court will be dismissed for a twenty minute recess. We will reconvene at eleven thirty to hear the other side of the case." Then she got up and walked off the bench and out of the court room.

Everyone got up and started making their way out into the lobby area. Charlotte and Caroline walked over to their mother's side and Charlotte said, "Mom I'm worried. Our case looks a little weak."

Lilly replied, "Don't worry. I have a plan. Just give me a second." Lilly walked out into the lobby and looked around until she spotted Tess Savoie. Tess was standing in a corner with her sister, Adele. Lilly went over to the two women and nonchalantly said, "Why hello Tess, Adele. It is so nice of you and your brothers to come today to support dear Mary. I know she must really appreciate it. God knows she and Jack's other children have been through so much with his death and all. It would be such a shame if they were to suffer another blow like, say, maybe finding out their father had cheated on their dear mother years ago when she was pregnant. Also, I could just imagine how much the two of you, not to mention the rest of your family, would hate it if such a story were to get out. I mean it could be so embarrassing for your family."

Adele just stood there with her mouth wide open, hardly able to move a muscle, but Tess had a much different reaction to Lilly's threat. She had had enough of this hateful woman's venom and she wasn't going to let her get away with hurting her family any longer. She said in the sweetest voice she could muster, "Why bless you heart, Lilly. It is so nice of you to warn us of something such as this getting out. You can rest assured you came to the right place with this bit of information. Adele and I know just what to do with it."

Adele looked at her sister as if she had just turned into an alien and stuttered, "W-w-we do?"

Tess said, "Why certainly we do, Adele. You know we would never let such an awful story as what Lilly just suggested hurt our beloved sister Maggie's children or tarnish our family's reputation. If such a story were to get out, poor Mary would not be able to show her face in town and it might even ruin her B&B business. Plus the Perot name means a lot in the community and we would never want to jeopardize that. After all what would the good people at Immaculate Conception Church think of us? You just leave it to us, Lilly. We will handle the situation discreetly and no one will ever have to know about this."

Lilly smugly replied, "I knew you would understand, Tess. You and Maggie were so close. I mean with being twins and all."

Tess looked at her watch and then at Adele. "Oh, Adele, look at the time! We better hurry if we are going to make it to the ladies room before the recess is up." She turned to Lilly and said, "Please excuse us."

Lilly replied, "Certainly" as the two sisters walked away but they didn't go in the direction of the ladies room. Instead, Tess grabbed Adele's arm and literally drug her over to where Mary and HB were talking. She immediately told them the whole story.

The bailiff came out in the lobby and said that court would be back in session in two minutes. Everyone, quickly, started filing back inside. As they walked to their seats, Charlotte and Caroline asked their mother what she was doing talking to Mary's two aunts.

Lilly answered, "Oh, I was just putting a little bug in their ear." Lilly smiled mischievously at her two daughters as she sat down. Just then Judge Parker walked back into the court room and resumed her seat at the bench. The bailiff called the court to order and the judge asked HB if he was ready to present his case.

HB replied, "Yes, Your Honor." Then he said, "Before I call any witnesses to testify, I would like to enter into evidence the deposition for Mrs. Sue Ellen Turner. Mrs. Turner is the supervisor for Helping Hands Home Health Care in Natchitoches, and she testified in her deposition that Nicole Renee Banks worked as a nurse's aide for her company and that Ms. Banks went to the Bordelon house on April 1, 2014 to do a routine home visit on Jacques Bordelon. Ms. Banks is one of the witnesses to the will in question but has moved out of state. I would also like to enter into evidence the employee work log for Helping Hands Home Health Care on the day of April 1, 2014. It shows Ms. Banks' work hours and the locations she worked on that day, including the residence of Jacques Bordelon on Perot Road."

The judge accepted into evidence the two records HB had just submitted and asked him if he was also providing a deposition for the other witness to the will in question.

HB replied, "No, Your Honor, but I would like to enter into evidence the medical file of the other witness, Mr. Douglas Lambert Sr. In the file it states that Mr. Lambert was diagnosed with the onset of dementia in November of 2014."

Judge Parker accepted the medical file for Mr. Douglas into evidence and asked Mr. Babin if he was ready to call his first witnesses. HB said that he was. He said that he would like to recall Lillian Bordelon to the stand. There was a slight murmur in the court room as Lilly got up and started walking toward the witness stand as she once again, put on her theatrics.

After Judge Parker reminded Lilly that she was still under oath, HB began questioning his witness. He asked Lilly whether or not she was present when her husband signed the will dated September 15, 2010. Lilly said that she was. Then, HB asked if she witnessed her husband reading the said will before he signed it.

She indignantly replied, "Of course he read it!" Then HB asked Lilly whether or not she had ever threatened to leave her husband if he did not leave her everything he owned in his will.

This question seemed to throw her off a bit, but after gathering her composure, she emphatically answered, "Absolutely not! The last question he asked Lilly was whether or not she and Jacques Pierre Bordelon Sr. had ever had a romantic relationship while she was married to Samuel Johnson and Jacques was married to Margaret Bordelon."

The whole court room broke out in loud murmurs as Lilly gasped, then shot a glaring glance at Tess and Adele.

Mr. Landry quickly jumped up and shouted, "Objection, Your Honor! This line of question has nothing to do with the validity of the will in question!"

However, before the judge could rule on the objection, HB said, "I'm sorry, Your Honor. I withdraw the question. I have no further questions of this witness."

Mr. Landry sat back down, clearly shaken by the question. HB walked back over to his table and sat back down next to Mary.

HB leaned over and whispered, "Well, she opened the can of worms, now we are going to make her eat them, one worm at a time!"

Mary smiled at HB and he winked back at her. Then, she turned around to look at her Aunt Tess and Aunt Adele. The looks on their faces were resolute.

The noise in the court room had not calmed down yet so the judge banged her gavel and sternly said, "Order in the court room!" Everyone quieted down except Charlotte and Caroline.

Caroline, not so quietly, asked Charlotte, "Did our mother have an affair with Jack when she was married to Dad?"

Charlotte answered, "If she did, this is the first I've heard of it."

Just then the judge banged her gavel again and yelled, "I said order in the court room!"

Charlotte and Caroline stopped talking and turned back towards the judge as she said, "Mr. Landry, would you like to ask the witness any questions?"

Mr. Landry stood up and, shakily replied, "Umm, no, Your Honor."

The judge told Lilly she could step down and she asked HB if he had any more witnesses. HB said that he did and he called retired Louisiana Senator Theodore William Perot to the stand. Uncle Teddy got up and walked across the room as briskly as his 84 year old legs would allow. After the bailiff swore him in, he sat down and HB asked him, "Did you sell to Jacques and Margaret Bordelon fifteen acres of land located on Perot Road and, if so, when?"

Uncle Teddy answered, Yes I did. I sold it to them in 1978."

HB continued, "And at that time, did Jacques make any statements as to what his intentions for the property were?"

Uncle Teddy replied, "Yes. He said that he wanted to have it to pass down to his children and grandchildren so that he and my sister, Margaret, God rest her soul, could carry on the legacy that the Perot family had with the land over the last two hundred some odd years."

HB asked, "And did Jacques ever state to you this same intention after his wife, Margaret passed away?"

Uncle Teddy answered, "Yes. He promised me in 2008 right before he married Lillian Johnson that he would definitely be leaving the land to his and Margret's children who were Perot family descendants."

HB said, "And did he ever repeat that promise after he married Lillian Johnson?" Uncle Teddy again responded, "Yes, he promised me again on July 16, 2012, and again on October 21, 2014, that he would be leaving the land to his children."

HB asked, "How do you remember the exact dates that he made the promises to you?"

Uncle Teddy said, "Because, on both occasions, I wrote it down in my daily appointment calendar book when I got home."

HB stated, "Your Honor, I would like to enter said appoint books for the year 2012 and the year 2014 into evidence at this time."

HB handed the books over to the Judge. After briefly looking at them she instructed him to continue. HB stated that he did not have any further questions for Senator Perot, and he walked back to his chair and sat down next to Mary. Judge Parker asked Mr. Landry if he had any questions for the witness. He said that he did not, so the judge dismissed the Senator. Then, she asked Mr. Babin if he had any other witnesses.

HB said he did and he called Paul Robichaux to the stand. After the bailiff swore Mr. Robichaux in, HB asked him if he and his wife were at the residence of Jacques and Lillian Bordelon on March 8, 2015 shortly before Mr. Bordelon passed away. Mr. Robichaux said that they were. He asked Mr. Robichaux if he heard Lillian Bordelon make any statements concerning her husband's mental condition, and if so, what did she say. Mr. Robichaux stated that he did hear Lillian Bordelon make such statements and that she had said Jack was "as sharp as a tack and as mentally competent as the day is long." HB said he did not have any more questions for the witness. The judge asked Mr. Landry if he had any questions for the witness and he replied again that he did not. She turned to Mr. Robichaux and told him he could step down. Then she asked HB if he had anymore witnesses.

HB replied, "Yes, Your Honor, I would like to recall Mary Frances Bordelon to the stand."

Mary got up and walked back to the stand and sat down. The judge reminded her that she was still under oath. Mary nodded and, then turned her attention to HB. He had walked back to the desk where he and Mary had been sitting and picked up a folder. He walked over and handed the folder to Judge Parker as he said, "Your Honor, I would like to enter into evidence this hand-written letter dated June 10, 2014, and a certified handwriting analysis that was conducted on the letter by Armstrong and Associates. They are an accredited Handwriting Analysis Company out of Shreveport. The handwriting analysis states that the person who wrote the letter was Jacques Pierre Bordelon Sr."

You could hear a pin drop in the court room as everyone's attention was on what was happening in the front of the room. Judge Parker looked over the two documents that were in the folder, then, she accepted them into evidence. She said, "You may continue with your cross examination of your witness, Mr. Babin." HB replied, "Thank you, Your Honor." Then, he turned to Mary and handed her a copy of the letter that he had just entered into evidence. He asked, "Mrs. LeBlanc, does this letter appear to you to have been written by your father, Jacques Bordelon, Sr.?" Mary replied, "It definitely looks like his handwriting to me."

Mr. Landry stood up and said, "Your Honor, I object."

The judge replied, "On what grounds, Mr. Landry?"

Mr. Landry responded, "On the grounds that Mrs. LeBlanc is not a handwriting expert."

The judge somewhat impatiently replied, "We know that Mr. Landry. That is why Mr. Babin just entered into evidence the certified handwriting analysis of the letter done by Armstrong and Associates. Would you like to see the analysis Mr. Landry?"

Mr. Landry said, "Yes, Your Honor, and I would also like to see the letter."

Judge Parker turned to the bailiff and said, "Would you please hand these documents to Mr. Landry?" The bailiff did as the judge asked. As Mr. Landry started skimming the documents, his eyes widened and his face became flushed. After a few minutes, the judge interrupted his reading and said, "Mr. Landry, do you have any other objections at this time?"

Mr. Landry mumbled, "No, Your Honor," as he slumped back down in his chair.

The judge turned to HB and said, "You may continue, Mr. Babin."

HB responded, "Thank you, Your Honor. Then he turned to Mary and asked her, "Mrs. LeBlanc, can you tell me how you came to be in possession of this letter?"

Mary replied, "When my sister, Madeline, found the will in the manila envelope, there was also a white envelope inside of it."

Mr. Landry jumped up and yelled, "Your Honor, I object!"

The judge replied in exasperation, "On what grounds this time, Mr. Landry?"

Mr. Landry quickly responded, "I questioned Mrs. LeBlanc about what she and her sisters found in the envelope at her deposition and earlier this morning in this court room. Both times Mrs. LeBlanc was under oath and she never mentioned a white envelope or a letter!"

HB turned to Judge Parker and explained, "That's because Mr. Landry never asked my client if there was anything else in the manila envelope. If he had, she would have told him about the white envelope and the letter. My client answered all of Mr. Landry's questions truthfully, Your Honor, and I object to him insinuating otherwise."

Judge Parker shook her head and, then, said, "Mr. Landry, Mr. Babin is correct. You never asked Mrs. LeBlanc if there was anything else in the manila envelope; therefore, she did not lie under oath as you are suggesting. Mr. Babin you may continue questioning your witness."

Mr. Landry, again, slumped down in his chair.

As HB started questioning Mary again, all eyes in the court room were on her. "Mrs. LeBlanc, would you please read out loud to the court room what the letter you are holding says."

Mary began reading and the more she read, the more murmurs among the observers could be heard. At one point the judge had to use her gavel to quiet everyone down. When Mary finally finished reading the letter, the room went dead silent and everyone's eyes turned towards Lilly, Charlotte and Caroline. When the sisters noticed everyone staring at them, they stood up and stormed out of the room. Lilly jumped up and ran after them. Instantly, the murmuring resumed and Judge Parker again banged her gavel to quiet everyone. When they were finally silent, she asked HB if he had any more questions for Mrs. LeBlanc. HB said that he did not. Then, she asked Mr. Landry if he had any questions for Mrs. LeBlanc.

Mr. Landry hung his head as he said, "No, Your Honor."

The judge told Mary she could step down and then asked HB if he had any more witnesses. HB said he did not, to which, the judge mumbled under her breath, "Thank God!" Then, she regained her composure and said, "After I review all the evidence entered into court today and all the testimonies heard here today, I will render a judgment." Then the judge banged her gavel one last time as she stood up and yelled out, "Court dismissed!"

Immediately, everyone else in the court room got up and started talking at once. It took the bailiff a while to clear the room. However, most lingered in the lobby still discussing what had just happened. Roy Landry, Lilly and her two daughters were standing in one corner of the lobby. Neither Mary, nor any of her relatives, were trying to eavesdrop on their conversation, but the volume of their voices was loud enough that everyone in the lobby could tell they were arguing. Mary and the rest of her family decided they needed to get away from the feuding women and their lawyer, so they decided to all meet over at Aunt Tess' for a family pow wow. Uncle Robby volunteered to stop off at Johnny's Pizza to pick up pizzas for everyone since it was almost one o'clock and no one had eaten lunch yet. On the way there, Mary texted her siblings and told them the hearing went well and that she would be holding the conference call at six o'clock as planned.

At Aunt Tess' house the relatives gathered in the kitchen to eat as they discussed the hearing and made predictions as to what the judgment would be. The conversation and visiting was so lively that Mary was surprised when she looked at her watch and realized it was almost five o'clock. She promised she would let them know as soon as she heard anything from the judge as she and Todd worked their way to the door hugging everyone along the way.

When they arrived back at the B&B, Ellie was still there. She had been waiting for Mary to get home so that she could find out what happened at the hearing. Mary tried to quickly summarize everything that had happened but Ellie kept asking her for more details. When Mary got to the part about reading the letter her father had written out loud and how Lilly and her daughters had reacted, Ellie screamed, "I knew I should have gone! I can't believe I missed all the fun! I would have given my last dollar to see the looks on all those hussies' faces!"

Mary laughed as she tried to rush her darling housekeeper out the door so she could make her phone call on time.

When all of the siblings were connected via phone, Mary gave them a slightly more descriptive play by play of what had transpired in the court room than she had given Ellie. Everyone praised Mary for how well she had done representing them all and they expressed high hopes for a judgment in their family's favor. Mary once again reassured them she would call them as soon as she got the news.

By the time Mary got off the phone, Todd had prepared them a light supper of soup and salad. After eating, Mary put in a call to Blake to give him the news of the day. Blake couldn't believe Lilly had been so vindictive. He told his mom how sorry he was that he could not be there to support her in all that she was going through. Mary thanked him for his concern but promised him that she was doing fine and told him not to worry about her. She said all that she needed for him to do for her was to pray that they got a judgment quickly and it was in their favor. He said that he would certainly do that.

Mary was too tired to call her other boys and go through everything all over again so she asked Blake to pass the news along and he promised his mother that he would. When Mary got off the phone with Blake, she went to her room, changed into her pajamas, brushed her teeth, washed her face, and climbed into bed. She tried to read for a while, but she was so exhausted from the eventful day that before she knew it she was fast asleep.

CHAPTER NINETEEN

THE JUDGEMENT

Tuesday morning, the sun was shining and the weather man had promised it would be a beautiful day. Mary was in the kitchen putting together an apple cobbler and Todd was outside doing some yard work. About ten o'clock the phone rang and, to Mary's delight, it was Sara. She had just returned home from her three week European vacation with her husband and was calling Mary to find out what had happened while she was away. After the two friends exchanged excited hellos, Sara invited Mary to lunch so that they could catch up. They made plans to meet at one o'clock at Maglieaux's.

When Mary hung up the phone, she put her cobbler in the oven and went looking for Todd. She wanted to tell him her plans and see if he would be home all afternoon in case they got any walk-ins. She found him out in the garage working on his weed-eater. When she told him what she wanted, he said he didn't have any plans to go out and that he would be inside in a little while.

By the time Mary's cobbler was done, Todd had come inside and was in the shower. While she waited for him to get dressed, she fixed him a ham sandwich with some chips, a glass of tea and a bowl of cobbler. When he came in the kitchen and saw the lunch sitting on the snack bar, he gave his wife a kiss and sat down to eat. Mary stood across from him as she gave him a few last-minute instructions before leaving for her lunch date.

Mary arrived at Maglieaux's a few minutes early, so she requested a table for two on the restaurant's outdoor patio. The weather man had been right. It was a beautiful spring day and perfect for an outdoor lunch. Sara arrived right on time and, as soon as she saw Mary, the two friends hugged each other as if they hadn't been together in months instead of weeks.

Sara told Mary all about her trip and showed her the amazing pictures she had taken. In turn, Mary filled her in on all that had been going on with Lilly, the crazy aunts, uncles and cousins, and the will since she left town. Sara laughed and laughed at Mary's stories about the skunk incident and the cousin's contest and she went from sheer excitement over hearing about the new will to disgust in learning about Lilly's blackmail scheme. When Mary told her about Jack and Lilly's affair years before, Sara was immediately concerned for her dear friend not knowing how she or her family had taken the news. Mary assured her they were all taking it in stride. Mary told Sara it seemed that Lilly's daughters were the ones taking the news the hardest, and with that, she went on to tell her all about the hearing. The friends talked so long that, before they knew it, it was four o'clock!

On the way home Mary stopped at the store to pick up a few groceries. When she got home she noticed a black BMW parked in the B&B parking lot. As she was putting away the groceries, Todd came in the kitchen and informed her that the car belonged to a lawyer from New Orleans who had come to town to visit his friend, HB Babin, and that HB had sent him to their B&B to get a room. Todd said that the guest would only be staying one night. He also mentioned that HB was supposed to be coming to pick up his friend at seven o'clock to take him to dinner.

Their guest came downstairs a few minutes before seven. He introduced himself to Mary as Peter Lockhart but told her to just call him Pete. He complimented her on how lovely her home was and said that he would have to come back some time with his wife, who loved historical homes and B&Bs.

HB knocked on the back kitchen door right at seven. After greeting his friend, he spoke to Mary for a few minutes. He told her that he had not heard anything from the judge yet, but he hoped he might hear something in a day or two. He said that he had, however, heard that Roy Landry could be in some hot water with the ethics board concerning the information that was released in Jack's letter, especially since it seems to have also come to light that he and Lilly have been seeing each other for some time now.

After a few more minutes of conversation, HB and Pete left and Mary went into her office to check her email. About nine o'clock Pete returned and Mary asked him how his evening had been. He said it had been great. Mary asked him what time he would like breakfast in the morning. He told her eight o'clock would be fine and to please not go to any trouble. He said he never ate a big breakfast and that he was more of a coffee and bagel kind of guy. Mary told him she would fix something simple and she asked him if he needed anything else. He replied, "Not a thing." as he headed up the stairs to his room.

The next morning, at eight o'clock sharp, Pete came downstairs and Mary was waiting for him. She asked him if he had slept well and he said that he had. She served him a breakfast of banana nut muffins and a bowl of fresh fruit mixed with granola and topped with yogurt. A few minutes later Todd came into the dining room and the two men talked a while about life in New Orleans, pre-Katrina and post-Katrina. Pete checked out just as Ellie was coming in.

Mary busied herself the rest of the morning working in her office going through the never-ending pile of mail on her desk. While working she had a couple of phone calls from people inquiring about rates and room availability. Around noon, Ellie stuck her head into the office doorway to ask Mary if she wanted to come join her for lunch. Mary looked up from her paperwork and smiled as she replied, "Yes, that sounds great. I need a break. I'll be there in just a minute."

As Ellie walked back to the kitchen, Mary shredded the last stack of junk mail on her desk, then got up, stretched her stiff back and went to join Ellie in the kitchen. Just as the two women were finishing up their lunch of red beans and rice the phone rang once again. As soon as Mary said hello, HB's voice boomed in her ear, "We won!"

Mary excitedly replied, "You mean the judge ruled in our favor?"

"That's exactly what I mean! She ruled that your will is the legitimate Last Will and Testament for Jacques Pierre Bordelon, Sr., which means you and your family will be inheriting all your father's property and remaining assets."

Mary sat back down at the table next to Ellie and took a few seconds to let it all sink in. Ellie was jumping up and down and singing "Praise be to Jesus!"

Mary tried to quiet Ellis down as she asked HB, "What do we do now? I mean do we just tell Lilly she needs to move out? What about the succession process?"

"Well, I have to warn you that Lilly could file an appeal but I really don't see that happening. I already called Roy just to make sure and he told me that he will be advising her against it. He knows it would be a frivolous appeal since in the judgment it makes clear that our will was your father's Last Will and Testament. Besides, if she decided to go against her lawyer's advice and file an appeal, she would have to put up a bond and pay legal expenses. It could get pretty expensive and she does not have a leg to stand on so she would just be wasting her money and prolonging the inevitable. It wouldn't be in Roy's best interest, either as he doesn't need any more attention put on him concerning the contents of Jack's letter."

Mary said, "I don't know. Lilly can be very obstinate and unreasonable when she doesn't get her way."

"You are the executor of your father's will and as your lawyer I will handle everything for you. If she files an appeal, then we will address it then, but for now I am going to get the succession process back on track, and I will send a certified letter to Lilly informing her of the request that she vacate the property. We need to give her a deadline and I recommend we make it short. You don't want her dragging her feet getting out. I would only give her thirty days if I were you. If I get the letter to her by Friday, May 1, that would give her until June 1 to move."

Mary replied, "Are you sure that will be enough time to give her to move?

HB assured Mary that one month was all the time she was required to give Lilly and he reminded her that Lilly did not deserve any sympathy from the Bordelon family after everything she had put them through. Mary agreed with HB in that regard and instructed him to go ahead and send Lilly the letter with the terms he had recommended.

Mary's head was spinning. She thought to herself, "How would they make sure Lilly didn't take anything that belonged to her mother or her father when she moved? What about Charlotte and Caroline's cottages that were on the property? What about her father's rental property that Lilly was still collecting rent on?" She gathered her thoughts before asking HB all the questions that were floating around in her head. First, she asked him about the cottages and he said he would send certified letters to both Charlotte and Caroline informing them that they needed to vacate the property also. He recommended giving them thirty days, too, to have their cottages moved and Mary agreed.

Next Mary asked HB about the rental property. He said that the rent is usually paid on the first of the month so he would send his investigator over to each property tomorrow which was April 30 and have him hand deliver a letter to each tenant notifying them of the change in ownership and giving them his address to mail their rent to. He said she would need to decide pretty quickly if she wanted to manage all the property herself or if she wanted to hire a rental company to do it for her. Once she decided this, she needed to evaluate each tenant and the rent they are paying to decide if she wants to keep renting to them and, if so, how much rent she wanted to charge them. Then she will need to get each tenant to sign new leases as soon as possible listing her and her siblings as the new landlords.

This opened up a whole other issue. HB told Mary that she and her siblings would need to decide whether or not they wanted to form an LLC to own the properties or to just do it as joint owners. At that point Mary stopped HB and told him not to go any further. She was getting overwhelmed. She said, "I think I need to talk to my siblings and let them know about the judgment first. Then I need to meet with you in your office in the morning so that we can go over all of this face to face. I have been so worried about keeping the land in the family that I never even thought about all of these things."

HB replied, "I understand. It's a lot to digest all at once. Do you still want me to move forward with the certified letters to Lilly and her daughters or do you want me to wait until after we meet tomorrow?"

Mary, answered, "Yes, you can definitely do that and you can have your investigator deliver the letters to the tenants."

Mary and HB agreed to meet at ten o'clock the next day. As soon as Mary hung up the phone, Ellie wrapped her arms around her and the two women danced around the kitchen laughing and crying all at once. Todd walked in, took one look at his wife and housekeeper, and decided they must have both lost their minds. As soon as Mary saw him, she let go of Ellie, rushed over to her husband, wrapped her arms around him and gave him a huge kiss.

After catching his breath he asked, "And what was that for?" Mary preceded to tell him about her conversation with HB while Ellie, intermittently, added phrases of, "Thank you, Jesus!", "Praise the Lord!", and "Glory Hallelujah!" to the conversation.

By the time Mary had finished telling Todd about everything Ellie was plumb worn out from the excitement. Mary told Todd and Ellie she wanted to drive over to her Aunt Tess' house to tell her the good news in person. Ellie said, "You go right on ahead, Sugar. I got everything here under control."

As soon as Mary pulled up in her aunt's driveway, she jumped out of the car and ran up the porch steps. She didn't bother knocking on the door or ringing the doorbell. She burst into the house yelling excitedly, "Aunt Tess, where are you?"

Aunt Tess came rushing into the living room, "What's wrong, Mary?"

Mary grabbed her aunt and hugged her tight as she said, "We won, Aunt Tess, we won! We got Belle Rose back!"

Aunt Tess started shaking in Mary's arms as her eyes welled up with tears. Mary led her trembling aunt over to the couch and sat next to her as she talked softly to her and wiped away her tears with a tissue. When Uncle Isaac walked into the room and saw his wife crying, he immediately came to her side. He sat next to her and worriedly asked, "Sweetheart, what's wrong?"

Aunt Tess replied in a shaky voice, "It's OK, Isaac. I am crying tears of joy. Mary just came to tell me the good news that the judge ruled in our favor and Maggie's children will be getting our family land back."

Isaac replied, "That's great news, Sweetheart!" Then he turned to Mary and congratulated her. Mary relayed to them all that HB had told her except the part about the possibility of Lilly filing an appeal. Since HB had said that was not likely to happen, she decided there was no use in worrying her aunt about it. She asked Aunt Tess how she wanted to handle giving the news to the other aunts and uncles. Aunt Tess said that Tommy and Robby probably would not be coming inside for a while as it was still early in the day. She said that she would call Pauline and Doris and tell them the news over the phone. Then, she would have them promise not to tell their husbands when they came in, but instead, tell them that she had fallen and sprained her ankle and that they needed to come over and check on her. Then when they came over, Mary could deliver the new to them herself.

Aunt Tess called her two sisters-in-law, gave them the good news, and swore them to secrecy. After she hung up, she asked Mary if she wanted to call Teddy and Adele since they would not be able to deliver the news in person to them as they had returned home after the hearing. Mary replied that she wanted Tess to do the honors so Tess called Teddy first, then Adele. Mary and Isaac sat by listening to her deliver the news to each of her siblings and watched her cry each time she did. Afterwards, Mary texted her siblings and told them to call in to her house at six o'clock for a conference call.

While they waited for Uncle Tommy and Uncle Robby to come, Mary and Aunt Tess walked out to the cemetery to visit Maggie and Jack as well as their other loved ones buried there. Then they walked back to the house and sat on the porch swing for a while drinking glasses of lemonade and enjoying the cool breeze.

Finally, around four o'clock the two women went inside and Mary began getting really anxious for her uncles to arrive. Luckily, they arrived together and a little earlier than Mary and Aunt Tess were expecting them. Uncle Tommy knocked on the front door and Isaac went to answer it. He welcomed his brothers-in-law inside and led them into the kitchen where Tess and Mary were waiting for them. As soon as they walked in and saw Tess and Mary sitting at the table and Tess showing no signed of a sprained ankle, they knew something was up. Mary wanted to deliver the news in a "witty" fashion but she couldn't contain herself enough to do it so she just blurted it out much as she had with Aunt Tess. The looks on both of Mary's uncles' faces were priceless. Within seconds everyone was hugging each other and there wasn't a dry eye in the room.

After everybody regained some amount of composure Tommy said, "Well, I hope that Black Widow doesn't take her good old time clearing out of Maggie's house but, just in case she does, I'm sure Robby and I can come up with some ways to convince her otherwise."

Robby seconded his brother's statement and added, "And you can bet they won't be pretty."

Mary warned her uncles to let her and HB handle the eviction process without any inference from them. They said they would hold off on doing anything for now, but they weren't going to make any long term promises. Mary figured that was the best she was going to get from them so she left it at that.

When Mary arrived back at the house, Ellie was gone and Todd was on the phone with her son Brett. He looked up at Mary and said, "Oh, here's your mom now. I'll let her give you the good news herself."

Todd handed the phone to Mary and, as soon as she picked it up, Brett asked, "What is the good news Todd was talking about? I hope it is that you got the judgment and it was in our favor!"

Mary laughed and said, "Yes, you guessed it."

Mary had to pull the phone away from her ear as Brett yelled out a resounding, "I can't believe it! He continued, Are you sure, Mom? Are we really going to get Belle Rose back?"

"Yes we are but it may take a little while as we have to go through the eviction process."

"That's great, Mom! I can't wait to tell Danielle when she gets home."

Mary told Brett she needed to go so she could call all her sisters and brothers. When all the siblings were on the phone line together, Mary delivered the good news. They were all ecstatic! She quickly explained the appeals issue to them but she reiterated what HB had told her about Lilly not having a leg to stand on. When Mary told them about the certified letters HB was going to send to Lilly and her daughters, they agreed that needed to be down immediately. Her brothers echoed her uncles' ideas about what should be done to Lilly and her daughters if they dragged their feet moving out or if they decided to file an appeal.

Mary, not wanting to encourage them, quickly changed the subject and started explaining to her siblings all the issues with the rental properties. They all agreed that they had some serious decisions to make. JJ recommended they set up a family LLC to deal with the rental property and that the proceeds from the rent be put into an account to fund the repairs on the properties. The funds could also be used to maintain Belle Rose and to pay for insurance and taxes on all the properties. He said that once sufficient funds built up in the account to take care of most any emergencies that may arise with the properties, they could decide whether or not they wanted to start drawing individual monthly or yearly stipends from the account or use the money for other purposes. Everyone agreed that this idea made a lot of sense.

Joe recommended that Mary ask Richard to stay on to look after Belle Rose. Everyone agreed to that suggestion, too, and Mary said she would call Richard tomorrow, right after she met with HB, to ask him to stay on.

Jake mentioned that Uncle Tommy might be interested in leasing some of the thirty acres to grow more hay on. Mary said she would ask him if he was the next time she saw him.

Myrié suggested that they ask Sara to manage the rental property since she and her husband owned a property management company. Mary said she couldn't believe she had not thought of that earlier. She said she would call Sara tomorrow, too.

Martine had been fairly quiet through most of the conversation but she suddenly spoke up and said, "You know, the Perot family still holds their family reunion at Aunt Tess' house every 4th of July. If all of you could find a way to make it home for the reunion, it would really be a great way to celebrate getting the property back."

Everyone thought that would be a great idea and promised they would all do their best to clear their calendars and make the trip home for the family reunion. Mary was so excited at the prospect of having all of her sibling home again so soon, especially since the 4th of July just so happened to be her birthday too. What a wonderful birthday present it would be to have all her siblings home for a happy celebration.

After her call with her siblings, Mary called Beau. As soon as she delivered the news to him, he solemnly said, "Mom, that is the best news you could have given me. Now Eva and I can really start making our plans to move back home when I retire in two years."

"And that's the best news you could give me! I can't wait to have you, Eva and the kids home again!"

"I know, Mom. Won't it be great?"

"Yes it will!"

Mary's heart skipped a beat with the thought of having one of her children and some of her grandchildren home again.

Mary repeated the call to Blake and he was just as excited to hear the news as his two brothers had been. By the time Mary finished all of her phone calls, she realized it was nearly eight o'clock and she was starving! She went into the kitchen to see what she could find to eat.

CHAPTER TWENTY

ANGELS AMONG US

Thursday morning Mary sat down across from HB's desk in the chair she had grown accustomed to over the last couple of months. She immediately informed him of the decisions she and her siblings had made concerning the rental properties. He told her that he would get busy right away drawing up the necessary paperwork to set up the LLC for her family. Then, he updated her on the things he had done. He said that he had sent the certified letters by mail to Lilly and her daughters and that they should be receiving them in a day or two. He also prepared letters for the tenants of the rental properties and had his investigator hand deliver them yesterday evening in hopes that they would all be home from work. He said that all had been but one and that the investigator had left that letter with the tenant's teenage son. Mary thanked him for his prompt attention to all her family's business, then she asked him what she should tell Lilly or her daughters if they called her. He replied that she should tell them that they needed to call him if they have any questions and that she should avoid engaging them in any conversations. Mary said that she would be more than happy to do that as she wanted as little to do with the women as possible. They discussed a few more minor details before Mary left.

As she pulled out of the parking lot, she realized she felt much less overwhelmed than she had the day before. She decided to surprise Sara by stopping in at her downtown office and, if she wasn't too busy, she would invite her to lunch. If she said yes, Mary could talk to her about taking over the management of the family rental property.

When Mary walked in to Sara's office on Front Street, her husband, Terry, greeted her as Sara was on the phone. They made small talk while Mary anxiously waited for Sara to finish her phone conversation. Finally, Sara hung up the phone and walked over to hug her friend. The first thing Mary told her was the news about the judgment. Sara was so happy for her that she hugged her again as she said, "We have to go out and celebrate!"

Mary laughingly replied, "Funny you should mention that because I was thinking the same thing. I came over here to invite you to lunch so you could celebrate with me."

Sara said, "That sounds like a great idea to me!" She turned to her husband and asked, "Can you cover for me for a couple of hours?"

Terry answered, "I think I can handle it! You two girls go out and have a good time."

Sara gave her husband a kiss on the check as she said, "Thanks, I owe you one."

He responded with a sly smile, "I love it when you owe me."

Sara smiled back at him then she turned to Mary and asked, "Can you just give me a minute to take care of a couple of things?"

Mary replied, "No problem. I need to call Todd anyway and let him know I won't be home for a couple of hours.

Mary made her phone call while Sara went back to her desk to wrap up a few things. Ten minutes later they were walking out the door, arm and arm, down the historic century old bricked street talking and giggling like a couple of teenage girls. They had decided, since it was such a beautiful day and neither one was in heels, they would walk the two blocks to Maglieaux's. When they arrived, they were pleasantly surprised to be greeted by Kathy, the owner of Maglieaux's as well as the owner of Sweet Cane Inn B&B down the street. All three women had been friends for years. Kathy escorted Sara and Mary to their usual table on the patio and visited with them for a few minutes until their waitress arrived. After they ordered, Mary started telling Sara about the rental property situation and asked her if she could manage the properties for her family.

Sara replied, "Of course I can! I will get on it right away. I don't suppose you have copies of the current leases or the names of the tenants do you?"

"Unfortunately, I don't and I don't dare try to get them from Lilly."

"I am with you on that. Don't worry about it. Just give me the addresses and I'll send my assistant over to each property to meet with the tenants and see if they can get copies of all the leases. After I go through them and do the comps for rental properties in the area, I will call you and we can go over my recommendations for the new leases."

"That would be great."

Mary told Sara she wanted to run background checks on all of the tenants before having them sign new leases. Mary commented, "I don't even know what kind of people are living in the houses. I have no idea if they are taking care of the property or if they pay their rent on time or if they have pets or anything."

Sara replied, "Absolutely! I always do both financial and criminal background checks on everyone I rent to. And, as for pets, I recommend you have a "no pet policy" but, if you decide you want to allow them, you really should consider allowing only small dogs with a big non-refundable pet deposit. Also, when my assistant goes to the houses to get the copies of the leases, he will be able to check out the outside of the property. Then hopefully the tenant will invite him in. If they do, he will also be able to get a glimpse of how the property is being cared for inside.

"Thanks, Sara! I am so relieved to be able to put this all in your lap to take care of. I don't think I could handle dealing with all of it myself. I am going to have my hands full just dealing with getting Lilly and her daughters off our family land. I am not looking forward to that but, at least, I have HB running interference for me, so hopefully there will not be any hiccups. I had to make my uncles promise to keep out of it, but they warned me if Lilly didn't comply with our eviction notice, all bets would be off."

Sara laughed as she said, "Your uncles are great, Mary. If I were you I would be happy to know I had them in my corner!"

"You are right about that. I really do feel blessed to have the support of my mom's family as well as my own family. I don't know how I would have gotten through all this without them."

"I agree with you one hundred percent. You are truly blessed with a wonderful family!"

"And with wonderful friends!"

"I'll toast to that!"

Both women laughed as they raised their water glasses and clicked them together. The two friends continued talking as they ate their meal. Afterwards, they indulged in a slice of cheese cake topped with pecan praline sauce for desert, rationalizing that they could both afford the calories since they had only eaten salads. And besides, it was necessary since you couldn't have a proper celebration without cake.

When Mary arrived back at the house, she asked Todd if anyone had called requesting reservations. He said yes and that it had been her friend, Sylvia, from New Orleans. He said that Sylvia and the gang were all planning a girls' getaway trip in a couple of weeks and thought it would be nice to drive up to Natchitoches and visit Mary.

Sylvia had been one of Mary's best friends when she lived in New Orleans. They met shortly after she and Todd had married. Sylvia and her husband belonged to a dance club in New Orleans that held weekly dance lessons at a local night club. Todd had heard about the dance club lessons and had convinced Mary to go try them out. When they arrived, Karen Miles, the secretary at the school where Mary worked, noticed her and Todd standing by the door looking lost, and had walked over to welcome them. After Mary introduced Karen to Todd, Karen brought the couple over to her table and introduced them to her husband, Logan, and the other three couples setting at the table. Todd recognized Sylvia's husband, Dean, from a job he had worked on several years back and they started up a friendly conversation. Todd and Mary were, instantly, accepted into the close knit group of friends and the rest is history. They had done so much together, from dance lessons and weekend dances, to dinners out together, to holiday parties at each other's homes to crawfish boils, to even going on cruises together. Mary had gone on several girls get-a-way trips with all the wives over the years and they had made an occasional trip to her B&B, usually in November when Natchitoches' annual Christmas Festival started up.

When Katrina hit New Orleans in 2005, Mary and Todd's friends had all followed them to Natchitoches and Mary's parents had put them up for weeks until they could all return home to their own houses. During that time they had all grown close to Mary's parents and had over the last ten years followed closely the trials and tribulations of Mary and her parents and their intertwined lives.

Before Todd even finished talking, Mary went straight to the phone and called Sylvia. After the friends finished catching each other up on the latest news, Mary asked, "So what's this Todd tells me about you and the girls planning another girls' getaway trip to Natchitoches in a couple of weeks?"

Sylvia replied, "Yes, we are thinking about it if you don't already have our cottage booked for May 13 through the 15. You know Mother's Day is May 10 and Gail's birthday is May 13. Plus you know that she lost her mom a couple of months ago, the same week that you lost your dad, and this will be her first Mother's Day and birthday without her mom. Gail has been taking her death really hard so we thought we would get her mind off of it by taking her out of town. When we were discussing where to go, we naturally thought about you."

Mary couldn't believe the day she was having. The blessings just seemed to keep coming. "Well, you are in luck because I do not have y'all's cottage booked for the nights of May 13 and 14."

"Then, it's settled. Put Karen, Gail, Claire and me down for the 13th and 14th and we will all be there come hell or high water!"

Mary went to find Todd, as he was no longer in the kitchen. She found him in the game room practicing trick shots. Mary told him what days her friends were coming and, then told him about her conversations with HB and Sara. He only half listened as he continued to concentrate on his pool shots. Finally, she gave up and went to her office to call Richard.

When Mary asked Richard if he would consider staying on to take care of Belle Rose for the family, he said he would be honored to work for Jack and Maggie's children and that it would be a pleasant change after working for Lilly. After that was settled, Mary asked Richard about the general condition of the house and the property.

Mary knew from her visits to see her father over the years that the family home had become run down and needed a lot of things fixed and/or updated, things that her father had either put off or ignored. Adding to the problem was the fact that Lilly was not nearly as neat of a personal housekeeper as Mary's mother had been.

In answer to Mary's inquiry, Richard told her that the house was a mess as Lilly had fired the last housekeeper over a month before. He said that he had done his best to keep up the outside of the property but that Lilly was no longer allowing him to charge supplies at Kaffie Frederick General Store like Jack had, and that every time he asked her for money to buy things like grass fertilizer and weed killer, she gave him a hard time. Plus, he said that the pump in the pond had gone out, but since Lilly found out she might have to move, she told him she wasn't about to put out the money to buy a new one.

Mary told Richard to go ahead and get the pump and charge it to her account at Kaffie's. After he thanked her, she was just getting ready to tell him goodbye when he offered up a little tidbit of information regarding Lilly and her daughters. He said that Charlotte and Caroline were almost as upset with Lilly about the affair she had had with Jack as they were about losing the Bordelon property. He told Mary that they even threatened to put her in an assisted living home. Upon hearing this news, Mary had to gloat just a little.

She said, "Well, bless their hearts. I hate to hear they are having family problems."

After Mary hung up the phone with Richard, she went into the kitchen to start cooking supper. While she cooked, she thought about the day she had had and she said a silent prayer thanking God for all the angels he had put in her life over the years in the form of friends and family members.

CHAPTER TWENTY-ONE

AN INTERESTING PHONE CONVERSATION

Friday morning HB called to tell her it was official. Lilly was definitely not filing an appeal. He said that he had spoken to Roy Landry and he said that, although it had been difficult, in the end he convinced Lilly that an appeal was not in her best interest. As soon as she got off the phone she sent an email to her brothers and sisters relaying the good news. Afterwards, she went back to working on getting the rooms ready for her weekend reservations.

The Cane River Music Festival was this weekend and Mary had several guests coming in for it. She and Ellie worked all morning. They finally stopped about one o'clock to take a short lunch break. They were talking and laughing and enjoying their meal of chicken salad on Ritz crackers when they were interrupted by the ringing of the phone. Mary failed to look at the caller ID before answering it. She started to rattle off her business greeting of, "Hello, this is A Bed of Roses,..." but before she could finish, she was rudely interrupted by Charlotte..

Without even as much as a hello, Charlotte began, "Mary, Caroline and I just received notices from your family's lawyer about having to move our cottages. There is no way we are going to be able to arrange that in just thirty days. Do you have any idea how expensive it is to move cottages let alone find someone who can do the job? When your father allowed us to build the cottages on the property, he assured us our mother would be inheriting Jack's land so we would never have to move them. You know, you should at least honor his promise to us by letting us keep the cottages on the property. It is bad enough what he did to our poor mother after she took care of him all those years."

Mary knew she had promised HB she would not engage with Lilly or her daughters if they called but she couldn't resist saying something. As soon as she could get a word in edgewise she interrupted Charlotte and said, "Charlotte, my father specified in his will that the fifty thousand dollar life insurance policy your mother received upon his death was supposed to pay for his funeral AND the cost of moving yours and Caroline's cottages off of our property. My sisters and I made the arrangements for our father's funeral, so I know how much Lilly paid for it, and I know that she should have plenty left over to pay for moving your cottages."

Charlotte huffed and puffed as she tried to regain control of the conversation. She told Mary that even if she and Caroline could get their cottages moved in thirty days there was no way they were going to have time to find Lilly a new place to stay and get her completely packed up in the same length of time.

Mary replied, "Well, Charlotte, I guess you and Caroline will just have to have her move in with one of you. Of course, there is always the option of assisted living to consider. I really don't care where she goes just as long as she is off of our property by June 1."

Charlotte whined, "I can't believe you can be so callous! Isn't it bad enough that Jack lied to our mother about taking care of her and us in his will, then he added insult to injury by writing that awful letter claiming that she had had an affair with him while she was married to our father and, to top it off, accused her of blackmail! You could have at least had the decency not to drag our family and yours through the mud by making that letter full of lies public at the hearing!"

Mary should have cut Charlotte off earlier but she was kind of enjoying listening to her rant about how awful everything was for her and her family. It was refreshing after everything she, Caroline and Lilly had put her family through for the last seven years. The more Charlotte went on the more hysterical she sounded.

Finally, though, Mary decided enough was enough and she said, "Charlotte, if you have any more issues to discuss concerning the eviction letters you need to contact my lawyer. Would you like me to give you his number?"

"No, that will not be necessary! I just thought you and I could have a civil conversation and that you might have a little compassion for our family after all that our mother did for your father. You know your family would have really been in a bind having to take care of him if it wasn't for our mother."

Mary had had it with Charlotte's constant referral to all that Lilly had done for her father. Now she was the one that was getting angry. As she started to reply to what Charlotte had just said it was as if suddenly a stranger had taken over her voice and she couldn't stop herself as she spoke, "Look, Charlotte, I don't know who in the hell you think you are kidding but Lilly was highly compensated for what she did for our father. My father provided for your mother financially and paid all of her bills. Plus, Lilly had total access to his bank accounts and she went through his money like it was water. There was nothing she wanted that she didn't get. Even so, my father generously saw fit to leave her two hundred fifty-two thousand dollars which comes to thirty six thousand dollars a year for all the tender loving care she gave him. He did this despite the fact that she tried to blackmail him out of his property and make him disown his own children. Not to mention the fact that she had an affair with our father while he was married to our pregnant mother! She is lucky we aren't kicking her ass out of our mother's house today and that is the last thing I am going to say about the matter! As I said before, you can call my lawyer if you need anything else!"

And with that, Mary, slammed down the phone. As soon as she did, she realized she no longer felt angry. Instead, she somehow felt liberated. She turned to Ellie who was staring at her as if she had just grown horns and had steam coming out of her ears. She had gotten so caught up in her battle of words with Charlotte that she had forgotten Ellie was even in the room. Ellie finally found her voice and said, "My goodness alive, Sugar! Are you Ok?"

Mary thought about Ellie's question for a couple of seconds, then replied, "You know, Ellie, I've never been better! Maybe I need to get angry more often."

"Well I hope you don't ever get angry at me because I sure don't want to be on the other end of the likes of what you just dished out to Charlotte. But, it sure made my day hearing you giving it to her with both barrels. She and her mama deserve every bit of it and then some."

Mary said, "I think you are right about that. They have deserved it for some time now and I don't feel one bit bad about giving it to her. I just wish I could have given it to Lilly, too. I think I feel like celebrating. After we finish lunch, I am going to make us one of my coconut praline pies and when it's ready you and I are going to eat a big slice of it. How does that sound?"

"Sounds great to me! I been craving one of your coconut pies for weeks."

After Mary and Ellie ate their pie, they had just enough time to put the finishing touches on the rooms and cottage before their weekend guests arrived.

CHAPTER TWENTY-TWO

LANDLORD HEADACHES

By Sunday morning Mary and Todd were ready to have their house back to themselves. They enjoyed having guests, but this weekend pushed them to their limit. Several of the young guests attending the music festival had been unruly and the family staying in the cottage had three small boys who only knew one speed, fast. One of the little boys was allergic to any kind of nuts so Mary and Ellie had to be extra careful of everything they cooked to insure it did not have any nut contamination. This proved to be very difficult because Mary put pecans in just about everything, but somehow they pulled it off as the child did not get sick on their watch.

The family of five was the last to check out and they left right at 12:00 noon. Mary and Ellie immediately stripped all the beds but, when they were finished, Mary told Ellie to go home. She said that she would do all the laundry herself and they could finish cleaning the rooms in the morning since they did not have any reservations for Sunday or Monday night. Ellie was so tired she did not put up an argument.

Mary spent the rest of the afternoon relaxing in front of the TV with Todd watching old John Wayne movies. At five o'clock she got up and went to get dressed for evening Mass. When she returned from church she ate supper, checked her email for reservation requests and went to bed early.

Monday morning Mary woke up refreshed after sleeping almost nine hours. When Ellie arrived at nine, she had almost finished washing the sheets and towels and was all set to start helping her make the beds and clean the rooms. However, her plans were interrupted by a phone call from Sara. Sara told her she was sorry to bother her but there were a few problems they needed to discuss concerning the tenants in a couple of the rent houses. She said that her assistant had gone to see all the tenants Friday and that he had managed to get copies of all but one of the leases but he had encountered a couple of issues that needed Mary's attention right away. Sara asked Mary if she could come to her office sometime today so that they could discuss the problems.

Mary knew from the sound of Sara's voice that the problems she was referring to were serious. She told Sara that she would be there in thirty minutes.

When Mary arrived at Sara office, Sara ushered her in and got right down to business. Mary hardly had time to grab a chair before she started telling her all about what her assistant and she had uncovered concerning the Bordelon rental properties. She summarized the situation into the good, the bad, and the ugly and asked Mary where she wanted her to start. Mary thought about it for a second and, then, told her to start at the top with the good and work her way down.

Sara said the good news was that three of the houses were rented by good, long-term tenants who had steady jobs and claimed to be paying their rent on time. She had not gotten back the credit and criminal reports yet, but she did not see any red flags on these three tenants and expected their reports to come back clean. Furthermore, she said that all three houses seemed to be well-maintained and only one of the three tenants had a pet, which was a small poodle. She told Mary that the rent these three tenants were paying was about right according to the comps she had run for the area and she recommended that Mary keep all of them at the same rate for now.

Mary thought everything Sara had just said was really good news so she figured whatever was wrong with the other two properties she could handle it. She said, "OK, that all sounds great, so give me the bad news."

Sara began, "Well the bad news concerns the biggest property Jack owned. It is an old, two-story house with four bedrooms, three baths and a garage apartment. It is currently being leased by a non-profit teen pregnancy shelter called Tough Choices. The shelter has been renting the house from Jack for nearly twenty years and during that twenty years Jack never raised their rent. When he died, he was still only charging them four hundred dollars a month."

Mary knew what property Sara was referring to. Her mother had done volunteer work for the shelter for years and she was the one who had gotten Mary's father to buy the house and rent it to the shelter for a minimal fee. Mary was not surprised that her father had not gone up on the rent even after her mother had passed away and she was sure her siblings would honor the arrangement, so she didn't see that there was a problem until Sara continued, "The problem is that the house is in need of a lot of repairs. On top of that, the shelter's lease has never been renewed since it was originally written. They had been paying it on a month-to-month basis and whenever their funds were low Jack would just let them skip that month. However, after he died, Lilly immediately informed them that they were going to have to sign a new lease and that she would be raising their rent to nine hundred dollars a month. Since the shelter cannot even come close to raising that amount of money, they have been stalling Lilly for as long as they could without signing the new lease. Finally, they had to tell her they could not come up with the money, and as soon as they did, she slapped them with an eviction notice. They are supposed to be moving out June 1 but they have not been able to find another location to move to, so they are considering shutting the shelter down altogether which means the pregnant teenagers staying there will have no place to go."

Mary was furious! She wasn't really surprised about the situation considering Lilly's track record, but she was furious just the same. She would love to tell Sara this very instant to inform Tough Choices that she and her siblings would honor their parents' original arrangement with them for as long as they wanted to stay in the house and that they would immediately take care of all the necessary repairs to it but she knew a decision like that would require a consensus vote from her brothers and sisters.

"Sara, I understand the situation and I am going to talk to my family about it as soon as possible and get back to you. I will be recommending to them that we continue the arrangement my parents had with Tough Choices and that we authorize all the repairs needed, but I will need their approval before I can have you make such promises to them."

Sara replied, "Mary, that is very generous of you, but I have to recommend to you as your property manager that you consider at least a modest rent increase so that you can be compensated at some point for the expenses of the repairs. Plus, I would definitely have them sign a new lease so that you have options should they not be able to make their payments on time going forward."

Mary understood both of the points Sara was making and she said that she would take both of them into consideration when she spoke to her siblings and get back to her. In the meantime, though, she told Sara to inform the shelter that they did not need to make any arrangements to move right now as her family would not be evicting them. She also asked Sara to send a contractor over to the house immediately to start making the repairs that were the most critical for the safety of the tenants.

With the "good" and the "bad" news taken care of for now, Mary braced herself for the worst of the news, the "ugly." She said, "OK, get it over with and give me the ugly."

Sara replied, "The tenants in the last house are Lilly's sister's pregnant granddaughter and her boyfriend and their two children and their two cats."

Mary did not see this coming. It never occurred to her that one or more of the tenants in her father's rent houses would be a relative of Lilly's. How could she not have thought about this before?

Sara continued, "The couple does not have a current lease and they have not been forthcoming with any information on the rent they have or have not been paying. Of course the granddaughter is not working as she is eight months pregnant. From the little information we have gathered from them, the boyfriend is a guitar player in a rock band and does construction work on the side to support them. The house is in decent shape on the outside but there is an old, broken down car in the driveway and the lawn needs to be mowed. I doubt they even own a lawnmower, so that is going to be a problem. However, the inside of the house is the real problem. According to my assistant, when he walked in the house, he was immediately hit with the odor of dirty diapers and cat urine. The living room walls have crayon marks and what not all over them and the carpet is soiled. Oh, and the granddaughter informed my assistant that he needs to send over a plumber because the hall bathroom toilet will not flush."

Mary completely understood now why Sara had referred to this as the ugly.

"Well, you are the expert in these matters. What do you recommend we do?"

Sara replied, "The first thing we need to do is address the plumbing problem. Under normal circumstances such an issue is the tenant's problem, but I am afraid if we wait for them to handle it, we could have a bigger problem on our hands. We would probably be better off just sending the plumber I keep under contract for all my properties over to fix it."

Mary agreed with Sara on the plumbing matter, so they moved on to Sara's second recommendation.

"Personally, I would immediately start the eviction process, but the woman is eight months pregnant and I know what a softy you are, so I will leave that decision up to you. At the very least, we need to evaluate the credit and criminal reports as soon as we get them back and determine if we can even feasibly allow them to stay. If so, we will need to get them to sign a lease right away. I will use one of my standard leases which will stipulate the amount of rent and the policy regarding payment and non-payment. I recommend you set the rent at nine hundred. If you end up evicting them, I would fix the place up and raise the rent to at least one thousand for any new tenants."

When Mary didn't respond, Sara continued, "The lease will also have some basic guidelines addressing what will be expected of the tenants regarding the maintenance of the property, what the pet policy is and a host of other things."

Mary took a deep breath as she tried to take in all that Sara had just said and figure out how she and her siblings were going to get out of this mess. She noticed Sara had stopped talking and was looking at her like she was waiting for her to say something so she asked, "When do you expect the reports to be back?"

"Probably tomorrow. I wasn't able to send the inquiries in until this morning since we only got the information back on the tenants on Friday and just received their signed release forms on Saturday."

Mary told Sara to let her know as soon as she got the reports in, and in the meantime she would talk to her family so they could make some tough decisions.

Sara apologized for having to be the bearer of bad news but she quickly added, "Welcome to the rental business! If you are going to be a landlord, you had better get used to it. It isn't always going to be an easy road. You are going to have a lot of pot holes along the way."

Mary thought about it and decided it was a lot like her mother's motto that life was not always a bed of roses. Well, she was going to make the best of it. She was going to be thankful for the three good tenants her family had and be happy that they had an opportunity to carry on their mother and father's legacy with helping out the teen pregnancy shelter. The house with Lilly's relatives in it was just one little pothole and she was going to figure out how to fill that hole with the best patch possible.

By the time Mary got home, Ellie was almost finished with the upstairs rooms. Mary called up to her from the bottom of the stairs, telling her to take a break and come down to eat some lunch. After they ate Mary sent Ellie to start on the cottage while she finished the upstairs. By three o'clock they were both finished and back in the kitchen drinking a glass of iced tea as they went over the upcoming reservations when the phone rang. Not wanting to take any more chances, Mary looked at the caller ID before picking it up. She saw that it was HB so she answered it.

HB barely said, "Hello," before he started chastising Mary for not taking his advice. He said that he had gotten a call from Charlotte and she had informed him that Mary had been very rude to her when she had called. He went on to say that Charlotte said she had called Mary to have a nice, civilized conversation about the cottages and that Mary had practically cursed her out for no apparent reason.

Mary innocently replied, "Now, HB, do I seem like the kind of person that would curse anyone out? In fact, in all the years that you have known me have you ever heard me use such inappropriate language?"

"Look, Mary, I have no desire to get in the middle of some cat fight between you and Charlotte, but please, if she, Lilly or Caroline call again, take my advice and DO NOT engage them in any conversation."

Mary promised HB she would be a good girl from now on and follow his orders if anyone of the three women called her again.

With the matter of Mary's "cursing" out of the way, HB went on to tell Mary that Charlotte said the reason she had originally called Mary was to ask her if anyone in her family would be interested in buying Caroline and her cottages. He said that they would be willing to sell them for seventy thousand dollars each. He said according to Charlotte the price is a steal considering all that they have put into them.

Mary replied, "I just bet it is. It is more likely that the price is about twenty percent more than what they have in them. I am sure they wouldn't be offering to sell them unless they think they can make a profit. I will have to ask my family about it but I know, even if they are interested in them, they are not going to give her near what she is asking. I'll let you know after I talk to them."

HB said, "OK, in the meantime, I sent you an email with a request for some information I need on filing your LLC paperwork. Please, get that back to me as soon as you can."

Mary went in her office to email HB the information he had just requested. When she finished with that task she texted her siblings to let them know to call in for a conference call at six thirty. Then she went into the kitchen to see what Ellie was up to. She was folding the last load of towels for the guest bathrooms. Mary told her when she was done she could go ahead and leave for the day.

After Ellie left, Mary put together a shrimp salad for her and Todd's supper. She wanted to be finished with supper in plenty of time to make her conference call with her family. Todd came home from the pool hall at five thirty and they were finished eating by six o'clock. Mary washed the few dishes they had used before going back to her office to get ready for her call. She wrote down a few notes to help her organize her thoughts. She expected this would be a long call as she had so much to cover.

Everyone called in on time except Joe. He had texted Mary while she was eating supper to say that he had to go visit one of his parishioners who just had a death in the family. Mary greeted her siblings, then got right down to business. She started with her phone call to Richard. Everyone was happy to hear that he had agreed to stay on to take care of Belle Rose and even more happy to hear that there was turmoil among Lilly's family members. As for all the repairs that were going to be needed on their family home, they decided to cross that bridge after Lilly was off the property for good.

Secondly, Mary told her siblings all about her phone conversation with Charlotte. When she told them what she had said to Charlotte, none of them could believe Mary, had actually used such colorful language.

Myrié, laughingly, said, "I think JJ and my bad habits may be rubbing off on you."

JJ replied, "Now, wait a minute, Myrié. I don't agree with that. I think it is more like we have increased her expressive vocabulary skills and that we have enlightened her in the art of being assertive when necessary."

Everyone laughed and joked for a few minutes until Mary brought the conversation back to the subject at hand by telling them of the follow up call she got from HB. When she told her siblings that Charlotte wanted to sell them their cottages for seventy thousand dollars each, they exchanged some colorful vocabulary of their own. Maddie was the first one to say anything constructive regarding the possible purchase of the cottages. She asked Mary if she had any idea how much the cottages were worth. Mary replied that she had no idea but she thought that seventy thousand was probably an inflated price just because

Charlotte would have most likely padded the asking price. She went on to say that she had only been in the twin cottages once and that was right after they had built them. Maddie asked her how big they were and Mary told her she would have to guess about eight hundred square feet each and that they both had two bedrooms, one bath, a small efficiency kitchen and a living area. She added that the best feature of the cottages was the front and back porches. Jake commented that they may not be able to keep the porches intact when they move the cottages as is often the case with such structures.

Maddie suggested that they should consider the opportunity to purchase the cottages as they would come in handy down the road if they had a lot of family members in town or they could even be used for short term rentals during the peak tourist seasons in Natchitoches.

This idea caught Mary's interest because she knew she was always booked solid during the period between Thanksgiving and New Year's when the town had its annual Christmas festival. She could always use extra cottages to rent out during that time of the year. She quickly decided that if her family was not interested in them, she would discuss the idea of purchasing them herself with Todd. After discussing the pros and cons of making an offer on the cottages, it was decided that they would table the idea for now until Mary could get Sara to go out and assess the actual value of the structures.

Speaking of Sara, that brought Mary to the topic of the rental properties, which was the most pressing issue on her list of topics to discuss with her family. She started off with the information on the three properties with the good tenants. They were all glad to hear the positive news and Mary quickly went on to explain the situation with the teen pregnancy shelter. When she finished they all agreed to let the shelter stay in the house but they had differing opinions on raising the rent to help fund the repairs. They finally decided that they would raise the rent but by only one hundred dollars a month for now and that they would pay to have the house fixed up to a decent standard.

Mary saved the discussion concerning the rent house from hell for last. When Mary first told them the tenants were relatives of Lilly's, JJ and Jake immediately said they should be evicted, and by the time she explained the extent of the situation, her sisters were calling for the same. Mary completely understood their reasoning, but the fact that the young woman was eight months pregnant had been weighing on her conscience ever since Sara told her about the situation. She promised her siblings that, if there was anything negative in the criminal or credit reports, she would immediately start the eviction process, but if not, she implored them to give the tenants a chance, at least for a couple of months until after the young woman had her baby. After a heated discussion on the matter, they all reluctantly agreed to let it ride for two months, but they stressed to Mary that if the tenants could not come up with the full amount of the rent, they would have to evict them.

Mary said she understood and quickly changed the subject to the upcoming family reunion in July. She asked if any of them had decided whether or not they would be able to come. Of course Martine said she and her family would be there. Jake said he would try to make it but, if he did, he would have to fly in on the morning of the 4th and fly out the following morning. JJ said that the week of July 4th was a busy time of the year for him as his restaurant did a lot of catering during the holiday weekend so it would be tough for him to make the trip but he would see what he could do. The others said they were still working on making the arrangements and couldn't make any promises yet. Mary thanked them all for even considering making the trip as she knew they had just taken time out of their busy schedules to be in town for their father's funeral. Before hanging up, JJ said he would get in touch with Joe to fill him in on all that they had discussed. Jake asked Mary if she had spoken to Uncle Tommy about whether or not he was interested in using any of the property for growing hay. Mary said she had forgotten all about it but that she would give him a call right after she hung up.

As Mary promised Jake, she immediately called Uncle Tommy. The phone rang twice before Aunt Doris answered it. When Mary asked her if her uncle was still up, her aunt told her she had caught him just in time because he usually went to bed at eight o'clock sharp, right after he watched the O'Reilly Factor on Fox News. Aunt Doris handed the phone to her husband and Uncle Tommy's gruff voice came across the line.

"Hello, Mary. Are you calling to tell me the Black Widow is giving you a hard time about moving cause, if she is, mine and Robby's offer still stands."

Mary, quickly, assured her uncle that was not the reason for her call. After she explained to him what she had actually called about, he told her that at his age taking on more farm land was not something he wanted to tackle. However, he suggested she call Robby as he said that he had recently bought a few more horses and had just told him the other day that he needed more grazing land. Uncle Tommy added that Robby had told him he was having to consider clearing some of the land he now uses for his riding trails to make more grazing land.

Mary's head started spinning when she heard this news! If Uncle Robby was interested in using some of their land, maybe she could talk her sisters and brothers into going in with him to invest in a barn and a riding arena. Maybe they could even put in a riding trail. She had been wanting to ask Uncle Robby if he would consider selling her Sunny for a while now, and this would give her a perfect opportunity to ask him. As soon as Mary thanked Uncle Tommy for the information and got off the phone with him she called her Uncle Robby.

The phone rang several times and Mary was just about to hang up when Uncle Robby answered. As soon as he did, Mary rushed into telling him why she had called.

"Well, that sounds like a perfect solution to my problem, Mary. How many acres do you think your brothers and sisters would be interested in leasing to me?"

Mary said she didn't think to ask them that earlier but that she would guess around fifteen acres.

When she told him about her idea to maybe eventually put a barn, a riding arena and a riding trail on the property as well, Uncle Robby said, "Well, it sounds like you have it all planned out."

"Not really, Uncle Robby. I just thought it would be nice to have a place of my own to go horseback riding on after all these years. Honestly, I am not even sure my brothers and sisters would be for the idea. The only one that likes riding besides me is Myrié and I don't think she has been on a horse in years.

"Uncle Robby interrupted her to say, "Honey, I am just teasing you. I think that is a great idea. I would be happy to build the barn and riding arena in exchange for the lease of the land. Besides, they will come in handy for me to use as well. As for the riding trail, I will see what I can do. Maybe I can have the trail run from your property to mine using the dirt road Tommy put in."

Mary couldn't believe her ears! She would talk her brothers and sisters into going along with the idea if it was the last thing she did! She excitedly accepted her uncle's offer and asked him how quickly he needed access to the land. He told her as soon as possible, as he had already purchased four new horses and they were being delivered next week. Mary told him she would get back to him as soon as she could. Then she timidly asked, "Umm, Uncle Robby, do you think you might consider selling Sunny to me, and if so, how much do you think the price would be?"

Uncle Robert thought about Mary's question for a few seconds while she held her breath, then he replied, "Well, let me think on that a while, Mary. As soon as you let me know when I can get access to the land, I will give you my answer."

Mary had hoped that her uncle would give her an answer right away but she didn't want to push her luck so she thanked him for agreeing to the other parts of her plan and told him she would call him back as soon as she had an answer for him on when he could access the land.

Mary fired off an email to Myrié right away telling her all about her conversation with Uncle Robby. She figured Myrié would be the easiest one to get on her side. Then she would get Myrié to help her with their other siblings. When she was finished writing her email, she left her office and went to the den to see what kind of a mood Todd was in. If he was in a good mood, she would tell him all about her conversation with Uncle Robby. However, when she got there she realized it was not a good time as he was engrossed in a documentary about World War II. She decided to wait until later so she went to take a shower instead. Her day had ended on an even better note than it had started, even though it had some pot holes in the middle.

Todd's Shrimp or Crawfish Étouffée

Ingredients

1 cup butter or margarine	½ cup milk
1 cup chopped onion	½ cup water
1 cup chopped celery	1 tbsp. parsley
3 to 5 cloves garlic, chopped	½ tsp. salt
¼ tsp. cayenne pepper	1 tbsp. flour
1 to 2 lbs. shrimp or crawfish	Cooked rice

Melt butter. Add celery, onions and garlic. Sauté until soft. Add flour and mix well. Mix milk in a little at a time and stir well. Add cayenne, salt to taste, parsley and shrimp or crawfish. Simmer until done and serve over hot cooked rice.

Note from Todd: This is an easy Étouffée recipe you can make when you need to put a meal together in a hurry. Plus, it is so simple just about anyone can make it whether they are "Cajun" or not. Try it the next time you have company and they will swear you must have some "Cajun" blood in you whether you do or not!

CHAPTER TWENTY-THREE

HATCHING A PLAN

On Tuesday morning Mary called Sara to see if she had gotten the reports on the tenants back yet. Sara said she hadn't and that it would probably not be until later in the day. With that question out of the way, Mary told Sara about the cottages Charlotte and Caroline wanted to sell her family for seventy thousand each. Mary asked her if she could go with her to look at them to help her figure out if they were worth the asking price and, if not, how much they were worth.

Sara said that she was tied up all day today but that she could do it the next afternoon. Mary told her that would be fine because she would have to call HB and have him set up an appointment with Charlotte as she didn't dare call her directly after the last fiasco.

Sara asked her what she meant by that and Mary replied, "You mean, I didn't tell you?"

"No, you didn't tell me. Out with it right now before I have to beat it out of you!"

Mary laughed as she told Sara about the conversation she had with Charlotte. Sara couldn't stop laughing.

When she finally caught her breath, she said, "Well, maybe there is hope for you after all."

"And what is that supposed to mean?"

Sara, quickly, apologized and, then told her she hated to cut the conversation short but that she had to run. Before hanging up, she told Mary to text her later to let her know what time she needed to meet her to go look at the cottages.

After her conversation with Sara, Mary called Aunt Tess and invited her over for coffee and cake. She had not spoken to her aunt since she had gone over to her house to give her the news about the judgment. She had a lot to tell her and she thought it would be nice to do it over a cup of coffee at her own house for a change. Aunt Tess, gladly, accepted her offer and said that she would be there in about an hour. While Mary waited for her aunt to arrive, she threw together a coffee cake. After she put it in the oven, she placed a call to HB. She asked him to call Charlotte and tell her that their family was somewhat interested in the cottages but that she needed to come look at them first. She told him that she wanted him to arrange for her and Sara to go over to see them sometime tomorrow if Charlotte was available. He said that he would see what he could do and get back to her. He also volunteered to accompany them, as he thought it was best for Mary not to be around Charlotte, Caroline or Lilly without legal representation. Mary gladly accepted his offer.

Aunt Tess arrived about ten thirty, just as Mary was taking the coffee cake out of the oven. She and Mary visited, while they drank their coffee and ate more slices than they should have of the warm, buttery cake. By the time Mary had filled Aunt Tess in on all that had happened over the last week, it was noon. She had discreetly left out the part about her use of the slightly colorful language in her conversation with Charlotte but she told her about Charlotte wanting to sell them the cottages.

Aunt Tess responded, "I wouldn't buy them from her unless you can get them for a really good price. I would hate to see any of that family make one more dollar of profit from my sister's children. They have already taken far too much from y'all!"

Mary understood her aunt's feelings on the matter and she assured her they would not buy the cottages unless they could get them for a good deal.

When Mary told Aunt Tess about all that she had learned concerning the rental property, she had much the same reaction as Mary. She definitely wanted Mary and her brothers and sisters to do all they could to keep the teen pregnancy shelter open as she knew how much it meant to her sister, and while she did not relish helping a relative of Lilly's, she was as softhearted as Mary and did not want to put a pregnant woman and her family out on the street.

Mary shared with Aunt Tess her last bit of family gossip about Uncle Robby and his horses, but she was disappointed when her aunt did not share in her excitement over the arrangement. Instead, she expressed concern that Mary had gone forward with the deal without first consulting her siblings. However, Mary told her not to worry. She said she knew she would be able to convince them that it was a win, win for everyone involved. Secretly, Mary prayed that would be the case.

Right after Aunt Tess left, Jane, called to let Mary know that she had contacted Charlotte and set up an appointment with her for two o'clock tomorrow afternoon for Mary to look at the cottages. She also told Mary that HB wanted her to come by his office before going out to the property so that he could follow her there. Mary was pretty sure HB knew how to get to Belle Rose so she suspected he just wanted to be sure she didn't get there before him and get into a confrontation with Charlotte, Caroline or Lilly. After hanging up with Jane, Mary texted Sara to let her know she would pick her up at one thirty.

Around three o'clock Mary checked her email box and saw that she had an email from Myrié and one from Sara. She opened the one from Myrié first. In it Myrié said she thought the deal with Uncle Robby was great but she said she was a little worried they were going to have a hard time convincing the others to go along with it. She said she would call Mary later so they could plan out a "Divide and Conquer" strategy. Mary was glad she had at least one sibling on her side. Now, if only she could convince six more.

When Mary opened the email from Sara, she saw that it contained the background reports on her tenants. All three of the "good" tenants reports had come back clean just as Sara suspected they would. Sara had told her earlier that she had not run a report on the shelter and Mary had agreed with her that it was not necessary. Mary had saved the report on the young couple for last fearing the worst, however, it actually wasn't that bad. Neither one had a criminal record, and the credit report was neither good nor bad as it didn't have much of anything on it. According to Sara's notes, she concluded that the couple must have done most of their business transactions in cash so far in their short adult life which would explain why they didn't have much of a credit history. This news meant that, according to the agreement she had made with her siblings, she could at least offer the couple a lease agreement. If they refused to sign it or said they couldn't afford to pay the nine hundred dollar a month rent or the one thousand dollar deposit, then it would be their decision to move. Mary emailed Sara back and asked her to set up an appointment sometime this week with the young couple so that she and Sara could visit them and get a first-hand look at what they were dealing with. Then, if all went well, they could get them to sign the lease. Since she was going to see Sara tomorrow she figured she would talk to her more about it then.

Mary answered a few more emails from various people requesting reservation information and before she knew it was five o'clock. She got up and went in the kitchen to put the potato casserole she had prepared earlier in the day in the oven for supper. She was putting a green salad together when Todd came back from the pool hall around five thirty. While they waited for the potato casserole to finish cooking, Mary told him about the rental property issues and he warned her against renting to the young couple. Mary told him she understood his concerns but that she had to at least give them a chance. He just shook his head at his softhearted wife as he poured himself a glass of iced tea. Mary took the potato casserole out of the oven and they both fixed their plates. While they ate, she casually mentioned the cottages and the deal she had made with her uncle. Again, her husband warned her but this time it was against getting her hopes up that Charlotte would reduce the price of the cottages or that her siblings would go along with the horse arrangement. By the time she finished talking to Todd, she was feeling downright gloomy. She had to remind herself that she had God on her side and that, with Him, all things were possible.

After dinner Mary cleaned the kitchen while she waited for Myrié to call. Finally, at seven fifteen the phone rang. Mary grabbed it on the first ring without even looking at the caller ID. Luckily, it was Myrié and not Lilly or Charlotte. As soon as Myrié started talking, Mary could tell she was almost as excited as she was about the prospect of having horses on their property. When Mary told her that she had asked Uncle Robby if she could buy Sunny, Myrié said, "Do you really think Uncle Robby would sell Sunny? You know how much he loves him."

Mary replied, "I know he does but he loves all of the horses that he has raised from colts. Besides, it's not like Sunny is his or Amanda's personal horse and Aunt Pauline doesn't even ride. His personal horse is Major, and Amanda has a paint named Apache. If he doesn't, though, maybe, he will at least board him at our place. That would be almost as good."

Myrié said, "OK, well, I'm in, so do you have a plan as to how we can convince the others?"

"Not really. I was hoping you would think of something."

"I've been thinking about it since I got your email but I haven't come up with much. You know it is going to be tough because it means we aren't going to see any kind of cash flow from the deal since it is a tradeoff arrangement, the use of the land for the barn, riding arena, riding trails and the use of the horses."

"Yeah, that pretty much sums it up. I'm thinking we might have a shot at convincing our sisters and maybe Joe but JJ and Jake are probably going to be the hold outs."

Myrié interrupted Mary to say, "I just thought of something. What if, instead of telling them how much we want the deal, we give them the impression that Uncle Robby really wants the deal and that he needs the land right away for his horses? We will make it all about Uncle Robby. We can tell them that after everything Uncle Robby and our other aunts and uncles did for us after Dad died, it is the least we could do. I mean, after all, they had our backs and now we need to pay them back by helping out Uncle Robby."

Mary exclaimed, "Myrié, you're a genius! I knew you would come through for me!"

Myrié, quickly, replied, "Wait a minute now. We don't know if it is going to work yet."

"I know, but it's a good plan. We need to start working on it as soon as possible because Uncle Robby said he needs the land ASAP."

"Why don't you write an email to everyone tonight explaining the situation? Lay it on really thick. Tell them how much of a bind Uncle Robby will be in if we don't help him out and tell them he needs an answer by, say, Friday. That gives them roughly two days to decide. We don't want to give them too long to think about it. You know, it's the pressure sales technique."

"Good idea! I can do that. I'll get on it right now. Thanks Myrié! You're a life saver. I owe you one."

"No you don't. Just make sure the horses are saddled up and ready to ride when I come to town."

Mary laughed as she told her sister it was a deal. Before hanging up she said, "I love you a bushel and a peck!"

And Myrié responded back, "And a hug around the neck!"

Mary went to her office and started working on the email right away. At nine o'clock she hit send as she said a prayer that the email would be convincing enough to get the job done.

CHAPTER TWENTY-FOUR

STEREOTYPES

Wednesday morning Sara called Mary to tell her she had spoken to the young pregnant woman related to Lilly in the rent house about the lease requirements and, quite surprisingly, she had assured her that they could afford the nine hundred dollars a month rent and the thousand dollar deposit. She said that she and Mary could come by the house this afternoon at four o'clock to get the money. Mary hoped this was good news as she didn't know if renting to the couple was going to work out. However, if they had nineteen hundred dollars to put down, they must have something going for them. Mary told Sara that it shouldn't be a problem for her to go to the house at four o'clock as their meeting with Charlotte was at two o'clock which should give them plenty of time to make the later appointment.

When Mary walked into Sara's office, Sara met her at the door, purse in hand. Mary turned around and followed her back out into the parking lot where they both got into Mary's car. As Mary pulled out she told Sara she had to swing by HB's office so that he could follow them out to Belle Rose.

Sara asked, "Doesn't HB know where your parent's property is? Better, yet, doesn't he have GPS?"

Mary replied yes to both questions, then, explained, "I think he is afraid of what I might say or do to poor little Charlotte. It seems she has convinced him that I am a dangerous woman that cannot be trusted."

Sara said, "You're kidding me, right? You, dangerous? That's like calling a week old puppy dangerous."

Sara's comparison made Mary smile. "Thanks for your vote of confidence in me. It's very much appreciated."

"You're welcome! Just don't make a liar out of me when we get there."

"I promise to be on my best behavior! Scouts honor!"

"Now, on the other hand, no one said anything about how I should behave and you know my reputation..."

"Yeah, I do and, if a skirmish breaks out, my money is on you. Charlotte won't have a chance."

They both laughed as Mary pulled into HB's office parking lot. Mary put the car in park, turned to Sara and said, "Do you want to wait here? I won't be but a minute."

Sara replied, "Yes, that's fine."

Mary got out of the car and went inside the office building. She returned five minutes later with HB trailing behind her. As he got into his car, Mary got back behind the wheel of hers. They both pulled out of the parking lot with Mary in the lead.

On the way to Belle Rose, Sara went over with Mary the things she would be looking at to determine a fair price for the cottages. When Mary pulled into the familiar driveway, she felt a slight tug at her heart. She was so relieved to know that all this would soon be over and Belle Rose would be back in the hands of the Bordelon family. She drove around the back of the property where the cottages were and parked the car in the gravel parking area. There were two other cars parked in the area and HB parked his car in the last spot. As they got out of their cars, Charlotte and Caroline came out of the cottage on the left. Charlotte addressed HB as if the two women standing next to him were not even there.

"Hello, HB. So glad you could make it."

Before HB could respond, Mary said, "Hello, Charlotte, Caroline. HB tells me you are interested in selling your cottages to my family. Would you mind if my property manager and I took a look around?"

Charlotte replied, "Well, I guess not. Isn't that why you are here?" Mary didn't bother to answer the rhetorical question.

She just walked up onto the porch, brushed past the two sisters and walked through the open doorway of the cottage.

Sara took a small notebook and pen out of her purse, as she followed Mary into the cottage, commenting along the way to Charlotte and Caroline, "These cottages sure are cute. Who built them for you?"

Charlotte, Caroline and HB followed Sara and Mary into the cottage as Caroline replied, "Our cousin, Shelby Fuller, built them. He's a contractor in town. Maybe you've heard of him?"

Sara responded, "I don't think so but the workmanship looks very good. Do you think I could get his number from you? I am always looking for a good contractor in my line of work."

Mary knew exactly what Sara was doing. She was trying to get Charlotte and Caroline off guard while she discreetly gathered information from them about the cottages and took notes on her observations. As they walked around the cottage, Sara asked several casual questions and Caroline readily provided answers to them. At the same time HB engaged Charlotte in conversation using his gentlemanly southern charms to distract her. With Sara keeping Caroline occupied and HB doing the same with Charlotte, Mary was able to do her own snooping without much interference from either of the sisters.

When Sara and Mary had finished looking at the first cottage, they started to walk towards the second cottage. However, Charlotte quickly stopped them saying there was no need to go in it since the cottages were virtually identical. If Charlotte had been anyone else, Mary may have taken this statement at face value but being that it was Charlotte, she immediately saw a red flag. She sensed that Charlotte must be hiding something. She took a sideways glance at Sara and could tell she was thinking the same thing.

Sara turned to Caroline, the obviously more mild mannered of the two sisters, and, sweetly, said, "Caroline, I understand the cottages are the same but I would really like to see what you have done with the other cottage. I just love all your decorating ideas. You have such a good eye for color schemes. Did you take interior design classes?"

Caroline blushed as she replied, "No, I didn't. I just like decorating."

As Sara talked to Caroline she continued to walk towards the other cottage and Caroline followed closely behind her. Charlotte started briskly walking towards the other cottage in an effort to catch up with Sara and Caroline.

As she walked she started to protest again but Mary interrupted her with a question concerning the asking price for the cottages. "Charlotte, HB tells me that you are asking seventy thousand for each cottage. Does that include all the furnishings, window dressings and other items currently in the cottages?"

Charlotte stopped walking towards the cottage on the right and turned towards Mary who was still standing on the porch of the cottage on the left. She responded. "No, but we would consider selling the cottages, turnkey, for an additional, five thousand."

In an effort to keep Charlotte's attention so Sara could get a good look inside the other cottage, Mary, quickly, responded back, "So are you saying five thousand more per cottage or five thousand more total?"

Charlotte took a second to think about Mary's question, then answered, "I mean five thousand more per cottage."

Mary said, "I see. Don't you think that is a little much? I mean the furnishings are nice but they definitely aren't high end pieces or antiques."

Charlotte replied, "I'll have you know that all the furniture in the cottages is high end!"

Mary knew this was a lie but she needed to keep Charlotte talking so she said, "I don't suppose you have receipts?"

Charlotte slowly replied, "Well, no. I didn't see a reason to keep the receipts but I assure you the furniture is high end."

Mary tried to think of something else to ask Charlotte to keep her attention. She quickly asked, "Umm, do you know how many square feet there are in each of the cottages?"

Charlotte replied, "I think they both have about a thousand."

Thank goodness Sara and Caroline walked out of the cottage on the right just then because Mary was running out of questions. She turned to Sara and said, "Have you gotten everything you need?

Sara replied, "Yes, I think so." Then she turned to Caroline and said, "Thank you so much for putting up with all my questions. You have been so helpful."

At that moment, HB spoke up and said, "Well, ladies, if you don't need anything else, we need to be on our way. We don't want to keep Charlotte and Caroline tied up all afternoon."

Charlotte interrupted him to say, "Well, do we have a deal or what?"

Mary replied, "Oh, I can't make a decision right now. I need to discuss with Sara her recommendations, then I will have to talk to my family before I can make you an offer." Charlotte impatiently asked, "How long do you think that will take?"

"Well, let's see. Today is Wednesday and it may take me a few days to reach all of my siblings so I'm thinking maybe by the first of next week."

Mary's answer clearly did not set well with Charlotte. She replied, "The first of next week? That's too long. We need an answer by Friday at the latest."

Caroline added, "Yeah, you know, if we can't make a deal, we have to make our moving arrangements and that could take a while. We don't even have a place to move the cottages to right now."

Charlotte shot Caroline a dirty look, clearly upset that she had let that bit of information out of the bag. Obviously, it did not help her negotiations with Mary for her to know that they did not have a place to put the cottages. On the other hand, Mary was quite pleased to hear this bit of information as it would be very helpful to her in the negotiating phase of the deal. In fact, she felt so grateful to Caroline that she said in a consolatory tone, "Well, in that case, I will do my best to get you an answer by Friday."

Then, she walked over to her car and got in without so much as a thank you or good bye.

Sara rushed over to the passenger side of the car and got in as HB went over and shook hands with the two sisters and graciously thanked them for their time. Then he got in his car and followed Mary out, down the driveway and off the property.

As Mary drove, Sara filled her in on what she had observed and what she thought about the fair market value of the cottages. First of all she told Mary that the second cottage was in worse shape than the first cottage. This didn't surprise Mary as she had suspected as much from the way Charlotte acted when they asked to see it. Over all, though, she said the cottages appeared to be well built and most of the issues were cosmetic. She said that all they really needed was a little TLC and a fresh coat of paint.

When Sara finished with her assessment of the cottages, Mary asked, "So what do you think would be a decent price for the two cottages together?"

"I think their asking price is a little high, especially since they are sitting on your family property." I would say a good counter offer for both cottages together would be one hundred twenty thousand considering you are not buying the land with the cottages."

"Well, in that case, I think I will offer them one hundred thousand."

"That's pretty low."

"Maybe not. Their cousin may have given them a discount. Besides, they are the ones that need to sell. My family is doing them a favor by offering to taking them off their hands."

"You are right about that. Just be aware that if you offer them one hundred thousand they are going to counter with something higher. Mary responded, "Well, they can counter all they want but my family only has so much money to offer. We don't have a lot of cash flow right now as Lilly got most of our father's cash assets and you know the situation with the rental property."

"I understand. You do have a good bargaining chip because, if you don't buy the cottages, they will either have to pay to have them moved or sell them to someone else who is willing to put out the money to move them. Plus they probably will not be able to move the porches so they will lose the value of them in the move."

"My thoughts, exactly!"

Mary pulled into Sara's office parking lot and they both got out of the car and went inside. It was three thirty and they needed to be at the rent house for four o'clock. Sara told Mary she just needed a few minutes to check her messages and to get the lease paperwork she had prepared for the tenants. Fifteen minutes later they pulled out of the parking lot in Sara's small work truck and at four o'clock on the dot they pulled up to the rent house.

As they got out of the truck and walked towards the house, they noticed the old car in the driveway that Sara's assistant had described, but the grass looked like it had been recently mowed. Sara knocked on the door twice before a tiny, young woman with what looked like a beach ball under her blouse, opened it. She had a heart shaped face and big blue eyes with long eyelashes. Her light brown hair was pulled up in a ponytail on the top of her head and she had wispy bangs. She shyly smiled at the visitors as she invited them in.

As Mary walked inside she held her breath in anticipation of the foul smells she was expecting from what Sara's assistant had told them, but instead all she smelled was a strong floral fragrance that must have been coming from a candle nearby. She suspected that it was masking any other lingering odors that may have been in the room. She was definitely relieved that no cats were present as she hated cats. She knew they were probably around just hiding somewhere but, at least, they weren't purring around her legs. The carpet was soiled looking, one wall had coloring marks on it and the furniture was shabby but the room was fairly neat except for one corner that had toys piled up in a laundry basket.

Sara introduced herself and Mary. The young woman said her name was Dixie Owens and then she turned to a tall muscular young man with a tattoo on his forearm. He had long hair and a short beard and was wearing a tank top and faded jeans. Dixie introduced him as her boyfriend, Trevor Gardner. There were two small children, a girl and a boy, sitting on the floor watching a Disney movie on the television. Dixie said their names were Violet and Noah. Trevor turned to the children and asked Violet to take her little brother to her room to play. The little girl, who looked about four years old, said, "Yes, Sir," as she got up and took her little brother's hand and they walked down the hallway to the back of the house. Trevor walked over and turned off the television as Dixie asked them if they wanted to sit at the dinette table at the far end of the room adjacent to the kitchen. Sara said that would be fine and all four of them walked across the room and took a seat at the table.

Dixie clasped her hands in front of her as she turned to Mary and said in a barely audible voice, "Ma'am, I understand you might have some reservations about letting Trevor and me stay in your house after what happened between my Aunt Lilly and your family, but I promise you we are honest, hardworking people and we won't disappoint you."

Next, it was Trevor who spoke up. He cleared his throat and, then said, "I know it might not look good, Dixie and me living together not being married and a kid on the way but I mean to do right by Dixie and her two kids and the baby. I love Dixie and I couldn't love Violet and Noah any more than I do now if they were my own. As soon as I can save up enough money to buy Dixie a nice ring and give her the wedding she deserves we are gonna get married."

Mary was glad she had not judged this young couple too quickly. They seemed to be breaking the stereotypes one tends to have in such situations.

Trevor pulled an envelope out of his back pocket and took a wad of cash out of it. As he handed the money to Mary he said, "It's all there, nine hundred for this month's rent and a thousand for the deposit. I just finished doing a carpenter job for Dr. Stevens and Dixie just got her tax refund check so we put our money together and, like I said, it's all there."

Mary took the money Trevor handed her as she asked, "Did you say you do carpenter work?"

Before Trevor could answer Mary's question, Dixie proudly replied, "Trevor can do anything with his hands. He can do carpenter work and plumbing and electrical and painting and all kinds of things. He's what they call a jack-of-all-trades. He would have fixed the toilet if we had had the money to rent the Roto-Rooter. There are a lot of things in this house that were broken and messed up when we moved into it a month ago. Trevor told my aunt he would do the repairs but she never bought the materials for him to do the work, and we didn't have the money after we paid Aunt Lilly for the rent."

Mary interrupted Dixie to ask, "What if I buy whatever Trevor needs and he does the work? Then I'll give you credit off your next month's rent."

Trevor gratefully, replied, "It's a deal, Mrs. LeBlanc!"

Mary didn't stop there. She said, "Trevor, I have a job you might be interested in. I have another rent house that needs a lot of work on it. Would you be interested in doing some of it for me at, say, fifteen dollars an hour and I'll buy all the materials?"

Trevor, quickly, answered, "Yes, Ma'am! I sure would!"

Sara shot Mary a warning glance as she interrupted her to say, "No electrical or plumbing work, though. You have to be certified to do that, and you'll have to work under my general contractor."

Trevor said, "I understand, no problem."

Mary said, "Sara is my property manager and she will coordinate everything with you."

Sara gave Trevor her card and told him to call her at her office first thing in the morning. Then Sara took out the lease contract and proceeded to go over it line by line with the young couple. When they came to the part about no pets, Dixie said, "Trevor gave the kids both kittens for Christmas. I told him it was a bad idea but he didn't listen to me. I was worried because Violet has a lot of allergies, and just like I suspected, as soon as we got the kittens, we found out she is allergic to cats too. We plan to get rid of them just as soon as we can find someone to take them."

Mary told the couple that she understood and, that she would give them a month to find the animals a new home. Sara went on to explain the rest of the lease in detail.

After the couple said that they understood what was expected of them, they signed the papers and Sara gave them a copy and put the original back in her folder. As Mary and Sara got up from the table, Mary asked Dixie when her due date was. Dixie said it was May 26th. Sara asked her if she knew what it was going to be yet. Dixie replied that she didn't and Trevor added that they wanted it to be a surprise. Mary and Sara shook hands with both of them and said good bye as they walked to the door and out to Sara's truck.

On the way back to Sara's office, Sara warned Mary about not getting too taken in by how sweet Dixie and Trevor appeared to be, as she knew all too well how deceiving tenants could be. Mary assured her friend that she would be on high alert.

When Sara and Mary arrived at Sara's office, it was nearly five thirty. Mary thanked Sara for all that she had done during the day for her. Then, the friends said goodbye and Mary got in her car to go home. As she pulled out of the parking lot she realized she was starving so she stopped at Lasyone's and picked up two shrimp po'boys and an order of fries. She resisted the temptation to also order a slice of pecan pie.

When Mary got home, Todd was waiting for her and he was happy to see she had brought po'boys for supper. As they ate, Mary told him all about her day. Afterwards, she went in the office to check her email. She was hoping she would have some emails from at least a few of her siblings in answer to the one she had sent them the night before but there wasn't even one. There were, however, a couple of reservation inquiries so she answered them. Then she started writing a new email to her siblings telling them all about the cottages and the young tenants. When she finished, she hit send and started to close her email box just as a new email popped up. It was from Mallory. Mary quickly clicked on the email. She was delighted when she read that Mallory agreed with the idea of Uncle Robby putting the horses on their family land. Mary thought, well, that's two sibling down. I just have five more to go.

CHAPTER TWENTY-FIVE

A LITTLE MISUNDERSTANDING

By Friday, Mary had received emails from all of her siblings and they had all weighed in on the pending issues. To Mary and Myrié's delight, everyone had, in the end, agreed to allow Uncle Robby to use the land for his horses. At first, JJ, Jake and Martine had been hesitant about the idea but they finally agreed to the plan after Mary and Myrié put the squeeze on them by stressing how much Uncle Robby needed the land and how they really shouldn't let him down. In other words, Myrié's idea worked like a charm.

Mary called Uncle Robby as soon as she got the go ahead from her siblings and let him know he could move the horses on to the property whenever he was ready. He thanked her and told her he would need to put up the fencing and feeding sheds first before he could move the horses. He said that he would probably go over to the property tomorrow to check everything out and see what needed to be done to accommodate the horses. Mary told him to do whatever he needed to and that she would contact Richard and let him know to be expecting him.

Then Mary asked her uncle the question she had been dying to ask him from the start. She asked if he had made a decision about letting her buy Sunny. He said that he had made a decision but he was sorry it wasn't the one she wanted. He said he didn't want to sell Sunny right now, but he softened the blow a bit when he told her that he would be putting the palomino horse at Belle Rose along with four more of his older horses and that she could ride him whenever she wanted. Mary was a little disappointed, but she was happy Sunny would at least be boarded at Belle Rose and she thanked her uncle for that.

As far as the cottages were concerned, only Maddie was interested in buying them. She made a proposal to Mary that if none of the other siblings had any objections to the cottages remaining on the family property, they go in together and make an offer on them. Mary liked the idea as she had already thought about buying the cottages herself but was afraid she would not be able to talk Todd into letting her buy both of them. None of the others had any objections to the plan so Mary ran it by Todd, and after some tense negotiation, she finally convinced him to at least allow her to make the offer as long as she didn't have to pay any more than fifty thousand dollars for her share. Maddie and Mary decided to offer one hundred thousand for both of the cottages as a package deal. If Charlotte and Caroline turned it down, then the deal was off. Mary told Maddie she would call HB and have him make the offer as she was afraid that, if she made the call directly it might get ugly. Maddie said she thought that was a wise decision.

When Mary told her siblings about her visit with Dixie and Trevor, none of them were as impressed as Mary had been. However, they agreed to let the couple stay for now since they had paid the deposit and the first month's rent and signed a new lease, but they warned Mary against getting sucked into the young couples' sob stories. JJ and Jake were especially concerned about Mary offering Trevor a job working on the other rent house, but Mary promised him that Sara's general contractor would be keeping a close eye on him. Speaking of the other rent house, Mary told her siblings that the pregnancy shelter had agreed to rent the two-story house for five hundred dollars and had signed the new lease.

Friday afternoon Mary called HB and asked him to make the offer on the cottages for her. He said that he would and that he would let her know as soon as he got Charlotte's answer. It didn't take long as a couple of hours later he called her back and said, "Mary, I am going to spare you all the interesting details of my enlightening conversation with the charming Charlotte Spencer as I don't think her comments bear repeating, but I can tell you that she rejected your offer and countered at one hundred and thirty thousand."

"Thanks for saving me from having to hear what she had to say. I am sure I am better off not knowing. As for the counter offer, you can tell her I don't really need the cottages, so I am not interested in negotiating the price. If she wants to sell, tell her my original offer stands but only until the end of the month when she is supposed to have the cottages moved. If she doesn't have them moved by then, I will start charging her rent for the land they are sitting on."

"Man, you drive a hard bargain!"

"Actually, it is Todd that is driving the hard bargain. He told me I can't offer her a penny more than fifty thousand for my half of the deal."

"Well, I will let her know and get back to you."

Mary thanked HB for his efforts and hung up the phone just as Ellie walked in the kitchen. She had been dusting the furniture in the front of the house. She asked Mary what else she needed her to do and Mary couldn't think of anything so she told her she could leave an hour early. Ellie protested a little bit but, in the end, she decided to take Mary up on her offer.

After supper, Mary went to her office and called Richard to let him know to be expecting her uncle some time tomorrow. After she explained to Richard the arrangement that she had made with her uncle to use the back fifteen acres of the property for his horses, she asked him if he had gotten the pump for the pond. He said that he had and that he had already installed it. She thanked him, and then asked him how things were going with Lilly. He said that she was in a real tizzy over having to move. He went on to say that her daughters were pressing her to move to the assisted living home in town but that she was trying to convince her new boyfriend, Roy Landry, into allowing her to move in with him. It seems Charlotte and Caroline were not that happy about their mother's new fling as they thought it was a tad unseemly that she would be dating a younger man, much less moving in with him.

Saturday morning, Mary fixed breakfast for her guests, then, went into town to get a manicure, pedicure and massage. Her children had sent her a Mother's Day card earlier in the week with a gift card for a day of pampering at the Rejuvenation Spa. She was thrilled with the gift as she figured she deserved some "pampering" after the stress she had been under lately. Just as she was leaving the salon, she got a phone call from Richard. He said that Robby had come over to take a look around the property but Lilly was having a conniption fit about it and was trying to make him leave. He said Lilly told Robby the property belonged to her until June 1 and he had no right to be on it until then. He said things were getting really heated between her uncle and Lilly and he didn't know what to do about it.

Mary didn't know what to do, either. She didn't want to call HB on a Saturday to ask him what her legal rights were, but she was pretty sure Lilly couldn't keep her off her family property. She told Richard to tell her uncle she was on her way over and to stay put but to stay clear of Lilly!

Mary drove as fast as she dared trying to get to Belle Rose. When she arrived, she found her uncle leaning up against his truck and Richard standing next to him. She didn't see Lilly anywhere, so she thought that was a good sign. She parked her car next to the truck, got out and immediately asked the two men what the situation was with Lilly. Richard said that she had gone in the house to call her lawyer.

Mary replied, "That's just great! I guess I don't have a choice now. I'm going to have to call HB, weekend or not."

Mary went back to her car, took her cell phone out of her purse and pressed the contact number for HB. When he answered she quickly explained the situation she was in. He told her that he couldn't come over right then but for her to tell Roy to call him if he had a problem with her being on the property. He went on to say that she could escort her uncle around the back of the property so that he could check things out but to tell him not to bring any equipment, building supplies, workers or horses onto the property. Mary thanked him, hung up the phone and walked back over to her uncle to tell him what HB had told her. However, before she could finish, she was interrupted by the sound of sirens blazing. She, along with her uncle and Richard, all turned to face the driveway as the sheriff's car came barreling towards them and right behind him was another car that Richard said belonged to Roy Landry.

Sheriff Jackson got out of his vehicle and strutted over to where Mary, Robby and Richard were standing as Roy Landry got out of his car and went into the house. When the sheriff got within a few feet of the three of them, he tilted his Stetson cowboy hat towards Mary, and then turned towards the men and said, "Hello, Robby, Richard." Both men responded back with a cautious "Hello, Sheriff."

Then the sheriff said, "Lilly says Robby here is trespassing on her property."

Mary jumped in between her uncle and the sheriff and proclaimed, "Sheriff, my uncle is here as my guest and this is my family property. My family has graciously given Lilly until the first of the month to move out of our family home, but that does not entitle her to all of the land surrounding the house."

Sheriff Jackson responded, "Look, I don't want any trouble but there is no reason to get a little old lady all upset. Why don't y'all just wait until after she gets moved to do whatever it is that y'all are wanting to do? It can't be that all fired up important that you can't wait a few weeks."

Mary was flustered but she wasn't going to give in so easily. "Sheriff, with all due respect, I'll decide what is important and not important for me to do on my family property, and I'll decide who can come on my family property and who cannot. My Uncle Robby and any other members of my family are welcome on this land anytime, day or night, and you can tell that to your Aunt Lilly!"

Just then Lilly came storming out of the house with Roy Landry close behind her. She started waving her arms and yelling something about having them arrested for trespassing while Roy seemed to be trying to quiet her down. By the time they reached the spot where the sheriff and the others were standing, she and Roy were in a heated argument over what she could or couldn't do in the eyes of the law.

Sheriff Jackson turned to his aunt and said, "Now Aunt Lilly, you need to calm down and let me handle this. You are going to get yourself all worked up for nothin'. Why don't you go on inside out of all this heat and let me do my job?"

Lilly looked up at her nephew, pointed her finger in his face and replied, "Daryl, don't talk to me like I am some old lady. I want Robert Perot arrested right this minute!"

Mary glanced over at her uncle and noticed the mischievous smile on his face. If she didn't know any better she would think that he was enjoying the whole ordeal.

"Sheriff, I hope you aren't seriously considering arresting my uncle. If you so much as try, I will have my lawyer on your case like white on rice!" Mary said.

Uncle Robby, finally, spoke up in his own defense. "Now, Mary, you can calm down. Thank you for wanting to defend me but I am perfectly capable of defending myself." Then he turned to the sheriff and said, "Daryl, if you want to arrest me, you go right ahead, but I must warn you that, if you do, Richard here will call my brother, Tommy, who in turn, will probably call our brother, Senator Perot, and I am sure you do not want to involve the good Senator in this little misunderstanding."

Sheriff Jackson looked like he had just swallowed a whole wad of tobacco. He knew all too well how popular and well-connected retired Senator Theodore Perot was in Natchitoches, not to mention in the whole state of Louisiana. He, quickly, turned to Lilly and said, "Aunt Lilly, there isn't going to be anyone gettin' arrested today. You go on inside, now like I told you, and I'll be in in a little while to talk to you."

Roy Landry took Lilly by the arm and firmly escorted her back to the house as she continued to protest. Sheriff Jackson turned back to Mary and said, "Like I said, before. I don't want any trouble here. Please, just do what y'all need to do and be on your way." With that he tipped his hat to Mary again, and then turned around and started walking briskly toward the house. Mary turned to her uncle and to Richard just as they both burst out laughing. She immediately joined them.

Mary walked around the property with her uncle and Richard, and the three discussed the best options for the fencing and sheds and the best location for a small barn and riding arena. They all agreed, however, that it would probably be best if Robby waited until June 1 to start making the additions to the property to accommodate his horses. Afterwards, Mary and her uncle left the property quietly without any more confrontations with Lilly.

Mary's Pecan Muffins

Ingredients

2 cup packed light brown sugar   1⅓ cup butter (softened)

1 cup all-purpose flour   4 eggs (beaten)

2 cups chopped pecans

Preheat oven to 350 degrees. Grease cups in a cup cake pan or line with paper liners. You can also use mini muffin pan. (Makes 18 cup cake size muffins or 36 mini muffins.) In a medium bowl beat the butter and eggs together. Add the brown sugar, then flour and pecans. Spoon batter into prepared cupcake/muffin cups. Cups should be about 2/3 full. Cook for 20 to 30 minutes depending on which size cups you are using. The mini muffins will take less time to cook then the cupcake size muffins will.

Watch closely as they will cook faster in some ovens than in others. Take out of oven when they are golden brown on top. If you are not using liners take out of mini muffin pan and let cool on a wire rack.

Note from Mary: I keep these on hand all the time for my B&B guests. They are so easy to whip up and they stay fresh for a long time. I can also make a lot of them at one time and freeze them in small bags of a dozen or a half a dozen. Then, whenever I need them, all I have to do is take them out of the freeze and pop them in the microwave for a few seconds. I have never had a guest not rave about them, unless of course they did not like pecans, but there are only a few people in this world who do not like pecans!

CHAPTER TWENTY-SIX

NEW ORLEANS FRIENDS

Sunday Morning after Mary's guests checked out, she and Todd went to church and then to Aunt Tess' house for a Mother's Day dinner. Aunt Tess' children were hosting what had become an annual family event and they had invited Mary and Todd over as they had done every Mother's Day since Mary's mom, Maggie, had passed away. With Mary's mom no longer alive and all of Mary's boys living out of town, it just seemed the most logical place for Mary to go on Mother's Day. Not only because Aunt Tess was Mary's mother's twin sister, but also because she was who Mary was named after and her godmother.

While Mary was at Aunt Tess', she went over to the family cemetery and put a vase of yellow roses she had picked from her garden in front of her parents' bench. She said a prayer that they were getting along in heaven and that her mom had not killed her dad all over again when he got up there for putting her children and siblings through so much.

Sunday afternoon Mary and her sisters texted back and forth wishing each other Happy Mother's Day. Mary's boys and their families also called her to wish her Happy Mother's Day and to tell her how much they wished they could have been with her. Mary thanked them all again for the wonderful Day of Pampering gift card and she wished all of her daughters-in-law Happy Mother's Day too. Afterwards, Mary said to herself the same thing she said every Mother's Day, "Maybe next year I will get to see at least one of my boys for Mother's Day,..."

On Monday, HB called Mary to learn the status of the situation with Lilly and her uncle. Mary told him about their encounter with the sheriff but assured him all was calm for now. However, she told him she wasn't sure how long the truce would last. She said she and her entire family would be happy when Lilly and her daughters left Belle Rose for good. HB said he completely understood how they felt and that he had some news of his own concerning that subject. He said that he had spoken to Charlotte at length about the cottages, and she said that she and Caroline could not take a penny less than one hundred twenty thousand dollars for the cottages.

Mary asked, "Did you tell her one hundred thousand was my final offer?"

"Yes, I did, but I don't think she is getting it."

"Then tell her she and Caroline better have their cottages moved by June 1, or they will not be getting a penny from me for them!"

"I told her that too, but like I said, I don't think she is getting it."

"OK, then call Roy Landry and tell him to explain it to her. I don't want any theatrics on June 1st when I go out to Belle Rose to make sure all three of them are off of my family property."

HB said, "I will give him a call, but I don't know if he will have any more luck with that woman than I did. She's almost as stubborn as her mother."

When Mary hung up the phone, she was not in a good mood. She tried to find something to do to get her mind off Lilly and Charlotte. She decided to go to her office and make a few phone calls. First, she called Sylvia. She knew if anyone could cheer her up it was Sylvia. Plus, she wanted to be sure there had not been any changes to her friends' plans and that they were still coming on the thirteenth. Sylvia said that they were definitely coming Wednesday and that they should be arriving around two o'clock in the afternoon. The two friends talked for a while and by the time Mary hung up she did feel much better. As soon as Mary hung up she called Lola's bakery to order a birthday cake for Gail.

Last, Mary called Sara to check on the progress with the repairs to the rent houses. Sara said that she had bought some paint for Trevor so that he could start painting the rent house, but it hadn't occurred to her that Dixie couldn't be around paint fumes while she was pregnant, so they had to put that on hold until after the baby was born. In the meantime, though, he had steam cleaned all the carpets and found new homes for the cats. Now he was at the other rent house working with her general contractor, Tony, and Tony had reported back to her that Trevor was doing an excellent job. He said they should have all the repairs on that house finished by the end of the month. Mary thanked her friend for taking care of the repairs and, then, she filled her in on the latest news with Lilly and her daughters. Sara got a kick out of the story about Lilly, the sheriff and Uncle Robby and she said she wasn't surprised Charlotte didn't want to accept Mary's offer to buy the cottages. She again told Mary that it was a low offer, but Mary again reminded her that she couldn't go any higher and that if Charlotte didn't want to accept the offer, she could sell them to someone else or move them before June 1.

After Mary's conversation with Sara, she went to the kitchen to see what Ellie was up to. Ellie was washing dishes and singing to herself. When she heard Mary come in the room she stopped singing and started talking. She told Mary a story about something one of her great grandchildren had done and that her granddaughter had posted on YouTube. The story was so funny that Mary forgot all about Charlotte and was laughing uncontrollably when the phone rang.

As soon as Mary said hello, she wanted to kick herself once again for not looking at the caller ID. On the other end of the line Charlotte's voice sang out. She went into a whole list of reasons why Mary should be more than happy to buy the cottages for one hundred twenty thousand. As soon as she took a breath, Mary jumped in. "Charlotte, as HB already told you, hardly anyone in my family wants the cottages. You are lucky my sister, Maddie, and I are agreeing to take them off your hands for one hundred thousand. If you don't want to sell them for that amount, the simple solution is for you to move them."

Charlotte whined, "But it's going to cost us too much to move them."

"Well, I am sorry but that is not my problem."

"You don't suppose you could give us an extension..."

"No, I do not."

"I can't believe how unreasonable you are being! You know, you used to be a pretty nice person but you've turned into a real jerk!"

Mary couldn't believe this prima donna had just called her a jerk! No one had ever called her a jerk before. She slammed the phone down and turned to look at Ellie as she said, "You aren't going to believe what she called me!"

Ellie replied, "No matter what nonsense that women is talkin,' you shouldn't let it upset you. Just consider the source."

Mary thought a few seconds about what Ellie had just said, then, she responded, "You know what, Ellie, you are exactly right. I'm not going to let her get to me. She isn't worth it. I've got wonderful friends who think I am a very nice person and they're coming to see me in just a couple of days. I am going to focus my attention on getting ready for their visit and forget all about snotty Miss Charlotte."

"Now, you're talkin,' Sugar."

With that, Mary turned her attention to planning for her company and never gave Charlotte another thought.

Wednesday morning Mary and Ellie put the finishing touches on the cottage. They put a mixture of fresh picked flowers from Mary's garden in vases in every bedroom and on the kitchen table. They put baskets of fresh fruit, snacks and individually wrapped pralines in each bedroom too. They stocked the refrigerator with soft drinks, bottled water and juice. At ten o'clock, Mary left to go pick up the birthday cake at Lola's. When she got back, she made a batch of pecan muffins so they would be fresh from the oven when her guests arrived. Finally, at two fifteen, they pulled into the driveway. Mary was out the door in seconds running to greet her friends. She hugged each one and told them how much she appreciated them coming to visit her. Sylvia said they wished they could have come sooner and the others echoed her sentiments.

When Mary got to Gail she told her once again how sorry she was about her mom and Gail said the same about Mary's dad. They all went into the house where Ellie was waiting and the ladies greeted the housekeeper like she was a dear friend as well. Since all of them had been to visit Mary on several occasions, they had met Ellie before and to know Ellie was to love her. They all sat around the table as Ellie poured cups of coffee for everyone. They snacked on the freshly baked muffins as they talked about everything from husbands to kids to the latest gossip. Todd came in and hugs were shared all around before he excused himself and left the women to go back to their gossiping. Before they knew it, it was nearly five o'clock. Ellie said her goodbyes and left, then the ladies, with Todd's help, went out to the car to get their luggage. When they went inside the cottage, they all profusely complimented Mary on how nice everything was and told her she should not have gone to so much trouble, but of course, they knew there was no use saying it because she always did. At six thirty Sara came to the house to join the party and they all went to The Landing for dinner and then to a movie. When they returned home, Mary brought out the birthday cake. After Claire led the women in a chorus of Happy Birthday and Gail blew out the candles, they had cake and wine for a midnight snack.

Thursday the friends spent all morning shopping at the local shops along Front Street. They went to Magieaux's for lunch, then did some sightseeing. By the time they returned home everyone was exhausted. Todd prepared a delicious dinner for the women and they all ate until they couldn't eat another bite. Then they went to the cottage and drank some of Karen's homemade Amaretto with pineapple juice while they talked like school girls until midnight.

Friday morning came too soon. Mary made her signature Praline French Toast for breakfast and her friends all raved about how delicious it was calling Mary the "Hostess with the Mostest." When the women got ready to leave, Mary cried as she promised them she would return the favor by coming to visit them soon. As they pulled out of the driveway, Mary wiped her tears from her eyes and went back inside to get ready for her weekend guests.

Todd's Jambalaya

Ingredients

1 bell pepper (green or red) chopped

1 onion, chopped

1 tbsp. olive oil

1 clove garlic, chopped

1 bay leaf

1 sprig thyme

¼ cup parsley

1 link andouille sausage, sliced

1 lb. small peeled shrimp

1 can RoTel tomatoes

1 cup uncooked rice

salt and pepper

2 cups chicken broth

Using a large covered skillet, place oil, peppers, onion, salt and pepper in skillet and simmer for 5 minutes. Add sausage and garlic and cook for another 5 minutes. Add tomatoes, bay leaf, thyme, rice and broth. Bring to a full rolling boil then add shrimp. Stir and cover reducing heat to a low simmer. Do not stir or open lid. Cook for 40 minutes. Let sit for 10 minutes then add parsley, stir and let sit for another 5 minutes. Serve and enjoy!

Note from Todd: This is a warm, stick to your ribs kind of meal. Toast some buttered French bread and make a salad and you'll have a feast!

CHAPTER TWENTY-SEVEN

WHAT GOES AROUND COMES AROUND!

Monday, May 18, was Maggie's birthday. That afternoon, Mary was putting another bouquet of yellow roses and spring flowers together. She was going to go out to Aunt Tess' house so that she could swap the flower arrangement out with the one she had put by her parents' bench on Mother's Day. She was almost finished with the arrangement when the phone rang. She was careful to check the caller ID this time not wanting anymore surprises from Lilly or Charlotte. When she saw that it was Sara, she picked up the phone and cheerfully said "Hello."

Sara sounded so excited on the other end of the line as she delivered the good news to Mary that Dixie had given birth to a healthy, six-pound, two-ounce baby girl earlier that morning. Mary told her that was indeed good news and asked Sara how Dixie was doing. She said that mother and baby were both doing fine. Mary asked Sara if she knew what Dixie and Trevor had decided to name the baby. Sara replied that they had named her Emily Grace. Sara said she planned to order some flowers to be sent to the hospital and she was sending a case of diapers to the house. Mary asked her to please put her name on the cards for the gifts, as well, and she would give her the money for them when she saw her. Sara said of course she would be more than happy to do so. After Mary got off the phone, she tied a ribbon around the vase with the roses and told Ellie she would be back in a couple of hours.

When Mary got to Aunt Tess' house, they walked out to the cemetery together and Mary swapped out the vases of roses next to her parents' bench. Mary said a short prayer, and Aunt Tess did the same. Then they walked back to the house where Tess invited Mary inside for a cup of coffee. Mary thanked her for the offer but said she had some errands to run. She didn't mention that one of them was to take a ride by Belle Rose to see if Charlotte and Caroline had done anything about the cottages yet and to see if Lilly had started packing.

Mary drove down the long driveway thinking to herself that in two weeks she would, once again, be able to drive down it feeling like she had when her mother was alive. Then, she had always felt like she was coming home, but since her father had married Lilly, whenever she came to Belle Rose, she felt like she was a visitor. All that would be over with in just fourteen days. As far as she was concerned, it couldn't come soon enough!

Mary drove around to where the cottages were and parked her car. She didn't see anyone so she got out and started walking around, but all of a sudden, she heard Lilly's shrilled voice yelling "Where do you think you are going!" She turned in time to see the golf cart speeding towards her with Lilly behind the wheel. Mary stood still as the cart got closer to her. When it was within a few feet of her it suddenly came to a stop.

Lilly sounded out of breath as she continued in her shrilled voice, "What do you think you are doing out here? You can't just come here unannounced!"

Mary replied in the sweetest voice she could manage, "Well, hello to you, too, Lilly. Isn't it a lovely day? Oh, and in answer to your question, I am here checking on the property for my family. You know the property that we own since our father left it to us in his official will. By the way, how are you coming along with your packing? Did you decide where you will be moving to?"

Lilly replied, "Where I will be moving to is none of your business! Besides, I may not be moving at all. I am continuing to explore all my legal options. So if I were you, dear, I wouldn't be counting my chickens before they hatch. You may think your family owns this property, but you know what they say, when it comes to ownership, possession is nine-tenths of the law!"

With that, Lilly turned the golf cart around and sped back to the house as quickly as she had come leaving Mary stunned. She should have known Lilly was not going to go easily. Mary got back in her car and headed straight for HB's office. When she arrived at her destination, she walked right past Jane and into the lawyer's inner office. HB was on the phone but he took one look at Mary and knew something was definitely wrong. He quickly told the person on the other line he would get back to them, and then hung up the phone as he addressed Mary.

"Mary, are you OK? You look like you just saw a ghost. Here, sit down."

Mary was too upset to sit. She paced around the office as she angrily explained to HB why she was so upset. When she finished, HB calmly said, "It's going to be OK, Mary. I know for a fact that she definitely has not filed an appeal. I will send another certified letter to her and to Roy reminding them that we fully expect her to be off the property no later than June 1. Furthermore, I will notify them that we intend to be at the property with law enforcement back up at nine o'clock sharp on June 1 and that we intend to take possession of the property at that time."

"Have you forgotten that her nephew is the sheriff? How do you intend to get him to back you up?"

"Well, he may be her nephew but, as the sheriff of Natchitoches Parish, he cannot refuse to enforce a court order, which we have."

Mary still wasn't convinced, so HB promised her he would go talk to Sheriff Jackson and give him a heads up about the situation with his aunt. He figured that the sheriff would like as little fireworks as possible concerning this matter and would probably do what he could to convince his aunt to vacate the property before Mary and HB arrived on the morning of June 1. However, HB advised Mary that it would be a good idea if she stayed off the property until then. Mary finally agreed to let HB handle it his way and to not go back on the property, but she told him to be sure to call her as soon as he spoke to the sheriff. After HB promised her that he would, she left the office a little less upset than she had been when she arrived but she was still not going to sleep easy until Lilly was off Belle Rose for good.

Mary went straight home after her meeting with HB. She wasn't in any mood to visit Sara while she was in town or to do any shopping. When she walked into the kitchen, Ellie instantly noticed something was wrong. At first she thought maybe Mary was depressed about it being her mother's birthday but she didn't notice her being upset when she had left the house earlier. She asked Mary what was wrong but she denied being upset about anything. Ellie, however, didn't give up and after a few more attempts, she was able to drag it out of her. Once Ellie heard what had happened, she was just as upset as Mary.

She exclaimed, "That no good for nothin' hussy!"

"See, I knew I shouldn't have told you. There is no use in the both of us being upset. It isn't going to solve anything. We just need to let HB handle it."

Ellie, countered, "No, what we need to do is tell Mr. Tommy and Mr. Robby what that hussy said. They'll put a fire under her and in no time she'll be high tailing it off y'all's property for good!"

"Oh, no you don't! Don't you dare tell my uncles about this!"

Mary made Ellie promise she wouldn't tell her uncles a word about what had happened between her and Lilly. Ellie grumbled about it but she, finally gave her word. Before she left Mary reminded her about her promise just in case she were to somehow forget about it after she left. When Todd came home she told him what had happened but he merely responded that letting HB handle it was the smart thing to do.

As Mary had feared, she didn't sleep much Monday night and Tuesday morning she woke up with a migraine headache. Thankfully, she didn't have any guests to attend to so she took some Excedrin and went back to bed. She didn't get up until almost noon. That afternoon, HB called to tell her that he had spoken to both Roy Landry and the sheriff and they had both assured him that Lilly and her daughters would be off the Bordelon property by June 1. Plus he had sent the certified letters as he had said he would just as an added precaution.

After her phone conversation with HB, Mary felt a little better. When Todd came home from the pool hall, she talked him in to taking her out for dinner, and when they returned, he talked her into watching a movie with him. That night she slept much better than she had the night before.

Wednesday, Mary decided to go visit Dixie and her new baby. She called Sara to see if she wanted to join her and she said that she did. Mary went by Ya Ya's Children's Boutique to pick out a cute outfit for the baby before going by Sara's office to pick her up. When they arrived at the rent house, they immediately noticed the broken down car had been replaced by a used but nice looking Red Ford Explorer. They knocked lightly on the door instead of ringing the doorbell as they did not want to risk waking the baby if she happened to be asleep. Trevor answered the door and welcomed them both inside. Dixie was sitting on the couch holding the baby and the other two children were sitting on either side of her admiring their new little sister. Dixie and Trevor both thanked the two women over and over again for the flowers and diapers and for giving Trevor a job.

Sara replied, "It is us who should be thanking you. My contractor, Tony, tells me you are the best carpenter he has ever worked with."

Trevor blushed as Dixie said, "I told you he was good with his hands." Mary and Sara laughed as Trevor blushed even more.

Mary decided to help Trevor out by changing the subject. She asked him about the new car in the driveway and he told her that he had bought it from Tony. He said that it had been Tony's wife's car and that Tony had just bought her a new one so he sold her old one to him. He went on to explain that Tony wanted to make sure he had a way to get to work on time so he sold the car to him really cheap and he was letting him pay for it in monthly installments. Dixie said that she really liked the car because it had safety locks and plenty of room for all three of the kids' car seats. Then she asked Mary and Sara if they wanted to hold the baby. Each one took a turn holding Emily Grace and they oohed and aahed over how beautiful and precious she was. After Dixie had unwrapped the baby gift Mary had brought and sincerely thanked her for it, Mary and Sara said their goodbyes to the young family and left.

Mary and Sara went to lunch at Maglieaux's, then Mary dropped Sara back off at her office. On the way home Mary stopped off and picked up some much needed groceries. When she got home, Ellie told her she had had several phone calls, mostly from people wanting reservation information but one call had been from Caroline. Mary's ears perked up as soon as she heard the familiar name. She asked Ellie if Caroline had mentioned what she was calling about. Ellie said that Caroline was calling to offer her a deal on her cottage.

Mary asked, "Did she say what that deal was?"

"No she just asked me to have you call her. I wrote her number down and left it by your phone in your office with the other messages."

Mary went to her office to return the calls. She saved the one to Caroline until last. When Caroline answered the phone, she sounded very nervous. She told Mary that Charlotte had warned her not to call Mary and offer her any kind of deal but she said she really needed the money as she had two kids in college to pay for. Mary once again asked where the money was that they were supposed to get from her father's fifty thousand dollar life insurance policy. She said that her mother had spent the money on legal fees and paying off her extensive credit card debts. She told Mary that her mother had a couple of credit cards that she had since before she married Jack and she had maxed both of them out.

Then Caroline dropped the real bombshell. She said that Lilly should be receiving the money from Jack's IRA account soon but that she didn't want to give her daughters any of it because she needed it to support her and her new boyfriend. It seems Roy had not been a very good steward of his own finances and was in a lot of debt. Caroline and Charlotte were afraid he had started seeing their mother in an effort to get her money. He agreed to let Lilly move in with him only after she agreed to pay off the second mortgage on his house. Caroline went on to say that Roy planned to retire in a month, and when he did, he and Lilly were going to go on a cruise to Alaska. Lilly already booked the vacation and Caroline said her mother was paying for the whole thing. Not to mention that Roy was making all kinds of other retirement plans with Lilly, all of which would, undoubtedly, be funded by her mother. Caroline ended the saga by lamenting, "It's downright disgusting, Mary! They are acting like two teenagers in love and, all of a sudden, our mother only has eyes for Roy! We have never seen her like this before. Charlotte and I tried to talk some sense into her, but she won't listen to anything we have to say!"

Mary had sat, quietly, listening to Caroline talk for the last several minutes, and when she finally finished, Mary was almost too stunned to respond to all that she had revealed. She suspected Roy Landry's sudden retirement plans had something to do with the ethics board's investigation HB had mentioned. Mary heard Caroline say, "Mary, are you there?"

Mary replied, "Yes, Caroline, I'm here. I'm sorry to hear what's happening to your mother. It seems Lilly has fallen head over heels in love with the dashing young lawyer and he is using his masculine charms to take advantage of your poor, unsuspecting mother. Does that about sum it up?"

"Well, yeah, that's about it in a nut shell. Can you believe he would do such a thing to our mother and to our family?"

Mary, sarcastically, replied, "No, I cannot believe anyone would do such a horrible thing to an innocent elderly person such as your mother."

It took a few seconds for what Mary said to sink in and for Caroline to realize Mary was comparing what was happening to Lilly to what her mother had done to Jack and his family. When she finally got the connection, she was a little embarrassed, so she quickly, changed the subject. She asked Mary if she would be interested in buying just her cottage for fifty thousand dollars. Mary asked her which cottage was hers and she said the one on the right. Mary thought about it for all of two seconds before declining the offer saying that she would only be interested in both of the cottages for the one hundred thousand she had previously offered. She told Caroline she needed to talk to her sister and convince her to accept her offer or they would both need to move their cottages by June 1. Caroline complained that she had already tried but Charlotte wasn't budging even though they still did not have a place to move the cottages to or the money to have them moved.

Mary replied that that wasn't her problem and that she needed an answer by the end of the week if she was to make the arrangements for the sale and the transfer of the money before June 1. Mary hung up the phone and walked back into the kitchen to tell Ellie what she had learned from her conversation with Caroline.

When Mary finished her story, Ellie commented, "You know what they say, 'What goes around comes around.' Miss Lilly just got what she had comin' to her and so did her daughters!"

CHAPTER TWENTY-EIGHT

THERE'S NO PLACE LIKE HOME

Friday afternoon Mary got another call from Caroline. She said that she had finally convinced Charlotte to take Mary's offer but it wasn't easy. She said that she had to agree to take only forty-five thousand for her share of the money and to let Charlotte have the other fifty-five thousand. Mary thought it wasn't that bad of an arrangement for the sisters as Charlotte's cottage was in better condition than Caroline's was so it made sense for her to get more for hers. Mary told Caroline she would have her lawyer draw up the necessary paperwork and that his secretary would call her when she and Charlotte could come in to sign it and get their checks.

After Mary hung up from talking to Caroline she called Maddie to let her know that they had gotten the deal for the two cottages. She explained to her sister that one cottage was in better shape than the other and that they would be paying fifty-five thousand for it and forty-five thousand for the other cottage. She asked Maddie which cottage she wanted and she said she would prefer the one that was in the better condition as she didn't want to have to do too much to it. That worked for Mary because it meant she would not have to explain to Todd that she would have to pay five thousand more than what they had agreed on for their cottage. Mary told Maddie she would have HB call her to let her know what her total cost would be and to arrange the purchase paperwork.

With the cottage business settled, Maddie asked Mary how things were going with Lilly. Mary told her what had happened earlier in the week but she said that HB had assured her everything would go smoothly on the first. Maddie said she really wished she could be there to see Lilly actually leave Belle Rose, but she told Mary she had some news that was almost as good. She told Mary that she would be in between projects from June 20 to July 10 so she would have some time off. She said that she had already decided to come to Natchitoches for the family reunion on July 4th, but now that they knew they were going to get the cottages, she would try to come in at least a week early and they could renovate the cottages together while she was in town. Mary thought that was a wonderful idea and she told Maddie as soon as she took over the property she would send her pictures of the cottages so they could start making plans for what they wanted to do with them.

When Mary hung up the phone, she was on cloud nine. She was so excited about Maddie's upcoming visit she almost forgot to call HB to let him know she needed him to draw up the paperwork for the deal. After she made the call and gave HB all the necessary information, she went to give the good news to Ellie. They didn't have much time to celebrate, though, because they were expecting several guests for the Memorial Day weekend.

The three day weekend flew by with all the guests to attend to. Mary barely had time to send an email to her siblings updating them on the latest developments concerning the property and Lilly and to remind them about the family reunion. She got a return email from Jake saying that he would not be able to make it after all as he was going to have to work through the holiday. JJ and Joe sent similar emails so it looked like it was just going to be the sisters. Mary knew she, Martine and Maddie would be there so that just left Myrié and Mallory. By Sunday night she had not heard back from them yet so she hoped that was a good sign that they were still working on trying to make arrangements to come. As for Mary's kids, it didn't look like any of them would be coming in town for the reunion and her birthday. However, they said they were all going to try to make it sometime in August so she was happy about that.

Tuesday Mary spent the day catching up on the laundry after the big weekend, and Wednesday she and Ellie spent the day cleaning the guest rooms and cottage. Wednesday afternoon Jane called and asked Mary if she could come in on Friday morning to sign the papers for the transfer of ownership for the cottages. She said that HB had already had her schedule Charlotte and Caroline to come in Friday afternoon so that they would not have to be in the office at the same time as Mary. Mary said that that was very thoughtful of him and that she would come in at ten o'clock Friday morning. Jane told her that she had already arranged to have all the paperwork for Maddie done electronically. Mary thanked her and asked her to thank HB for her, also.

Thursday Mary had a couple of walk-in reservations which she was thankful for because it gave her something to occupy her mind instead of focusing on the fact that June 1 was less than four days away. Friday morning, after she went to HB's office to sign the paperwork for the Caroline's cottage, she went to Sara's office to check on her family rent houses. Sara told her everything was going fine. She said that all the tenants had signed the new leases and that Tony and Trevor had finished the repairs on the two story house. The two women visited for a little while, then Mary got up to leave as she didn't want to take up too much of Sara's time while she was working. As she turned to walk out of the office, she noticed a striking painting of a mother and child hanging on the wall. She didn't recall the painting being there before so she asked Sara where she had gotten it.

Sara replied, "Oh, that was a gift from Dixie."

Mary was a little surprised by the answer as she thought the painting looked to be pretty expensive. She asked, "Do you know where she got it?"

Sara laughed as she said, "Nowhere. She painted it herself."

Mary looked amazed as she commented, "My goodness! That couple is full of surprises! Dixie kept telling us how good Trevor was with his hands and she never said a word about how good she was with hers!"

"You are right about that. I offered to buy the painting from her but she wouldn't hear of it. She said it was the least she could do after everything I had done for her and Trevor. I didn't want to offend her so I didn't push it but she could really make some money selling her paintings, especially if she got them framed. I got this one framed myself at Cane River Gallery. I am going to ask Meredith at the Art Guild down the street to take a look at some of her work."

Mary told Sara that was an excellent idea and she said she would be Dixie's first customer. Sara said she didn't want to spoil Dixie's surprise but she was pretty sure she was already working on a painting for Mary. Mary tried to press Sara to tell her what the painting was of, but Sara said she had already said more than she should have. So, Mary left the office and headed to Lola's Sweet Creations Bakery to get a few treats for her guests.

Saturday, Mary rode out to Uncle Robby's house to go over with him his plans for the barn. When she arrived, Aunt Pauline greeted her with open arms and told her she was just in time for lunch. After they ate a hearty meal of field peas, corn on the cob, creamy mashed potatoes and fried chicken, Mary and her uncle went into his den to go over the plans. Mary loved her uncle's ideas for the barn and couldn't wait for him to get started building it. Uncle Robby seemed almost as excited as she was about the project and he said he wanted to get started as soon as possible. Mary told him she was supposed to meet HB at Belle Rose at nine o'clock sharp Monday morning. She told him Sheriff Jackson was supposed to come along just in case they had any problems from Lilly but that she didn't think there would be any as a little bird had told her Lilly was making plans to move in with her new beau. She went on to tell her uncle about her phone conversation with Caroline. Uncle Robby just smiled and said that God works in mysterious ways. If Mary didn't know any better she would have thought from her uncle's comment that he had something to do with Roy Landry and Lilly's budding romance, but she knew that was impossible so she just told him to meet her at Belle Rose at nine thirty Monday morning.

Mary had a hard time calming her nervous energy Sunday. She did what she could to keep busy but nothing seemed to work. She went to bed early in an effort to make the morning come sooner but she couldn't sleep so she got up, went to her office and searched online for ideas of ways to renovate her new cottage. Around midnight, she went back to bed and tossed and turned some more until she finally fell asleep.

As soon as her alarm clock went off Monday morning, she jumped out of bed, showered and got dressed. When she went to the kitchen Todd was there fixing breakfast. By the time they finished eating, Ellie had arrived. She had come in an hour early so that Todd could go with Mary to Belle Rose. At eight thirty Mary couldn't wait a minute longer so she and Todd headed out in his truck to Perot Country.

When they arrived at Belle Rose, it was still ten minutes until nine o'clock and neither HB nor Sheriff Jackson were in sight, so Mary waited impatiently at the front of the property until they arrived. At exactly nine o'clock they both drove up and the sheriff led the way down the long driveway. About halfway down Mary spotted the moving truck behind the house and her heart sank. She had been praying she wouldn't have to see Lilly today, but it looked like she would be after all. They all got out of their vehicles and walked towards the house as Lilly came out looking more frazzled and worn out than Mary ever recalled seeing her before. Roy Landry was behind her carrying a big lamp. Sheriff Jackson was the first one to speak.

"Aunt Lilly, I thought we went through this the other day and you promised me you would be out of the house no later than Sunday."

Before Lilly could respond, Roy stepped up and replied, "Daryl, I'm sorry but this is all my fault. You see, the moving company came on Saturday and loaded up most of Lilly's things and brought them to my house but there just wasn't enough room for all of her stuff so I told them not to come back and get the last load until I could figure out where to put it all. Of course, they don't work on Sunday so they had to wait until this morning to get the last load."

Lilly added, "We have been working all weekend and I am exhausted! This is just too much work for someone my age!"

Mary asked, "Where are Charlotte and Caroline? Why aren't they helping you?"

"Because they seem to have a problem with me moving in with Roy. I don't know why they don't want me to be happy! I spent the last seven years nursing Jack and before that it was Wayne and before that it was Sam. Now I just want to live a little!"

Mary rubbed her forehead as she said, "How much longer do you think it is going to take for you to get the rest of your stuff out of the house?"

"Well, I'm not sure. Can't you just come back later this afternoon or tomorrow morning?"

Mary didn't know what to say. Luckily, HB stepped forward and said, "Sheriff, what do you plan to do about this situation?"

Sheriff Jackson looked bewildered as he tried to come up with a solution. Finally, he turned to Mary and asked, "Do you think you can give her until noon?" Mary just stared back at the sheriff so he continued, "I know it is asking a lot but it's just three more hours. I'll get some man power out here and we'll help get the rest of her stuff loaded up. I promise you we'll do whatever it takes to have her out of here by then."

Mary turned around and started walking back to the truck without saying a word. Todd followed her and caught up with her right before she got in. He, gently, turned her around to face him and softly said, "Mary, it's going to be OK. It's just three hours. You have waited this long so three more hours isn't going to kill you."

Mary replied through her tears, "I know, I know. I should have expected as much. Let's go over to Uncle Robby's and wait there."

Todd opened the truck door and helped her inside. As he walked over to his side of the truck, HB came up to him and said, "How is she?"

"She'll be okay but you and Daryl better make sure that woman is gone when we get back or I'll throw her off the property myself!"

Todd drove in silence as Mary just looked out her side window. When they pulled into the driveway, Uncle Robby was just getting ready to pull out himself. When Todd explained to Mary's uncle what was going on, Robby swore under his breath but he didn't say anything else about the situation as he didn't want to upset his niece any more than she already was.

Instead he said, "Well, that gives us just enough time to saddle up Major and Sunny and go for a trail ride." He knew if anything could cheer Mary up it was horseback riding.

Mary halfheartedly replied, "I don't have my riding boots."

"That's OK. Amanda's got a pair in the barn you can borrow. Come on, I know Sunny is going to be so happy to see you!"

Mary turned to Todd and asked, "Do you mind?"

"Not a bit. I'll just go inside and see what Pauline's up to."

Mary gave Todd a quick kiss and headed to the barn with her uncle.

The day was perfect for riding and Mary had such a good time she almost forgot about being upset. Before she knew it, it was eleven thirty, and by the time they unsaddled the horses, brushed them down and put them back in the pasture it was almost noon. They went in the house and found Todd in the kitchen with Pauline cooking a big pot of jambalaya. Aunt Pauline asked Mary if she wanted to stay for lunch but Mary didn't want to take the time to eat, so she politely turned down her aunt's invitation. Five minutes later she and Todd hopped in the truck and headed back to Belle Rose with Uncle Robby right behind them.

When they pulled up in the driveway, Mary saw that the moving truck was still there. She got out and walked over to where the sheriff, HB and Richard were standing but before she could say anything Sheriff Jackson said, "Don't worry, Mary. The movers are all loaded up and ready to go. Lilly and Roy already left so they could meet them at the storage unit Lilly rented."

Mary ran in the house to see for herself that Lilly was in fact gone for good. Sure enough, there was no sign of Lilly, but the house was in shambles and trash was everywhere! Mary didn't know if she should jump for joy that they finally had their house back or cry because of the shape it was in. It was going to take an army to get the house looking decent again, but she quickly decided it was worth it. She walked over to the kitchen sink, looked out the window and said, "Mom, I'm home!"

EPILOGUE

Mary's alarm clock went off as usual on Saturday morning. As she sat up in bed, she thought about the fact that today was her birthday and she was, now, fifty seven years young. The last five weeks had been so full of activity that she had not had much time to think about her upcoming birthday or how old she was going to be. As soon as she had gotten Belle Rose back from Lilly, Uncle Robby had started working on putting up the fences and building the barn and sheds for the horses. He finally moved Sunny and four of his older horses to the property the week before. In between going out to Belle Rose to check on the activity there, Mary had been busy with her B&B guests and helping Dixie plan her wedding, which was going to be July 18 at A Bed of Roses. She had also been working with Maddie, via phone and email, planning the renovations on their cottages. Mary hired Trevor to do the construction end of the work in exchange for her hosting his and Dixie's wedding and he had completed most of it by the time Maddie arrived in town ten days ago. Since then, she and Mary had been working non-stop putting their decorating plans into action. It had been hectic, but they enjoyed every minute of the quality time they spent working together.

They had just put the finishing touches on the cottages as Myrié, Mallory and Martine made it into town to attend the family reunion. Mary was so excited that all of her sisters were able to make it for the reunion and would also be with her to celebrate her birthday but she was especially glad they were here to help her celebrate getting Belle Rose back. The night before they had all stood together in their mother's kitchen, wine glasses in hand, and made a toast to their parents for all the happy memories they had shared in the house and on the property and for giving them each other. They also made a toast to their three brothers who they wished could have been present to share the moment with them. Last, they made a toast to all their aunts and uncles who had been in their lives as long as they could remember and who had supported them all in the difficult years after their mother's death, but especially in the last four months.

Mary got up and quickly showered and dressed. She didn't have any B&B guests to take care of as she had decided not to book any rooms for the 4th of July weekend. She wanted to be able to devote her time solely to her family. When she walked into the kitchen at seven thirty, Todd, Maddie, Martine and Myrié were already there drinking coffee. They all greeted her with Happy Birthday wishes and hugs as Todd walked over and gave his wife a birthday kiss. Mary thanked them as she made her way to the coffee pot.

Mary smiled with delight when she noticed the platter of homemade beignets sitting on the table. She knew they must have been Myrié's handiwork and that she had probably made them especially for her as a birthday treat. Their mother always made her children a special breakfast treat for their birthdays and her daughters had often done the same for their children.

Mary went over to Myrié and hugged her as she thanked her for the sweet gesture. Then she picked up one of the sugary pastries and bit into it. Powdered sugar went everywhere. Mary licked her lips and her fingers as she savored the sweet taste of the fried pastry.

A few minutes later Mallory made her way to the kitchen and the sisters and Todd ate breakfast as they excitedly discussed the upcoming day's events. Maddie, Myrié and Mallory had not been home for a family reunion in so long that they couldn't even remember how many years it had been.

The family reminiscing was interrupted by a knock on the back door. When Mary answered it, she saw Dixie standing there holding a large, flat, gift-wrapped package almost as big as herself. Mary quickly motioned her to come inside as Todd rushed over to help her with the large package. Mary introduced Dixie to everyone and asked her if she would like a cup of coffee. Dixie declined the offer and apologized for interrupting her family time. She said that she had come early because she wasn't sure what Mary's plans were for the holiday and she wanted to make sure that she had a chance to give her her birthday gift. Mary replied that she wasn't expecting a gift and that she hoped that Dixie had not gone to any expense or trouble to get her anything.

Dixie said, "Oh, but it wasn't any trouble and it didn't cost much at all."

Mary replied, "Well, I guess I should open it then."

She went over to the package and pulled the paper off of it. Mary gasped as she saw the beautiful painting of A Bed of Roses in a mixture of muted and bright colors all perfectly combined to look exactly as the house looked on a spring day with flowers blooming. Mary hugged Dixie as she thanked her from the bottom of her heart for the amazing birthday gift. Dixie smiled proudly as she told Mary it was the least she could do for all that she had done for her and her family but she was quick to point out that Sara had supplied the frame. When Mary explained to the others in the room that Dixie had painted the picture herself, they were all amazed and they complimented the young woman on how talented she was. Dixie shyly accepted the compliments. Mary invited her to stay and have some breakfast, but Dixie politely excused herself saying she had to get home before Emily Grace woke up.

By the time Todd finished hanging Mary's present over the fireplace in the living room and everyone finished getting dressed, it was almost eleven o'clock. Everyone piled into the SUV and headed to Perot Country. When they arrived at Aunt Tess' house, they were surprised to see how many of their relatives were already there. Dave had arrived with his and Martine's two kids and they came over to greet the others.

Tables and chairs had already been set up outside in a shaded area under some pecan trees. The tables were covered with checked table cloths and two of them were piled high with food dishes of every kind. One table was covered with every dessert imaginable and another had pitchers of tea along with paper plates, napkins, plastic cups and plastic silverware. Next to it were coolers full of ice, soft drinks and beer. Over to the side was the fire pit where Jason was supervising some of the cousins in a Cochon De Lait, or what northerners would refer to as a pig roast.

Todd, Mary and her sisters all dispersed themselves into the crowd of people as they started greeting their relatives and visiting with them like old times. All the aunts and uncles were there along with a slew of the cousins and their families, many of whom the Bordelon sisters had not seen in years if at all. As the sisters greeted each one of the relatives, they were congratulated over and over again on the regaining of their family land. The sisters were all quick to point out each time how much they had appreciated everyone's support through the difficult ordeal.

The festive activities of the day included horse shoe throwing competitions, sack races, pony rides and a softball game, just to name a few. The main event was the traditional talent show which was always hilarious and this one was no exception. The last event was the crowning of the new King and Queen of Perot Country.

Each year two family members were elected King and Queen and they were responsible for organizing the following year's reunion. Last year's King and Queen, Jason and Lola, took their final walk around the make-shift staging area, then they did the honors of announcing the new King and Queen. When they called out Mary and Todd's names, no one was more surprised than Mary and Todd! Everyone clapped and cheered as Jason and Lola came over and bestowed the costume jeweled crowns on the new royal couple's heads and draped the homemade silk capes over their shoulders. Then Mary and Todd took their walk around the staging area as their reign over Perot Country began.

Before everyone knew it, the day was almost over. Towards the end, Lola brought out a beautiful birthday cake decorated patriotically in red white and blue. Everyone started singing Happy Birthday to Mary as she stood there still in her royal attire and tears running down her cheeks. Mary didn't think the day could get any better until Uncle Robby walked over to her and her sisters and said he had something he wanted to give them. He handed Mary an envelope, and when she opened it and took out what was inside, she couldn't believe her eyes. Inside was a bill of sale for one registered fifteen-year-old palomino gelding horse named Sunny for the amount of one dollar to the Bordelon family. Mary handed the bill of sale to Myrié and then they were both crying.

After Todd and the sisters helped with the clean-up and hugged all their aunts and uncles as they said their good-byes, the sisters rode over to Belle Rose. They went out to the barn and, after a lot of coaxing by Mary, they saddled up the five horses with Myrié on Sunny and they rode around the property as they talked about their plans for it. Maddie mentioned her idea again to sell her producers on doing a show in Natchitoches for their small town segment next season and she suggested that the Bordelon house would be a great option for the project. The other sisters had to admit it wasn't a bad idea as the house definitely needed a makeover. They told Maddie that they would think about it but warned her not to make any moves until they could discuss the idea with their brothers.

They rode back to the barn and unsaddled the horses as they continued to talk and laugh about all the different things that had happened throughout their lives together here at Belle Rose.

Myrié said, "You know, we could write a book about all of our stories."

Martine replied, "And who of us is capable of writing a book?"

All eyes turned to Mary as Maddie exclaimed, "Mary could do it! She's a wonderful writer!"

Mallory responded, "She's got my vote!"

Mary suddenly realized her sisters were serious. She, quickly, replied, "There's no way y'all are going to talk me into any such thing so forget it."

Myrié, pleaded, "But Mary, what if we all helped you? We have so many good stories you could write about."

Mary knew she needed to put a stop to Myrié's impromptu idea before her sisters got carried away with it. She gave all of them a no-nonsense look as she flatly replied, "No, and that is my final answer!"

Maw Maw's Squash Patties

Ingredients

4 average size squash vegetables
½ to ¾ cup chopped vegetables
(onions, celery, bell pepper, etc.)
Creole seasoning such as Zatarains

2 eggs beaten
½ cup milk
2 cups self-rising flour
¼ to ⅓ cup sugar

Wash and slice squash. Put in pot and cover with water. Add seasoning vegetables and creole Seasoning. Boil until squash is tender. Remove from stove and drain. Mash squash until a smooth texture. Add eggs, milk and sugar. Add flour a little at a time until mixture is consistence of cornbread batter. Pour oil into frying pan or electric skillet and heat. Drop squash patty batter one spoonful at a time in to hot oil. Fry until brown on one side, turn over and cook on other side. Remove from skillet when golden brown on both sides. Place on plate covered with paper towels to drain. Let cool slightly and serve.

Note from Mary: My mom learned how to make these delicious patties from her mom, Olivia, and she passed the recipe on to all of her children. She even taught Ellie how to make them soon after she came to work in the Bordelon household. They are a Perot and Bordelon family favorite!

Mary's Potato Casserole

Ingredients

5-6 medium to large size potatoes   ½ cup milk
1 can cream of mushroom soup   ¼ cup butter
1 lb ground hamburger meat   2-3 cups grated cheese
½ cup chopped onions   Creole Seasoning to taste

Peel and chop potatoes. Put potatoes in pot, cover them with water, sprinkle them with Creole seasoning and boil. Drain potatoes and mash. Add milk and butter. Add in can of soup and stir until well blended. Pour mixture into greased baking dish and set aside. Brown hamburger meat, onions and creole seasoning in skillet. Drain off grease and stir into potato mixture. Add in a cup of grated cheese to mixture. Cover top of casserole with remaining cheese. Bake at 350 degrees for approximately 30 min. or until cheese is melted.

Note from Mary: There are several good Creole seasonings on the market these days you can choose from. Some of my favorites are Zatarain's, Tony Chachere's and Slap Your Mama. (Yes, there really is a seasoning brand by that name!)

ABOUT THE AUTHOR

Ann Marie Jameson was born in New Orleans, Louisiana, and has lived in various areas of the state her entire life. Her mother's side of the family came from France and settled in Natchitoches, LA. Her father's side of the family also came from France but they passed through Canada before settling in Cottonport, LA. Therefore, Ann Marie proudly considers herself to be of "Cajun" French heritage. She, like her character, Mary, is the second child of a large family of eight children. Ann Marie is a retired teacher and is married with three grown sons, one grown step-son and eight grandchildren. Ann Marie has always loved reading and writing and she first started her career writing children's stories. A Bed of Roses is her first novel but it is unlikely to be her last! She already has more plans for Mary and her siblings, their crazy aunts, uncles and cousins and the wonderful people of Natchitoches, LA, so be on the lookout for another Ann Marie Jameson novel coming soon!

Made in the USA
Columbia, SC
06 November 2018